a PACK *of* BLOOD *and* LIES

OLIVIA WILDENSTEIN

a PACK of BLOOD and LIES

USA TODAY BESTSELLING AUTHOR
OLIVIA WILDENSTEIN

A PACK OF BLOOD AND LIES
Book 1 of THE BOULDER WOLVES series

For information contact:
OLIVIA WILDENSTEIN
http://oliviawildenstein.com

Cover design by *Ampersand Book Covers*
Editing by *Krystal Dehaba & Josiah Davis*

ISBN 13: 978-1948463140

TO WOMEN.

IT'S NO LONGER JUST A MAN'S WORLD.

PROLOGUE

T he astringent tang of ammonia and glass cleaner stung my nose, but I powered through the smell, rubbing the glass table until it reflected the modern high-rise across the street. Six years ago, I could barely be in the same room as a spritz of Windex, but distance had dimmed my acute sense of smell.

Stretching my stiff neck from side to side, I moved away from the table to pack the cleaning supplies and roll them out of the conference room.

"Evelyn, I'm done!" When I spotted a dyed-black mane, I released my cart and draped my forearms over the top of the cubicle's laminated wood siding. "Want help out here?"

"No. I'm done, too, *querida*." The bright silk scarf knotted around Evelyn's hair tonight made my throat constrict.

Mom had owned few things of value—her wedding band embedded with diamond chips that I wore on a leather cord around my neck, and the designer scarf Evelyn never parted with since Mom had gifted it to her. I was by no means jealous that Evelyn had gotten it. If anyone deserved such a beautiful present, it was the woman who'd taken care of us since our arrival in Los Angeles six years ago.

Our neighborhood was, to put it nicely, rough, which meant I was to open the door to no one. When Evelyn knocked two days after we had moved in, I stared at her through the peephole and told her to go away. She did, but then she returned.

The next time she came, she slipped me a folded piece of stationery on which she'd scribbled her name and unit number. When Mom got home from a job interview and saw the paper I'd left out on our dining table, she shot up the stairs like a bullet, racing past the poorly rendered violet boob graffiti that graced the concrete stairwell, and then pounded on Evelyn's door to demand what interest she had in an eleven-year-old girl.

Turned out, Evelyn just wanted to help. Mom had flown back down, a blur of red cheeks and crazed eyes, yelling that we didn't need anyone's charity...that we were *fine!*

We weren't fine.

Thankfully, Evelyn remained persistent and returned again, placating my mother with dishes suited for a crowd and clothing that had been gathering dust in the back of her closet. Naïvely, I'd determined Evelyn was a hoarder with terrible math skills.

Evelyn unplugged the vacuum, then limped back to it and toed the knob that wound up the cord. It coiled into the belly of the apparatus as quick as a prairie rattlesnake. Before she could bend over, I grabbed the handle and heaved it onto her cart. Together, we walked our carts back to the janitorial closet, Evelyn gritting her teeth the entire way. Although she never complained, her right shoulder had been bothering her for some time now. Coupled with her constant limp caused by the stray bullet that had hit her calf two decades ago, Evelyn had slowed down considerably.

"I made your favorite tacos, but do not feel obliged to eat with me, *querida*. If you have a date—"

"Nope. No date." I hadn't gone on one since Mom passed away.

At first, I stayed away from boys because depression was eating me whole, but then paying rent and bills overtook my life, and I picked up as many hours of cleaning jobs as I could find. Some days, the commuting wore me down more than the actual workload and chemical odors. I found no solace in rolling on buses through gray city blocks, leaning away from passengers who smelled like the lunch they'd put away hours before or the perspiration they'd accrued during the day.

Tonight, at least, Evelyn sat next to me, large-knuckled fingers clasped in her lap, chin dipped into her neck, lids closed in rest. A couple seconds before we reached our bus stop, I gently rubbed her forearm and murmured, "We're home."

She startled awake. Hooking her arm through mine for support, we got off the bus. The deep-blue streets were not especially busy at this hour. The regulars were out, though—the army vet with the thick aura of liquor fumes, talking to his runt of a dog that perpetually bared his fangs at me; the two sex workers sporting torn fishnets and caked-on drugstore makeup, who reeked of sweaty vinyl; and the hooded men sought out in equal measure by the police and their twitchy customers.

Except for the dog, they were all pleasant enough.

One of the hooded dealers whistled at me. "When you gonna give me some sugar, Ness?"

Months ago, I'd stupidly worn my name pinned to my chick-yellow cleaning uniform.

Smile tugging at the corner of my lips, I flipped him off, which had his two associates snickering. Every night I passed by them, they'd either whistle or make kissy noises, and every night I'd show them what I thought of their subtle advances.

One night, one of them hadn't been on the corner, and I worried the cops had nailed him, but Suzie the prostitute assured me the boy's pops had gotten out of jail and come to collect his son to start a new life.

Sometimes I wished someone would whisk me away to start a new life, too.

As we stepped into the dirty cement cube we called home, I pushed away thoughts of desertion and told Evelyn, "I'll be up in a minute."

The elevator was out of order...*again*, so she started her slow ascent to her second-floor unit, the menthol salve she rubbed into her sore joints wafting over the tang of fresh urine. Her shoulder wasn't the only thing that worried me. Her bad leg, too, seemed to be causing her pain.

Once I heard her keys jangle over the shouting match of my next-door neighbors and the cartoons blaring from Mrs. Fletcher's place, I walked toward my apartment and pulled out my keys, but then I froze in the middle of the hallway.

I sniffed the air—cigarette smoke, potpourri, and evergreen. The tangled scents jolted my pulse.

My front door was closed, but yellow light slanted onto the steel-gray floor. I turned the knob, then gave a hard shove.

Two people were crowded around my flea-market dining table.

The man jumped to his feet so fast his chair skidded backward on the linoleum. He caught the wooden top rail before it hit the ground. "Ness."

"How did you get in?" I sounded calm, which was surprising, because I was *not* calm. Every nerve in my body twitched.

My uncle tipped his head toward the window over the denim couch. Shards of glass glittered on the threadbare seat cushions.

I backed up. Smacked into a wall.

Not a wall.

Hands came around my biceps and pinned me in place. "Hi, Cuz."

I twisted my neck and gaped up into a familiar set of hazel eyes, then stared back at Uncle Jeb and Aunt Lucy.

"We've come to take you home," Lucy said, finally heaving herself out of the chair.

When I'd hoped for a new life, this wasn't what I'd had in mind.

I shrugged my cousin Everest's hands off and tried to lope around him, but his body filled the exit path. "Like hell I'm going back there!"

"Why didn't you call us when Maggie died?" My aunt wiped the corners of her eyes with a tissue. She hadn't cared about Mom when she'd been alive, but now Lucy was suddenly heartbroken? *The nerve of her.*

"Why *would* I tell you?"

"Because we're your family," Jeb said.

"You lost that title the day you forced us out of Boulder."

My uncle scratched a spot behind his ear. "Ness, there were reasons we urged your mother to leave."

"Oh, I remember them: *Ness is fragile. She shouldn't run with boys. It's dangerous.* Am I misquoting you, Uncle?"

Jeb flushed.

"But now you suddenly want me to come back? Why would I go with you?" My voice rang so loudly in the corridor that my neighbor stopped beating up his wife long enough to stick his head through the door. Probably to check for cops. He didn't ask if I was okay. He wasn't concerned with my well-being; he was scum.

Just like my uncle and aunt.

"You have to come with us. You're a minor," Lucy said.

"I'll be eighteen in September."

Lucy balled the tissue in her dimpled hand. "Until then, we're your legal guardians, so we call the shots."

Disbelief raked over me. "How did you even find out about Mom?"

"News travels," Everest said.

I had no more ties in Boulder, which had me wondering if Mom's death certificate was on the internet for all to see.

"Your school principal called," Jeb said. "You neither attended your graduation, nor picked up your diploma. He was trying to reach your mom, but her phone was disconnected. Since I was listed as next of kin, he phoned me."

Anger and shock warped my sight. Anger that Mom had listed my uncle on my school file, and shock that it was my own error that had led these people to me.

"How long have you been living like"—Lucy wrinkled her nose—"*this*?"

Where I lived wasn't a palace. I was aware of that, but having her state it with such distaste raised my hackles. Her gaze roved over our faded couch, over the chipped white veneer of the countertop, over the yellow water stain that had bloated and cracked a piece of the ceiling.

"Move your arm, young man." The familiar voice had me wheeling around. Evelyn held out a can of pepper spray to Everest's face.

"Whoa, chill out, lady." My cousin lowered the palm he'd planted on the wall to corral me.

Keeping the can directed on Everest, she said, "Get behind me, Ness."

When I didn't, she stretched out her arm and tried to force me back. Worried about my uncle's reaction, I pressed her arm down and whispered, "It's okay," even though it wasn't.

A frown worked itself onto my aunt's smooth, milky skin. "Who's she?"

Evelyn glared at her. "Who are *you*?"

"People I used to know," I muttered.

"We're her family," Jeb said.

Evelyn cocked a penciled eyebrow up.

"They're the reason Mom and I had to leave Boulder."

"And you are, Ma'am?" my uncle asked.

"Evelyn."

Lucy crossed her thick freckled arms, and a column of metal bangles clinked against each other. "And you know Ness *how*?"

"She's been playing the role you guys failed so miserably at," I said through gritted teeth. "If anyone should be my legal guardian, it should be her, not you."

Evelyn glanced over her shoulder at me, then back at my uncle. "I will gladly be her legal guardian. Entrust her to me."

My heart bounded at the possibility.

"I'm not entrusting Ness to a person I don't know from Eve or Adam." Jeb shook his head.

"Why not?" I asked. "*I* know her."

Jeb slapped the kitchen countertop. "That's not how it works. Now you start packing right away, young lady, or—or—"

I could tell from the strain around my uncle's eyes that I was chipping away at his patience, but he had to understand I wasn't the submissive pup he could kick around anymore.

I raised my chin. "Or what?"

"Or Everest will carry you out to the car," Jeb said in a quiet roar.

"He wouldn't dare."

Everest shot me a brazen smile.

Crap. He *would* dare.

"Evelyn's been here for me when you guys haven't! I am not leaving her."

She wrapped her calloused fingers around my wrist. "Shh, *querida*."

"Then I guess we'll be taking her along," Everest said.

I blinked at my cousin. "No one's taking any—"

Jeb tipped his head toward Everest. My cousin slapped the can of pepper spray out of Evelyn's fingers, then shackled the fists I swung at him, pinning them against my back.

"Take your hands off me!" I tried to tear my wrists out of his grasp, but the action was as futile as a hanging man trying to loosen a noose.

"Sorry, Cuz. No can do."

"We are not the enemy, Ness," my uncle said, stepping on the can of pepper spray Evelyn was reaching for.

"Well, you're sure acting like it!" I bit out.

I tried to headbutt my cousin, but he must've predicted my move because he added space between our bodies, all the while keeping my wrists in a vice. "I don't want to hurt you, Ness."

"I will go with her." Evelyn's declaration made everyone freeze.

"What? No." Lucy's head jerked back, and it made her double chin wobble. She'd gained weight since I'd last seen her; not that she was ever a size eight, but she used to be firmer.

"You surely can't just up and leave, Ma'am," Jeb said.

"I surely can and surely will. Now release her before I call the police and have them observe how unfit you are to be her guardians."

"We're not afraid of cops," Everest said, a lilt to his voice.

I was so furious I wanted to spit on him. On him and on his pride.

My uncle raised an open palm. "Release her, Everest."

Everest let me go. I rubbed my wrists and glared at him, funneling everything I thought about him and his little stunt into that one look. I didn't spit though.

"Can you cook, Ma'am?" Jeb asked. At first, I assumed the drive had made him hungry—my uncle and cousin were always hungry—but then Jeb added, "We need a new cook at the inn."

Lucy startled. "Jeb, we can't just—"

"She's an incredible cook," I said.

"But—" Lucy started again.

"Dad's right. We need a new cook, and Ness won't come without Evelyn. It's a win-win."

Lucy gasped. "We can't just pick someone off the street."

"We're not *on* the street, Mom," Everest said.

My cousin's support was startling and reminded me of another time when he'd stood up for me, but my gratitude whizzed out like air from a popped balloon when I recalled how he'd just manhandled me.

"We can't promise it will work out," Jeb said.

"But she'll stay with me until I'm eighteen even if it doesn't." Evelyn was my life. At fifty-eight, living alone with decreasing mobility, there was no way in hell I'd let Jeb kick her to the curb. "You'll give her a room in the inn."

"You're a very demanding girl," my uncle said.

"You're uprooting me from my life." *Again.* "I have a right to be demanding."

Jeb glanced at his wife, but Lucy was too busy scowling to meet his gaze. "We'll supply her with a room, but it'll impact her salary. *If* it works out."

Lucy finally flicked a creamy hand, contaminating the air with the essence of nicotine that had yellowed the white crescents of her nails. "All this is well and good, but shouldn't we sample the woman's cooking first?"

"The woman has a name. Evelyn. And she made fish tacos," I said.

"I could eat," Everest chirped.

Of course he could. My cousin's appetite was a monstrous thing when we were growing up.

"I'll go fetch the tacos with her," I offered.

"No. I'll go," Everest said.

"Like I'd trust you to do that," I said.

"Everest goes with you." Was Jeb afraid I'd make a run for it?

The thought had crossed my mind, but another one had quickly taken its place: Evelyn wouldn't be able to run. Besides, where would we go? I had never made good enough friends I could phone for help. I'd tried back in middle school, but kids found me odd and kept away. I remembered wondering if they could somehow sense what I was, smell what I was the same way I could smell their acne serums and tinted lip balms. I'd never dared ask Mom. I was afraid she'd burst into my school and punch the kids for shunning me, which wouldn't have improved my social status.

Evelyn, Everest, and I went upstairs, and then we came back with the taco dish. While Evelyn warmed it in my microwave, I packed. Gathering everything I owned took me fifteen minutes and two blue Ikea bags.

"That's it?" Jeb picked up one of the bags and tried to wrestle the second one from my hands, but I held on tight.

"That's it."

As Jeb and I walked to the black van with the golden Boulder Inn logo, we discussed my last rental payment and the cost of a new window, and then he asked if I had a car, and I shook my head. I didn't even have a license.

"A boyfriend or friends to say goodbye to?"

I thought about my drug-dealing admirers and the sympathetic prostitutes for all of a second. "No."

"Really? No one?"

His concern surprised me. I supposed acting as though I hadn't had a life here wouldn't serve him.

"I have Evelyn," I ended up saying so he would stop pitying me.

Lucy and Everest were sampling the tacos when we returned. Evelyn offered my uncle a plate and watched as the tangy goodness vanished down his throat.

"If all your food tastes this good, you won't have to worry about job security," he finally said.

Evelyn smiled at me, and her expression dissolved some of the tension that had gelled inside my veins since I'd busted open my front door and set eyes on the past.

A past I dreaded revisiting.

ONE

one month later

T he inn was packed.

Brawny men of all ages had arrived sometime before lunch, alone or accompanied by their wives, girlfriends, or sons.

I recognized many of the men, but they didn't recognize me. In my gray housekeeping uniform, I blended with the rest of the staff. Every time someone looked my way, I disappeared into the kitchen where Evelyn was cooking up a feast, or entered one of the unoccupied bedrooms I'd helped prep for the occasion.

Energy crackled in the carpeted hallways, in the living room with its high-beamed ceilings and two-story glass panes, and in the tartan-covered adjoining dens. Every Adirondack on the sprawling porch held a reclined body. Voices chirped. Laughter rang. It was as though the Boulder Pack hadn't come together in years. But I knew for a fact they met once a week. Well, the men did. The women and children were not invited to regular pack gatherings.

"If you go at it much longer, the metal will start peeling."

I froze, and the feather duster I'd been using on the sconce next to the elevator tumbled onto the burgundy runner.

That voice...

Deeper, but nonetheless familiar.

Slowly, I turned to face Liam Kolane, one of the men who'd opposed my plea to join the pack the day my father was shot. I wasn't short for a girl—five-seven like Mom—but I still had to crane my neck.

I hid my loathing for him underneath a smile. "Sometimes the filth is not visible to the naked eye, but it doesn't mean it's not there."

A small crease appeared between the dark brows shadowing his reddish-brown eyes.

I picked up my feather duster and continued down the hallway, swiping the long gray feathers over the other sconces.

He didn't move. "Have we met?"

I looked over my shoulder at him, fake smile still in place. "Not in this lifetime."

That made his entire forehead groove. I tossed him a wink as I turned the corner.

The second I was out of sight, I dropped the smile and hurried to the bedroom my aunt and uncle had loaned me. I shut my door and sidled against it. My heart was thumping so hard it threatened to derail. Liam hadn't recognized me. I was safe.

At least, that was what I believed for the next few minutes.

Two knocks on my door made me spring away from it.

"Open up."

I sniffed the air. Evergreen. *Not Liam*. I turned the knob to let my cousin in.

It had taken his girlfriend almost dying for me to forgive my cousin for being such an ass back in LA. I hadn't forgiven his parents, though. They'd yanked me out of my life one too many times to forgive.

"I just overheard Liam mention to his buddies that he ran into a hot blonde housekeeper." Everest dropped into the flannel-covered armchair in the corner of my bedroom. "Was it you?"

I crossed my arms. "I'm offended you need to ask."

"Only reason I'm asking is 'cause I thought you were planning on holing up in your bedroom until the pack left."

"Can't a girl change her mind?"

"You *can* change your mind, but if I were you, I'd stay the fuck away."

"Noted."

"I'm serious, Ness. Especially from Liam Kolane. He's cut from the same cloth as his dad."

A chill whorled beneath my ribs. "He rapes women too?"

"There are rumors…" Everest dragged his long fingers through his red hair.

I hated that I'd just reminded him of his girlfriend's fate—raped by Liam's father, Heath…the horror.

I sat on the edge of the duvet I'd fluffed upon waking, folding one leg underneath me. "Go against Liam."

"What?"

"For Alpha. Go against him."

Everest exhaled a rough breath. "I have no desire to lead the pack."

"You'd rather have Liam lead you?"

"No."

Ever since Everest's girlfriend had attempted suicide the week I arrived in Boulder, I'd softened toward my cousin. His pain, although different, reminded me acutely of my own. Maybe that was why I'd found it in my heart to overlook Los Angeles. Gone was his cockiness, replaced by this oppressive despondence that had turned him into a bit of a recluse.

"I can't stop thinking about what Heath did to Becca," he whispered, hazel eyes slickening with emotion. Not many things got to me, but a man crying…yeah, that got to me.

I leaned across the narrow space and touched his clasped hands. "Heath is gone, Everest. He got what he deserved."

Even though Heath had died a week ago, the realization hadn't settled in Everest yet. Perhaps because Liam had decided to bury his father in an intimate ceremony to which only a handful of pack members had been convened. Although brutal, seeing my mother's body lowered into the earth had brought me closure.

"He may be gone, but so is Becca," he muttered.

"She's not gone-gone."

He cocked an eyebrow. "Her odds of waking are fucking ridiculous."

"Ridiculous is better than no odds at all."

He snorted. "Can't believe *you're* the optimist."

He was right. I was a half-empty sort of girl.

He sighed then stood. "I should go. The meeting starts soon."

"Think about what I said. About tossing your name in the hat."

"There won't be a hat. No one's going to go up against Liam."

"You don't know that."

He shot me a *how-many-shades-of-clueless-are-you* look.

And here I thought the pack had balls. Many pairs of them. Was there truly no one to challenge a Kolane?

TWO

T he second Everest left, I swapped my gray housekeeping uniform for skinny jeans and a white tank top. Mom's wedding band drummed against my chest as I headed for the inn's common area. Conversations and laughter frothed through the closed doors and filled the hallway. Steeling my nerves, I pumped the sculpted copper handle and drew the door open.

Squares of sunlight dappled the airy room. People were huddled in large groups, either sprawled over the leather sofas, or standing by the buffet of sweets and drinks set up next to the massive stone fireplace. No fire snapped in the blackened hearth, and yet the room smelled of warm smoke, as though the scent of winter fires had penetrated the pale-yellow stucco walls and Native-patterned area rugs.

As I dragged my gaze over the crowd, I caught Lucy's attention. She shot me a look that could've withered one of her prized rose transplants. She wasn't the only one glaring. I garnered many a glare. For example, Liam and the two guys standing on either side of him gave me the stink-eye.

I was the new kid all over again. Good thing it didn't frighten me.

Lucy elbowed her way through the sunlit room toward me, then latched onto my bicep and tugged me aside. "What are you doing here?"

I shrugged her off. "I've decided you were right. That I should get out and meet people."

Lucy dipped her chin into her fleshy neck. "Ness…"

"Yes?"

Her warning died in her throat. My aunt wouldn't dare make a scene, and considering how quiet it had gotten, she chose silence over a messy confrontation.

One of the guys broke away from Liam's little group and approached me, black eyebrows slanting over piercing green eyes. He stopped mere inches from me and tipped his head down. I crossed my arms, expecting him to tell me to beat it.

"Dimples? Is that you?"

If I were the type of girl to blush, I would've turned crimson at the nickname. Not because it wasn't true…I had deep dimples—craters really—but because it was spoken loudly.

"I go by Ness now. And you are?"

He grinned. "Shit. Ness. You're all grown up."

"Six years does that to you." I raised an eyebrow as I studied his face, took in the light-brown skin with the dusting of freckles, the prominent but straight nose, the dark stubble, the cropped black hair, the hazel eyes. "August?" I asked hesitantly. "August Watt?"

He smiled wider.

And then I smiled, because August had been my absolute favorite person in Colorado after my parents. When I'd asked the pack to allow me into their ranks, he and his father had fought in my favor, joining their voices to Everest's. They'd been drowned out by the chorus of *absolutely-nots*.

A girl in an all-male pack? What a revolting idea.

I couldn't help that I'd been born a girl. And it wasn't like I could pledge myself to a neighboring pack, because werewolves couldn't switch packs. The only thing werewolves could do was either be a part of their own pack, or move away—far away—so the distance prevented their bodies from changing. Those who stayed—lone wolves— were loose cannons hunted down by all.

August shook his head. "I didn't think you'd ever come back."

"I wasn't planning on it, but shit happens."

He got that look that drove me insane. Pity. I probably shouldn't have mentioned the *shit-happens* part.

"You okay?"

"I've had better days, but I've also had worse ones."

His frown deepened.

I ran my hand through my long hair because, heck, now *I* was uncomfortable.

Slowly, slowly, his chiseled face smoothed out. "Are you here to stay?"

"Haven't decided yet." My skin pebbled from the vent blasting cold air over my head. I hugged my arms to my chest. "Want to take the conversation outside?" I was chilly, but I also wanted to get away from my aunt's prickly glower.

"Sure."

As we walked through the open sliding-glass doors onto the overhanging porch that was almost as spacious as the living room, I said, "You don't *need* to talk to me by the way."

He draped an arm around my shoulders and tucked me into his side. My entire body tightened at the contact.

"Shut up. I just got my favorite girl back. Let me enjoy her."

I snorted softly. "Favorite girl?"

He amended, "Woman."

I peered up into his face. His freckles seemed to have darkened. "I imagined you'd have plenty of *new* favorite girls. I mean, look at you. You're like a real man now."

"A real man?" He chuckled. "If everyone wasn't staring at us right now, I'd put you in a headlock and rough up that pretty hair of yours."

"Don't you dare."

"Fine." He looked down at me, still grinning. "Seriously, it's so good to see you."

"Likewise." When we reached the guardrail fashioned from a tangle of sanded branches, I ducked out from underneath his heavy arm. "How've you been?"

"Pretty good. I enlisted a year after you left. It paid for college."

"Navy or army?"

"Marines."

I ran my fingers over the knots in the tawny wood that Dad and August's father had put in after Jeb bought the inn. Dad had been a talented carpenter. He'd taught his trade to August's father who purchased Dad's company after he died.

I placed my forearms on the thick balustrade and squinted at the dense copse of pines running up the sharp ridges of the Flatirons. The view from the inn definitely beat the one from the unit I used to call home. Not that I would *ever* admit this to anyone.

"Heard you were working with your dad now," I said.

"Yeah." August stroked the wood, his fingers moving carefully over the knots, and then he turned and leaned against it.

"How's business?"

"Booming. Want a job?"

"A job?"

"I remember you loved whittling wood."

"That was"—Dad's face flashed inside my mind—"a long time ago. Besides, I have a job. I work here."

I wanted my uncle to pay Evelyn her full wage, so I'd offered to help with the housekeeping. My suggestion had made my prim aunt balk, but rather rapidly, when she observed how effective I was, she changed her mind. If Evelyn caught wind of this trade, she'd unleash a torrent of Spanish on me. Every time she became emotional, her mother tongue spurted out like steam from a geyser.

At the beginning, I'd helped with the actual cleaning, but after a week, my sense of smell had gotten so acute I had to stay away from cleaning products. I stuck to laundry and ironing and occasionally helped out with vacuuming and assisting Evelyn in the kitchen.

August's thick black eyebrows almost joined together. "Something just occurred to me."

"What?"

"Did you run into Liam earlier?"

"Why?"

As his gaze settled on a spot behind me, a vein throbbed in his temple.

"I do believe we've met in this lifetime, Ness Clark."

Speak of the devil. I turned around slowly.

Liam glowered at me. I swear…little lightning bolts were zipping out of his eyes. "Where's your feather duster?"

I cocked my head to the side. "Did you want to borrow it?"

The lightning bolts turned into electrical discharges.

A loud clap resounded, disrupting the thick tension, and then Lucy exclaimed, "All pack members are asked to make their way to the conference room."

Reluctantly, August pressed away from the balustrade. "Catch you at dinner?"

I nodded. He'd *catch me* sooner than that.

Liam's jaw moved as though he were about to say something. In the end, he backed away without speaking.

I watched the men leave, allowing them a head start. Whether they liked it or not, I descended from this pack, so their decisions would affect my life. I hadn't had a say in returning to Boulder, but I wanted a say in what would happen now that I was back and out of hiding.

THREE

I forded through the clusters of women sipping drinks from copper goblets, the heady mix of perfumes and spirited juices making my nose twitch.

"Ness?" Someone tapped my shoulder.

I pivoted.

"It's me. Amanda."

I studied the brunette with the bluntly cut curly hair, the long-lashed tawny eyes, and the heart-shaped face.

"Amanda Frederick," she went on.

At last, I placed her. Miss Popular back in elementary and middle school. Not a mean girl. Just someone interested in everything I wasn't.

Her lips bent into a satisfied smile once she noted the recognition. "Are you back for the summer or longer?"

"Not sure yet."

Two other girls pushed in beside her. They tossed their names at me. *Taryn* and *Sienna*. Sienna reminded me of a piece of pale silk with her wispy blonde hair, latte-colored eyes, and flawless complexion. Taryn, on the other hand, was all harsh angles and stark contrasts. Her face was as narrow as an axe blade, her hair tar-black, and her eyes an icy blue.

"Who did you come with?" I asked.

The pack didn't have daughters—hadn't had any for over a century until me—so these girls had to be plus-ones.

Taryn raised her pointed chin. "Lucas Mason."

I remembered Lucas: shaggy black hair, serious acne, and surly attitude. He used to be Liam's best friend. Maybe still was.

Amanda said, "I'm with Matthew Rogers."

The name conjured up a blond giant.

"Sienna..." Amanda tilted her head toward the delicate blonde. "She's with August." It sounded like a warning.

"You and August seem close." Sienna's voice gusted softly toward me. I'd never met anyone whose voice matched their appearance until today.

"August is the brother I never had," I explained.

"You have Everest," Taryn snapped.

What was that supposed to mean? That I shouldn't hang out with August? "If you'll excuse me, I have somewhere to be."

I started back toward the doors of the living room when Lucy stopped me. I was about to utter an exasperated *what*, when she asked, "Where are you going?"

"To my bedroom."

She scrutinized my face. "Evelyn could use some help in the kitchen."

Without a fight, I walked in the direction of the kitchen until Lucy moved to the buffet. Then I doubled-back and set course for the basement. When I burst into the conference room, forty faces spun my way. Expressions ran the gamut: I got annoyance, anger, shock, curiosity.

But mostly annoyance.

"Ness?" my uncle said in a strangled voice. "Is everything all right?"

The salty, tangy scent of male was overpowering.

"Great." I looked for a free chair but found none. "Sorry I'm late, but Matt's girl is a talker."

A large blond boy with a neck as thick as his face crossed his beefy arms in front of his fridge-sized chest. I suspected he could crush a tree trunk with those arms.

"What are you doing here?" Jeb asked me.

"It's a pack meeting, isn't it?"

"It is."

"You have to be a member of the pack to sit in on it," someone said.

"Good thing I am, then."

An elder with bushy white hair and bushier white eyebrows linked his hands together before him in a business-like manner. "Ness Clark, you're not part of the pack."

"But that was under Heath Kolane. Now that he's gone, you've surely amended your misogynistic ways."

Everest made a little sound in the back of his throat. He wasn't the only one. Matt turned a shade darker, as though soaked with wood stain. August and his father gaped at me. Where Nelson tapped his fingers nervously against the laminated wood, August fought off a smile.

"You would have had to pledge yourself before puberty to become part of the pack," one of the elders said.

The mix of nerves and anger loosened my tongue. "What makes you think I hit puberty?"

Half the room checked me out. In their defense, I'd invited the attention.

"Okay, fine. I hit puberty. But it's a dumb rule. Besides, I was physically absent from Boulder, so I should get a free pass."

"Rules are rules." The declaration delivered by a bald elder was like a whip. Scorching.

Bastards.

Silence descended upon the room, punctuated only by the sound of denim rustling against leather.

Jeb turned pained eyes on me. He was going to ask me to leave. I could sense it in my bones. "Ness—"

Everest blurted out, "Alphas can bring new pledges into the pack at any age, as long as they have pack blood and can change at will."

All eyes were on him now. Everest's cheeks, neck, and ears glowed crimson.

I mouthed a *thank you*.

"You've been away a long time. Can you access your wolf form at will?" Liam asked.

"Yes," I lied.

I hadn't changed in six years, but now that I was back in Boulder, in proximity to the pack, I supposed it was a question of days until my nails turned to claws, my hands turned to paws, and the fine hair on my limbs thickened to fur.

"When was the last time you became a wolf?" he continued.

"Three days ago." From the corner of my eye, I could see Everest's lips pinch. Hopefully no one else caught his expression.

"The issue remains that there is no Alpha yet," the white-haired elder said. "Once one is chosen you will be able to plead your case. Until then"—if he said *shoo* or flicked his fingers, I would punch him—"you are not privy to pack discussions."

"Who are the contenders?"

Exasperated sighs grated up corded necks.

"Liam Kolane." The elder gestured to Liam as though I didn't know who Liam Kolane was.

"And?"

"That's it."

I scanned each and every face around the table. Didn't all wolves long to be leaders? Especially when the opportunity to become an Alpha so seldom arose? This would probably be our generation's one and only chance. After forty, a werewolf was no longer eligible because his body couldn't morph at will.

I looked at Everest. Challenged him to give Liam a run for his money. Heath would've hated that.

The elder with the gleaming bare scalp cleared his throat. "Kindly leave."

Jerk. "What are the requirements?" I asked. "Besides the age, what are the requirements?"

"The requirements for what, Ness?" Nelson asked, his ebony skin crinkling.

"For becoming Alpha."

"You must be under forty and have pack blood in your veins," Everest said.

"So I qualify?"

The planes of my uncle's face tautened. "Ness—"

"It's just a question, Uncle."

"It's a very specific question," Bushy-Eyebrows said.

August had paled, or perhaps it was the contrast to his father's much darker complexion that made my friend seem paler.

"You qualify," Everest declared.

The realization that I ticked all the boxes drummed against me like soft rain. But like rain, it also splashed a good deal of sobriety into me. What exactly was I thinking?

To put my name into the proverbial hat to annoy Liam Kolane was a dangerous game. One I wasn't sure I wanted to play, and not because I was afraid of losing—I had *nothing* to lose—but because, what happened if I won? I'd have to stay in Boulder and lead a pack I abhorred until I died or was demoted.

That wasn't the life I wanted.
At least, I'd never wanted it before.

FOUR

A s I applied a thin coat of mascara to my lashes, someone pounded on my door. Pounding was never good. It meant I was in trouble. After the stunt I'd pulled, I wasn't surprised. Actually, that wasn't true. I'd assumed the deafening knocks would've come earlier. Then again, I'd been helping Evelyn out in the kitchen, so maybe my haters hadn't known where to find me.

Lips squeezed into a smile to hide my hammering heart, I drew the door open. My rigid lips slackened. I'd expected Jeb or Everest.

I leaned against my bedroom door, draping on an air of boredom. "To what do I owe the pleasure of your visit, Liam?"

He shoved past me.

I pressed away from the door but didn't close it. "Come right on in…"

He whirled on me. "What the hell was that?"

I cocked an eyebrow.

"Are you seriously entertaining the idea of challenging me?"

"Oh. *That*." I strolled back into my bathroom and lined the insides of my lower lids with kohl.

Oblivion irritated people. I had every intention of irritating Liam and trampling his inflated ego.

He filled the open doorway, eyes flashing to mine in the mirror.

"I'm thinking about it," I said sweetly.

"If it's just to get into the pack, I'll consider your candidacy once I'm Alpha."

"How generous of you." I tossed my eyeliner into my makeup bag and spun, leaning back against the cold porcelain sink top and crossing my arms.

He lowered his brows. "Do not go against me."

"Or what? You'll hurt me?" I walked up to him and jabbed my finger into his chest. "I lost both my parents *and* was forced to come back to this hellhole where people look down on me because I wasn't born with the right blend of chromosomes. What exactly do you think you can do that will hurt me, huh?"

He stared down at my finger. Stepped back so it fell off his rock-hard chest. "I wouldn't *hurt* you, but you'll lose."

"You don't think very highly of me, do you?"

His eyes darkened.

"What if *you* lose?" I asked.

"I won't."

I hadn't decided what to do yet, but that...*that* decided me. "I see cockiness runs in the Kolane family."

He scowled as he backed out of my bedroom. "You know what? Go for it. Challenge me." He rolled his fingers into fists and cracked his knuckles. "It'll be my pleasure to teach you a little humility."

I felt the color rise in my cheeks. When he left, I slammed my door shut and stared at the wood paneling until my breathing no longer came in rough pants.

I DEBATED A LONG while whether to head down to dinner. Going would show Liam I didn't care that he'd come inside my bedroom to threaten me. But going also meant having to bust out small talk, and I was in too foul a mood to carry on any conversations.

I yanked off my jeans and black swing top, then pulled on leggings, sneakers, and an exercise bra. Sticking my hair into a ponytail, I tore through the empty hallway, down the deserted stairs, and straight for the cavernous gym.

I shut the door then flooded the room with light and music. I dragged the dummy from where it lurked in the shadowy corner like a stalker and thrust my hands into a pair of boxing gloves. Jeb and Lucy stocked this place with more exercise gear than the shoddy gym I'd spent hours in before Mom got sick.

I squinted at the dummy, replacing its blank face with Liam's. I kicked and jabbed at it. It shifted on its springs as I pummeled my fists and feet into it, but it didn't bleed and it didn't bruise.

Liam thought I didn't stand a chance. He was wrong.
Wrong.
Just because I was a female didn't mean I was weak.
Asshole.

I pounded my fists at dizzying speed into the dummy. Sweat slicked down my spine, soaked the back of my exercise bra, dripped down the sides of my face. I swiped my forearm over my brow, then wound my arm back and let my fist fly. A hand hooked around my bicep and wheeled me around. I reacted with a direct punch to the gut. A breath whooshed out of August's mouth as my glove connected to his abdomen. He released me and rubbed the spot.

"I'm so sorry," I yelled over the thumping music.

Tearing my gloves off, I crossed the room toward the water fountain to saturate a towel with ice-cold water, then brought it back to him, but he shook his head at my offering.

A crooked smile replaced his grimace. "Where'd you learn to punch like that?"

"Self-taught." I used the towel on my face and neck, chilling my flushed skin. "Is dinner already over?"

"No. We're at the main course."

"Then why are you here?"

"Because the seat I saved you was empty."

I lowered my gaze to the black rubber flooring. "I wasn't hungry."

"You're not hungry or you're mad?"

"Maybe both."

"What did Liam tell you?"

I whipped my gaze back to his. "How do you know he came to see me?"

"I heard him ask your aunt for your room number."

So that's how Liam knew where to find me... The fact that Lucy had doled out this information peeved me. Did she think his visit would be pleasant, or was she happy to encourage his intimidation technique? Probably the latter.

"Yeah. He dropped by."

"Look, I didn't come down here to discuss him."

"I hope you didn't come down here to drag me to dinner, because I'm not going."

"As much as I admire your spunk, I think you shouldn't go up against Liam. You don't want to be Alpha, Ness. Even *I* wouldn't want to lead the pack."

I tried to steady my breathing, but my larynx felt snarled. "Why not?"

"Why not what?"

"Why don't you want to lead the pack?"

"Because dealing with overblown egos and temperaments takes a toll on you. Even though Heath was...*well*, not the finest specimen...he gave a lot to the pack."

"He might've given a lot to the pack, but he took a lot from people who weren't part of the pack."

August's full mouth thinned.

"Everest's girlfriend tried to take her own life from shame," I continued.

"He's gone now." August's voice was low. "He paid for what he did."

"*He* might be gone, but Liam Kolane isn't."

August touched my bare shoulder. "Liam isn't Heath." When I didn't shrug his hand off, he closed his fingers over my rotator cuff and squeezed gently. "Let him have this."

A new aroma ribboned over August's sawdust and Old Spice scent—flowery, watery. In the open doorway, I spied a pale face set with glittery eyes.

"Your girlfriend's here," I muttered.

He didn't release me. "If you want a place in the pack, I'll make sure you get it, but don't do this."

The beat-heavy Drake song faded. Just before a new song came on, Sienna spoke August's name. He didn't acknowledge her.

"You will lose," he said.

Like claws, his words scraped against my self-esteem. I straightened my spine and squared my shoulders. "Did Liam put you up to this?"

"No."

I backed away from him.

A shadow muddied his green irises. "Ness—"

"I'm a big girl, August. I'll make up my own mind." I walked toward the hamper and chucked the towel inside. "Thanks for your concern, though."

"You're going to go through with it, aren't you?"

"I like proving people wrong."

"This isn't a game."

"I'm aware of that." I drew the door wide.

Sienna scrambled out of my way and flattened her back against the mirrored wall. At least I inspired fear in someone. Not the right someone, though.

"Sorry to have kept your date away," I muttered.

Not that it was my fault. I hadn't asked August to come and tell me how foolish I was.

From anyone else, I wouldn't have cared. But August…August's opinion mattered.

I hated that it mattered.

I hated that it made me question my decision.

Halfway back to my bedroom, I crossed paths with Everest. "If you're here to talk me out of it, don't waste your breath."

He kept up with my hurried strides. "Are you kidding? I'm totally on board with you going up against Liam."

That took me by surprise. I stopped. "You are?"

"Hell yeah. But if you're sure, you need to tell the elders before midnight."

"Why? Do they turn into pumpkins after that?"

Everest smirked, and it shook off the cloying anxiety that had marred his face since Becca swan dove off her roof. "The blood oath happens at midnight."

I remembered my father telling me about blood oaths, but it was in the context of electing the Alpha. Pack members needed to slash their skin, then touch their seeping wounds to the Alpha's. Once the contact happened, the magic took place and turned an ordinary wolf into a true beast. I wasn't sure how it worked in terms of competing for the title.

"Get cleaned up and meet me on the deck," Everest said.

In front of the dining room entrance, I spied Liam exchanging words with Matt, the blond giant, and another boy who was as tall as Matt but built narrower, with shaggy black hair and an ugly scar across one of his eyebrows.

When they caught me staring, I turned my attention back to Everest. "I'll be there in a sec." And then I jogged away to get ready.

I'd give the jerk a run for his money.

Did I want to win? Sure. Who wanted to lose? Did I want to lead a bunch of jerks? No. But if I did win, I could probably nominate someone else to run the pack. I wondered what my father would've thought of my decision. Would he question my sanity, or would he be proud?

My mother had raised me to go after what I wanted. And what I wanted was to stop another Kolane from being in a position of power. I held on to that as I readied to fight for my beliefs.

FIVE

D essert and drinks were being served on the spacious deck when I arrived. Flickering candles in giant hurricane holders cast eerie glows and moving shadows over the faces angled my way. Conversations halted. The only sound was the instrumental jazz whirring from hidden ceiling speakers.

Jeb shifted toward me, a tumbler of whiskey clutched between his fingers.

"Sorry I missed dinner," I said.

"You want to eat something?"

"I'll eat later."

He lowered his glass to his narrow hip, and the ice clinked. "Ness—"

"Please, Uncle. Don't tell me what to do."

"A month ago, you didn't want to come back here. You wanted nothing to do with the pack, and now you're vying for—for Alpha." He joggled his hand, and whiskey splashed out.

"Let me guess… I shouldn't compete, because I'm a girl, and according to you, girls are mangy little things."

Color crawled up his throat.

"I might've been weak when you kicked me out of Boulder, but I'm not anymore."

"Stop saying I kicked you out, will you?" he hissed.

"Well, it's true."

Through gritted teeth, he added, "It was to protect you."

I dropped my voice. "Because of what Heath did to Mom?"

White appeared around Jeb's iris rings.

Although people were near, they were too busy gossiping to listen to us. Or maybe they'd heard.

Like. I. Cared.

More whiskey dribbled along his wrist. "You—You—"

"Know about it? Yeah. Mom told me. I also know you didn't do shit about retaliating. Besides getting us to leave, that is. Better Mom not tempt your revered Alpha again, huh?"

At first, I'd believed the cancer had made Mom delirious, but then Everest had confirmed it during one of our late-night chats after Becca's attempted suicide. The confession came out almost at the same time as Mom's last breath. Once she'd untethered herself from the lurid secret, her soul slipped out of her body and left me to deal with the aftermath of the terrible truth.

I'd been angry with her. But then Evelyn reminded me anger was one of the stages of grief, so I allowed myself to feel angry. With Mom and with Heath. Where I'd forgiven my mother for not telling me, I hadn't forgiven Heath.

"So this—you entering the contest—it's a personal vendetta?" Jeb asked.

"Not only."

His Adam's apple bobbed. "Liam is not like his father."

Gosh, how many people were going to tell me that? I gave a sharp nod and went to find Everest. Crossing the deck was like walking past a firing squad. Even though the slanted gazes pricked, I raised my chin and pretended to be unaffected by the petty glares.

"I'd forgotten how friendly Coloradans were," I muttered once I reached my cousin by the stainless-steel drinks dispenser.

He poured coffee into a mug, then handed it to me. "Did Dad try to talk you out of it?"

"I didn't give him time to." I took a sip of the charred-tasting beverage. "He knows I know. About Mom."

The clink of metal against glass interrupted our quiet conversation.

The bushy-eyebrowed elder stood from his Adirondack. "Usually pack matters are discussed among the pack, but since the choice of Alpha affects all our lives, not only our fellow members but also our partners, we decided to discuss the subject with all of you. As you're all aware, Liam Kolane offered to replace his father as Alpha, but he's been challenged." The elder's gaze slid to me, but then it skittered toward the beefy blond beside Liam. "Matthew Rogers"— next, the elder tipped his head toward the lanky boy with the mean white scar and mop of black hair—"and Lucas Mason have decided to go up against Heath's boy."

My shoulders pinched together. I bumped my arm into Everest's. "Did you know?"

My cousin shook his head.

The elder's gaze returned to me. "I believe they aren't the only contenders, though."

Silence entrenched the patio.

While Matt and Lucas leered at me, Liam's face was blank, calm. Too calm. Too blank. If anything, his expression bothered me more than theirs. And then it hit me that he must've orchestrated this, asked them to enter their names in the contest to dissuade me from entering mine.

Smart.

If I hadn't spied them talking, I would most probably have been swayed to drop the charade, but I could bet anything Lucas and Matt were going to suddenly back out and leave Liam in charge.

The elder's gaze was cemented on me. "Anyone else interested in the role of Alpha, speak now or forever hold your peace."

August was standing on the opposite end of the deck next to his father. Both had their arms crossed tightly, but only August scowled. His father kept wetting his lips, nervous, concerned. For the briefest of moments, I shut my eyes. When I opened them, determination chased away the hesitation.

I stared at Liam, and in a clear voice I said, "Sign me up."

Intakes of breaths traveled through the women, followed by breathy exclamations. No one looked more surprised than my aunt, though. Her face, which she already kept out of the sun, had become as white as the sheets I'd spent all morning ironing.

Jeb downed the dregs of his whiskey in one long gulp.

Contempt was stamped in many a gaze. And then there was the look August shot me. Disappointment. If I'd learned one thing about life, it was that pleasing everyone was impossible.

I lowered my gaze to the black liquid rippling inside my mug, rippling because my hands were shaking. I tightened my grip.

"You are one ballsy chick," Everest murmured.

"Anyone else?" the elder asked.

I raised my chin and scanned the faces surrounding me. So many of them were still looking my way. So many still whispering. Amanda and her two besties were smirking. Would they have smirked if they'd been werewolves or would they have supported a sister's endeavor?

"I will convene with the elders to discuss the rules of this competition. After breakfast, we will deliberate with the four contenders in the conference room. But before we leave, we need to collect a drop of your blood to guarantee your candidacy."

Bushy-Eyebrows crooked a finger. I handed my mug to Everest and joined the other three who'd already approached the white-haired elder.

"Wrists." His nail had lengthened into a claw.

Liam, Matt, and Lucas extended their arms.

"Ness?"

I jutted my hand out.

"With blood, you will bind yourselves to me so I may know your whereabouts and keep track of your vitals during the contest. Once an Alpha rises, your connection to me will be severed."

He slashed his wrist, and then slashed all of ours in turn. I gritted my teeth at the shock of pain. Bushy-Eyebrows pressed his blood to ours.

"Well, that's sanitary," I mumbled.

"Wolves don't carry disease, Ness," the elder reassured me.

The wolf in me knew that; the human still saw blood as a vehicle for disease.

Almost instantly, the edges of the boys' skin knitted together.

Lucas snorted at my still-gaping nick. "Not healing very fast, are you? Want a bandage for your boo-boo?"

Shooting him a glare, I returned to the table set with desserts and grabbed a paper napkin, pulse pounding against the torn skin. *Heal*, I instructed my wrist; it didn't. That wouldn't help my street cred. I pressed the napkin to my wrist and watched the white turn crimson.

"We will meet in the morning to discuss the contest." Trailed by four other elders, Bushy-Eyebrows walked off the terrace.

Amanda tore away from her friends and strutted over to me, her heeled booties clucking against the hardwood floor. "Hun, hun, hun. Going against our boys is one dumb idea."

"*Your* boys?" I asked.

"Yeah, *our* boys. We grew up with them; we stuck around; we were there to comfort them when they needed some TLC."

My fingers cinched around my wrist tighter.

"We are as much part of this pack as you are. Actually, that's not true. You're not part of the pack."

"Enough, Amanda," Liam said.

So engrossed was I by her pettiness that I hadn't seen him advance.

She twirled, and her curls fanned out around her, littering the air with the aroma of apricot. It blended with the smell of the coffee cooling in my discarded mug, the scent of the blood drying on my wrist, and Everest's evergreen cologne. My stomach swished from the sensorial assault.

"I was just voicing everyone's thoughts," Amanda chirped.

Liam's lips were pressed so tight that when he said, "Leave her alone," I thought it was Everest speaking.

Liam was defending me? Surely I'd heard him wrong. Or he had an ulterior motive. After being a bastard, the only reason he'd act kind would be to confuse me. "I can fight my own battles, Liam."

"I'm sure you can, but we don't talk down to each other. Other packs might, but not us." He sounded so freaking noble. I understood why no one challenged him. He spoke like he was already an Alpha. But if he'd learned that from

Heath, then I could only imagine the rest of what Liam had been taught.

Amanda pursed her glossy lips just as a large hand landed on her shoulder. She tipped her neck up and smiled up at Matt, who stood a full head and a half taller.

He extended one large paw. "Don't know if you remember me—"

"I do." I stared at his hand a long while before shaking it.

He didn't crush my fingers like I imagined he would.

As though the contact with Matt's hand had thawed the invisible ice encasing me, others approached. Introduced themselves, *reintroduced* themselves. Six years changed teenage faces, yet I recognized most...remembered most.

A smile crooked Lucas's lips. "We should bond."

My spit went down the wrong hole, and I coughed. "Excuse me?"

"We should do a bonding exercise." He tucked Taryn into his side, his hand almost on her breast. Classy.

His words combined with his sly smile had caused my mind to form indecent images full of leather fetters and iron chains. Why in the world was I thinking about bondage?

"Paintball," a young boy with shoulder-length copper hair said.

"Exactly what I was thinking, little J. We should totally go paintballing tomorrow." Lucas was still simpering at me. "Ever paintballed, doll?"

"Don't call me doll."

Lucas's white scar writhed at my reproof.

"And *no*, I never paintballed."

Amanda stroked Matt's thick fingers, while Taryn whispered in Lucas's ear. I looked for Sienna, found her speaking quietly with August. Unlike the other two couples, they weren't touchy-feely. If anything, their rigid body language told me they were arguing.

There were other girls on the terrace, but they were chatting away, either oblivious or uninterested in participating in the conversation going on around me. I wondered if Liam's girlfriend was among them. I assumed he had a girlfriend, considering the number of girls who'd come to the pack event.

I returned my gaze to Lucas. "Is *everyone* going?"

Lucas's smile snuck back over his lips. "Just the pack and *you*. Feeling intimidated by so much testosterone, Clark?"

What I felt was hot. Probably from the wall of massive bodies encasing me. Or from the blood loss. I lifted the reddened napkin and noted the cut was shallower, the skin less puckered. The wound was closing. That was a good sign.

I retied the tissue, then pressed my palm against the nape of my neck, but my clammy hand did little to cool me down. "Not much intimidates me, Lucas. But thanks for your concern."

That seemed to make Liam smile, or at least I thought amusement had contorted his lips, but I must've imagined it.

Man, it was hot. I needed air. And space. I backed up, bumping into a chest. Brackish sweat and floral perfumes assailed my senses.

I concentrated on breathing through my mouth. "You all have yourselves a good night."

My stomach swished harder, and my head... My head felt as though my brain were being kicked around with cleats.

"Excuse me." When no one moved, I elbowed my way through the throng of bodies.

My sneaker caught on a big foot, and I stumbled, knocking into Liam. His drink sloshed from the glass and spilled over his black T-shirt.

"S-sorry."

He wrapped a hand around my arm to steady me.

Had someone slipped something into my coffee? I bristled and yanked my arm out of Liam's grasp, then traipsed across the deck like a drunk. I made it into the living room without vomiting, and then I bolted to my room on legs that felt detached from my body.

What was going on with me?

SIX

C old sweat slicked down my tingling spine. I jammed my key against the lock, but the metal slid uselessly against the wood. I tried again. Again I failed.

"Ness! Wait up." Everest was barreling down the hallway.

There were two of him.

Three.

I didn't want to be sick in the hallway. He grabbed the key from my fingers, opened my door, then helped me in. I scrambled to the bathroom and knelt in front of the toilet just as a jet of vomit spewed out of my mouth.

"Did you eat something bad?" Everest asked.

I hadn't eaten anything since lunch. I shook my head, but that angered the throbbing.

Another wave of sick spurted out of me.

My vision blurred and readjusted. Unfortunately, my sense of smell didn't blur. The acrid stench of vomit was so acute it made my nostrils flare.

Everest took a seat on the edge of the bathtub. "Was it true what you said earlier? That you changed three days ago?"

"Are you really grilling me right now?" I hoisted myself from the floor, flushed the toilet, and turned on the tap.

"No, I'm not grilling you. I'm asking because I have a theory. Did you or didn't you change yet?"

I splashed cold water over my face then squinted at my reflection. My eyes looked wrong. I blinked. My irises glowed like the neon sign over the ice-cream parlor August would take me to on hot afternoons when our dads needed to work.

I spun toward Everest. "It's—It's happening!"

He sighed. "I take it you didn't change three days ago…"

I lifted my hands in front of my face and slowly turned them. My nails had lengthened and were curving.

I stared in horror at Everest. I couldn't become a wolf here. Not in my bathroom. I would destroy it. In beast form, my muscles would grow and my movements would become choppy and rough. When I'd changed for the first time at eleven, I'd destroyed my bedroom and clawed through the living room couch. It took me weeks to master my wolf form.

Would it take me weeks again?

As though someone were carving out my vertebrae, blinding pain vaulted up my spine. I arched backward and gritted my teeth. Pointy canines dug into my lower lip and split the soft tissue. Blood dribbled down my chin. As my shoulder blades popped out of their joints, I bit back a scream and fell forward, landing hard on my palms and knees.

The seam on my wrist burst open and blood gushed out. A crimson river trickled in the grout between the stones.

"It's going to be okay, Ness. I'm right here. It's going to be okay…" Everest's voice sounded like it was coming from another room. He crouched beside me, his palm cool against my scorching neck.

The blood from my lip slopped onto the slate flooring and mixed with the blood from my wrist. I sagged and blinked. Had it been this painful six years ago, or was the pain augmented because of the years I'd deprived my body of its transformation?

Tears dripped off my cheeks and tangled with the blood. "I can't. It hurts…" My voice was more howl than words.

My mind turned hazy with ache, and my elbows gave in. I yelped and flailed forward, smacking my cheek against the cold stone floor. The blow felt as though it had shattered the cartilage in my face, but perhaps it was the wolf within that was shattering my face, just as it was altering my bone structure, dislocating my joints, and hardening my sinews. I closed my eyes and willed it to stop.

Begged for it to stop.

And it did.

THERE WAS AN INCESSANT jangling inside my skull. *Ugh.* I pressed a pillow over my face and squashed my lids tight, my lips tighter. Searing pain radiated over my mouth. I pitched the pillow off my head and sat up so fast my bedroom swam before my eyes. I touched my throbbing lower lip. My fingers came away red, wet with blood.

It hadn't been a dream.

The night poured back through me. I shivered, even though I was still fully clothed. Everest—I assumed it had been him—had put me to bed, but he hadn't stripped my clothes off. The seams of my jeans dug into my skin, and the wire frame of my bra felt engraved into my ribs.

I peeled myself from the warm bed and padded to my bathroom. I flicked on the lights, smelling blood before spotting it. Balled pink tissues littered my wastebasket. I moved to the sink and peered at my hellish reflection. My bottom lip was split and swollen, my right cheek was bruised, and my wrist, although no longer torn, sported a purple hematoma.

I turned the shower on and stripped. Red lines streaked my skin, but the imprint of clothing would vanish quickly, unlike my tattered flesh. That would take a couple more hours to heal—if I was lucky. The worst part was that, even if I managed to camouflage the bruise on my cheek, there was nothing I could do about my lip. Everyone would see it. If they learned I'd bit my own self, they'd realize I had no control over my wolf form, which could disqualify me from the Alpha contest.

I returned to my bedroom, grabbed my cell phone that was snoozing, turned off the alarm, and typed a message to Everest. **I passed out because I was sick, and my lip split from the fall. Come see me in the kitchen when you wake up.** I sent that off, then added: **Thank you for staying with me. And for putting me to bed.**

And then I got ready for the long day ahead, feeling like my body had been rubbed against the metal ridges of the washboard nailed to the wall of the laundry room, a memento of early life in Colorado.

SEVEN

The second I entered the kitchen, Evelyn gasped. *"Dios mio!"*

She clapped a hand over her mouth and set down her whisk. The runny milk and eggs dripped onto the scratched but gleaming stainless-steel island.

"Who did that to you?" Even though we were alone in the kitchen and probably the only ones awake in the entire inn, her voice was quiet.

I didn't move my gaze off the trickling whisk. "I fell."

She narrowed her eyes at me, irises darkened by skepticism. "Against whose fist did you fall?"

"No one. I promise. I was sick, and you know how I get when I'm sick…I pass out." Which was true. I always passed out when I threw up.

She walked around the island and caught my chin between her fingers, turning my face left and right, inspecting my cheek. I bit down on my lip before remembering the tiny stab wound. I released my lip instantly, then removed my face from her hands.

Her thin, penciled-in eyebrows drew together when her gaze moved over the rest of my body and spotted bruises on my elbows and wrist. "The truth, *querida.*"

The truth... Could I tell her the truth, or would she run back to LA screaming? Or worse, would she stop loving me for who I was? Why hadn't these things occurred to me before I made her leave everything behind for me? Did I think I could hide my dual nature from her forever?

"It is why you left Boulder in the first place?" she asked. "Someone was hurting you?"

"No one was hurting me." Had Mom told her about Heath? "But it's the reason we left Boulder."

Her eyes glittered furiously as she took in my skin that carried the same camo pattern as the tank underneath my gray uniform. I should probably have gone with long sleeves.

I sighed. "Can you promise not to hate me once I tell you the whole truth?"

She pressed a hand against her chest, over her heart. "Hate you? It is too late for me to hate you."

I sank onto the stepladder Evelyn used as a chair when her knees ached and hung my head in my hands. "You're going to think I'm crazy."

"I would never think such a thing."

"Yes, you will. And you'll leave." I'd told Liam nothing could hurt me anymore, but that wasn't true. Evelyn shunning me, leaving me, that would cause me tremendous pain.

"I will never leave you."

"You swear?" I tipped my head back to stare into her gentle eyes.

"On the Lord above, I swear it. Now tell me."

"I'm a"—I gulped—"a...*werewolf*." My voice was quieter than the fan whirring over the stove.

Evelyn's rouged mouth gaped. Closed. Gaped again. She reminded me of the trouts Dad and I used to catch fly fishing in the mountain streams. "*Un lobo?*"

She'd taught me enough Spanish for me to understand *lobo*: wolf. Even to me, who'd grown up with the knowledge that such fantastical creatures existed, it sounded outrageous.

With shaky fingers, I tucked a strand of hair behind my ear. "Yes."

She didn't back away from me, didn't run screaming, but confusion rippled over her features.
"How hard did you bump your head?"

"I'll show you." Concentrating hard, I lifted my unsteady hands and willed my nails to turn into claws. Nothing happened. I tried again. Still nothing. I tucked both my hands underneath my thighs. "I used to be able to change at will, but being away—"

"Oh, sweetheart..."

"Evelyn, please. I'm telling you the truth."

She shot me a look filled with such pain and sympathy that I grabbed the phone from my tunic pocket and dialed Everest.

After a couple rings, his sleepy voice came on. "Hello?"

"Come to the kitchen now," I said.

"Ness, it's not even six."

"Please."

He grumbled. "Fine."

Silence slipped between Evelyn and me. I could tell a thousand words formed on the tip of her tongue, but she didn't utter any of them. She just stared, her face stamped with as much worry as the day we'd finally let her into our ground-floor unit.

Five long minutes later, Everest arrived. "What?"

"Show Evelyn," I asked him.

"Show her what?"

"What we are."

His eyes widened. "Ness..."

"I can't keep this a secret from her any longer."

He turned his face toward Evelyn. Alarm deepened the little lines around her eyes and mouth.

"Please," I whispered.

"Okay." He raised his hands. In seconds, his nails lengthened and curled, and then his fingers retracted into his palms.

Evelyn became as pale as her pancake batter. She crossed herself, and then...and then she fainted.

Everest caught her before her head could knock against the tiles. I scrambled off the stepladder and helped him situate her there. I rushed to the sink, wadded up some paper towels, and wet them.

"Why did you *have* to tell her?" Everest muttered, his voice still a bit groggy.

"Because she would've found out. It's not like our existence is that much of a secret in this part of the world."

"Just because people suspect we exist, doesn't mean they all believe it."

I crouched beside her and moved the damp compress across her forehead. "I needed her to believe it."

Her eyelids fluttered, and then her mascara-laden eyelashes lifted. She blinked as she came to. And then her black eyes settled on me. An emotion—I couldn't tell if it was fear or astonishment—flitted through them.

"Please, say something, Evelyn." I dabbed the wet towel along her neck.

"Breakfast," she murmured. "I need to make breakfast." She pressed my hand away, latched onto the island for support, and wobbled onto her feet. Everest hadn't released her, but she brushed his hands off as though they were spiders.

She picked out a serrated knife and turned toward me. I backed up and fell, my buttocks hitting cold tiles. Was she going to kill me?

"Can you cut the bread, Ness? Make thick slices."

Working on evening out my thudding pulse, I scrambled back up to my feet and reached out to seize the knife. The serrated blade whispered through the air and gleamed in the bright lighting.

Evelyn returned to her batter and picked up the whisk as though my reveal hadn't happened, as though Everest's hands hadn't morphed into paws.

"If I'm no longer needed, I'm going to go crash a couple more hours." Everest pivoted toward me. "Unless you want me to stay?"

"No. Go. Thank you." Before he left, I told him, "Read your messages."

"I read them."

I plastered on a weak smile as he passed through the swinging door, and then I walked to the cutting board topped with three loaves of challah.

"Evelyn, are you—" I was about to say angry when she stopped me with a raised palm.

Tears pricked my swollen lids. She didn't want to talk to me. She was horrified, and how could I blame her?

We worked in silence next to each other. While she tossed thick slabs of bacon in a cast-iron skillet, I soaked the slices of bread I'd cut in egg and milk, prepping them for the griddle Evelyn had already buttered. Not once did we look at each other. I was afraid of what I would see there, and probably, so was she.

While she cooked, I sunk my hands in rubber gloves and soaped up the toppling tower of bowls and cooking paraphernalia. Then I aligned the stainless-steel containers and helped Evelyn arrange the golden triangles of French toast, the fluffy pancakes, the crispy hash browns, the fried sausage, the glistening bacon, and the scrambled eggs.

As I carried the lidded metal containers into the deserted dining room, dawn fanned out over the mountains and raked through the majestic pines, tinting the rock lavender and the bristly leaves blue. Dawn had always been my favorite time of day. Perhaps because it was the quietest, or perhaps because it felt like a piece of blank paper upon which anything could be drawn.

But not today. Today its blankness felt barren and smudged by Evelyn's silence.

After I slotted all the dishes into their cradles and lit the small candles that would keep them warm until the pack descended upon the dining room, I brewed coffee and tea in the pantry and filled several thermoses with the dark, steaming liquids, going through the motions robotically.

The swinging door flapped.

"Do you know where I could get—" Liam's gaze collided into mine.

I raised a thermos. "Coffee?"

Slowly, he nodded and extended the ceramic mug clutched between his long fingers.

I filled it for him. "How do you take it?"

"What happened to your face?"

I licked the scab on my lip. "I fell. Do you want milk? Sugar?"

His dark eyebrows pressed together. "Just milk."

I poured some into his mug. "More?"

He was still looking at my mouth.

"Do you want more milk?"

He shook his head, then tugged a hand through his brown hair, mussing it up. I didn't remember his mother in great detail—she died when I was five and he was nine—but I remembered she was a beautiful, gentle woman.

Instead of looking for Heath in Liam, I looked for her, but the square, chiseled jaw, the brown eyes, the dark eyebrows, those were all Heath.

"Ready for today?" Liam asked as I set the milk down on the large wooden platter.

"For the meeting with the elders or the paintballing?" I lined up the jugs and thermoses, then filled glass pitchers with ice and tap water and placed those on the platter.

"Both."

I shot him a cocky smile, which sent a jolt of pain through my face. No more smiling for me today. "I was born ready." I latched on to the horn handles of the tray and heaved it up.

"Want help with that?"

Even though my joints smarted a little, I said, "I don't need anyone's help." I gave him a wide berth so our arms wouldn't graze, then pressed my shoulder into the swinging door.

The only thing I needed was for Evelyn to keep loving me in spite of the beast I was.

EIGHT

I changed out of my work uniform before meeting with the five elders. I slid on skinny jeans and a pair of much-loved, scuffed-up Timberlands that seemed appropriate footwear for paintballing.

Lucas, Matt, and Liam were already in the conference room when I arrived, lounging on the springy office chairs.

"Close the door, Ness," Bushy-Eyebrows instructed.

Even though the idea of being locked in a room with eight men was unpleasant, I shut the door before making my way to the free seat next to Matt. I felt his gaze rake over my face. Lucas looked too.

The bald elder leaned forward and clasped his hands. "Did someone…hurt you?"

"No." I didn't offer details. "So what's on the agenda?"

Chairs squeaked as bodies shifted.

Bushy-Eyebrows took a swig of water from the glass in front of him. "Okay. Let's get down to business. There will be three tests. The first, endurance. You will have to run twenty miles in wolf form over a terrain set with obstacles and traps. The last person to arrive at the marked destination will lose. And anyone who switches into his or her human form will be automatically disqualified."

My pulse jackhammered inside my veins. To compete, I would need to change. Fully change. Not the pathetic attempt I'd gone through last night.

Praying the assembled werewolves' heightened senses wouldn't pick up on my nervousness, I asked, "When will this take place?"

"The sooner the better. Would next weekend work for everyone?"

That gave me one week to master my wolf form. Not ideal but better than a couple hours. I toyed with Mom's ring, slotting it around one finger, then slipping it over another.

Everyone nodded.

"We will test your cunning next. The details of that trial will only be given to the three winners of the first contest," Bushy-Eyebrows said.

I could do cunning. I released Mom's ring and tucked it back into my tank top where the warmed metal rested against my heart.

"And then we'll end with a test of strength. A fight between the last two contenders."

"A fight?" I croaked.

"Did you think this was some sort of beauty pageant, Ness?" Eric asked.

I squashed my aching lips tight to seal off the sharp comeback that threatened to pop out. A fight wasn't fair, but I supposed the elders knew that. Even though I was strong, how much damage could a hundred-and-twenty-pound girl inflict on a two-hundred-plus-pound monster like Matt? I could hurt him, sure, but beat him...unlikely. But maybe Matt wouldn't be the one in the ring.

Maybe *I* wouldn't be the one in the ring.

Bushy-Eyebrows leaned forward in his seat. "Does anyone have questions?"

The other three shook their heads. I neither shook my head nor nodded. I stayed perfectly still.

"Now let's talk rules. Eric?" Bushy-Eyebrows nodded to the bald elder.

Eric started, "Non-pack members—"

I bristled. "So these rules only apply to me?"

"Just the first one. If you lose, Ness," Eric said in a voice that sounded like he'd eaten gravel for breakfast, "you cannot ask the future Alpha to bring you into the pack."

I narrowed my eyes. "Which means I'll have to leave Boulder?"

"Yes."

Even though I'd planned to leave, I wanted it to be my choice. Not theirs. "But if any of the others lose, they get to stay in the pack?"

"Correct."

Well, that's fair.

"You will all be civil to each other. We don't want any fighting outside of these trials," Eric said.

Bushy-Eyebrows continued, "Internal discord will only weaken the pack. Already not having an Alpha for such a prolonged period of time has hurt us and bolstered the self-worth of neighboring packs. Let's not give them more ammunition."

Last night, they'd all been civil to me. This morning, Liam had been borderline kind. Would this go on? The pack had shunned me when I'd needed help after Dad was shot. I had a long memory, and that memory had wedged deep trust issues inside me.

"Okay, Ness?" Eric asked.

I didn't appreciate being singled out. *Again.* I shoved my shoulders back hard against the leather seat. "I can be nice."

"Can you?" Lucas asked.

I shot him a taunting smile. "If I want to be, yes."

"Well, we do hope you'll want to be," Bushy-Eyebrows said. "Any uncivil behavior reported to us will incur serious consequences. Elimination being the gentler consequence."

His name suddenly slotted into my mind. *Frank.* Frank McNamara. He used to be the Alpha when my father was my age. Dad had always spoken highly of him. I wondered if Frank would've allowed me into the pack had he been Alpha instead of Heath. But I quit wondering fast because what was the point in musing over something that couldn't happen?

"I believe you kids have something fun planned, so we'll adjourn this meeting."

Yeah, fun. Not.

"Next Saturday, come to the pack headquarters at noon. Don't be late." The elders rose.

As Frank passed behind my chair, he placed a palm on my shoulder. "Jeb told me about your mother this morning."

Great. Lucy was giving out my room number to strangers, and Jeb was informing people of my loss. So much for respecting my privacy. Sadly, my aunt and uncle were meeting my expectations…my very low expectations.

"Maggie was a good woman," Frank added.

My throat felt like someone had gone at it with a fist.

Frank squeezed my shoulder once, then went on his way.

"What'd she die of?" Matt asked as I got up.

I pushed a lock of hair behind my ear. Even though I didn't want to discuss my mother with anyone, I also didn't want them to get their information from other places. "Ovarian cancer."

"Is that why you're so bitter?" Lucas asked.

Matt and Liam both shot him a look.

Lucas raised his palms in the air. "I was just wondering if she was biting off our heads because she couldn't stand the look of them, or if her behavior was out of the ordinary. Am I not allowed to ask?"

"*Damn*. And here I thought I'd been coming across as charming." I smiled. "I should probably work on my social skills." My phone vibrated in my back pocket. I fished it out, but when I saw the number on the screen, I rejected the call and shoved it back inside my pocket. "So, paintball?" I asked, my heart loping around my chest.

If only I could've quieted it with a press of a button, too.

A SMALL BUS WAS waiting outside the inn, already crammed with animated pack members. Sucking in a breath, I climbed on, Everest close behind. I slid into the first row so I didn't have to ford through the entire bus. Everest dropped down next to me.

I caught sight of August across the aisle. He seemed intent on deciphering the slogan in bold block letters on the driver's cap.

Everest bent toward me and dropped his voice to a low whisper, "He broke up with Sienna last night."

That explained the surly curve of August's mouth.

"How long were they dating?" I murmured back.

"A couple months. Wouldn't know why he ended things, would you?"

"Me?" I frowned. "Why would I know anything?"

Everest gave me a *come-on* look.

"I didn't even know her…"

He narrowed his eyes so much they looked about to collide against the bridge of his nose.

"What?"

"*Dimples*?" he whispered.

"You think it's because of *me*?"

Everest shrugged. "Maybe they were having trouble before he called you his favorite girl."

I jabbed my elbow into his ribs because he'd said that way too loudly. So loudly that August glanced my way. I highly doubted he'd broken up with his girlfriend over me. Everest was giving me way more importance than I had.

The bus door closed after Liam, Lucas, and Matt walked on. Matt slid in next to August, while Liam and Lucas sat behind me. I sank a little lower in my seat. I heard Matt ask August how he was holding up.

August grunted. "Fine."

"How was the meeting?" Everest asked.

As the bus pulled out of the inn's driveway and rolled west, I told him about the first trial and the rule—the one that only applied to me. And then I told him about the last trial. And his eyes went as wide as his mouth.

"You can't win a physical fight," he whispered.

"Thanks for the vote of confidence." He was probably right, though.

Lucas leaned forward, his greasy black hair flopping in my peripheral vision. I half expected him to mention the trials. He didn't. "I was remembering the last time I saw you in your wolf form. You were this scrawny ball of white fur."

The bus went over a pothole, and my breasts jiggled. I folded my arms to block them in place. "You sure you didn't mistake me for a kitten?"

He smirked. "I know the difference between a cat and a wolf. Both have claws, but only one bites."

My phone vibrated in my lap. I could tell Everest had recognized the number from the stiffening of his body. I flipped the phone over.

"Who you avoiding? An ex?" Lucas inquired.

"Exactly."

"Got many exes back in... Where was it you lived again?"

Matt filled in for him, "Los Angeles."

"Got many exes back in LA?" Lucas asked.

"Maybe."

"You know, Ness, the elders didn't state this rule, probably 'cause there hasn't been any girls in the pack for over a century, but there's no dating among the pack. We don't shit where we eat, if you get the gist."

I cocked an eyebrow. "In what screwed up world do you think I'd be interested in dating *any* of you?"

He tipped his long chin toward Everest. "You and your cousin look awfully chummy."

Shock rushed through me that he would think I would screw my own cousin.

Everest spun and smashed his fist into Lucas's simpering grin, which had Lucas shooting to his feet.

Liam grabbed a fistful of his friend's T-shirt and yanked him back into his seat. "Enough!" His eyes gleamed dangerously. He probably didn't want his little friend to be kicked out of the running for Alpha for being *uncivil*.

"You punch like a girl, Everest," Lucas muttered under his breath.

"Stop being a dick, Lucas." August's retort rumbled like thunder.

The bus had gone extremely quiet, so quiet I could hear Everest's leaden breaths. I wound my fingers around his wrist, but he ripped his hand away, then sulked the rest of the trip to the paintball arena.

Lucas didn't try talking to us again, but he did talk. To Liam. Told him about the explosive orgasm he'd given Taryn that morning, which had me wrinkling my nose. And then he asked Liam if they were still on for tonight, 'cause Tamara was *extremely* eager to see Liam.

I wasn't the type of person who eavesdropped, but this conversation was in no way a secret. I bet Lucas was thrilled I was hearing it. I bet he thought it made them look appealing. All these girls throwing themselves at shifters because they were muscled and powerful and could turn into fierce creatures.

Few humans were privy to our existence. Most people still believed we were fictional beings, which packs perpetuated because not everyone was hot and bothered over a person who could morph into a beast. There were those who despised what we were.

Like the hunter who'd killed my father with a silver bullet.

People often hated what they didn't understand.

No one understood why a girl was born to the pack, and that inspired hatred.

NINE

T he paintballing arena resembled a post-apocalyptic junkyard. A rusted old bus with blown-out windows sat at the center of muddy earth strewn with various corroded car parts and scraps of metal tall enough to shield a body—and sharp enough to slice through one, too. A plastic tunnel linked the north part to the south part of the arena. A row of brick walls arranged like a labyrinth ran the length of the western fence. A log cottage sat along the arena's northern fence. The rooms were dusty, the furniture disemboweled and overturned, the cabinets crooked and broken, their doors flapping like broken bird wings.

On the east side, there was a narrow tower with a winding staircase, and a platform with a plank leading down into a wooden boat that seemed to have washed up from a playground. The round windows were grimy and the corridors tight and dark.

A couple minutes ago, we'd been given long-sleeved overalls, walkie talkies, helmets with visors, heavy guns loaded with paint pellets, and a mission. Besides defeating the enemy team, we had to locate five clues hidden amidst the junkyard.

Everest's grumpy mood lifted. Even August seemed somewhat less encumbered. These boys loved playing wargames.

Everest was on my team, but not August. He was on the red team with Lucas. Liam and Matt were greens like me. The teams had been predetermined before we showed up. Not that I would've chosen to be on the red team. I was plenty happy to have Lucas on the enemy team.

I had my back to the brick wall. On the walkie talkie tuned into a special bandwidth only accessible to our team, I heard Liam's voice crackle, asking for Matt's position. Matt mentioned the tower. I looked up and spotted him, and then I spotted the barrel of his gun aimed straight at me. Something hard blasted against my stomach.

The bastard shot me!

I was his freaking teammate. He grinned, and then his voice grizzled on the walkie talkie, "Oops. I shot one of ours. Sorry, Clark."

I glared at him, which just increased his wolfish grin.

I walked off the field, gun and hands raised to indicate I was on a timeout. Two pellets flew at me. One from a red. The other from a green. Did these assholes not know the rules? I'd never played before, but I'd listened to the briefing.

I sat in the green camp, waiting for my coach to give me the go-ahead to return to the field—not that I wanted to return. I listened to the voices crackling over the walkie talkies. Heard one of my teammates announce that they'd located item number two and were bringing it back to the camp. Then heard another one announce he was on a timeout. A couple seconds after he walked in, I went back out and raced toward the wooden boat, where I found Everest.

"Fucking Matt shot me."

"I heard." He pulled open a trapdoor just as footsteps sounded above our heads. Dust flaked off the low ceiling. "The rusted pipe's somewhere in the boat apparently. Search the back."

I walked toward the hull, bumping into a hard body steeped in shadows. The green light on his helmet told me he was on my team, even though I couldn't see his face.

A pellet burst against my back. I jerked, then gritted my teeth as I turned. Through the fog forming on my visor, I met Lucas's pleased leer. "You're out, Clark."

Lucas didn't shoot my teammate. He kept the gun leveled on me. "Better run along before I shoot you again."

"Play nice, Lucas," I heard the person behind me say. *Liam*.

He circled around me and then retreated, the weathered boards groaning beneath his footfalls. I hadn't expected him to stay, but I had expected him to be shot. He wasn't.

I marched past Lucas, shoving him with my shoulder, and he chuckled.

"Asshole," I muttered.

I walked back to the camp, not bothering to lift my gun. I was hit six more times, once on the jaw. The pellet broke the skin.

After a minute of stewing inside the camp, nursing my newest wound, I decided that if they weren't going to play fair, I would play dirty too.

The second I was back in the game, I went to find Lucas, disregarding direct orders from our team captain—lo and behold, that was Liam—to assemble on the north side to strategize. I noticed Lucas's black hair first, peeking out from underneath his helmet, and shot him square between the shoulder blades. He turned, arms raised. I shot him again. And again. I took great pleasure in seeing the colorful paint splatter his overalls.

When I was blasted on the waist by one of his teammates, I didn't even care. I stalked back to the camp and refilled my ammo.

"Don't know north from south, Clark?" Liam asked, barging into the camp seconds after me, a large splash of paint on his chest.

"Are we playing as a team now? Because if memory serves me, Matt and two other people from the greens shot at me. You probably didn't notice, though, too wrapped up in barking orders."

"Matt thought you were—"

"Oh, don't give me that! I have a freaking green light flashing on my forehead." I wiped the fog from my visor. "Who got you?"

"August."

I smiled.

We didn't speak after that. Liam was way too busy studying the video feed of the arena. Our coach radioed in that I was clear to reenter the field.

"We're still missing the compass and the pair of yellow pliers," Liam said without turning away from the monitor. "I think the compass is in the tunnel. Want to come with me to find it?"

"Are you planning on shooting me in the back?"

"I don't shoot people in the back."

Sure you don't.

He held my gaze. "I'm not sure what you heard about me, but from the way you've been treating me, I'm guessing it's all bad."

I didn't answer him.

"I'll cover you," he said. "Come to the tunnel with me."

"Whatever. Fine. But know that if you shoot me, I'll make your life hell."

He had the audacity to smile. "More than it already is?"

I erupted from our bunker and headed toward the plastic tunnel. While Liam radioed in our position and asked if anyone had eyes on the exit, I peered inside. An, "all-clear," crackled over the walkie talkie.

"Search the middle of the tunnel," Liam said.

"Sending the girl in first. How gentlemanly."

Liam's eyes flashed behind the fog in his goggles. He pushed past me and flopped onto his stomach and started creeping down the tunnel. "Cover *me* then."

So I shielded him. I thought I caught the glow of red. Sure enough, someone from the enemy team shifted inside the dilapidated cottage. I raised my gun and fired through the window. My pellet hit its mark. The guy turned in my direction. I couldn't see who it was, but did it matter? He retreated into his camp's bunker with his gun and hands raised. On the other side of the tunnel, I noticed another red light. I clambered over the dirt piled atop the plastic tunnel and shot at the person before they could duck and locate Liam.

I hit the person's helmet.

He raised his hands and gun just as a pellet smacked the base of my spine. "Got you again, Clark."

I grabbed my walkie talkie. "I'm out. Lucas is at the south entrance of the tunnel, Liam."

Just as I spoke that, Lucas raised his gun to me again, but before the jerk could get another shot in, a pellet hit him on the thigh.

I wheeled, half expecting one of my teammates to have shot him, but found one of his own instead.

"Stop picking on her, Mason," August growled.

Lucas glowered at him before prowling off.

"Thank you, but you didn't have to do that," I said.

"This is a preview of the trials, Ness. They'll stab you in the back the first chance they get. Drop out. You hear me? Drop. Out."

"I drop out, and I have to pack my bags this afternoon."

"I'll talk to the elders."

"I'd rather you didn't."

He huffed. "I won't stand around to watch you get hurt."

I laid a hand on his forearm. "It's a game, August. They're not going to kill me."

"They might not kill you, but they'll—" His body jerked as a pellet smacked his back.

Liam had crawled out the other side of the tunnel and opened fire.

"What will we do to her, August?" His voice was as harsh as his close shot.

"You won't hesitate to hurt her," August bit out.

"Didn't you hear? Nothing can hurt her." Liam was tossing my words back at me with such a derisive tone, that for a second, I tightened my gloved grip on the gun, tempted to shoot at him.

But I took the high road; I spun and walked away.

If this *was* a preview, then at least I knew what to expect.

TEN

M y body resembled a sheet of blotting paper. Like ink smudges, bruises marbled almost every limb on my body. The worst one was on my inner thigh.

My team ended up winning. Not that I'd felt in a celebratory mood. After the game, I'd vanished into my bedroom to take a hot bath, then donned leggings and a super soft off-the-shoulder tee. I skipped wearing a bra because the wires dug into my bruised ribs. On the upside, my cheek and jaw were looking a lot better. My werewolf blood was kicking in and working its magic.

I simply prayed my body wouldn't decide to change tonight. I didn't think I could take any more pain.

A text from Lucy had me heading to the laundry room in the late afternoon. Now that the weekend was over, all the beds had to be changed.

I loaded up the industrial-sized washers with sheets and pillowcases and duvet covers, trying not to gape at certain stains. I washed my hands twice then started on the ironing of the loads that had already been washed and dried. I fed sheet after sheet through the rotary iron, watching the furrows smooth out of the fabric, feeling them smooth out of me, too.

I cracked my neck, working out the kinks brought on by lugging heavy gear and constantly watching my back. As I reached for a bulky duvet cover, I felt a disturbance in the air, caught a whiff of sawdust and Old Spice. I turned to find August standing in the doorway, knuckles raised.

He froze. Without knocking, he slid his hand into the pocket of his sweatpants. "Your aunt told me I might be able to find you here."

Of course she did. "Did you come to tell me how stupid I am again?"

Surprise carved his face. "I never said you were stupid."

I grabbed the duvet cover, folded it in half, and thrusted it into the iron. I heard him approach...smelled him approach.

"Ness"—his voice was on my neck—"I don't think you're stupid."

I didn't turn. "So why are you here?"

"I'm here to tell you that I've decided to return to active duty."

I let go of the duvet and whirled. "You're going back out there?"

"Just for a few months."

"Why?"

His eyes raked over my face. "I miss it."

"Is that why you broke up with Sienna?"

"News travels fast."

"Is it?"

"It's part of the reason. The other part is that she's a sweet girl who deserves a good guy."

"And you're *not* a good guy?"

"I'm not good"—he watched the rotary iron spin—"for her." He wet his thick bottom lip.

I'd never noticed August's lips before. He had really nice lips.

"Will you give me your phone number?"

"You want my number?" I breathed.

"Yeah. You know"—he smiled—"so I can call you."

"You're not leaving because of me, are you?" I realized how conceited that sounded only after it popped out of my mouth. I raked my hair back. "You know, because you don't want to see my ass handed to me." A spot of heat spread over my jaw and throat and spilled into my chest.

Shut up, Ness.

Shut. Up.

A groove appeared between August's eyebrows. "No," he said after a long pause. "I just need to get away from Boulder for a while. I've been here for three years. I don't like staying in the same place for long stretches. I have my entire life to grow roots, but until I have to, I'd rather run wild."

"And going to fight in... Where are you going?"

"It's classified."

"And going to fight is your idea of running wild? Why can't you run wild in the Rockies or in the Appalachians?"

A smile grew on his face. "Worried about me?"

"Um, *yeah.*" I felt the tips of my ears heat up. "You're going God knows where to fight God knows who. Of course I'm worried."

Amusement twinkled in his eyes. "Quit stalling, and give me your number."

He had his cell phone poised in his hands. It was unlocked, so I lifted it from his fingers, created a new contact, and typed in my number.

"Don't run too wild, all right?"

His Adam's apple bobbed in his throat. "You too."

I felt all torn up over his departure. Ten years my senior, August Watt had been like a big brother to me way back when. He'd taught me to play backgammon while our parents had never-ending meals. He'd taught me to climb my first tree. He'd walked with me to the ice-cream parlor, and when the weather was crap, he'd collect me from school in his pickup.

Before good sense could knock into me, I hooked my arms around his neck and pressed my cheek against his chest, against the heart that beat there, strong and steady.

"Thank you for being nice to me. Since I came back, but also during all those years before I left."

For a second he didn't move, but then his arms wound around me and pulled me in tight. "Don't ever thank someone for being nice. Especially not me."

We stayed locked together until one of the dryers beeped so incessantly I broke the embrace to power the machine off.

"Keep in touch, okay?" His voice was a little thick.

I raised a paltry smile—the best I could muster. "I'd need your number for that."

He pressed on his phone's screen, and my cell phone started ringing.

"Pick up," he said.

I frowned. "Okay." I swiped my phone off the top of a pile of clean sheets, then slid my finger across the screen. When I saw him raise the phone to his ear, I raised mine too.

"Hey," he said, and then he winked and turned around, disappearing the way he came. "What are you up to?"

Silly. This was so silly. But it got me smiling. "Laundry."

"That's always code for something else."

"Is it?" I laughed. "What's it code for?"

"Everyone knows what it's code for."

I touched my navel, which suddenly felt tight and hot. "Enlighten me, why don't you?"

THAT NIGHT, JUST AS I was falling asleep, a knock resounded softly through my bedroom. Since the pack had left, I imagined it would be Everest, but as I walked toward the door, I smelled menthol and bacon grease.

Evelyn.

Had she come to tell me she was leaving? My heart thumped as I drew open the door. Hugging her arms, she stood in the darkened corridor, her face free of her usual heap of makeup. The red rims of her eyes told me she'd been crying.

My fault.

My *selfish* fault.

She pressed her arms tighter in front of the plush black bathrobe Mom had given her for Christmas a few years back. To avoid parting with it, Evelyn had mended almost every seam. Would she impart on our relationship the same treatment she'd given her robe?

As her eyes raked over the bruises marring my skin, she pursed her lips.

I wanted to explain, but when I opened my mouth, a tiny sob lurched out instead. Evelyn's arms came loose, and then they laced around me. She pulled me against her chest, combing my hair back as I soaked the fluffy fabric with my tears.

"You won't leave me?"

"No, *querida*. I will never leave. Just as I could never hate you, even if you transformed into a dragon."

A wheezy chuckle glided out between my blubbering. "Those don't exist."

"*Gracias a Dios.*" If she hadn't been holding me, I was certain she would've crossed herself.

The corridor lights flickered and buzzed.

"I am ready to hear...*more*. Will you tell me?"

I nodded and tugged her inside. Once the door was closed, once she'd settled on the bed next to me and dragged her lotion-softened fingers through my hair, I told her about how I'd tried to become part of the pack after my father was shot in his wolf form by a hunter. I told her about Heath and what he did to Mom when she'd begged him to train me.

What I didn't tell Evelyn was that I'd entered the contest to become Alpha. I neither wanted to worry her nor have her tell me how dumb it was.

ELEVEN

When my phone rang on Wednesday morning, I answered without even checking the number. For the past three days, all my calls had originated from August. We talked every day, and when we didn't talk, we texted.

I'd never communicated with anyone as easily. He made me laugh. He also made me feel things...things that were apparently against pack rules. Things that made me wish he'd come back to Boulder sooner than planned.

"Candy, you're alive!" a chirpy voice said.

I rolled into a sitting position so fast I had to clutch the nightstand to avoid keeling over. "Hi, Sandra."

"I've got a job for you, girl."

"A j-job?"

"A client saw your profile—"

"I thought you took it down!"

"I did, but he screenshot your pic and begged me to get in contact with you."

Creep. "I'm not interested."

"Hun, you got gypped out of your last payment because of the unfortunate demise of the customer. This is me trying to make it up to you."

"It's okay, Sandra." It's not like I would've taken said customer's money.

"What about all those bills you still need to pay?"

I let go of the nightstand. I did need money for the overdrafts on the joint bank account I'd shared with Mom, but I didn't want to earn it doing...*that*.

"Why d'you think Everest insisted I pair you up with Heath Kolane?" she continued.

Sandra believed my cousin, whom she'd met through Becca—one of her *girls*—had pimped me out so I could earn fast cash. I hadn't played escort for Heath's money, but explaining my true intentions would've earned me a restraining order instead of a job.

"Real shame he died. He was one of my best customers. Real shame. Anyway, the customer I'm calling 'bout is offering three grand."

I coughed. "Three grand?"

"You interested now, hun?"

Escort was a job like any other, right? Besides...*three grand*. I couldn't exactly turn that down. I still had debts, plus I wanted to reimburse Evelyn for the money she'd loaned me to pay for Mom's funeral. Even though she insisted she would never take a dime for it, the funeral had been pricey, because we'd wanted to give my mother an ending worthy of the woman she'd been.

"Can you tell me more about the gig?"

"Dinner at Pelligrini's."

"No sex, right?"

"*Absolutely* no sex! I don't run a brothel."

I could do dinner. Dinner was safe. "Why would someone pay three grand for dinner?"

"Can't give you any details until you agree to it. So, what'll it be?"

If Evelyn found out... I couldn't even finish that thought without shuddering. I wasn't a prostitute—this was just about being arm candy to men who didn't want to spend time getting to know a person—but most people wouldn't see the distinction.

I hadn't, until Everest explained it to me. He'd met Becca through the agency. Too shy to ask a girl out on a date, he'd paid someone else to do it for him.

"Okay. But, Sandra... Don't keep me on the roster after this, okay?"

"You got it, Candy."

She finally proceeded to give me the details of my date, which I jotted down on the small pad of paper next to the bed, and told me to wear something fancy.

I had two nice dresses: one was the black sequin number I'd worn for my "date" with Heath Kolane; the other was a cherry-red silk slip with spaghetti straps that used to be Mom's.

Even though donning something of hers sent a chill straight through my breastbone, I went with the red.

I didn't want to be reminded of Heath tonight.

I WAS READY EARLY. I'd applied foundation to my fading bruises. Most had already vanished anyway. And I'd swiped mascara over my lashes and lipstick as red as my dress to my healed lips.

Instead of lingering inside the inn and incurring more of Lucy's inquisition: "Where was I going dressed up like a...like a..." She hadn't finished the sentence, but I'd heard the end loud and clear. I told her I had a blind date and not to wait up. Not that she would have waited up. She told me not to get knocked up. I thanked her for her unsolicited advice.

I waited in the inn's driveway, eyes closed, face raised toward the dying sun. The weather was unusually warm for early July, which suited the LA girl in me. Winter in Boulder—if I stayed that long—would be especially brutal now that I was used to mild temperatures.

"Someone's looking mighty fancy."

I snapped my lids open and found Lucas hopping out of the passenger side of a dark Mercedes SUV decked out with oversized off-roading tires. And then Liam was there, too, in a short-sleeved, black V-neck, his hair artfully tousled, as though he'd finger-combed it back with styling wax but missed a couple locks.

How I wished he was covered in warts; it would've made disliking him way easier.

"Where you going, Clark?" Lucas drawled, coming to a stop in front of me.

I was glad I'd worn heels, glad for the extra inches. "I'm going to dinner with a friend."

"You have friends?" he asked.

Jerk.

Liam jabbed his companion. "You look nice, Ness."

I frowned, unsure what to do with the compliment. I tightened the black leather jacket I'd added to my dress. "Thanks?" Why, oh why, did it have to come out as a question? "What are you guys doing here?"

"We just came to have a couple beers at our favorite inn," Lucas said. "Did you think we were coming to hang out with you?"

I balked. "Why would you ever think I'd want to hang out, Lucas?"

He disregarded my comment. "Ready for trial number one?"

"Absolutely." I wasn't ready. I still hadn't changed into my wolf form—I hadn't even tried. I'd been too busy licking my wounds from paintballing to worry about much else. I'd worry about it tomorrow, and if by Saturday I couldn't change, I'd fake an illness. They wouldn't force me to compete sick.

Or would they?

Lucas rubbed his hands. "So…excited to go back to LA?"

"Why is everyone so convinced I'm going to lose? And don't you dare say it's because I'm a girl."

His stupid grin widened.

"Leave her alone." Liam shoved Lucas toward the revolving doors just as a black limo pulled into the driveway.

My ride had arrived. I traipsed down toward it. An impressively large driver came out and drew the back door open for me.

I thanked him and got in.

"Mr. Michaels is waiting for us at the restaurant." His voice was as big as he was.

I'm pretty sure Liam and Lucas, who were rooted by the entrance of the inn, had heard the driver speak. They seemed star-struck by the limo, which I guessed wasn't a common car to see in Boulder.

Sandra had sent me a little background information about Mr. Michaels. He was a hotel promoter who owned five-star resorts in Denver, Beaver Creek, and Las Vegas. An extremely wealthy sixty-year-old who'd grown up in Boulder but dropped out of high school at seventeen and moved to Vegas, where he worked his way up to management, then gambled his way to a large bank account, before receiving a consequential amount of money from a deceased grandmother.

I was sort of excited about meeting him, not because of his wealth or status, but because I assumed that anyone who could ascend so far up in the world was worth meeting…worth learning from.

The restaurant was thirty minutes away, in a barn that had been refurbished with cowhide banquettes and lacquered black tables. Modern glass chandeliers swathed the dim interior in a tawny glow that made everyone look handsomer.

The romper-clad hostess led me to a table all the way in the back, toward a man sipping an ochre drink with a snowball-sized ice cube.

Aidan Michaels stood when I arrived, looking me over through wire-rimmed glasses. "Your picture doesn't do you justice, Candy."

"Thank you, Mr. Michaels."

"Sorry I couldn't pick you up myself, but I had an important call with my lawyer."

"That's fine."

He walked around and held out my chair. "Would you like some wine? Or maybe a glass of champagne?"

"Champagne would be nice."

He asked the hostess for a glass of their best champagne, and then he tucked my chair under the table before returning to his seat. "You don't look like a Candy. What's your real name?"

"You're not paying me enough to get my real name."

His gaze tightened, but then his teeth flashed, and he laughed.

"Can I ask *you* something?"

He leaned back in his chair and raised his tumbler to his lips. "Go ahead."

"Why does a successful man like yourself go through an agency to find a dinner date?"

"Aha. The million-dollar question. I was married once, and she broke my heart. So I decided never again, and I've stuck to that thanks to treating dating like I treat my businesses." He shifted forward and placed his drink down. "A tidy social transaction."

His honesty had my shoulder blades un-pinching.

"My turn. Why is a pretty young thing like yourself doing this?"

I unfolded my napkin and laid it on my lap. "I need the money."

He nodded his understanding. "How much is it that you need?"

I bristled. "That's private."

"I apologize. It was brash of me. I was simply considering how many more dates I could get with you." He ran a hand through his silvery hair, then readjusted his glasses and leaned in. "So tell me about yourself, Candy."

Candy wasn't Ness. I didn't want her to be anything like Ness. "I lived in New York until a month ago."

"What a fabulous city! Did you enjoy it?"

"Yeah. I had a great place on the Piers."

He frowned a little. "The Piers? You mean, *Chelsea* Piers?"

Without breaking eye contact, I said, "Yes."

"And what brought you back here?"

I'd been about to say college, but I was supposed to be twenty-one. "Family."

"*Ah*...family."

"Do you have family?"

"My wife's gone, my father's dead, and my mother has Alzheimer's. So no. No family. I have a dog though." He handed me his phone, where he'd prepped a slideshow of images showcasing his pet.

I liked animals—after all, I was one—but Aidan's love for his dog was something else.

"Do you like hunting?" he asked.

I sucked in a breath. "Hunting?" I took a bread roll from the basket and chomped on the chewy crust. Hunting reminded me of my father. I swallowed the lump of masticated dough. "Not especially."

"You're not a Greenpeace advocate, are you?"

"No. I'm just...I don't like guns." *Act normal, Ness,* I chastised myself. "What do you hunt?"

"Bears, cougars, deer...wolves. Have you noticed how many of them we have in our forests?"

I forced myself to look him straight in the eyes. "I never noticed," I said, just as the waiter came back to take our order.

My appetite had vanished, so I ordered a salad, which led Aidan to ask if I was watching my weight, because if I was, it was silly. I answered that I wasn't, and he went on to tell me about all the diets he had to go on when he was married because his wife was a terrific cook.

"Only damn thing she was good at." A smirk ghosted over his reedy lips. "I take it back. She was good at keeping secrets."

I stiffened. The man had serious baggage. What he needed was a shrink, not a date. But I supposed, for three thousand dollars, I could provide him with a dinner's-worth of therapy.

TWELVE

After the main course, I excused myself to go to the bathroom, even though what I really wanted was to bolt. Before each bite of food, Aidan would wipe his fork down on his napkin. And then, every couple seconds, he'd rub his earlobe.

I felt his heavy gaze on me as I crossed the crowded restaurant. I eyed the exit with longing, but I'd sat through most of the meal. Only dessert remained—I wouldn't order any and hopefully he wouldn't either—and then I'd get paid.

I asked a waiter where I could find the bathroom, and the man pointed me toward the bar. As I walked past it, a pulse erupted in my temples. There, aligned on the cowhide barstools, sat Liam, Lucas, Matt, and Cole, Matt's older brother, another massive blond with a buzz cut.

I crossed my arms. "Did they run out of beers at the inn?"

Lucas spun on his barstool. "How's your date? Looks mighty cozy." He twirled the neck of his beer bottle between his long fingers.

"Is it a coincidence you're all here?" I asked.

Cole cocked one of his honeyed eyebrows up. "Aidan Michaels is as sleazy as they come, Ness."

"And what? You came to warn me?"

Matt leaned back against the bar. "Yeah. We take care of our own."

"Your own? I'm not even part of the pack."

"You could be, if you drop out before Saturday," Liam said.

"Like I'd ever trust your word."

"Ouch." Lucas slapped a hand over his heart.

"Look, thanks for the warning, but I'm fine."

Liam and Cole hopped off their barstools and walked over to me.

"You *will* be fine." The smell of cold cigarettes clung to Cole's sunburned skin. "If you come back with us."

"I can't."

Liam frowned. "Is he forcing you to be here?"

"No one's forcing me to do anything, but I can't leave."

I tried to step around him to go to the bathroom, but Liam clamped his hand around my bicep. "*Why* can't you leave?"

"Sorry. Did I say can't? I meant I don't want to."

"You can't hang out with a guy like Aidan Michaels."

I shrugged Liam off. "No one tells me what I can or can't do."

He glowered down at me.

"The dude is sixty and only dates whores and call-girls," Cole said.

"Maybe that's why she's here," Lucas drawled.

Liam's eyes widened.

"I'm not a whore," I snapped.

Lucas raised a cocky grin. "Which leaves call-girl."

"He's paying you to be here?" Liam's voice was dark, as though the shadows crowding his face had creeped down his throat.

"Just leave me alone. All of you. And stop fucking pretending like you have my best interest at heart. None of you do."

I started toward the bathroom, but Liam grabbed my arm. *Again.* "Do you need money?"

"That's none of your concern."

"You're a Boulder wolf, so it is our concern," Matt said.

"I'm not a Boulder wolf," I bit back.

"Is there a problem, miss?" the bartender finally asked.

"I'm fine," I gritted out. Then, to Liam and the other three, I said, "You...*all of you*...you all better be gone when I come back out."

"Or what? You'll throw a tantrum?" Lucas sneered.

"Maybe I will."

Finally I went to the bathroom. When I was done, they weren't gone, but at least they were sitting back down. I returned to the table where the waiter had set out a giant chocolate sundae and a thick slice of apple tart topped with cinnamon cream.

"I didn't know which you'd like, so I ordered both."

I glowered at the desserts.

"We can order something else if you—"

"No. No. It's fine. Thank you." I dunked my spoon into the sundae and took a bite to settle my swishing stomach.

"Are those boys friends of yours?"

My breathing hitched a couple notches.

"I noticed you chatting with them." He rubbed his ear.

"They're not friends. Just acquaintances."

"I own a lot of land and concessions. Money and power attracts detractors." Even though he smiled, it looked strained...and I felt a twinge of pity for the man who had no friends and no family, just a dog, a couple rifles, and a real estate empire. His smile vanished, and his eyes deepened to navy as he tilted his neck. "If it isn't Liam Kolane in the flesh."

My gaze climbed up the length of Liam's rigid body and then landed on his incendiary glare.

"My deepest condolences," Aidan continued.

"I'm taking Ness home."

I cringed at the use of my real name.

"I'll be the one taking her home." Aidan reached under the table and crinkled the red silk hem of my dress.

I jerked my knee so hard his hand fell away. *Just yuck.*

"Have you considered that she might not want to go home?" he continued.

I hoped Aidan had said that simply to annoy Liam, because there was no way in hell I was going anywhere else.

"Ness, now." Liam's voice brooked no argument.

"Liam, you're being rude. I'll grab a cab." Dinner was minutes away from being wrapped up. I couldn't leave now. Because he was still standing there, glaring, I said, "Liam's been very emotional since his father…passed away."

"It's understandable. Especially considering the way he died. Have the police caught the murderer yet?"

"Murderer?" I blurted out. "I thought Heath committed suicide."

Liam's face turned to stone.

I blinked at him, then blinked down at the pool of cream surrounding the half-eaten slice of pie. Heath *hadn't* committed suicide? Someone had killed him? A chill curled deep inside my belly.

"Oh, no." Aidan's eyes sparked. "Apparently someone killed him."

Liam muttered something under his breath and then yanked me up by the bicep.

"Liam!" I tried to bat his hand away, but he held on tight.

Aidan didn't cause a scene by interceding, but he glowered. I dug in my heels as Liam tugged on me. Even though Aidan was a strange man, the least I could do was be polite. Plus I needed my bag and jacket.

I grabbed both. "Thank you for dinner, Mr. Michaels."

Aidan studied the place where Liam's fingers connected with my skin. "I see you treat your women the way your father did."

Aidan's comparison made Liam free my arm. Staring at the skin he'd gripped—the skin I was now rubbing—he muttered, "Let's go. *Please*." It sounded painful for him to add that last word.

Without hesitation, I headed toward the exit.

The second we were outside, he said, "I can't believe you went out on a date with that…that rat."

I stopped rubbing my arm and fished my phone out of my bag.

"What are you doing?"

"Calling a cab."

He gestured to his mammoth-wheeled car. "I got a car."

"I make it a point not to get into cars with strangers."

"And yet you got in that limo earlier."

"That was different."

"Get in, Ness."

I started scrolling through my cell for the number, but Liam plucked the phone out of my hands. "Hey!"

"Just get in already."

"No."

"Look, if you don't get in, I'll toss you in."

"You wouldn't dare."

A bold smile appeared on Liam's dusky face. "Do you want to test that theory?"

I huffed a breath, trod to his car, and climbed in. "You're a real pain, you know that?"

He pitched the phone on my lap before I shut the door. As I strapped myself in, he climbed into the driver's side.

"Where did the others go?"

"I don't keep tabs on my buddies."

"Just on me, then?"

He didn't answer, but his eyes flashed to mine before settling back on the road.

"Lucky me," I grumbled.

Music drifted from his stereo, punctuating the silence with a heady beat.

In the darkness, my phone flashed with the agency's number. I sighed, anticipating the reason for the call. I turned toward the window and answered in a low voice, "Hello."

"Candy, is everything all right? I just got a text from Aidan to complain that you'd rushed out on him."

"Family emergency," I grumbled.

"Oh. Okay. Anyway, hun, he asked for a discount, and since he's a real good customer, I had to grant it. I hope you understand."

"How much less?"

"Half."

I squeezed my fingers around the phone.

"He was happy with you otherwise. Asked if you'd be interested—"

"No."

"If you change your mind—"

"I won't."

"Okay then. I'll wire your wage to your account. Bye, Candy."

A deep sigh rattled out of me. I'd sat through an entire dinner, all the way through dessert, but the dude had the gall to haggle. And it wasn't like he didn't have the money to pay me. I was incredibly tempted to tell Liam to turn around so I could give Aidan a piece of my mind.

"How long have you been doing this?"

"Doing what?"

Liam's eyes gleamed in the darkness. "Dating for money."

"Just this once," I lied.

"Do you have debts?"

"Doesn't everyone?"

"How much do you owe?"

I plopped my elbow down on the armrest and cradled my head. "A lot."

"A lot is not a number. Fifty grand? A hundred?"

I blinked at him in horror. "No!" If I owed a hundred grand, I would...I would... God, I didn't even know what I would do. "Six grand."

"For college?"

"No."

"Credit card bills?"

I huffed. "Past rents. Mom's funeral. Not everyone has an unlimited supply of money like you."

He braked so suddenly my seatbelt dug into my chest. "Ness, can you give me a break? I just lost my father too, all right? I've got my own shit to deal with. But I don't go around being nasty to everyone and debasing myself for a couple of bucks."

Shame surged through me.

He put his hazard lights on and heaved a ragged breath. He clenched his fingers around the steering wheel. "I'm sorry. That came out harsher than intended."

He touched my leather sleeve, and I shifted my arm away.

"Don't touch me." I stared at the crimson flashes punctuating the darkness. "Can you please drive me home?"

"Do you want me to loan you the money?"

I whipped my head around. "And be in *your* debt? No thank you."

"You'd rather keep doing…?" He gestured to the back of his car, but I knew he meant being an escort.

"No. I'm going to look for a real job."

"Don't you already have one?"

I frowned.

"You're working at the inn, aren't you?"

"They're not paying me."

"Why not?"

"Because. I'm not doing it for me."

"Who are you doing it for?"

"For someone else."

He wet his bottom lip that was thinner than his upper one, and it glinted in the darkness. "Do your aunt and uncle know about your debts?"

"They're aware of some of them."

"And they won't help?"

"I would never accept their help." Jeb offered to loan me the money for the rental payments, but I'd refused. I'd let him foot the bill for the window he'd broken, though. "By the way, they don't know about what I did tonight, so don't you dare tell them."

"I won't say anything about your *date*." He spoke the word as though it tasted bad. After a long moment, he asked, "Would you have slept with him if he'd paid you extra?"

I wrinkled my nose. "I would never sleep with someone for money."

Even though I could barely make out his face in the dim light of his dashboard, I could tell he was weighing my words.

"Why?" I asked. "Would you?"

"Sleep with someone for their money?" He let out a soft snort. "Thankfully, I don't need to resort to that."

"I meant, have you ever paid for sex?"

"No."

"Your dad—"

"I know what my dad did. But just because *he* did it doesn't mean I do it." He made a sound halfway between a growl and a sigh. "I'm *nothing* like him."

"That's what everyone says. That you're not like him."

"But you don't believe it?"

"I like to make up my own mind."

He finally angled the car back on the road. "Seems like you already did."

My pulse sprang like a livewire inside my veins and knocked against the side of my neck. I almost apologized, but he was a Kolane. He might not be *all* bad, but he was still the flesh and blood of the man who'd laughed at an eleven-year-old girl in need of guidance and who'd raped a bereft widow after she'd begged him for help.

THIRTEEN

After an uncomfortably quiet ride home, I left Liam without saying goodbye, my throat and chest too congested with anger and grief.

I headed straight to my bedroom, to the small terrace with the single Adirondack. I dropped into it and watched the heavy starlight bathing the serrated crowns of the pines.

Maybe I wasn't being fair to Liam. After all, his father had been murdered. Not that Heath's death was my fault. I'd simply gone to his place posing as an escort so that he'd let me in. If I'd gone as Ness Clark, he would've turned me away at the door. After playing nice for an agonizing stretch of time, Candy told him she knew what he'd done to Ness Clark's mother, to Becca Howard, and to a handful of other women, and warned him she was going to press charges. Heath laughed at her.

At *me*.

And so I'd slapped him. Hard. Which turned his dark eyes frosty. But at least he hadn't shifted, thanks to the crushed pills I'd slipped into his Manhattan. I drugged him, afraid he'd kill me once I revealed my true identity.

In skin, he was frightening, but in fur, he was a monster.

When I told him who I was, he growled, "Get…out," and I got out.

And someone must've gotten in right after me.

Murdered.

The eight-letter word iced me. I wrapped my arms tighter around myself and stood to go inside when a howl echoed deep in the night.

A shadowy shape moved at the edge of the forest—a large black wolf with glowing eyes. The wolf looked at me across the grassy expanse and howled again, and his howl scattered goose bumps over my forearms, over my entire body. Another deep keening made my muscles spasm and my nails turn into claws.

"*Shit. Shit. Shit,*" I whispered, backing into my room.

I yanked off my jacket, threw off my dress as my torso twitched, and tore my necklace off. Heat engulfed my skin, and then fur—white, silky fur blanketed my burning arms and sprouted over my legs. My thighs hardened and shortened. My teeth sharpened. I felt them with the tip of my tongue that had grown thicker, longer.

I tried to pull off my underwear, but my hands were paws.

Paws with sharp claws.

A bolt of pain hit my spine. I arched and threw my head back as my lips stretched and stretched, like my nose, like my ears. I growled, and it vibrated against my narrow, rubbery muzzle. My bones shifted underneath my skin, my shoulder blades turning in.

I dropped to my knees hard. The black pads that had replaced my palms absorbed the brunt of my weight. A tail surged from my backbone, shredding my underwear, whipping against my desk and bed. My knee joints cracked, snapping inward, until they became lupine hocks.

Adrenaline shot down my spine and into my limbs, electrifying every inch of skin, sharpening each one of my senses. I heard conversations from all the way inside the living room. I caught the hoot of an owl, the caw of a raven, the rustle of pine needles. I smelled Lysol and detergent and the green scent of the swaying forest beyond my first-floor balcony. I felt the heartbeat of tiny things—bugs and rabbits and owls.

I ran toward my open balcony doors, crouched low, and then sprang over the balustrade. I soared through the frizzling night air, body thrumming from the release of the wolf that had lain dormant beneath my human skin.

I hit the soft grass on all fours, and then I was galloping through the clearing that led to the forest, kicking up clumps of earth and grass. Behind me, on the large terrace, loud gasps and small cries rang out, followed by captivated chatter. I swiveled my head, and sure enough, a handful of bodies were pressed tight against the wooden railing, pointer fingers raised toward my receding form.

Wolf-watching was an attraction mentioned in the inn's brochure. Visitors were rarely disappointed.

I lifted my nose to the wind and sniffed to pick up on the other wolf's trail, but became distracted by the chitter of a squirrel spiraling up the trunk of a tall cedar. The furball stopped to watch me, its lithe flesh pulsing deliciously beneath the dusting of tawny fur. I'd hunted a squirrel once, had torn through its warm body and crushed its bones in my jaw. I was a sentient beast, but a beast nonetheless.

I observed the squirrel a while longer, until a new fragrance tickled my senses—sultry and spicy and fresh, like hot musk and crushed mint. I ran toward the scent, my paws kicking up pinecones, my claws digging into moss and clattering against downed logs, splashing into engorged, moon-lacquered streams. I dove into one, rolled on the bank, and then wrung myself out.

Free.

That's what I was...wild and untethered.

I sprinted. Away from the inn. Away from the girl I'd left behind. The girl weighed down by guilt and debt. I ran until my heart threatened to derail, and still I ran. Only when I passed under a rocky ridge did I slow. The seductive fragrance of mint and musk churned in the air above me. I craned my neck and met the gaze of an impressive black wolf pawing the stone ledge dozens of feet up from where I stood.

Beneath a cover of matted leaves, a mouse shuffled. I didn't chase it—mice were more cartilage than meat. The wolf made a soft keening noise that traveled toward me slowly. There were no words in that sound...or perhaps my lupine brain hadn't yet reawakened to our tongue.

Was it Liam?

If it was, had he tracked me, or was it a coincidence that he was there?

I thought of Heath again before remembering that wolves could read minds, so I sprinted away, the forest smudging into one long strip of wild darkness. Only hours later did the inaccuracy of my memory hit me—wolves weren't mind readers. They could, however, speak into minds, but only the Alpha possessed that ability, and I had no Alpha.

My secrets were safe.

FOURTEEN

O n Friday night, my stomach swarmed with butterflies. In less than a day, the first trial would begin…and end. Even though I'd managed to transform, did I stand a chance against wolves that hadn't been on a shifting sabbatical? I stared around my bedroom, wondering if I should pull the blue Ikea bags back out of my closet. My mother would be ashamed of my defeatist attitude. She was a staunch believer in mind over matter.

For all the good that did her.

I crushed her wedding band in my fist as I left my bedroom. On my way to meet Everest, I stopped by the kitchen. Ever since the night Evelyn had curled into bed next to me, and I'd confessed everything to her, we hadn't spoken about the pack. We'd discussed safe subjects like food and college—she wanted me to apply, but I hadn't done my SATs. Tonight again, she was on my case about colleges.

"I have some savings—" she began.

"No." I shook my head, and my hair brushed my bare shoulders. "I'm not taking your money anymore. Not unless you let me reimburse you."

"Ness…"

"Have you been to see the doctor?" I gestured to her knees. Lucy had given me the name of her physician, which I'd passed along to Evelyn.

"My arthritis is better." She ladled gazpacho into wooden bowls, then topped them with golden croutons, tiny squares of raw vegetables, and a drizzle of olive oil.

"Really?"

"Really." After finishing off the soups and ringing the buzzer to get one of the servers' attention, she busied herself with making my favorite dish: chicken quesadillas. "You're getting too skinny."

I *had* lost weight, but I'd gained back some of the muscle I'd lost working two, sometimes three, jobs back in LA. I gobbled up every last golden triangle filled with melted cheese set before me.

Evelyn checked the order sheet the server had dropped off, opened the fridge, and removed thick slices of creamy salmon which she laid on the already smoking griddle.

"Who is singing again tonight?" she asked.

"The Lemons."

"Are they good?"

"They—" The door swung open, cutting off my answer. Everest had arrived, but not alone.

"Frank wanted to meet our new cook," Everest said.

Evelyn dropped the metal spatula she'd been using to flip the salmon. The utensil clattered loudly against the tiled floor, festooning her white apron with oil. Ever since we'd arrived, Evelyn had barely strayed out of the kitchen, let alone the inn. She'd never been a particularly outgoing person, but moving to this unfamiliar town had made her downright skittish. And here was my insensitive cousin bringing someone—not just someone, Frank McNamara— into her safe haven.

Frank bent over to pick up the fallen spatula. "Evelyn, right?"

She gaped at him as he tendered it to her, but her fingers had balled into fists. He placed it on the island.

"I forced Everest to introduce me to the new cook. The Clarks are lucky to have found you."

Since Evelyn's feet had become part of the floor, I grabbed a handful of paper towels and wiped the tiles.

She finally moved, touching my shoulder. "It is okay, Ness."

As I straightened up, I raised my eyes to hers. Two pink spots had appeared on her high cheekbones, dimmed by her foundation, but still bright.

"We better get going," Everest said, "or we'll miss the opening act."

I waited for Frank to leave.

Frank's light-eyed gaze darted my way, then back to Evelyn. Finally, he moved toward the swinging door. "I hope you'll be staying, Evelyn."

Evelyn still hadn't said a word, but she nodded.

Frank offered her a demure smile, then left, the door flapping behind him.

"Are you okay?" I murmured.

Evelyn's lips were slow to unbuckle, but when they did, they arched upward. "I am fine." She slid a knuckle across my cheek.

"Ness?" Everest said.

His voice made the smile wilt off her lips. Where disgust no longer stained the way she looked at me, there was something guarded in the way she observed my cousin. It was as though she couldn't see him without seeing the beast inside. Would she look at me the same way if she bore witness to my other shape?

Note to self: never shift in front of Evelyn.

"Is all of Boulder going to this thing?" I asked Everest as we walked out of the inn and hopped into his convertible Jeep.

He'd taken off the black fabric roof, and the breeze twisted my hair. I wound it up and clutched the ends so that I didn't arrive at the music festival looking like I belonged in the band. Mullets and pompadours had been untrendy for years, but it didn't deter The Lemons from sporting them.

"You sure you want to go to this thing?"

"Yeah. I like The Lemons."

He side-eyed me, one lid a little lower than the other. "You really know who they are?"

"I wasn't living in a cave back in LA."

"Not a cave but—"

I hummed one of their songs as proof that I knew the band and to stop him from making an upsetting comment. Mom had worked hard for everything we had. At some point, I asked, "How's Becca?"

"The same."

A long line of vehicles had formed up ahead. Blinkers striated the dark woods. The drive to the field converted into a parking lot was a crawl, but we finally made it. Like ants, the cars trolled over the grass and dirt.

I climbed out of the Jeep and tugged at the hem of my short, white eyelet dress. A glance around reassured me that most girls were showing way more skin than I was.

"Well, well, if it isn't contestant number four." Lucas's oily voice had my spine straightening. "I bet Liam that you'd be catching up on your beauty sleep before the trial."

Giggling ensued. The girlfriends had come.

My pupils felt like they were warping. I snapped my eyes shut a millisecond, then opened them. "Did you think I was planning on distracting the three of you with my looks to win?"

Taryn, who clung to Lucas's waist as though her balance depended on it, narrowed her blue eyes at me. Of course Liam was there too. And next to him stood a ravishing redhead. Was that the girl they'd spoken about on the bus the other day? What was her name again? The outer corners of her green eyes slanted upward, which lent her this fierce feline look. God, I already disliked her, for no other reason than because she was stunning and surely knew it.

"Is that *her*?" she whispered to Liam, perky nose crinkling.

Liam didn't say anything. Didn't even look down at her. He was looking at me. No. Not at me. Through me. As though I wasn't even standing here.

"Hey, Tammy," Everest said, walking over to me.

Tammy latched on to Liam's hand. "Hey, Everest."

My ribs cinched at the sight of their twined fingers.

"Aidan couldn't make it?" Lucas asked.

Everest cocked an eyebrow. *Right.* I'd failed to mention my *date* with Aidan Michaels. Instead of answering, I spun around and threaded myself through the throngs of festival-goers. If I didn't lose the pack, tonight would be far from fun.

Everest caught up to me and tugged on my elbow. "What the hell was that about?"

"I had a date with Aidan Michaels."

"You what?" His eyes grew as wide as the flashlights the security guards were shining into bags.

I unzipped my cross-body bag. Once the guard let me through, I handed my ticket to the woman scanning them.

"How do you even know him?" Everest asked.

"How do you think I know him?"

"Sandra?"

"Bingo."

"I thought—"

"He offered 3K. Couldn't exactly turn that down."

"3K?"

"Yeah."

"He only paid half because Liam—who *happened* to be at the restaurant—made me leave. He says Aidan is a major creeper. Is it true?"

Everest's face creased, in concentration or in surprise or maybe in something else entirely.

"What?" I asked, combing the air to push away the thick smoke billowing from a food truck.

Slowly, as though he were trying out the words for size, he said, "Aidan Michaels hated Heath."

Bass jolted from nearby amplifiers, making my heart skip a beat. If Aidan hated Heath and I hated Heath, then maybe Aidan wasn't such a bad man.

"But is he a creeper?"

"I'd stay away from him." Everest rubbed his hands on his jeans. "Want a beer?"

"Sure."

He marched ahead of me toward a bar truck. Hollers and whistles pierced the purple air as the server filled two large plastic cups with the foamy liquid. I pulled a long swallow, then licked my lips. Exactly what I needed.

We traipsed through the thickening crowd. The opening notes of one of the band's most popular songs rang out, and people went crazy. Bodies writhed, people shrieked, hands came up and pumped the air. I drank more of my beer so that it wouldn't slosh all over me as we neared the stage. The drummer pounded on the percussions, and the orange-mulleted singer jumped in the air, belting out the lyrics.

I shifted my hips and raised one of my hands. The alcohol flowed through my veins, swirled through my body, and muted the thoughts and worries running on a loop inside my head. I drank deeper from my cup. By the third song, the entire content of my cup swished inside me, heightening the delicious beat and smoky voice of the band.

I felt a tiny bit happy. Even Everest smiled. He didn't dance, but his head was bobbing to the tune. I bumped my elbow into his side.

"Thanks for taking me! This is awesome!" I yelled so he would hear me over the group of chanting girls.

He grinned, then grabbed my empty cup. "I'll go get us refills. Don't move, or I'll never find you."

"Not going anywhere." I swung my head from side to side, the music thrumming against my bones. The night air was warm and pungent with a thousand smells—hot dogs, ketchup, grass, beer, sweat, jasmine, apricot...

I looked for the origin of that scent, fearing I'd find Amanda. Sure enough, she was standing a couple feet away, enclosed in Matt's beefy arms. Next to them stood the rest of the pack. A couple of the guys looked my way, eyes glowing in the darkness. Tamara was grinding up against Liam's rigid build. His hands didn't touch her body, but that didn't deter her. Maybe he wasn't into public displays of affection.

I'd promised Everest I wouldn't move, so I stayed put and tried to pretend they weren't all right there. As I directed my attention back toward the stage, my gaze landed on some guy in a white wifebeater and low-slung jeans. Instead of facing the stage, he was looking at me, and so were his two friends. I frowned when I saw them raise their chins and sniff the air. They whispered to each other, then casually approached me.

My spine clicked into alignment, all of my nerves on high alert. Before they'd even reached me, I knew they were wolves.

"Ness Clark?" Wifebeater asked.

I squared my shoulders. "And you are?"

"We heard the pack bitch was back, but damn, we hadn't heard how hot she was."

For the first time since I'd returned to Boulder, I disliked someone more than Liam and Lucas. "You might call your females bitches, but I prefer she-wolf."

Wifebeater smirked and took another step in my direction.

"Come any closer," I hissed, "and I'll make sure you can never breed."

"The bitch has attitude."

Anger dripped inside my veins like fuel. My limbs hummed. "Just leave me alone."

He raised his palms in the air. "One question, and then we go."

"I'm not answering any questions."

His head was so close to mine I could smell his ripe breath. "Is your ass very sore from being the only bitch in your pack?"

My gaze narrowed to a sharp point. I punched his Adam's apple and kneed his groin. Hard. And then arms were hauling me back, and a wall of bodies darkened the space between me and the asshole. I tried to shrug away from the arms, but they banded tighter.

"What did he say to you?" Liam's voice was low.

Like I would ever tell him. He'd probably wonder why I'd turned violent at such a petty taunt. Or worse, he'd use it as ammunition against me.

"Nothing," I grumbled.

"Justin Summix is an asshole, Ness. So I repeat, what did he say to you?"

Justin Summix. I committed the name to memory. "It doesn't matter."

Liam finally released me, and I turned to scan the sea of faces for Everest. When I couldn't locate him, I stared back at Liam, caught him nodding. I pivoted, just as Matt tore through the line of bodies.

"What was that about?" I asked.

"Nothing."

"My ass, it was nothing."

His pupils throbbed in the gleam of the strobe lights. "You don't talk; I don't talk."

"Ugh." I growled, raking my hands through my hair.

Yelps rose around me as the pack moved through the field of festivalgoers, chasing Justin and the other two. And then three security guards broke away from their postings around the stage to jog after the boys.

"They're going to get arrested!" I bellowed.

Liam gazed intently at his crew, lips thin, jaw set.

"Liam, call them off."

"I'm not Alpha. I don't give them orders."

And yet, that's exactly what he'd just done.

The singer from The Lemons stumbled on one of the lyrics as he witnessed the crush of bodies at the edge of the field, but then he flung his attention back to his twisting crowd and smoothed out the lyrics.

"Have you seen Everest?" I asked.

"Not since he left you alone out here."

"Liam," Tamara whined. "You're missing—"

Amanda elbowed past the redhead. "What the hell just happened?"

I wasn't sure if she was asking me or Liam.

His gaze raked over my face. "The Pines insulted Ness."

"What'd they say?" Amanda asked.

Goose bumps popped up on my flesh, and I rubbed my arms. Amanda tipped her head to the side as though trying to see inside my brain. She was a girl; she probably guessed what boys could say that would set a girl off.

I started sidestepping around Liam, but he caught my wrist. Tamara's eyes zeroed in on her date's fingers.

"Where are you going?" he asked.

"I'm going to look for Everest so he can take me home."

Matt and the others stalked back toward us, all of them a full head taller than everyone else. Their faces flashed with bloodlust and satisfied smiles. For a fraction of a second, I thought they might've killed Justin and the other two shifters, but then I chased that thought away. They were werewolves, not monsters.

"They won't be bothering you anymore, Ness," Matt said as Amanda skipped into his arms. He reeled her in tight and kissed her so hard I had to look away, but not before seeing the blood coating his knuckles.

Lucas's white T-shirt had a sprinkling of blood too. *Shit.*

I bit down on my lip, gnawed on it. "You guys didn't need to do…whatever the hell you did to them."

"I told you: we protect our own." Liam's voice was soft even though his grip wasn't.

"I don't need your protection."

He dipped his mouth toward my ear and said, his voice husky, "Well, you'll get it, whether you want it or not. That's the way the Boulder Pack operates."

My heart pounded unevenly. "I need to find Everest."

I didn't want Liam to be nice. Nice people were harder to hate.

I shook his hand off. "I want to go home."

"I was leaving. I'll drive you."

"No. Please. You have a date."

"I need to be on top of my game tomorrow."

Tamara, whom I'd all but forgotten, huffed. "Fine, let me say bye to the girls."

I would have rather snaked a clogged toilet than be stuck in a car with Liam and his girlfriend. Where the hell was Everest?

"Stay here, Tammy. Have fun," Liam said.

She batted her eyelashes at him. "I want to have fun with *you*."

That was a picture I didn't need in my head. I texted Everest, praying he would see my message and rescue me.

"Not tonight." Liam pried her hands off. "I'll see you tomorrow. Lucas will get you home."

"I don't want Lucas to take me home," she whined.

I checked my phone. *Seriously, Everest…* How long does it take someone to buy a beer? I texted him: **Are you OK?** Because now I was worried.

"I'm ready when you are?" Liam said.

I looked up from my phone and pushed a lock of hair behind my ear. Tamara was whispering angrily at Taryn. Even though I couldn't hear what was being said, from the way both girls glared my way, I guessed it had to do with me.

I sighed. "I should really find Everest first though."

"We'll look for him on our way out."

I chewed on the inside of my cheek, combing each food truck we passed for Everest. Just as I spotted him sitting at a picnic bench next to a girl, I got a text back: **I'm fine. Just ran into a friend. You OK?**

Liam must've followed my line of sight, because he said, "You want me to tell him I'm bringing you home?"

He started toward Everest, but I touched Liam's arm to stop him. "No. Don't interrupt him. He's had a tough month."

I typed back: **I'm fine.** I would send him a message once I was at the inn.

I walked alongside Liam, drained from the strange night. I was glad I was going home early. If I didn't sleep and relax, I'd be a complete mess for the run.

"Are you black?"

He cocked an eyebrow. "I think you have me confused with August."

"Funny. I meant as a wolf."

A lopsided smile formed on his lips. "Yeah."

Even though the air around Liam shimmied with the crisp, warm scent of mint and musk, I wanted confirmation. "Were you out in the woods on Wednesday?"

He nodded.

We passed boisterous groups of teens—slightly younger than I was—and it reminded me of high school, of the cliques I'd never been a part of. I wondered if Liam had been popular back in school. I bet he was. I bet all the guys in the pack were.

"Do you go to college?" I asked, turning away from the gaggle of tweens pointing at Liam, faces flushed from the sight of him.

"I graduated a month ago."

"And now?"

"Now?"

"What are your work plans?" I asked.

"I'm planning on picking up where my father left off."

"Real estate?"

He nodded. "What about you?"

I drew in a long breath of sweet, sticky air. "I don't know. I just want to get through this summer, and then I'll see where I'm at in September."

"Not so certain about winning anymore?"

I wasn't certain of anything anymore, but I didn't tell Liam this. Instead, I stared quietly ahead of me, at the long lines of parked cars bathed in starlight.

"How are your bruises?"

I blinked at him. "My bruises?"

"From paintballing." He glanced at my legs, which made me strangely self-conscious.

I frowned at his concern. "I'm healing quickly again."

"Again? Was that not the case when you were away?"

"I wasn't getting banged up much when I was away."

As he beeped his car open, something flickered through his eyes—remorse, or maybe it was just the reflection of his bumper lights. I could feel him hesitate to follow me toward the passenger side. In the end, he must've remembered I wasn't a date he had to impress, because he got behind the wheel while I opened my own door and climbed in.

As he pulled out of the lot, I asked, "How long have you and Tamara been dating?"

"We're not dating."

"Are you sure she knows that?"

"She knows it."

I didn't ask what they were doing if they weren't dating. I was a virgin, not an idiot. They might not have been dating, but they were most definitely hooking up. My phone thankfully pinged with a message, tearing me out of my strange deliberations. When I saw August's name in the message box, I smiled.

He'd sent me a selfie with some of his Army buddies. They were holding makeshift mics to their mouths— bananas. The picture was captioned: **You're missing one hell of a concert. How's yours?**

"What about you and August?"

I glanced away from my phone. "Me and August?"

"Are you together?"

"Me and August?" I sounded like a broken record. "No. We're just friends."

Liam's features were smooth as stone. "Are you sure he knows that?"

"Of course he knows that."

A sound scraped the walls of his throat, like a grunt, but not a grunt.

"What?"

"He just seemed awfully happy to see you, that's all."

"August used to babysit me, Liam. He's ten years older than I am. Trust me, he doesn't see me as anything other than a little sister." I picked at a loose thread on the hem of my dress. "Were you hoping *everyone* in Boulder would dislike me as much as you do?"

His dark gaze leaped off the road and ground into mine.

"Don't put words in my mouth." He didn't talk to me after that, just drove way above the speed limit.

The pines hedging the roads blended together in an endless juniper-colored smear. Someone was in a hurry to get rid of his passenger. Not that I wanted to spend a single minute more than necessary cooped up in a car with Liam Kolane. Why was I in his car again? *Right*...because Everest had looked like he was enjoying himself.

My cousin owed me big time.

When Liam came to a screeching halt in front of the inn, I pumped my door handle. Before jumping out, I said, "Thanks for the ride."

Liam didn't respond. He didn't even look at me as I climbed out, and the second I'd shut the door, he was off, tires squealing against the asphalt road, taillights burning blood-red in the black night.

FIFTEEN

I didn't sleep. Not a wink. I tossed and turned and tossed some more. The night spun on a loop inside my mind. Every damn part of the night too, from my encounter with stupid Justin Summix, to my drive home with infuriating Liam Kolane. Tamara popped inside my head a couple times too, and even though I tried to picture her with acne and buckteeth, somehow she always morphed into a gorgeous siren.

Ugh!

I finally got out of bed at the crack of dawn. Although I didn't want to overexert myself before the treacherous marathon the elders had set up, I hit the gym to stretch, and then I went to the kitchen and asked Evelyn for a high-protein breakfast. I mentioned I was planning on going for a run this afternoon. I didn't clarify in what form I'd be running or the reason I was running, and God bless Evelyn, she didn't ask.

She boiled three eggs, grilled fat slices of whole wheat toast, and fried two sausages. I took my breakfast back to my bedroom and ate on the small balcony, watching the sun rise and fill the world with color.

Trailing in the smell of fresh cigarettes, Lucy dropped by my room around nine, and it wasn't to wish me good luck. She came to ask me to tidy the guest bedrooms.

"But I have to be at the headquarters at noon."

My aunt had styled her red hair, and it fell in almost child-like ringlets over her milky shoulders. "Better hurry then."

She swiped her fingers across my desk as though inspecting it for dust. She wouldn't find any.

"What did you do with the potpourri jar?"

"What?"

"The mason jar I fill with potpourri. The one I put in every bedroom. What did you do with it?"

"Oh. It's on the balcony. The smell is a little…*strong* for me." Which was true, but the reason I'd set it on my balcony was because the desiccated, flowery scent reminded me of Lucy. Sharing a roof was grating enough without the constant olfactory assault.

"The petals will rot," she muttered as she traipsed to my balcony door and rammed it open. Heels clicking on the plywood floor, she scurried to recover her precious, eye-watering mix.

How could Jeb stand the smell? And Everest? Didn't it bother them?

She walked back into the room and then headed toward my bedroom door, clutching the jar to her bosom.

"Lucy, can I work tomorrow instead of today? Please? I'll put in a double shift."

"You might not be physically competent to work tomorrow. Besides, Saturdays are always busier than Sundays. You should know that by now." She leveled her hazel eyes on me, daring me to complain again.

She wasn't being fair, but perhaps this was the reason she was making me work. As I donned my gray uniform, I called Everest to ask him if he was still taking me to the meeting, but he didn't answer.

I texted him.

No answer.

An hour into my morning chores, I texted him again.

The headquarters was a good fifteen miles away from the inn, up mountain roads where driving faster than twenty miles per hour was downright treacherous. It would take me close to an hour to get there, and it was 10:30, which meant I would need to leave in thirty minutes to make it on time.

At 10:45, I finished cleaning the bedrooms and loped to my own room to change back into shorts and a T-shirt. I called Everest again, my patience dwindling. When five minutes later he still hadn't answered, I jogged toward his suite and then banged on the door.

No answer.

Fuck. I ran to the front desk, ready to grovel with Jeb to take me, but Lucy informed me he'd left with Everest on an errand.

"An errand?" It came out shrilly.

"Keep your voice down."

"Everest promised to bring me to—"

"He must've forgotten. Why don't you borrow one of the vans?"

A breath snagged inside my throat. "I don't have a license."

"You don't say." From the lilt in her voice, I gleaned she knew this.

The clock on the wall behind her ticked so loudly I felt it inside my chest. "Could you drive me?"

"I might not seem busy, but I have a business to run. I can't just get up and leave to take you to a silly contest."

Heat pricked my eyelids. "This isn't a silly contest."

"Isn't it?" She leaned over the check-in counter. "You've set your expectations on an unreasonable goal. Women don't lead packs of men; it's emasculating."

My scudding heart came to an abrupt halt. I blinked at my aunt, stunned to silence.

"Did you expect me to pat you on the back?" She shook her head. "You should've contented yourself with being their equal. Or married one of them."

I backed away because my fingers had closed into tight fists, and my nails were elongating. Before I started howling at my aunt or slashing at her tubby throat with my sharp claws, I pushed through the inn's revolving doors.

I dragged in lungfuls of air to calm my flaring anger and contemplated running, but racing fifteen miles before running a marathon was nonsensical. Besides, there was no way I could cover fifteen miles in one hour, even in wolf form. I whipped out my phone so fast I almost dropped it, and then scrolled to the saved number of a taxi company. I was put on hold before a woman informed me that my ride would arrive at the inn in ten minutes. It was already 11:05. I would never make it.

Never.

I wrote Everest a dozen hurtful text messages but deleted them all. Mom once told me communicating whilst angry was a terrible idea. Considering the things I'd written—things that could irreparably damage my relationship with Everest—she was right.

Finally, a yellow cab drove up the winding path. I tapped my foot. Before he'd even stopped, I lunged into the backseat and gave him directions. We were halfway through the drive when I realized I hadn't taken a bag, which meant I hadn't taken a wallet. I decided not to mention it until we arrived.

As the yellow cab climbed the mountain roads at a cautious fifteen miles per hour, I stared at the red digits escalating on the meter. "Could you drive any faster? I'm a little late."

The needle rose to eighteen miles per hour. How I wanted to jump in front and jam my foot on the gas pedal. I'd told Liam I wasn't sure what I wanted to do, but at this moment, I knew—I wanted to get a driver's license.

I researched this, since watching the minutes and dollars tick by was wreaking havoc on my fraying nerves. At 11:58, the Boulder headquarters rose before us like an oasis in a desert. The squat gray stone structure surrounded by the rusted fence and sunburned grass hadn't changed an iota.

"Word around town is that this place is crawling with wolves." The cabby was gazing at the large wooden sign carved up with the words: *Private Property*.

"I heard, but I also heard they aren't aggressive."

He grunted—obviously not sharing my belief—then turned in his seat. "That'll be forty-eight dollars."

"About that...I forgot my wallet. Can I pay you tomorrow?"

"What? No."

"But I don't have cash."

"Maybe your friends can pay me."

"My friends?"

He jerked his bearded chin toward Matt, who'd stepped into my line of sight. He glowered at the cab. Liam and Lucas came to flank him. Relief flooded through me when I noticed they were all still in skin.

"I'd rather not ask them, but I promise—"

"I got a family to feed, insurance to pay, not to mention taxes and schooling fees. If I accepted promises as payment, my family would starve and get evicted."

Geez. "Do you take PayPal?"

"No, I don't take PayPal, but even if I had an account, I wouldn't accept electronic cash."

"Fine." Cheeks heating up, I kicked the door open, then trekked toward my welcoming committee.

"You're late," Lucas chirped, chewing on a toothpick.

"Why isn't the cabbie leaving? Did you invite him to watch?" Matt asked.

Without taking my eyes off the overgrown grass that smelled like piss, I mumbled, "I forgot my wallet. Can anyone lend me a fifty?"

"Already spent all that hard-earned cash of yours, huh?" Lucas drawled.

I jerked my narrowed gaze toward him. "I forgot my wallet. If someone has PayPal, I'll wire them the cash right away."

"Here." Liam extended a green bill. "Get the guy out of here."

I took it from him, mumbling, "Thanks."

I ran back to the cabdriver and tossed the bill through his window, then waited for him to leave. Once his tires spun, spitting dirt and pebbles against my ankles, I made my way back to the others.

"You look like hell," Lucas said.

God, if only I could bash his tiny skull in. Sensing he'd riled me up, his smile grew grotesquely wide.

"What's your PayPal account, Liam?" I asked.

"I don't have one."

Why did no one freaking have a PayPal account? "I'll pay you back later."

"Sure." He shrugged without looking at me. He was entirely focused on Frank, who was traipsing back up the hill that led into the thick woods. "Should we get started?"

Frank nodded, slipping his phone into the holster hooked on his belt. "Get into your wolf forms."

Matt ripped off his T-shirt then pulled down his pants. Soon, Lucas and Liam, too, stood there only in their boxer-briefs.

Lucas leered at me. "Planning on ogling us or joining us?"

I went pale. Unless I wanted to tear my clothes apart, I would need to take them off also. My pride was dying a slow, agonizing death.

"Why don't you go change behind the building?" Liam offered as my fingers rolled up the hem of my tank top. "No one's inside."

"Alphas change with their packs," Matt said.

Liam glowered at him. "Ness isn't an Alpha."

I thought about turning around and going through the change with my back to them, but that had my stomach in knots.

As I hurried toward the back of the building, Liam's voice rose. "Watch out for the grate. It's pure silver."

A silver grate? I turned the corner, stepping lightly, carefully. I caught the metallic tang of silver before I even saw what Liam had mentioned. There, flush against the squat building was a grate twice the size of a sewer cap. I peered through the sturdy metal netting, at the excavation that was as deep as a well.

"Ness? Are you ready?" Frank's voice made me jerk away from the hole.

I put some distance between me and the silver grate, then chucked off my sneakers and clothes and concentrated hard.

Nothing happened.

I tried harder.

Still nothing.

After everything I'd gone through to get here. And now this! *Traitorous body.*

"Please," I begged.

But apparently beseeching my wolf was pointless. Minutes ticked by, and I remained pale flesh and taut human limbs.

SIXTEEN

I wasn't the type who gave up, but it had been ten minutes, and I was still in skin. Why the others hadn't rounded the building to find me yet was beyond me. I reached for my underwear just as a howl pierced the buzzing air.

And then another wolf howled.

And another.

The base of my spine tingled, and then my bones began to shift underneath my skin. Tears of relief coursed down my cheeks as my ears migrated to the top of my head and my mouth elongated into a muzzle filled with teeth that could scissor through bark and bone. The dusting of hair on my body thickened to summer fur. I fell onto my forepaws as my hind legs shortened and readjusted, as the wolf in me replaced the human.

In my four-legged form, I jogged around the house.

A large gray wolf with sharp blue eyes—Lucas, I imagined—howled, and this time I understood him. *Did you have to take a shit or what?*

I snarled at him.

Matt was more bear than wolf, butter-colored with vivid-green eyes. Next to him, I looked like a scrawny pup.

Liam was much larger up close than he'd seemed in the woods. His glowing yellow-amber eyes raked over my unimpressive body before settling back on Frank. The elder crouched beside us, a strip of crimson fabric gripped in his hands.

"You're going to head south." He pointed toward the thick forest coating the side of the mountain. "We've spread pieces of this throughout the woods. Follow the trail until you find Eric. The rest of this shirt is tied to him. He's your finishing line." He passed the piece of fabric around so we could soak in the smell—sweet cigar smoke and cedar. "Now, the quickest way is straight down the hill, but it's also the most hazardous. If you get stuck in a trap, we will free you at the end of the race. Remember: do not turn back to skin. I will feel it if you do." He tapped his wrist as he straightened and rolled the cloth up into his palm.

I was glad for the blood oath then, glad someone could track my whereabouts and vitals. I rotated my withers then crouched low, the tall grass tickling my thumping chest.

"Ready. Set." Frank's voice rang out like a starting pistol. "Go!"

We sprang into action.

Lucas's hind paws sprayed dirt into my eyes. I blinked wildly, slowed, then switched course. Frank had mentioned the shortest path was the most treacherous. Was it true or a trick?

Lucas dashed through the tree line, vanishing into the forest that spilled down the flank of the mountain. He was apparently not worried about the traps, or maybe he'd change course at a later point. Soon Matt and Liam were lost to the trees, too. Although I could hear the soft thuds of their paws and sense the hectic beats of their faraway hearts, I could no longer see them. Which was better. I needed to funnel my awareness onto the ground.

I ran almost leisurely, stepping lightly through the underbrush. Spooked raccoons scampered out in front of me, and birds flapped out of trees, wings dark against the dazzling sky.

At some point, I forgot this was a race and flew heedlessly down woodchip-covered trails. The distant rumble of a car reminded me to melt back into the forest. I cut across a billow of spiky ferns and came out crowned with a cloud of frisky black flies. I flicked my ears and swiped my tail, then growled until they buzzed off.

Dense brushwood raked over my chest and leaf litter snagged in my silky white fur as I jogged toward a stretch of glittering water. My muscles became greedy for speed, so I ran faster. When my paws hit the chilly stream, I halted and lapped my fill. And then I pounced inside to cool my flushed limbs. I bounded down the riverbank, hopping over rotting trees and smooth rocks.

I thought I saw a blur of black fur to my left, but when I looked, there was nothing but a giant boulder. If I hadn't drunk water, I could've blamed my delusion on thirst, but my mind was clear. I was making up company to comfort myself into thinking I wasn't lagging behind. *Was* I lagging behind?

I raised my face and sniffed the air, caught the musky scent of another wolf. I looked for him but didn't see him. I sped up, slaloming through the trees, sliding over patches of dry dirt. I sniffed the air again. This time, it was the blend of tobacco and cedar that netted my senses. Sure enough, tied to a low branch, flapped a piece of red fabric. At least I was heading in the right direction.

I ducked past the branch but stumbled when my paws tangled on something. I backed up. Transparent fishing line glinted in the sunlight. Was this one of their traps or a vestige of a fishing expedition at the nearby creek? I bucked to unravel the plastic filament, but the knot tightened around my pastern.

I growled at the increasing jumble of thread, slid my fangs between it and my skin, and tugged. The fishing line sliced through my skin before finally ripping on my serrated teeth.

I moaned with relief then backed up to change routes. Another thread, this time taut, pressed against my hocks. I bounded forward, but not before hearing something click.

The ground rumbled as though a herd of Mustangs were stampeding down the hill. I twisted my neck.

No wild horses galloped.

The noise was coming from rocks.

Huge rocks.

They smashed against each other as they rolled. Sharp debris rained down on me, whipping my back. I sprang into action just as a large rock skimmed my hind paw. I faltered but recovered my footing fast. Desperation converted to pure adrenaline. As the stones thundered closer, I sprinted, the world blurring green, brown, gray. Thorns and rough bark frayed the pads of my paws, but I kept running.

I tried to change course, but a small boulder arced through the blue air and pounded into my spine, shredding my breath. I went down, down…down, rolling over and over. As the world spun out of focus, as up became down and down became up, I thought of the elders and the cruelty of their little game. Were they watching? Were they enjoying my grievous fall?

My mom's face swam through my mind, eyes as blue as cornflowers, hair fluttering around her face like stalks of wheat caught in a breeze. I drifted in the beauty of the memory, finding comfort in her bright smile, in the low timber of her voice as she spoke my name. As my name transformed and distorted into something else entirely.

A roar.

An inhuman roar that had me snapping my lids. A black shape floated between sky and earth. Another boulder? I blinked, but shards of rock sprayed my face, spoiling my already poor sight. Another roar, more wolf than stone, shook me fully awake.

I dug my claws into the earth, but I wasn't on soft earth. I was on solid rock. And not just a rock. *A Flatiron*. Oh God…

From my vantage point, there was no telling how steep the fall. Calling on the last dregs of energy, I channeled all of my weight into my paws, mincing my claws on the searing rock. My muscles screamed as my speed decreased, as my claws were sanded down and my pads ribboned. I was still coming at the edge of the cliff too fast.

Gritting my teeth, I locked my muscles and dug what remained of my filed claws into the rock.

An inch from the edge, I came to a stop. I kept my head down until the rubble stopped walloping my battered body.

Shivering, shuddering, heart pounding against the sun-soaked Flatiron, I waited for silence to replace the pitter-patter of rock. Once it finally draped over the land, I lifted my head and squinted upward at the gritty trail of blood and chalky scratch marks.

I'd survived the fall, but would I survive the rest of this brutal contest?

SEVENTEEN

I licked my wounds a long time. It wasn't as though I could possibly win anymore. Unless another contestant had run into a trap more perilous than mine. I doubted it. The others were surer-footed and more attuned to the land than I was, thanks to the years of experience I lacked.

After a lengthy interlude of self-deprecation, I pressed my battered body up onto my shredded paws. I groaned, feeling as though I weighed a ton more than I had at the start of this godforsaken race. I took a step and whimpered. Another step. Another whimper.

Well, this'll be fun.

And slow.

I hope you're all enjoying this, you asswipes, I howled into the inert air.

Running was out of the question. Tripping repeatedly, I hobbled down the grassy sides of the Flatiron then headed back toward the evergreens. At least, at this pathetic speed, I couldn't possibly run into another trap.

The sun baked my hide as I traipsed clumsily toward the trees. After what felt like a day, I reached the dappled forest. Shadows cooled the bitter heat, and damp moss alleviated the pain that was each step. Moss and shadows could unfortunately do nothing for my sore spine. I wondered, more than once, if the stone that had landed on my back had dislodged a vertebra.

Could I still move with a dislocated vertebra?

I was no doctor, but I guessed my spine must be intact.

My breaths were no longer coming in short spurts. They were lengthening like the shadows as the sun dipped a little lower in the sky. I sniffed the air to make sure I was still heading in the right direction. I caught the sweet smell of tobacco and the crisp scent of cedar, but it was muddled by that of blood.

Fresh blood.

I stopped and sniffed my paws. It wasn't my blood I smelled.

I sniffed again.

Then I followed the tinny trail through the trees, through a shrub of wild roses that layered their sultry perfume over that of the blood. I pushed past them, their thorns snagging in my flesh, and almost tripped on a mound of blond fur.

Matt whipped his head toward me, leveling his green eyes on my face and letting out a low growl. I backed up, but then my gaze snagged on the metal snare jammed around his forepaw.

The jagged trap had bitten into his flesh, revealing bits of white bone and pink sinew. He snapped his teeth at me. I gnashed my own teeth and barked, *I didn't come to gloat. I mean, look at me.*

He looked me over. Grasping I wasn't a threat, he lowered his muzzle to the metal, trying to pry it open with his fangs, but all it did was steep the fur of his face in blood.

I stood motionless for a moment.

I could still win.

The realization fluttered through me as delicately as butterfly wings.

I could leave him behind.

Even if he managed to break free, he wouldn't be able to beat me with a mangled leg. I turned southward and stared at the green hollow covered in deciduous trees. The race would end somewhere in those woods. I could reach them in minutes—fifteen, twenty at most—and once I found Eric, I could inform him of Matt's whereabouts.

Low whines lanced through the air.

I closed my eyes.

Matt was crying.

This bear of a man was crying.

There goes winning.

I twisted back to find the brute gnawing on his forearm. Was he planning on chewing off his paw to get out of the trap? It wouldn't regenerate. We were wolves, not lizards.

I moved back toward him. *Stop.*

A pitiful snarl rose from his reddened muzzle. *Go away.*

I shook my head then dipped it toward the snare. I'd get no pleasure in winning if I left him behind. The smell of Matt's blood, of his agony, overwhelmed my senses. I almost retched.

Matt snapped at me with blood-soaked teeth. Growling, I rammed my head into his chest to get him to back off. *Stop your yapping, Hulk. I'm trying to help you.*

He froze. I placed my paws on either side of the snare and drove my weight down hard on the levers. Besides sending explosive bolts of pain into my bones, it created a thin opening, but failed to release Matt's paw. I tried again, wincing. Matt must've shifted his paw, because when the metal jaw clamped back shut, he let out a low, mournful keening, and fresh blood gushed down his fur.

Don't move, I grumbled.

He snarled at me. I shot him a look that must've translated well because he shut his muzzle. I heaved on my paws again, and again the trap opened, but not wide enough for him to shimmy out. Why the hell did he have to have giant paws anyway?

Ugh.

I tried again.

Nothing.

Again.

My attempts were paltry and clumsy. If I had hands instead of paws—

I sucked in a breath just as Matt's eyes took on a glassy sheen like the marbles I used to roll on the hardwood floors of my childhood home.

Whoomph.

Matt went down so hard I jumped.

Fuck. Fuck. Fuck.

Matt!

His flattened ears didn't flick.

I howled, hoping someone would come, but they hadn't come for me, so they most probably wouldn't come for him. Still, I waited. Wasn't Frank worried? When no voice answered mine, I loosed a rough breath, shut my eyes, and willed my body to change.

I would be disqualified, but at least I'd be able to live with myself, wherever it was I would be living.

EIGHTEEN

I' d been half-right about what my body would look like. Where I wasn't entirely mottled with bruises, my palms and soles were in bloody tatters. For the first time since Matt had become unconscious, I was glad for it. After all, I was standing over him in my birthday suit.

Even though I felt and looked like roadkill, I was still prudish roadkill. I kneeled next to his massive, inert form, and worked my blood-soaked fingers nimbly around the levers, prodding them. In one swift jerk, I jammed my palms against them and the trap's jaws opened like a night-blooming flower.

Sweat trickled down my neck, down my smarting spine, as I delicately lifted Matt's ravaged paw and set it on the grass next to his head. I tossed the trap aside, and it clinked shut.

"Piece of crap mousetrap," I grumbled.

Matt stirred, and I jumped behind the wild rose bush. They weren't dense enough to shield me, but beggars couldn't be choosers. The thorns felt like piranha teeth against my skin. I plucked them out, letting out a slew of choice words. Compared to the pain radiating inside my bones, being a human pincushion was peanuts, but still. A twig breaking had me snapping my gaze up, straight into a set of no longer glassy eyes.

I blinked dumbly at Matt. His paw dragged, yet he was already up! *How?*

Remembering I was naked, I spun around, willing fur to cloak my curves. I squinted so hard that anyone passing by would think me constipated. Thankfully, besides Matt, no one was even around.

When I felt a wet muzzle on the knobs of my hunched spine, I almost jumped out of my skin. "Go away!"

Matt made a noise my human ears couldn't decipher. And then he released a soft wail that made my skin pebble.

Not pebble.

Change.

His howl made me change back.

Once cloaked in fur, I turned and nodded to the paw. *Can you walk?*

Not well.

Want to stay here while I go get help?

And let you win?

My shoulders locked up. Hulk's competitive streak had apparently not suffered from the snare. *You're going to win anyway. I broke the rules, remember.*

To help me.

Still, I changed.

I swear he rolled his eyes at me. *Come on, Little Wolf.*

I snorted, which earned me an amused sideways glance. We began to limp down the hill. Where Matt no longer whimpered, I did, and I felt absolutely no shame. *I feel like I crawled through a garbage compacter.*

Your back is one solid bruise.

There goes wearing most of my wardrobe in public.

Wolves didn't laugh, and yet Matt made a sound that sounded almost like a chuckle. And then he asked how I'd gotten the bruise, and I told him about the rockslide.

Even though we moved at a slow pace, we moved nonetheless. Soon we'd reached the trees. I caught the scent of cigar and cedar. It was strong.

Almost there, Matt said, limping beside me.

A slash of red broke through the greenery. It flapped around Eric's wrist.

I can't believe we made it, I whispered.

Figures shifted through the trees like ghosts. I recognized Liam and Lucas and Cole and countless others.

Matt faltered beside me, then landed with a hard thump.

I stopped walking. *Come on, Hulk, get up.*

He whined.

I shoved my muzzle against his furry shoulder. *Get up.*

Slowly, like a mountain rising from two tectonic plates, Matt got up. And even slower, he limped beside me.

Don't tell anyone you saw me naked or I'll stick a snare in your bed.

He let out a small grunt.

Metal blinded me as I focused on the scrap of red fabric. There were cars. Lots of them.

Good, because I was done with walking.

Probably for the rest of my life.

I thought of my driver's license then. At least now that I was out of the stupid running, I'd have plenty of time to get it.

Matt slowed. I waited.

Just go, Little Wolf.

I shook my head. *Stop growling and move your furry ass. I'm out; I changed.*

But they don't know that.

I took the blood oath same as you. Frank knows.

Matt gave me a lingering look, then finally set forth toward Eric. We reached him at the same time. I was finishing this race for myself. I'd cheated, but at least I hadn't quit.

A shiver of pride pulsated through me as I collapsed at the man's feet. Sunlight and loud voices danced around me like dandelion florets. I made a feeble attempt at getting back up, but I...just...couldn't.

A paltry thought inserted itself inside my mind. If I changed while unconscious, everyone would see my naked ass. I almost laughed.

Almost, because I was still a wolf, and wolves didn't laugh.

But then, my muscles slid and slotted back. Unable to fight off the change, I let it sweep through me.

What a pitiful sight I must've been. Thankfully, darkness enveloped me before I could hear anyone laugh.

NINETEEN

I woke up to Evelyn glowering at me. If I'd thought her eyes were black before, they were a whole new shade of black now—sewer-hole-at-night-black.

"Thank *God!*" She lobbed the book she was reading on the table next to the armchair and stalked over to me on slippered feet. "Ness Clark, I am so mad at you! If you were my daughter, I would ground you until your thirtieth birthday! Rock-climbing alone! *Sola!*" Even through her layers of foundation, her cheeks were the same dark pink as the sky behind her. "When that *chico* carried you into the inn—"

"What boy?"

She blinked a great many times, seemingly startled I'd interrupted her rant for something as silly as the identity of the person who'd handled my naked body.

"Liam Kolane."

"Liam?" My neck felt hot; my jaw too. Fucking crap. I groaned from embarrassment.

"*Sí*, and you were unconscious and covered in blood. *Mi corazón* stopped beating. My heart stopped!" Her Spanish always bled through her English when she was agitated. "I thought…I thought your spine was *rota!*" Her brash voice was trembling. Her hands, too. All of her was quivering.

Even though I was still dying a little from the fact that Liam had carried me back, I reached out and enclosed her cold fingers in mine. The contact wasn't enough for her, and she sandwiched her other hand over mine.

Tears cascaded down her cheeks, dragging tiny clumps of mascara off her wet lashes. And then a sob racked her body. I sat up, and the momentum had her stumble and plop down on the bed next to me. The momentum also had me gritting my teeth. I don't know how long I'd been out, but apparently not long enough. My flesh felt like someone had clobbered it with a meat mallet before rubbing it against a cheese grater.

"I'm sorry, Evelyn. Sorry I put you through this." I let go of her hands so I could hug her. My arms felt like they were attached to fifty-pound dumbbells, but I fought through the pain to pull her in close.

She crushed me against her, and I yelped from all the bruises her grip awakened. She didn't loosen her arms—probably hadn't heard me yelping over her sobbing. "Never again. Never again. You promise? Two days of being by your side. Of watching you—"

I pressed her away. "It's been two days?"

"*Sí*, two days!"

"I've been sleeping for two days?"

"Yes!"

Whoa.

"Your bruises, they've been going away quickly, but—"

Abruptly, I stood. My legs felt wooden, but at least they held me up as I shuffled toward my closet. I pulled open the door to get a full view of myself in the built-in mirror. I lifted the hem of my tank and pivoted. The backs of my thighs and spine were tinged a yellowish-green. Could've been worse.

Could've been black. The worst part of me was actually my hair, which was crusty and tangled and matted in God only knew what. My nails were in pretty dire shape, too—ragged like pinecones.

Evelyn appeared in the mirror behind me, her face ghostly-pale compared to my tanned one. At least *rock-climbing* and slumbering for forty-eight hours had given me a healthy complexion. Mom was always on my case about finding silver linings. She used to say that was how she'd made it through life. *Here's to you, Mom.*

I turned away from the mirror and closed the door.

"I soaped your body, but I did not dare wash your hair. You had a big gash here." Evelyn pressed lightly on a spot on the back of my head that felt incredibly tender. I half expected her fingers to come away wet with blood. They didn't.

"Even though it is still hard for me—what you are"—she gave a small shrug—"I think that if you were not...I think you would not have lived." She wiped her red-rimmed eyes.

I gathered both her hands in mine. "I'm not going anywhere."

No more death expeditions on my agenda in the near or far future. But there would be an expedition. I was going to have to leave town now. Jeb would have to release me back into the world—minor and all. I didn't broach the subject with Evelyn. She'd had her fair share of stress for the day.

Instead, I said, "I love you."

Her crying started again, and even though it felt like I was being quartered, I hugged her.

AFTER SHE LEFT, WHICH took much prodding on my part—
Evelyn needed rest—I took a blisteringly hot bath. As I
steeped, I thought. Which made me anxious because most of
my thoughts revolved around how many people had seen
me naked after the run.

I slid beneath the bathwater, wishing soap could cleanse
my brain of its petty anxiety. After all, I'd almost died. *Died!*
And here I was worried about nudity. My priorities were
massively skewed.

After washing my hair, a task that felt tougher than
racing down a hill chased by boulders, I stepped out of the
bath, towel-dried my body, and patted lotion over every
inch of skin, as though moisturizing my sore muscles could
somehow soften them. It didn't, but at least I smelled good—
like toasted coconut.

I was about to pull on PJs when there was a knock on my
door. In my bathrobe, I pattered toward the door. I imagined
it was Everest. Evelyn must've told him I was conscious
again.

Note to self: stop assuming things.

It was not my cousin.

TWENTY

"Amanda?" I yelped.

"You're alive." She tucked a long curl behind her ear and shot me a cheery smile.

Why was she smiling at me? Was she playing a trick on me? I checked the hallway for a raised phone but found only a couple leaving their bedroom hand in hand.

"Why are you here?" I finally asked.

"One, to check if you were doing better. When I stopped by yesterday, your grandma said you were still recovering. And two, to thank you."

"Thank me?"

"For helping Matt."

I frowned.

She raised an eyebrow. "Do you have a concussion or something?"

"No."

"Well, then, you must remember you saved my baby's hand."

"Oh." I nibbled on my bottom lip. "Is it still... functional?"

"Uh-huh. They've stapled his skin. The nerves and tendons are regenerating."

My stomach flipped at the mention of stapling flesh.

"Anyway, we're all going out to play some pool and grab a couple beers."

I released my lip. "And you're inviting me?"

"No. I came to give you a play-by-play of my evening to make you jealous." She rolled her brown eyes. "Of course I'm inviting you! Scratch that. I'm here to *take* you."

"I don't really feel like going out."

"You're alive. And clean. You're going out, so get dressed."

I furrowed my forehead. My hair was still wet, and I hadn't had time to file my nails down—that last part felt superficially important.

"We'll wait for you in the car."

"Amanda—"

She tsked. "Would you rather we all come to you?" She snuck a look behind me at my bedroom. "Might get a tad crowded in here."

I blanched. "You're joking."

"I never joke." Even though one side of her mouth was pulled up in a smile, her eyes were deathly serious.

I sighed. "Fine."

"You got ten minutes."

"What happens in ten minutes?"

"I send Matt to lug you out of your bedroom."

The girl was not only crazy bossy but also mercurial. A week ago, she wanted me to stay away from *her* boys, and now she was forcing me to spend time with them. Since I was a little worried she'd throw a party in my bedroom, I finally accepted. "Fine. I'll get ready."

After I shut the door, I tried pulling on a pair of jeans, but the simple act of tugging them on felt like rubbing my legs with sandpaper, so I settled on leggings and a T-shirt. Wearing a bra was out of the question, but my nipples weren't *too* visible—I hoped. Okay, they were a little noticeable, but one really had to look.

Hopefully no one would. They'd all surely gotten enough eyefuls on Saturday.

Oh God...

And Liam had carried me back...

Oh great freaking God.

Trying to stifle my embarrassment, I swiped mascara over my eyelashes and red gloss over my lips, ran a brush through my damp hair, then filed my finger and toenails to the quick. I grabbed my bag, my phone—which Evelyn must've plugged in for me—and my room key. As I made my way down the corridor, I checked my messages. Found five from August.

Ness?

Call me back?

I heard what happened.

Ness? Send me some fucking news.

NESS CALL ME.

I smiled at my screen. He was roasting on some desert base or ambushing enemies, and yet he was thinking of me. August was as sweet as they came.

I feel like a freight train just rolled over me, but I'm alive. Thanks for checking on me.

I hesitated to send a heart emoji. August was my friend. Did girls send heart emojis to boy-friends? I'd never even sent one to Everest, and he was family.

"You gave us all a fright."

I looked up from my phone and locked eyes with my uncle who was manning the bell desk. He rubbed the back of his neck. Was he expecting me to apologize?

"Lucy was out of her mind with worry—"

"Lucy was worried?" My voice sounded slightly unhinged. "She tried to stop me, Jeb. She told me girls shouldn't play at boy's games. Wonder where she got that from."

Jeb blushed. Like a full-on blush. "We were trying to protect you, Ness. We didn't want you to get hurt, and you did. You weren't supposed to find a way of getting there."

"So that's why Everest vanished from the face of the Earth?"

He nodded.

"I may be your ward, Uncle, but this is my life."

"So we should just stand back and watch you kill yourself? You think this is what your mother would've wanted?"

"I'm not going to die."

"You kids… You think you're so invincible, but you aren't. Look at that sweet girl Everest was dating."

"She tried to commit suicide. I'm taking part in a competition. Besides—"

"A competition no one wants you to compete in! *No one.* And I'm not talking about Lucy and me. I'm talking about the whole"—his voice dropped to a hiss—"pack."

His comment hurt. "I'm out of the running anyway," I mumbled. "And for your information, the whole *pack* just invited me to go out with them tonight."

He drew his shoulders back until they formed a perfect T. "I thought you wanted nothing to do with them. I thought you weren't looking to fit in."

Outside, a car honked, and then Amanda waved from the passenger window of a silver Dodge sedan.

"I thought so too, but I'm trying to make the most of my time here. But don't worry. I'll be out of your hair soon."

What I'd wished for the most had finally come true, except leaving wasn't what I wanted most anymore.

Matt honked again.

"I'll see you later," I said.

Jeb pinched his lips together. Either he was all out of unsolicited advice or he'd understood giving me any was useless.

I pushed through the revolving doors, the deep-blue night air slapping my warm cheeks, then pulled open the back door of the Dodge. Someone was already sitting in the backseat.

Sienna. Her fingers worked the hem of her baby-doll top, rolling it over and over.

"Hi," I said.

Keeping her gaze cemented to her hand, she murmured, "Hey."

I wasn't certain why, but I felt guilty all of a sudden. As though entering the Alpha contest had prompted August to leave—which wasn't true. He'd left because he'd needed to get away. It had nothing to do with me.

Matt spun around and gave me a wolfish grin. "Little Wolf's in the house!"

I smirked at the nickname. "Should you be driving?"

"I'm a righty." He wiggled the fingers of his good hand. "Thank goodness for Amanda."

Amanda flicked his big arm and tittered.

I didn't catch the correlation between his fingers and his girlfriend, until Sienna said, "TMI, guys."

Oh. "Eww." I wrinkled my nose.

A soft smile settled on Sienna's face.

Matt belted out a laugh that was as large as his ribcage, then spun the dial of his stereo until a rap song shook the car. And then he revved up his engine and took off, headlights zipping over the darkened landscape as fast as laser beams.

"You might want to put your seatbelt on," Sienna yelped, strapping herself in. I think she added, "Not that you can die from a car crash," but the music was so loud and her voice so soft I wasn't sure.

Couldn't I, though?

Werewolves were stronger than normal humans, but they weren't immortal. If Heath could drown in a pool, couldn't I die from a car crash? Couldn't August perish from a detonating grenade? I filed the question away for later.

I would ask Everest.

After yelling at him for ditching me, I would ask him.

TWENTY-ONE

T he pack along with two bartenders and a couple grizzly-faced beer drinkers made up the small crowd at Tracy's.

As I walked inside, I started regretting coming along. Wherever my enthusiasm to hang out with the pack had stemmed from, the second I crossed the threshold, it shrunk like the Colorado River during hot, dry months.

I straightened my spine and raised my chin. I was here now. Might as well make the most of it. Besides, I was leaving, so it wasn't like they'd have to endure me much longer.

Several gazes raked over me as I trailed behind Amanda and Matt. Even though I was mad at Everest, I desperately sought him out, but encountered Taryn's narrowed blue gaze instead. She elbowed Lucas, who leaned on his cue stick as he turned toward me. On the other side of the felt table, Liam was lining up his pool tip to the cue ball. He was so concentrated on making the shot that a deep wrinkle plowed the spot between his eyebrows. Next to him stood Cole, and next to him, Tamara.

Whereas Tamara looked at me as though I were a leper come to contaminate her, Cole sent me a smile.

"You got Ness to emerge from her lair." Cole pumped his fist against his brother's uninjured one.

"Can't take credit for that. It was all Amanda's doing." Matt draped his arm around his girlfriend. "Everyone knows you can't say no to my girl." He craned his neck to look at me. "I tried when she pursued me. She was relentless."

"Poor baby." She pouted up at him. "You're such a victim."

He laughed and kissed her temple, then tightened his grip. "A real content victim," he purred into her ear.

"They're annoyingly cute those two," Sienna said, her tone slipper-soft. There was no jealousy in her voice, though, just genuine affection.

"When did you move to Boulder?" I asked her.

"In my junior year of high school."

"Where from?"

"Tucson."

"You like it here?"

She shrugged a freckled shoulder.

"First round's on me." Matt made a beeline for the bar that was decorated with sticky ring marks.

The hygiene freak within me cringed. How hard was it to wipe down a bar?

"Name your poison, Little Wolf."

That nickname. I shook my head. "Sam Adams."

"Coming right up."

I was tempted to follow him to the bar, feeling strange just standing here next to the pool table, especially after Sienna and Amanda had flocked over to Taryn and Tamara. I watched Liam finally hit his shot—miss it, to be exact. The tip of his stick skidded right off the cue ball, which spun on itself without making contact with any other ball.

"Performance anxiety, Kolane?" Lucas's gaze sparked with delight, while Liam scowled.

He straightened, studying the cue ball as though it were a live thing that had dissed him.

Cole chuckled, then lined up his stick. He hit the eight ball and sunk it in.

When he leaned over for another shot, I asked, "Isn't that a foul?" I wasn't a huge pool player but was pretty certain the black ball was supposed to go in last.

"We're playing cut-throat," Liam said, chalking up the tip of his stick.

"How do you play that?"

Without taking his eyes off the game, he explained the rules: each player had a section of pool balls and they had to sink their opponents' balls in. Matt arrived then and handed me a sweaty bottle of beer.

"Thanks." I took a sip and felt it drip into my empty stomach. I needed food. And I probably needed it before I drank the beer. "I should eat something," I told no one in particular, but then I offered to get the others food. I prayed no one would ask for anything, or my bank account would take a serious hit.

After everyone said they were good for now, I walked over to the bar, sat on a stool, and then grabbed a laminated menu that was as sticky as the bar. I ordered nachos with cheese and bacon, then spun on the stool and watched the pool game. Again, I wondered what got into me to come tonight. I heaved a sigh, then wheeled back toward the bar and took my phone out of my bag.

August had answered me. **Glad you're okay. Heard you're Matt's favorite girl now too.**

I smiled. **No. Still just yours. He has Amanda.** Only after I pressed send did I realize how flirty that sounded. I dragged a hand through my hair that was now completely dry.

August sent me a smiley face.

Not for the first time, I wished he were here instead of across an ocean. That thought filled me with abrupt guilt. Guilt that made me glance at Sienna. She was laughing at a story Cole was telling her. I studied her a moment, analyzing her body language. Her eyes glittered a little as she looked up at the mammoth blond with the buzz cut. Maybe her eyes always glittered. Or maybe she was over August.

I ducked my face back down and wrote: **You'd be proud of me. I'm at Tracy's with the pack. I'm trying to be social.**

A couple seconds later: **I hope they're on their best behavior.**

No one's called me any names yet.

And if any of them do, you tell me, OK?

I'll be fine. Concentrate on staying alive out there. Which had me thinking... **Are we as killable as humans?**

Don't get your question.

I took a swig of beer, then set it back down and typed: **Can we die of something other than drowning or silver poisoning?**

Dot-dot-dots appeared. Then: **Silver, fire, or asphyxiation. Why? Are you planning on killing Lucas?**

I grinned. **LOL. Even though I wish you'd taken him with you, no. No homicidal plans on my end. I was just wondering.**

Strange thing to be wondering about.

The bartender came back with my dish and the bill. As I dug out my wallet, I remembered I owed Liam fifty dollars. I paid for my meal, then took out the owed amount and slid it inside my bag's front pocket.

When I looked back down at my phone, August had written: **Want me to call you?**

I frowned.

One more line of dialogue appeared: **For a refresher course. Wolf 101.**

I did need one. I was about to type yes when Matt sidled up next to me at the bar. He ordered more beer and filched a soggy tortilla chip from my bowl. "Who you sextin'?"

The chip I'd been chewing on went down the wrong hole. I coughed, then grabbed my Sam Adams and took a long gulp.

"I wasn't *sexting*," I wheezed out.

A goofy grin slashed his jaw. "Sure you weren't."

"Seriously, I wasn't."

He snatched another chip. "Who were you *texting*, then?"

"Everest."

"Liar."

My spine tightened.

"You couldn't have been texting Everest 'cause he's right there, sucking face with some chick."

I spun on my stool. Everest was here? Sure enough, he was sitting on a brown leather couch in a dusky corner of the room, making out with the girl from the music festival.

"So? Who were you really talkin' to, Little Wolf?"

"No one, *Hulk*."

His smile grew larger. "As long as it ain't that creep you went out with the other day, I'm cool with it."

I snorted. "It wasn't, but thanks for your consent." Even though I would sooner swallow a live goldfish than admit this to Matt, I was sort of touched by his concern.

"You looked out for me, so now I look out for you... Only fair. Unless someone's already doing that?" He looked at Everest again then, and I did too.

Like the hunger crimping my stomach, Everest's fickleness pinched my heart. It had barely been a month since Becca's suicide attempt, and he was already kissing someone new. Sure, I'd thought it was healthy for him to be flirting, but making out with someone...that was too much too fast.

"August just wrote back," Matt said.

I whipped my face toward Matt and swiped my cell off the bar. I didn't check the text message, just stuffed the phone inside my bag. My heart had leaped a good couple inches into my throat. "We're just friends."

As he paid for his beers, he said, "I'm not judging. I like the guy."

I wanted to add don't tell Sienna, but that would've sounded incriminating. I scooped up some plasticky cheese and crunchy bacon bits with a chip and stuffed them inside my mouth.

"Lucas wiped me out." Liam was suddenly here, right next to me. He swiped a beer from Matt's stash and drank half of it. "Your turn, Mattie." As though just noticing me, he asked, "Unless you want to play, Ness?"

My heart performed a strange little twist as I looked up at Liam, as I imagined him carrying my limp, naked—*ugh*—body in his arms. They'd probably had to draw straws, and he'd gotten the shortest one.

"I can barely move my arms."

He settled on the stool next to mine, gaze roaming over my arms. "You got a serious thrashing out there. All those rocks."

Had he been there?

Before Matt left to play, he tossed out, "If Liam annoys you, call out my name. Or Hulk. I'll respond to both."

I smiled.

"Did Ness Clark just crack a real-ass smile?" Matt winked at me, which had me shaking my head. He scooped up the three beers and then returned to the others.

"I heard I had you to thank for getting back to the inn." I twirled a chip in the air, twisting the string of cheese glued to it until it snapped off.

Liam didn't say anything.

Without taking my eyes off the chip, I said, "Tell me I wasn't naked." Some people could sweep things under rugs; I was the type who'd rather vacuum them.

"You weren't."

I exhaled a long breath.

"They covered you up the second you changed."

Another breath rushed out of me. "I wonder how the other packs—the ones with females in them—I wonder how they…operate."

"You mean does everyone get naked together?"

Heat curled up my throat.

"I would imagine nudity isn't such a big deal for them."

I finally dared look away from my chip. Liam raised his beer to his lips and tipped it, his Adam's apple bobbing sharply under his dark stubble.

"At least I don't have to worry about that anymore."

He laid a long, muscled forearm on the bar. "What do you mean?"

"Now that I'm out of the pack." *Out of Boulder…*

"You're not out."

"They said that if I failed, I couldn't get into the pack."

"But you didn't fail."

"I did. I changed during the trial."

"Ness, you're still in the running. Matt's the one who's out."

I knocked my beer over, and it spilled onto Liam's jeans.

"Shoot." I grabbed a handful of napkins and dabbed his thigh.

He wrapped his hand around my wrist and stilled my fingers. I froze as something pulsed against my knuckles.

I snatched my arm back. "Sorry," I mumbled, ogling the row of backlit liquor bottles and wondering how many of those I should ingest to forget that my hand had just connected to a very private part of Liam Kolane's anatomy. I wiped my shaky fingers on a napkin. "I broke the rules..." My disloyal voice was wobbling. I prayed Liam would think it was the emotion of not being disqualified that was affecting my larynx and not—

"To save his hand," Liam said huskily.

I feigned great interest in the baseball game on the TV hanging from an articulated arm over the liquor shelf. "He wouldn't have gnawed it off."

"He might've. In wolf form, we can act like animals."

I side-eyed him.

Pale arms slid around his chest. "Baby, you abandoned me." Tamara tried to kiss him, but he twisted his face, and her lips landed on the hard line of his jaw.

I ogled my half-eaten basket of tortilla chips. When minutes later she was still trying to coax him off the barstool, I stood.

"Before I forget." I slid out the fifty-dollar bill and extended it to him.

Tamara stared at the bill, nose crinkled. "Are you paying him for his company?"

I frowned. "What?"

She shot me a sweet smile that was anything but sweet. "Isn't that how you make your living? Cash for company?"

She could've thrown a glass full of ice at my face, and it would've chilled me less than her comment.

Liam pried her arms off him.

"Excuse me?" I said, playing dumb in case I was reading too much into what she'd insinuated.

"The boys said you were a wh—"

"Tamara!" Liam's complexion went a little ruddy.

She pushed out her lower lip in a pout. "What?"

In what world did I think I had friends here? I backed up, and then I turned, emotion burning on my lids. My ears buzzed as I stepped onto the street. I felt drunk and sick to my stomach, but I was neither. What I was, was ashamed. And angry. It wasn't like I could explain what I'd been doing on an escort service website in the first place.

I started walking, not caring where I ended up. I just needed to get away.

"Ness!" someone called out.

Even though my legs ached, I quickened my pace, but someone stepped out in front of me, blocked my path.

TWENTY-TWO

I tried to sidestep Liam.

He shuffled, blocking me again. "Ness, I'm sorry."

"About what? Telling your girlfriend I was a whore? It's true, isn't it? So there's nothing to be sorry about." I walked off, but Liam stalked next to me.

"We never said you were a whore."

They'd probably used the word escort—big whooping difference. I started to cross the street to get away from him when a car honked at me.

Liam yanked on my arm, reeling me back onto the sidewalk. My shoulder screamed in pain from the sharp tug.

I gritted my teeth as I flung his hand off and rubbed my sore joint.

"Shit." Liam palmed the back of his neck. "Did I hurt you?"

"Don't give yourself so much credit."

"Oh, will you stop acting like you're fucking made of steel. A rock almost spliced your spine Saturday. You're allowed to be in pain."

So he had seen me... He *had* been there. "Thanks for your permission."

He grumbled some unintelligible words. "I don't get you. Really, I don't." He shoved a lock of hair off his forehead.

"What don't you get, Liam? Did you think I'd enjoy everyone finding out that I went on a date with a guy for money?" I hugged my arms against me, trying to squelch the tremors shooting through my limbs. I was cold and I was mad. Not a good combination.

"You said you didn't sleep with your customers, so there's really nothing to be ashamed about. Unless you do…sleep with them."

My stomach bottomed out. "*Them*?"

He held my gaze. Did he know about his father? He couldn't, could he?

Keeping my eyes fixed on his, I said, "I only went out with Aidan." Technically, it was true. I hadn't *gone out* with Liam's father; I'd stayed in. "But I'm not doing it anymore, so if you can stop telling people—"

"I'm sorry."

"Whatever." I tried to step around him again, but he whipped his arm out to stop me.

"Come back inside. Let me buy you a drink to make up for being a prick."

"In what world do you think I'd want to go back in there?"

"Then let me buy you a drink someplace else."

I tightened my arms. "God, Liam, I don't need a pity drink."

"It wouldn't be a pity drink. It'd be an apology drink."

I shook my head. "Thanks, but no thanks. I just want to walk around."

He lowered his hand, and I passed by him. But then he was striding next to me.

"The bar's the other way."

"Maybe I want to walk around, too."

"There are plenty of other sidewalks."

"I like this sidewalk."

"Liam—" I huffed.

"What? You don't have to talk to me."

"That's not going to be weird at all."

I thought I detected a smile, but it could've been a twitching nerve.

"Why?" I asked.

"Why what?"

"Why are you walking with me? And if you say it's to protect me from a handsy passerby—"

"My earliest memory is of your birth."

"My birth?"

He glanced down at me. "Your dad came over to our house to announce that he'd had a kid, and that kid was a girl. I remember how appalled my father was."

His strange confession unsettled me. "You were four."

"So?"

"That's young to remember something."

Liam's gaze dropped to my collarbone as though not daring to meet my eyes. "My father advised your dad to take a paternity test."

I gasped. "My mother would never—"

"It gets worse, Ness." Liam palmed his hair uneasily.

Worse than implying my mother had betrayed my father?

"He also told your dad that he should take you out into the woods"—the volume of Liam's voice dropped so suddenly I had to strain to hear the rest of his sentence—"leave you there, and then try again."

"Leave me in the forest? To do what?" I frowned but then I didn't. Then I opened my eyes so wide my lashes hit my brow ridge. "Oh… He told my father to *kill* me?" I all but shouted. "Because I was a girl?"

Liam's gaze finally climbed back to mine. "Your father was outraged. My mother, too."

"And you?" I snapped.

"Why do you think it's my earliest memory, Ness?" His voice was as thick and dark as the fur that cloaked his wolf form.

Heath had made my father doubt my mother and then suggested I should be murdered because of my gender! If Liam's father weren't already dead, I would've found a silver blade and wrenched it inside his black, black heart.

"What's *your* earliest memory?" Liam asked, whisking my mind off my homicidal deliberations.

I racked my brain. When the memory slotted into my mind, I blinked. It couldn't possibly be my earliest recollection. I hunted through my mind for another but found none.

"Your mother's funeral."

He flinched.

I'd been five at the time. I could still remember what I'd worn—a scratchy black wool dress with thick white stockings and black patent mary-janes. The air had smelled of overturned earth and tears, and there hadn't been a dry cheek.

Except Heath's.

He didn't weep, but Liam cried enough for the two of them.

Liam had been a gangly boy with features too large for his face. He'd grown into his body, grown into his features. He didn't even resemble the narrow-faced sixteen-year-old boy I'd last seen on the winter day I begged the pack to accept me.

"I remembered wondering if you had a hole in your heart," I said as we crossed the street toward a little park. "But now I know." Mom's gaunt face flashed into my mind. "I'm sorry."

He glanced down at me. "For what?"

"For reminding you of her."

"Because you think I forget? Not a day goes by where I don't think about her, Ness." His voice contained the same shadows that had collected over his face.

We carried around the same pain, he and I.

"You never forget the people you love, but I guess you know this now," he said softly.

A snare snapped around my heart.

I thought about my mother, about my father—who was *most definitely* my father—as we passed by the playground of my youth. It had changed, gotten a shinier swing set, but the monkey bars I spent hours scaling were still there. Dad would swing alongside me sometimes, while Mom looked on, shaking her head and laughing, telling him he looked ridiculous—a gorilla in a hamster cage.

I didn't realize I'd stopped walking, didn't realize I'd started crying, until I felt the swipe of a thumb over my cheek.

I drew in a sharp breath when Liam did it again.

Oh, no, no, no.

His face took on such an intent look that I jerked backward. His fingers slid off my cheek and fell slowly, curling into a fist at his side.

My heart whizzed around my chest like a stray bullet. I prayed he couldn't hear my pulse, prayed he couldn't see how it made the thin cotton of my shirt quiver.

He shifted his gaze to a plump tree dripping with lilac blooms. "I'm sorry about laying all this on you. I just thought you'd appreciate knowing."

"I do appreciate it, but it doesn't make me sorry your father is dead."

Liam didn't respond for a such a long time that I hesitated to apologize, but I just couldn't. I couldn't apologize for saying words I meant. His father was evil.

"Do you want to go home?" he finally asked.

Did he mean to the inn or to Los Angeles?

Probably to the inn… "Yeah, but I'll call a cab."

He shifted his gaze to me. His eyes were so dark, as though his pupils had stretched from lid to lid and corner to corner. "I'll drop you off. It's on my way."

Was it really? "Okay."

In silence, we made our way to his car that was parked across the street from the pool bar. I could see the pack through the glass façade, wielding cue sticks, laughing, and drinking. I prayed they couldn't see me. I didn't want new rumors to spread.

Liam pulled my door open, and instead of making a fuss, I got in. The tension inside the car was so thick it was stifling. I cracked my window open, but the brisk air did little to deflate the ripe atmosphere.

I rested my cheek against the headrest and watched the darkness unspool outside the car, the same way it was unspooling inside my mind: Liam wasn't attracted to me; he pitied me. He thought I was pathetic and sad and way too proud for my own good. Besides, I wasn't attracted to him. Sure, he was handsome, but plenty of guys were handsome. Just because my body reacted to his didn't mean I should encourage the feelings swarming through me.

"The elders want to meet on Wednesday." His voice jolted me out of my deliberations.

I turned to look at him, his profile lacquered by the glow of his dashboard.

"To discuss the next trial."

"I shouldn't be part of the next trial."

His jaw flexed as he slid to a stop in front of the inn. "But you are."

"But I shouldn't be."

"Look, if you don't want to take part in the contest anymore, go to the meeting and have it out with *them*."

I flinched from the harshness of his voice. "Fine. At what time will it be and where?"

"It'll be at my father's house at 6:00 p.m."

A shudder shot down my spine. "Why at your father's house?"

He cocked an eyebrow. "Do you have a problem with going there?"

I clicked my seatbelt and pumped my door handle. "No."

"Aren't you going to ask me for the address?"

"I remember where it is."

"Of course you do."

My pulse became a chaotic mess of heartbeats.

I didn't ask what that was supposed to mean, because I dreaded his answer. Had the agency told him I'd been the girl they'd sent to see Heath, or had Liam figured this out on his own? Or did his father have security cameras? I hadn't seen any, but that didn't mean the sleazeball hadn't installed some.

What did it matter? It wasn't as though *I'd* killed him with my three little anti-shifting pills. They were innocuous. I knew that firsthand, because I'd had to swallow one every day for the first three months after we left Boulder. Even though distance from the pack eventually blocked the change, Mom had used pills to drain the werewolf magic from my veins. The pills had belonged to my father, who'd taken them to avoid shifting while his bones mended after he'd broken both his legs.

I hopped out of the car and muttered, "I'll see you after tomorrow." And then I slapped the door closed, feeling the vibrations all the way inside my joints.

TWENTY-THREE

T he following day, Lucy stopped by my bedroom at sunrise to ask how I was doing. I wondered if she honestly cared. I shrugged and told her I was better.

"I heard they've kept you in the running," she said, pulpy arms folded in front of her Double-Ds.

"I heard that too."

I waited for her to tell me to quit the contest. She didn't. And I didn't share my intention to drop out.

Her hazel eyes combed over the bare legs peeking from my sleep shorts. "Can you work?"

"Yes." I stretched my arms. They no longer felt attached to dumbbells, but a faint soreness remained.

So she assigned me guest bedrooms, and I donned my gray uniform and tackled her task, scouring rugs with a vacuum, stretching sheets to their breaking point, dusting the mason jars filled with homemade potpourri. The physical exertion kept my mind off what Liam had insinuated.

But only for a while.

By the afternoon, after eating with Evelyn in the kitchen, I paced my bedroom like a tiger locked in a cage. At some point, I picked up the framed picture on my nightstand—a shot of me with my parents. I studied my father's face and compared it to my own. Besides our matching dimples and perhaps the shape of our mouths, I'd inherited all of my features from my mother.

I growled as I realized what I was doing. How dare the Kolanes insert doubt into my brain.

I was my father's daughter.

I was a werewolf, like him!

I set the frame down so hard the glass rattled. Thankfully, it didn't break.

A knock snapped my attention off the picture. I went to the door and then thrust it open. Crossing my arms in front of my chest, I scowled at Everest, then gave him a piece of my mind. I gave him *all* the pieces of my mind.

He dropped a shopping bag on my bed.

"What's that?" I grumbled.

"A dress. I hope it's the right size."

"What the hell? You bought me a dress?" I threw my hands in the air. "You think I'm going to forgive you because you got me a present?"

"I didn't buy it to cajole you. I bought it because you're going to need it tonight."

"Why am I going to need a dress tonight?" I realized I was yelling when Everest pressed a hard finger against my lips.

"Keep your voice down."

"Don't you dare tell me to keep my voice down. You don't get to tell me what to do! You ditched me." My voice caught on a sob.

Everest sighed and tucked me against him. "I'm sorry. My parents." He shook his head. "And then—then I found out something, and I was working on a solution before I came to you. Now calm the hell down, so I can explain."

I pushed him away.

"Liam hired a PI," he explained.

My throat became a dry husk.

"The man's been sniffing around to find out what happened to Heath. Guess where it led him? Straight to the escort agency." His whispers sounded like shouts. "Sandra didn't give him your name. She contacted me, though, when she couldn't reach you. Anyway, she promised not to give you away in exchange for some hush money."

"You paid her off?"

"Yes. I paid her off."

"How much?"

"Don't concern yourself with how much. I covered it." He palmed his mussy red hair.

"I think Liam already knows. Last night, he implied—"

"He doesn't know. He's trying to guess, but he doesn't know."

I dropped heavily into the armchair, rested my head back, and sighed. "I realize my being there the night Heath died doesn't look good, but I didn't kill him, Everest. I should just come clean."

When Everest didn't say anything, I propped my head back up. His lips were so thin and his cheeks so pale my heart stilled for a couple beats.

"What?"

He sat on the foot of my bed.

"You're scaring me… What?"

"Ness, I heard Lucas and Matt talk about Heath's tox screen. How the coroner found drugs in his system."

My spine went rigid. "So?"

"He drowned because those pills… They fucked up his nervous system."

"Are you—are you—" Tremors crawled over my arms and legs, rattled inside my chest, rippled over my skin. I lifted a trembling hand to my gaping mouth. "No," I whispered.

Everest hung his head then craned his neck and shot me the grimmest, most doleful stare in the history of stares. "Yes."

The room distorted. "You mean to say… You mean to tell me…"

"That you killed him? Yes."

My breathing halted as fear clambered down my throat and squashed my lungs.

I killed Heath.

For all my talk of murdering him, I would *never* have gone through with it.

I wasn't some blood-thirsty executioner.

Everest leaned forward and caught one of my hands. "I have a plan."

I tried to swallow, but jagged lumps clogged my airway like clumps of hair in a shower drain. "I need to…to run away."

"No."

I killed Liam's father. The pack Alpha. The pack was going to come after me and shred me to ribbons.

"I have a plan. A plan that will keep you safe. I promise. It's foolproof."

Nothing was foolproof.

Silver bars materialized in front of my eyes. The Boulders were going to toss me in that hole of theirs. I removed my hand from Everest's and massaged my temples. If the pack didn't kill me, the authorities would lock me up for involuntary manslaughter. It wouldn't matter that it hadn't been intentional.

Shit.

"Ness. I got a big player to help you," he said.

I didn't think the President of the United States could get me out of this mess.

"Julian Matz," Everest said, as though the name should've meant something to me. It didn't.

"Who the hell is Julian Matz?"

Everest flinched from my shrill tone. "The Pine Pack Alpha."

My skin broke out in goose bumps. His plan was to involve the Alpha of the greatest enemy pack? Ice spilled into my stomach as an even more chilling thought settled. "Did you...tell him?"

"I had to."

He had to. I was straddling the brink between fury and anger, and it was giving me a strong urge to gouge my cousin's eyes out. "You told him! How dare you!"

Everest blinked. "Ness, I did it for you."

Fuck. My life was fucked. Maybe I should attempt to fly off a roof like Becca. Or maybe I should turn into a wolf and travel to a distant mountain range and lose myself in the wilderness.

"Look, you're going to meet with Julian tonight, and he'll explain how he's going to go about clearing you." He gestured toward the shopping bag. "Wear the dress and meet me in the driveway at five. I'll take you to him." He checked his watch. "You have two hours to get ready."

He got up and started walking toward the door.

"Why do I have to wear a dress?"

"It's his nephew's engagement party."

Stab me through the heart. Not only did I have to meet with an enemy Alpha, but I had to attend an engagement ceremony where surely the entire Pine Pack would be assembled.

I'd almost rather have died.

Almost.

TWENTY-FOUR

T he dress Everest had gotten me fit like a glove…an actual glove. The stretchy black leather hugged each one of my curves, leaving absolutely nothing to the imagination. Nor did it leave any room to strap a knife to my thigh, which I'd considered.

But then I'd reconsidered it.

Bringing a weapon to a werewolf engagement party was surely in poor taste. What would I do with a knife anyway? If the blade wasn't welded from silver, it would do me little good. Everest's revelation made me bang a clenched fist against my mirror. A fissure streaked the glass. I stared at the crack as though it were an omen. What did breaking mirrors mean? *Right…seven years of bad luck.*

I was doomed.

I took one of the pins I'd sandwiched between my lips and stuck it into the bun that was supposed to look sleek but ended up resembling a ball of yarn a cat would've chased down a staircase.

When my updo was done, I grabbed my bag, cell phone, key, and then slid on my black heels. On my way out of the inn, I crossed paths with Jeb. I prayed he had no inkling of what I'd done.

He crossed his arms as I passed by the bell desk. "Where are you going?"

"I'm having dinner with Everest."

His forehead grooved. "Where's he taking you?"

"He said it was a surprise for having forgotten to take me to the first trial."

Jeb's pupils twitched with guilt.

"'Night, Jeb."

He peeked over my shoulder at the parking lot, probably to check whether I was telling the truth about going to dinner with his son.

I climbed into Everest's car with little grace, the dress constricting my movements. "I didn't know they made straitjackets out of black leather."

Everest cracked a grin, one of his incredibly toothy grins, and for a second, it made me forget that this was possibly one of the crappiest days of my existence. And I'd had my fair share of crappy days.

I hooked on my seatbelt. "So, who was that girl you were swapping spit with at Tracy's?"

"Just a girl."

"Same one from the music festival, right?"

"Right."

"And you met her...randomly?"

The tips of his ears flushed. "She's not an escort."

I hadn't meant to imply he'd met her through Sandra. "What's her name?"

He flicked his gaze to me. "Why do you want to know?"

I was a little taken aback by that. "Because I'm your cousin, and your life interests me. But if you don't want to tell me—"

"It's Megan. She's a freshman at UCB."

Glancing outside, at the narrow sunlit road hedged with pines, I rubbed my thumb over my bag's strap. "What about Becca?"

"What about her?"

"What happens if she wakes up?"

"It's been a month, Ness."

"So you're giving up?"

"I'm not giving up, but neither am I going to wait by her bedside for the rest of my life."

I was no relationship expert, but moving on from someone he'd loved after just a month felt incredibly brusque.

"I didn't mean to make you feel guilty," I ended up saying.

"I don't feel guilty." His answer was dry, brittle almost.

For a long moment, we both watched the ribbon of road we were traveling in silence.

When we crossed over into the Pine Pack territory—a border delineated by sour piss and a pristine, ten-foot metal fence guarded by two wolves in skin, I asked, "How come you went to the Pine Pack for help?"

Everest eased his window open and gave the guard our names. The man waved us through, and we set off down a cedar-shaded alley lined with floating white balloons.

"Because they hated Heath."

I mulled this over. "What's in it for them?"

"Julian will tell you."

"Why don't *you* tell me?"

"Because he'll explain it better."

"Do they want something—"

Everest slapped his steering wheel. "God, Ness, have a little patience, okay?"

I bristled from his snappishness. He was delivering me to a den of wolves—literally. The least he could do was hint at what was expected of me.

"Are you coming in with me?"

"No. It wouldn't look good if I were there."

"But my presence won't set off warning bells?"

"You are not a Boulder wolf. You have every right to be here. And if anyone gives you grief, tell them Julian paid you for your company. He'll corroborate the story."

I wanted to scream that I wasn't an escort but reined in my irritation.

He came to a stop in the looping driveway of the Pines' headquarters—an all glass and wood structure that resembled a luxurious country club. A cut above the simple gray stone building the Boulder Pack convened in. Then again, the Boulder Pack made good use of the inn, which was perhaps the reason they'd never invested heavily in expanding their headquarters.

A white-gloved waiter opened my door.

"Are you picking me up?" I asked.

"Julian will have someone drive you home."

"Can't you pick me up?" I sounded like a whiny child, but I didn't like being in unknown territory.

He sighed. "Fine. Call me when you're ready to go."

"Thank you." I shot him a weak smile. "Thank you for everything, Everest." My throat was closing up again.

He didn't look at me as he answered, "What's family for?"

Clutching my bag against me, I turned and ascended the wide, peony petal-dusted stone steps like a prisoner walking toward their execution.

TWENTY-FIVE

I'd researched Julian on the internet to find out what he looked like and what he enjoyed doing. He wasn't a particularly private person, so I'd unearthed plenty of shots of him surrounded by his "family." I even got to see my favorite Pine Pack member, Justin Summix, in a couple shots. I'd had the urge to print one out of Justin so I could stick pins into his face and crotch. Misogyny brought out the worst in me.

As luck would have it, Justin was the first person I laid eyes on. Perhaps I noticed him first because he was the only person I knew. Others were vaguely familiar, but grief and distance had blurred my memories of them. Justin elbowed the boy he was standing next to and pointed me out. *Subtle.*

A girl, not much older than me, with a mass of long kinky blonde curls and lips colored a bright pink, placed a hand on my forearm.

Her nostrils flared. "Excuse me, sweetie, but I believe you have the wrong pack gathering. I smell Boulder wolves all over you." She pressed on my arm to turn me around. "We don't take their leftovers here," she explained sweetly.

I pasted on a pert smile and brushed her hand off my bare arm. "Good thing I'm not a Boulder leftover then. I'm looking for..." His name withered in my throat when I spotted him at the center of the room. Like a pebble tossed into a pond, everyone rippled around Julian.

As though he sensed me looking at him, Julian turned his clear-blue eyes up toward me. A frown gusted over his face, followed almost immediately by a slow, slow smile.

I walked down the steps, my heels clicking on the stone. Nostrils flared, and more than one set of eyebrows hitched as I approached my *date*.

"Mr. Matz," I said.

"My, you are striking, Miss Clark." He picked up one of my hands and held it to his lips as though he were about to kiss it. His lips never met their mark, but his gesture did. The weres I'd felt closing in around me began to back up. He twirled me around so that I had my back pressed against his bordeaux-colored dinner jacket. A tiny gasp escaped my lips, and he loosened the arm he'd wound around my waist.

"Everyone, Ness Clark is our special guest tonight. I expect you all to be on your absolute best behavior."

My gaze crossed paths with many sets of wide, startled gazes. Everyone seemed to wait for an explanation as to why I was their special guest, but instead of adding anything, Julian released me and then offered me his arm. I supposed not taking it would be in bad form, so I looped my arm through his.

"Let me introduce you to the couple of the hour."

He led me through a set of open doors that gave way onto a sprawling, manicured lawn planted with perpendicular hedges. Their corners were so straight I imagined the gardener using a ruler to chop them.

Julian raised one of his hands, where a pinkie ring glittered with a diamond the size of his nail. "Robbie, Margaux!" he called out to the couple who were having their picture taken by a team of professionals.

The photography equipment looked as expensive as the bride-to-be did with her white lace dress and the river of diamonds wrapped around her swan-like neck.

Julian's nephew turned toward me first. He raised his nose the slightest bit and sniffed the air. His eyebrows slanted just like those of his fellow shifters. Obviously Julian had not announced my visit to anyone other than the guards at the gate.

"This is Ness Clark." Julian's pouty mouth curved, which accentuated his nephew's frown.

"Callum Clark's girl?" Robbie asked.

Julian nodded. "The very one." He released me and leaned in toward his future niece-in-law—or whatever she was to him. "Margaux, darling, you look ravishing tonight."

"As do you, Uncle."

"Always a kind word for your graying uncle."

"You are not graying." She let out a tinkling titter, as though her lips were made of crystal.

I sniffed the air, wondering what she was truly made of—skin or fur. She smelled like Robbie, as though she'd bathed in his scent.

When the camera crew asked if they could get a picture of her with Julian, he obliged.

Robbie crossed his arms as he watched his uncle dip his future wife over his arm. She laughed, her eyes glittering for the camera as wildly as her diamonds. I looked up at Robbie and wondered if he worried about the way Julian touched Margaux. After all, Julian was the Alpha, and Alphas liked to take things that weren't theirs for the taking…at least that had been true in our pack.

"You've grown up lots since the last time I saw you." Robbie glanced down at me. "How long has it been?"

"Six years."

"Six years…" he mused, his gaze back on his future wife who was now giggling because Julian had scooped her up. "I always wondered something."

"What?" I asked him.

"Why didn't your pack punish the hunter who killed your father?"

"Excuse me?"

"The last hunter who injured one of ours was mauled instantly. I thought the Boulders abided by the same rules as we did."

My body, which I'd angled toward Julian and Margaux, pivoted fully toward Robbie. "They do. The hunter was killed right after I left Boulder."

He frowned deeply. "The man's very much alive, Ness."

My heart, which had behaved until now, hurdled against my ribcage.

"You were with your father that night, weren't you?"

"I was, but it was dark, and it was one of my first runs, and my sense of smell was still developing, and—"

"So you don't remember the hunter?"

"I never even saw him. At least, I don't remember seeing him." I remembered hearing the gunshot, the hot spray of blood, the metallic smell of it, but that was all that remained of the devastating night. "But the pack sniffed him out. And they"—my voice caught—"they *killed* him."

The pity crinkling Robbie's expression made my skin crawl. "For a dead man, he looks and sounds awfully real."

Bang. Bang. Bang went my heart. Like the rifle that had stolen my father from me. Robbie was lying, trying to get a rise from me.

"How do you even know who it is?" I asked.

"You don't think we carry out our own investigations? The death of a shifter affects us all."

His words rubbed my nerves raw. "Why should I believe the man is still out there? For all I know, you're trying to rile me up so I go and kill an innocent man. A man whose death would be convenient to the Pines?"

"Passionate little thing, aren't you?"

"Answer my question. Why should I believe you?"

"Truth is, you shouldn't. But if I were you, Ness, I'd go ask your pack for the truth."

"I don't have a pack."

He tilted his head to the side. "So the rumors I heard that you were competing for Alpha are deceitful?"

"I'm not competing anymore. I have no interest in being a Boulder."

He folded his strong arms in front of his broad chest. "So a lone wolf it is?"

"No. I'm leaving Boulder."

"Not shifting will shorten your lifespan. It's unnatural for your body not to go through the change. It would be like a woman not menstruating."

His comparison had me wrinkling my nose.

Margaux burst back next to us as Julian posed for a couple shots by himself. She latched onto her fiancé's arm but then let go to fuss with the white ribbon wrapped around his short blond ponytail.

"We should return to our guests, Robbie."

He kissed her, and then to me he said, "Enjoy the party."

Hand in hand, they went back to the crowd that had spilled out the French doors onto the paved terrace where all the faces and finery blurred into a vibrant, glittery cloud.

A hand wrapped around my elbow. "They'd like to take a picture of us. Would you pose for one with me?"

I turned to Julian. "No."

He studied my expression, then flicked a hand toward the photographer's assistant who had trailed after him. The woman scurried away.

"Mr. Matz, who killed my father?"

Julian gave his head a little shake. "Robbie. Robbie. Robbie. Always sticking his nose in matters that don't concern him."

"Tell me his name. Please." I had a violent need for the truth.

He dipped his chin. "If I am not mistaken, you had dinner with him a few days ago."

"*I* had dinner with my father's killer?" My voice was loud, too loud. It echoed inside my ears.

Julian's lips settled into a grim line. "Aidan Michaels."

Every sound, color, flavor, and scent faded as the name sank into my mind.

I'd sat at a table with my father's assassin. I'd made conversation with him. I'd taken his money.

I raised a hand to my neck and gagged on the bitter taste careening up my throat. I clamped my teeth shut, and sweat broke out over my upper lip. An arm wound around my waist, steadying me. The world eddied, before coming back into sharp focus.

"I'm sorry to be the bearer of such dire news, Miss Clark."

Stupidity left a vile taste in my mouth. Here I'd thought my pack disliked me, but if they hadn't avenged my father, then their dislike ran deeper than I'd assumed. Loathing throbbed beneath my skin. Claws curled from my nailbeds.

"Breathe. Your eyes have shifted," Julian instructed.

I breathed, and the simple act of inhaling and exhaling managed to drive my claws back. What it didn't manage to do was ease my fury.

"Heath had too many business dealings with Aidan Michaels to afford killing him." Julian leaned toward me, his whisky-scented breath brushing my ear. "You did the world a great favor by killing him."

My heart felt like a shard of ice. "Everest said you could help me." For the first time since my cousin had informed me I was a murderer, I didn't care.

An amused, almost satisfied expression creased his eyes. Unlike what humans believed, werewolves aged at the same rate as humans, yet Julian looked ancient, like he'd been alive far longer than his forty-seven years.

"I am well acquainted with the PI Liam hired. One word from me, and he will direct the focus of the investigation off of you."

"What will that word cost me?"

"You don't beat around the bush, do you?"

I squared my shoulders, and the leather dress tightened around me like a second-skin. "What will it cost me?"

"You go on with that little game your elders have organized."

I jerked my head back. "I don't want to be part of my pack."

"You wouldn't just be a part of it. You'd rule it."

"I have no desire to rule a bunch of pricks."

"Why did you enter your name in the first place, then?"

"Because I didn't want another Kolane to have that sort of power."

"And you've changed your mind?"

"No."

A slippery smile eased over Julian's lips. "You go on with those silly trials then, and I will not only make sure that your name is cleared, but also that you win."

"How and why?"

"Don't bother yourself with the how. As for the why…" Julian closed his hand over my elbow and steered me up the lawn. "I want there to be peace between our packs, and I believe you are the instrument of that peace. There is something incredibly special about you, and not simply because you are the first female born to your pack in a century. Although, perhaps your sex does color my conviction." He pulled me to a stop on the first step of the grand stone staircase leading up to the terrace. "Do we have a deal, Miss Clark?"

His flattery and backing were honing my ego into a dangerous weapon. "The Boulders detest you. They believe you are the source of all evil."

"I don't doubt this." His eyes flared like silver bullets. "But would an evil man desire peace?"

I tried to glimpse the wolf lurking beneath the human casing of tanned flesh, pouty mouth, and powder-blue eyes that were Julian Matz. I sensed his wolf was an impressive specimen.

"I could sweeten the pot by having my weres deal with Aidan. Would you like that?"

"I like to clean up my own messes, but thank you for the offer."

"So, will you go on with the trials?"

Did I have a choice? Besides hitchhiking away from Boulder, I had no way out. "Yes."

Julian's teeth flashed. He lifted my hand to his mouth and laid a kiss there to seal our deal. "How proud you would've made your father."

Glass shattered against stone, and then screeching voices exploded above us. I wheeled around and found an almost unrecognizable man glowering down at me and Julian. Blood poured from Liam's temple and gushed from his nose.

"Get away from him, Ness!" Liam's voice struck me like a bolt of lightning, but instead of making me tremble, it electrified me.

With an almost clinical detachment, I cocked my head to the side and watched as he struggled against the three shifters restraining him. I wondered if they were the same weres who'd rearranged his features into a bloody, pulpy mask. Liam bared his teeth, then whacked the back of his head against one of them. His captor gasped and teetered back. Blood dripped from his nostrils, mixing with Liam's on the slabs of limestone.

"Release him." Julian's voice cut through the pregnant air.

Liam was freed so suddenly he stumbled forward, but he regained his footing instantly.

"To what do we owe the pleasure of your visit, Liam?" Julian asked.

Liam's eyes roamed over my face. "I've come to collect my wolf."

His wolf? I was *no one's* wolf.

Julian echoed my musings out loud. "*Your* wolf?" His voice cocked in time with his eyebrow.

Color prickled Liam's jaw. "Ness is a Boulder wolf."

"As far as I understand, your pack hasn't let her pledge herself."

"Ness, come on. I'll take you home." Desperation rolled off him and banged into my toughened shell.

Now he cared? I hugged my arms around my torso. In my mind, I whispered, *Go away. You're making a fool of yourself.*

Julian wound a possessive hand around my bicep. "Ness is my date for the evening."

Liam's gaze rocketed toward the Pine Alpha, then slammed back into me.

He waited.

And waited.

For me to deny this. Or perhaps he waited for me to scrub Julian's hand off.

I did neither.

I could see the exact moment it registered with him that he'd wasted his time playing the savior. His entire face hardened, and he backed away. And then he shook his head, lips curling in disgust.

I kept my face blank of emotion as he stepped back and back until he disappeared.

I'd made an ally tonight, but I'd also made an enemy.

TWENTY-SIX

I stayed at the engagement party another hour. I'd made it a point not to leave with him, just as I was making it a point not to stay too long. I wasn't looking for a replacement pack.

Not that this was a possibility. I dug my phone out of my bag to ask Everest for a lift, but Julian pre-empted my demand by clicking his fingers. "Sarah!"

The wild-haired werewolf who'd told me Boulder whores weren't allowed on Pine territory got tasked with bringing me home. From the annoyance tightening her brown eyes, I could tell she was as glad about this arrangement as I was.

Midway home, she asked, "Did you blow him?"

I pitched my gaze off the dark road and onto her. All her features were fine, especially in contrast to her mass of tousled curls, but I could tell her delicateness was skin-deep, and that her personality matched her wild hair.

I guessed she meant Julian, but I needled her anyway. "You'll have to be more specific."

She wrinkled her pert nose. "God, really? Eww." She narrowed her gaze on the starlit forest. "I meant Julian."

"No."

"But you did do something to him, or he would never have helped you."

"Do you know where Liam Kolane lives?"

She raised one of her already peaked eyebrows. "Is this a trick question?"

"No. I left Boulder when I was eleven. Liam still lived with his father then."

A dimple appeared in her cheek. She must've been biting it. "I do know where he lives."

"Can you drop me off there?"

"Why?"

"I don't owe you an explanation, Sarah."

"If you're two-timing my Alpha, you do."

"Two-timing your Alpha would mean I was one-timing him. Which I'm not. I just need a word with Liam."

"I'm not waiting on your ass, though. I'm not your chauffeur or anything," she grumbled.

"Because you think I'd want you to wait on me?"

"Are you screwing Liam?"

"Do I look like I'm screwing him?"

"Babe, you look like you're open to screwing a lot of things."

"What is that supposed to mean?"

"Who wears a dominatrix dress to an engagement party?"

My eyes snapped a little too wide. I realized I hadn't fit in with the tulle and silks in my skintight leather but hadn't realized what impression it gave others. Then again, I hadn't been too concerned with fashion when I'd donned it.

"I didn't buy it."

"One of your lovers got it for you?"

I tugged on the hem that was riding up. "My cousin bought it for me."

"Yuck. If my cousin ever bought me shit like that, I'd tell her to wear it herself."

I snorted as an image of Everest wearing my dress snuck into my mind. "It's a him, not a her."

"An even better reason to get him to wear it." She smiled, and it thawed some of the stiffness padding her small red Mini.

"You're a wolf, right?" I wasn't sure why I was asking. She smelled like one. Perhaps it was to get confirmation. Confirmation that I wasn't the only female werewolf in the world.

"Damn right."

"How many of you are in your pack? Females, that is?"

"Twenty-eight for seventy males."

The Pine Pack was more than twice the size of my pack. *My pack.*

The thought caught me by surprise. I shook my head, but like a fly, the thought stuck to the web of my mind. Boulder blood ran through my veins, but that was it. The Boulders weren't *my* anything. Even if I became their Alpha, I'd never truly belong.

I stuck my elbow on the armrest and cradled my head as what I'd agreed upon—becoming Alpha of a pack I loathed—dug its talons inside of me. My deal with Julian wasn't fair to the Boulders, but fairness wasn't a value upheld by my pack anyway.

I massaged my temple. What was I supposed to do? If only there was someone I could ask. I thought about speaking to Everest, but he'd all but forced me to meet with Julian, so his counsel would be far from objective. I thought of Evelyn next. Perhaps, in not too many words, I could paint a clear enough picture of what was going on so she could advise me.

"We're here. That'll be a hundred bucks." Sarah turned toward me in the car, her eyes glowing in the semi-obscurity.

I raised my head off my fingers. "You're kidding, right?"

"Depends. Do you have money to burn? I could really use new headphones."

"You'd spend a hundred dollars on headphones?"

"I like good sound." She lowered her hand.

"But a hundred bucks?"

"Ever heard of DJ Wolverine?"

"No."

"Have you *not* been to The Den?"

"What's The Den?"

She rolled her eyes. "Only the coolest club in the whole of Boulder. I deejay there on Thursdays and Saturdays. DJ Wolverine." She pointed to herself. "I can't believe you haven't been."

"If it's Pine territory—"

"It's neutral territory. The Boulders go there with their little bite-sluts."

"Bite-sluts?"

"Girls who want to get bitten." When I frowned, she went on, "Some people still believe that if you get bitten enough times by a shifter, you'll turn into one."

I blinked. I didn't remember seeing any bite marks on the Boulders' girlfriends.

"God, you really are a total newbie at this. Robbie wasn't kidding."

"Robbie wasn't kidding about what?"

"That you need an education."

"He told you that?"

She smiled, her teeth glowing so white in the light of the car they resembled pearls. "I'm his baby sister. Robbie tells me everything."

"You're his sister?"

She slapped a palm over her chest very dramatically. "I'm offended."

"That I didn't know you were his sister? Unlike you, I didn't study your family tree."

"What'd they teach you in werewolf school?"

"I didn't go to…werewolf school." Was there even such a thing?

She smirked. "Did you fall for that?" Her smirk became a smile. "You did, didn't you?"

"You're weird."

"Says the only female in her pack."

"That makes me unique. Not weird."

She went back to smirking.

A light came on in a sleek, wood-paneled cabin at the end of a short dirt drive. I caught movement in the floor-to-ceiling windows that boxed in one end of the house. Liam's place wasn't oversized like his father's but looked pricey nonetheless.

The click of the car doors unlocking made me jump.

Sarah squinted at the shifting, shadowy shape. "You seriously not tapping that?"

"I'm seriously not tapping that," I said, pumping my door handle. "Thanks for the ride."

"Yeah. Whatevs." She flicked her hand. Gold rings set with cut stones glinted on two of her fingers. "Ciao."

I got out and started walking.

"If you ever get bored"—Sarah's voice made me spin around—"or have questions about being a she-wolf, you can find me at The Den. Thursdays and Saturdays."

I gave a short nod. That was…*kind*. Sadly, kindness made me suspicious. This was the reason behind my detour. I wanted confirmation that Aidan Michaels *had* shot my father and an explanation as to why there hadn't been any retaliation. I twisted back toward the rectangle of glass and wood, moonlit dust blooming around my heels as I approached Liam's house.

TWENTY-SEVEN

I was about to knock when the door opened. Liam had probably smelled me, like I'd whiffed his distinctive musky scent halfway down the drive.

He stood there, a towel riding low on his waist, his dark hair dripping water from a recent shower. Even though he basked in shadows, I noticed that his nose and a large part of his jaw were bruised. The blood was gone, though.

I looked away from his face, focusing on the sharp-lined furniture arranged at ninety-degree angles on a cowhide rug. Liam shifted, his body filling the doorway, surely to block out the sight of his home from my prying eyes.

He crossed his arms. Sinews moved beneath his smooth, golden skin like mooring lines. "What do you want?"

I inched my gaze back up to his face. "Did Aidan Michaels kill my father?"

His expression emptied of its hostility. Clearly, he had not been expecting *that* question.

"So? Did he?"

Frowning, he said, "I thought you knew."

"I wouldn't be asking if I knew."

Liam's eyes raked the darkness behind me, which had me twirling around. Was Sarah still there? Before I could turn back to face him, he yanked me inside then released me and shut his door.

"What were you doing at Robbie's engagement party, Ness?"

My gaze dipped to his glistening, muscled torso before sliding to something safer, something inanimate—a lamp speared into a block of black marble that bowed over the couch's armrest.

"I repeat, what were you doing at a Pine gathering, Ness?"

I looked back up into his stern face. "How did you even find out I was there?"

"Frank sensed you were in their territory. And then I caught a picture of you on one of their Instagram feeds. The Pines are social media whores." His voice was as sharp and stark as his house.

For some reason, that last part made me snort. "You have Instagram?"

"What. The fuck. Were you. Doing there?"

"The agency sent me." The lie slid out as smooth as the leather that ensconced me.

"The fuck they did. Julian would never use a Boulder wolf as an escort. Besides, I thought you were done with that."

"I'm not a Boulder wolf. Plus it was easy cash. *And* it gave me the opportunity to meet them. They're lovely people. Way more civilized than *your* pack."

"I told you I can pay your debts."

"And I told you I don't want your charity."

His hands moved to the towel at his waist. "It wouldn't be charity if I fucked you, right?"

I blanched. "I-I just… It's just d-dates." My throat went dry. "I don't have sex."

He untucked the towel, his long fingers moving slowly. "I have trouble believing that." The gray cotton slid heavily to the floor and pooled around his feet.

I backed up. "I'm not having sex with you, Liam."

"But you'll spread your legs for Julian?"

That made me snap. "I don't spread my legs for anyone."

"Look at you. Look at what you're wearing." He gestured to my dress, and I burned with rage.

I pressed my palms against the leather at my hips, wishing I could transform it into something else, something that stopped giving the impression I was a whore. "You're a real jerk, you know that?"

"At least"—his voice was barely above a vibration—"I'm an honest one."

Nerves skittered underneath my skin.

He took a step toward me, and I took another step back. My tailbone hit smooth wood.

"First..." His lips shut then parted again.

My heart held perfectly still.

"First Aidan. Now Julian." He moistened his lips. "Do you have a thing for older men?"

"They were jobs." My shoulder blades knocked together as I flattened myself against the wall.

Liam pressed one hand on the panel beside my face. His breaths whispered against my forehead. "Prove it."

I gaped at him. How was he expecting me to prove it? It wasn't like I'd documented my evenings.

An inhuman glow devoured his irises and coated the whites of his eyes. And then his nails lengthened into claws beside my face. They clicked against the wood. He snapped his eyes closed. When he opened them, they no longer shone yellow and his nails had receded.

I became acutely aware of his nakedness, of his proximity. He was careful not to touch me with any part of his body, and yet I felt him…everywhere. Smelled him. Heard the blood pound wildly in his neck.

"Damn it, Ness," he growled. "Prove it!"

His tone broke me out of my daze. "I don't need to prove anything to you, Liam Kolane."

"You embarrassed me today."

"I never asked you to retrieve me."

"What's your game?"

A knot of fear pulsed behind my navel. "Get away from me."

I pressed my hands into his torso, but it was like trying to move a tree. An infernally hot tree. His body wasn't on fire but felt like it was, especially in contrast to my clammy palms.

He spun me around and pushed me against the wall until my cheek was flush with the glossed surface, then locked my wrists behind my back with one of his hands.

"Let me go!" I screeched.

"Not until you tell me the truth. Did you or didn't you fuck Julian Matz?"

"Go to hell." A tear snuck down my cheek. And then another. And another.

"You leave me no choice." His knees clicked as he crouched.

Horror shot through me, and I struggled against him. Was he going to rape me? Oh, God, Everest had been right. Liam *was* like his father.

Silence. And then a long inhale. He'd sniffed me!

White-hot rage undid me, and I spun, ripping my wrists out of his grip. He rose, and I slapped him. Not once but twice, and I would've slapped him again if he hadn't caught my flailing hands.

"You are a pig! No worse than a pig!" I shouted. "How. Dare. You!"

His expression went slack. I ripped my hands from his and punched him in the gut. I would've punched him lower, but I didn't want to violate him like he'd violated me.

A groove formed between his slanted eyebrows. "You didn't sleep with him."

I shook, trembled, quaked. "I hate you. Hate you!" I fumbled to find the door knob. "If you ever...*ever*...come close to me, Liam, I will injure you so badly even your wolf gene will be powerless to fix you."

Liam stood perplexed. I doubted it was my threat that was scaring him. I doubted he took me seriously. If he did, he wouldn't have defiled me.

"Ness..." His voice sounded scratchy.

"Don't talk to me." I wrenched the door open and fled into the night, tripping on my heels. I kicked them off.

Anger and humiliation throbbed against my spine, against my heart, against my skull.

"Ness!" I heard him call out to me.

I didn't stop, didn't turn around. I had no idea where I was, but I ran anyway. Any place was better than here. And as I ran, my muscles thrummed, my bones hummed, and my skin prickled. The claws came out first, and then the fur. My body changed so fast it tore my dress, and I fell hard against asphalt.

Headlights blinked into existence up ahead, and I seized up.

The car rolled closer, the light glinting like honey off the ends of my white fur, the beams burning into my retina. I blinked just as an enormous black shape rammed into me.

For a second, I flew and then I landed so hard on my rump I whimpered. The world spun like the car's tires, and everywhere I looked was drenched in the blackest darkness and the shiniest starlight.

TWENTY-EIGHT

F ear shot up my spine at the same time as tiny aches exploded around it. And my lungs... They could barely expand underneath the weight of the body crushing mine. I squirmed and the black wolf rose off me and dragged himself a couple feet away.

I waited with bated breath in the shadows of the ditch, half expecting car doors to click open and footsteps to pound the road. But the car didn't even slow, zipping past where I lay hidden, spraying gravel over my dirt-flecked white fur. Slowly, I stirred, pressing up onto my limbs that were once again shaking, and blinked the darkness away. When my sight cleared and sharpened, I made out the gleam of Liam's eyes.

He let out a low-pitched whine. I backed away, but my bruised rump hit the slope of the ditch.

Liam didn't advance on me. He also didn't back away.

In that instant, I realized I owed him my life, but saving me didn't erase what he'd done. I bared my teeth and growled.

He still didn't move.

I barked, *Get away from me.* He didn't, so I shot out around him and into the forest, my sense of smell going haywire as it picked up a myriad of aromas. Dank moss tangled with Liam's musk, and the cold sweetness of wood smoke blended with the crisp scent of insect bodies.

I stepped over rocks and splashed through a creek. At some point, I caught a whiff of white jasmine and something else. Something chemical—Windex. I was approaching a house.

You're going the wrong way.

I froze. I wanted to ask which way was the right way, but I'd chew off my paw before I would admit I was lost.

The Flatirons are to your left. Liam's low drone carried over to me like the buzzing fireflies flitting around my ears.

I'd been relying on my sense of smell but had forgotten to look. I tipped my head up and located the Flatirons. And then I raced over earth and downed logs, muscles smacking against my hide like elastics. When the inn materialized, I slowed my pace. Bodies moved on the spacious terrace, glasses clinked, and fire snapped in a wide copper pit set between the Adirondacks.

I scurried along the lip of the forest, hoping the centennial trees would keep my wraith-colored form hidden from the guests having dinner. The scent of chargrilled meat and tangy barbecue sauce wafted toward me. My stomach gave a violent growl.

I loped around the side of the inn toward the parking lot but froze before turning the corner.

I couldn't enter the inn in wolf form.

I would need to shift back, but I'd be naked. And my bag? Where was my bag? It must've fallen outside Liam's house. I squeezed my eyes closed, my tail whacking the wall in frustration.

Jeb would have a second key.

Craning my neck, I looked around for Liam—I'd lost his scent at about the same moment the inn had come into view.

He was gone.

Finally.

Taking in a deep breath, I closed my eyes and let my human form bleed over my animal form. In seconds, I was a girl again. A bare-assed girl covered in dirt, with twigs tangled in her snarled hair. Thankfully, it was long enough to hide my breasts, revealing only their underside. I rose from my crouch, and shielding my privates, I crept toward the revolving door.

A mother with her child walked by, and I slammed my backside against the wall, praying they hadn't spotted me. Once I heard their voices peter out, I peeked inside again. The coast was clear. I pressed my muddy palms into the glass and pushed the door, then sprang toward the bell desk and dove behind it. Feet—small with copper-polished toenails—appeared underneath my face.

I craned my neck and locked eyes with Lucy. A sigh of relief whooshed out of me.

Her irises were framed with so much white that I could tell the feeling wasn't mutual. "Ness," she hissed, but then she flinched at the sound of approaching voices and all but shoved me inside the back room that stank of potpourri from the shelves full of drying petals. "Are you insane?"

"I lost my bag. And my clothes." Which was self-evident.

"What do you think we run here? A kennel?"

Ouch. "I didn't do this on purpose, Lucy."

"Of course you didn't."

"Can I please get a bathrobe? Or a towel? And another key?"

"Another key?" Her cheeks were so red they looked like candied apples. "You lost yours?"

"It was in my bag."

"Which you lost."

"Which I misplaced. But I'll find it." I stood back up, slowly, covering myself with my hands again.

My uncle's voice floated from just outside. Lucy jumped to block the office entrance, her collection of metal bangles jangling wildly on her freckled wrist. "Jeb, can you grab an extra bathrobe from the linen closet?"

"A bathrobe. Why do you need a bathrobe?"

She shifted to hide the sight of me. "Ness needs one."

A beat. Then. "Oh."

Once he left, she walked to a wall with lots of tiny hooks and grabbed a key—I supposed it was a spare. The hooks weren't numbered, but her system didn't seem very secure. I sensed it wasn't the right time to offer advice, but it increased my longing to have my own place, a place I could stroll into naked if I wanted to.

I thought of my apartment back in LA, then of my childhood home here. I wondered if I would remember how to get there. Wondered if anyone lived in it.

A white bathrobe smacked me in the face. I hurriedly donned it, tightening the belt until it dug into my waist.

"You can come in," Lucy said, I supposed to Jeb.

My uncle stepped into the room. After he took in my disheveled hair and mud-splattered face, he said, "I thought you were going to dinner with Everest."

Right. "I did, but he had a date afterward. He asked me if I would be okay to walk home." I dragged my hair off my face. "I got lost. And then I changed...and well...I managed to find my way back."

Lucy was shaking her face in disbelief. "That's incredibly irresponsible."

I wondered if she was talking about me or about Everest. I didn't ask.

She huffed. "Oh, and she lost her key."

"Keys are replaceable," Jeb said.

"Was it a master key?" Lucy asked suddenly.

"No. I don't leave the inn with the master key." After cleaning the rooms, I always put it in the safe.

My uncle sighed, a deep, rattling sigh. I didn't think it had anything to do with the type of key I'd lost though. He sounded tired.

"I'm going to call Everest. I'm not pleased with him. Not pleased at all. We raised him better than this." He lifted his phone to his ear and watched me as he spoke into the receiver. Everest must've corroborated my story, because when Jeb hung up, he was shaking his head. "He says he's sorry." He exchanged a weighted glance with Lucy.

"Can I go?" I peeped.

He waved toward the door, and I slid by them, stepping quickly over the wine-colored runner, hoping the sconces weren't casting too much of a glow on my face. The second I arrived inside my bedroom, I sidled against the door and crumpled to the floor.

For a long moment, I didn't move, didn't flick on the lights, didn't take a shower. I just sat there on the floor with my knees tucked against me, and I breathed. Just breathed.

The adrenaline vanished from my body the same way it had come—quietly and completely.

TWENTY-NINE

L ucy had me start work early the next morning.
She stopped by my bedroom to ask that I
vacuum the common areas and rearrange the
furniture on the terrace. Neither of us mentioned the
previous night's happenings. It was easier to pretend that I
hadn't erupted into the inn like a wild animal.

I grabbed my earphones from my nightstand drawer
when I remembered I didn't have a phone, which meant I
had no music to listen to during my chores. I sighed. But that
was the least of my worries. I also didn't have my wallet.
And a key to my room was somewhere in the wilderness,
etched with my room number and the Boulder Inn logo,
which was basically an invitation to visit.

After I finished my chores, I would need to retrace my
steps to Liam's house. Would I even recognize the way?
Hopefully my wolf scent still clung to the forest floor, and I
would be able to follow it back.

The motor rumbled as I pumped my arms back and
forth, dragging the nozzle over the thick rugs and hardwood
floors. My shoulders ached, but I pressed on. At some point,
my body would adjust to my four-legged activities, and my

muscles would strengthen. Besides, the ache paled to the pain that had ravaged my body after the first trial.

Which reminded me that I had to meet with everyone this evening at Heath's old place.

Which reminded me that I would have to sit in the same room as Liam.

The thought made me vacuum faster and harder. I crouched to get the nozzle underneath the couches, then plucked off the throw pillows decorated with Native American motifs and vacuumed the seats, before fluffing the pillows and arranging them like dominoes. I turned to start on another sofa when I bumped into someone.

My first instinct was to apologize, but my first instinct fizzled out the second I saw who it was.

Liam's nose and jaw were almost healed. It was his dark eyes that looked bruised. I guessed he hadn't slept much, and I hoped it was because of me...of what he'd done. My thighs clenched as I remembered him sniffing me, and the urge to slap him frothed upward.

"Ness?"

I pretended I hadn't heard him. Heart thumping fast—too fast—I moved around the room, hauling the roaring nozzle over every inch of floor, even the areas I'd already scoured. If only I could suck him up inside the hose.

I heard his slow inhale again, and a bolt of indignation sparked inside my core. In my peripheral vision, I saw him step toward me. I put more distance between us. Finally, he got the message, because he walked out of the living room. It took several minutes for my breathing to return to normal.

I shut off the vacuum, and as I dragged it back through the double-storied room, I spotted something on one of the couches. Something that hadn't been there before.

My bag and my shoes.

Making sure the doorway was still empty, I strode over and checked the contents of my bag. I even unzipped my wallet. I didn't carry around much cash, but the little I had was there. I took out my phone, half expecting it would have died during the night, but it had a full battery. Liam had probably charged it to peruse its contents. Sure my phone was password-protected, but the code was my birthday—it wouldn't take a rocket scientist to crack it.

I had two new text messages.

One from Everest: **Need me to pick you up?**

One from August: **Heard you were still in the running. What's going on? Call me.**

I didn't answer either. I stuffed the phone back into my bag, returned the vacuum to the closet, and tidied up the terrace. Once I was done, I stopped by the kitchen for food. During lunch, I asked Evelyn if she would accompany me on a little trek: to my old house.

Although hesitant, she'd agreed. We left the inn in the early afternoon and walked up a long stretch of winding road that ended in a cul-de-sac.

"One winter, I skidded on ice and fell all the way down the hill. Mom almost fainted when she saw me. I had cuts all over my cheeks."

"Was it ghastlier than the way you were returned to me on Saturday?"

I flashed her a sheepish grin. "Probably not."

She looped her arm through mine, her bad leg slowing our pace. The skid of rocks underneath her sneakers worried me—she wasn't even lifting the foot attached to the damaged calf.

"Is this too hard on your leg?"

"No. It is good for my leg." The ends of Mom's silk scarf, which Evelyn had wound around her ponytail, fluttered in the warm breeze. "I do not exercise enough, and it is becoming stiff."

I kicked a pebble that landed noiselessly inside a clump of heat-bleached grass. The road, which used to be smooth, was pockmarked. I hoped that whoever owned my childhood home was maintaining the house better than the path that led to it.

When slate shingles rose in the distance, my heart sped up and so did my pace. But then I remembered Evelyn's leg, and I slowed.

No smoke curled out from the chimney. Then again, it was summer.

As we neared the house, I told Evelyn the story of how I forbade my parents from kindling a fire one Christmas, terrified it would char poor Santa. I'd believed he was real until we'd left for Los Angeles. After all, werewolves were real, so why wouldn't Santa be?

Moss flecked the purple-gray stone walls, making my house resemble a witch's hut…if witch's huts had broken windows.

I frowned at the shattered glass.

"Was all of the land your family's?" Evelyn ran her finger over the heavy purple blooms of the wisteria that wrapped around the beams of our porch and spilled their heady scent into the hot air. After Mom planted the vine, it took years for it to bloom, and then one summer, it purpled and pinked.

As bees pirouetted lazily next to the blooms, I peered through another cracked, dusty window. There wasn't a trace of life in the house. It was abandoned.

"This was my bedroom," I told Evelyn.

The previous owners had stripped the mint wallpaper from the walls and painted them a blaring sunflower yellow, but the floor was the same faded-honey color with scratch marks they hadn't been able to sand down. I remembered leaving them there the first time I'd changed.

The only feature that remained in the room was a built-in closet that hung open like a gaping, toothless mouth.

"And in here?" Evelyn asked.

I went over to her. "That was Mom and Dad's room."

Only a bare box spring and an iron headboard remained. Like my room, it was barren and grubby. My heart squeezed as memories trickled into my mind: dawn-tinted bedsheets, the space between their warm bodies, soft lips on my forehead, fingers running lazily through my hair.

They'd coddled me—their only child—with unyielding affection and infinite gentleness.

And Aidan had taken that from me. Desire to understand why he'd shot Dad and then insisted on dining with me made me shake with anger.

A hand wrapped around mine.

"Oh, *querida*."

I leaned into Evelyn, and she tightened her grip, tugging me around the empty house to a wall that was all sliding glass doors.

"The kitchen was Mom's favorite room."

Evelyn turned her gaze up to the strip of sunshine pouring through the mottled gray skylight Dad and Nelson had put in one summer. August had assisted our fathers while I'd served them extra-sour lemonade to show them what I thought about not being allowed to help. I'd felt immense satisfaction when they'd all squinted from the bitter taste.

My parents didn't want me climbing high, afraid I'd fall and break my neck. I hadn't shifted yet, so although everyone watched me closely for a sign that I'd inherited the Boulder gene, I was still deemed a delicate human.

One night, though, after Mom had headed into town for a girls' dinner, Dad had let me climb up on the roof with him. With our backs against the sun-warmed slate, we'd gazed up at the sheet of stars. He'd told me how he'd once wished upon a shooting star that Mom would marry him and bear him a healthy baby.

"Are you sad I'm a girl?" I'd asked him.

He'd fixed me with his eyes that resembled the surface of Coot Lake at sunrise—a deep gray that veered to silver—and stroked my cheek. "No, sweetheart. I am terribly happy you were born a girl."

I touched my cheek as his caress ghosted over it.

Evelyn stepped in front of me, the scent of menthol eddying thickly around her...around me. "Enough. We are leaving."

"I'm okay."

"You are not okay." She swiped her thumbs against my cheeks.

Finally, I relented with a deep, rattling sigh. She was right. I was experiencing a sensorial overload and needed distance. As we walked away, my phone vibrated inside my bag. I checked who was calling—*August*. I didn't pick up.

"Boy trouble?" Evelyn asked.

"No. I just don't feel like talking to anyone right now. Except you."

She snaked an arm around my waist and gave me a long squeeze.

"Are you liking it here?" I asked.

She bit her rouged upper lip before answering, "*Sí*. Jeb is a kind man."

"But Lucy isn't?"

"Your aunt is a little...*bossy*, which is not to say she is malicious. I just prefer your uncle." Once we'd reached the junction with the main road, she said, "The boy who brought you home on Saturday…he is handsome."

Her words flicked my heart. *Nope.* I was not touching the Liam subject with a ten-foot pole, or a fifty-foot one for that matter.

"He was very worried when he dropped you off…"

My cheeks burned with the memory of how he'd violated me. I would never dare tell Evelyn what he'd done. She'd be disgusted, but perhaps not only with him. Perhaps she'd be disgusted with me too. Because she'd ask what prompted him to do such a thing.

It was a can of worms I had no desire to open.

Not now.

Not ever.

THIRTY

I arrived for the meeting five minutes early, but I was still the last one there. I breezed past Liam sitting at the sleek wooden bar that separated the kitchen from the living room.

Lucas was his usual jovial, annoying self, leering at me from underneath the baseball cap he'd fit sideways on his head. "Have a good time at Robbie's engagement party?"

Instead of freezing up or ignoring him, I pasted on a fake smile. "It was awesome."

The five elders clenched their jaws, and gazes met and lowered to the chopped centennial tree trunk used as a coffee table. I guessed they'd all been brought up to speed about my visit to the Pine Pack.

Lucas's gaze tightened on the elders, their lack of condemnation obviously irritating him. "I have an ethical problem with Ness competing in this trial."

Eric shifted on the tan suede couch. "Perhaps she had a good reason for attending." The clear glass globe pendent suspended over the living room cast a white sheen on his bald head.

"I did. I wanted to get to know our neighbors," I said. "Isn't that required of Alphas? To be aware of everything and everyone around them? Besides, wouldn't it be nice if the Boulders and the Pines could interact without violence?"

"They're calculating pricks," Lucas hissed.

"Because you're not?" I tossed back into his face.

Lucas scowled.

"*You've* been plotting my downfall since I signed up for this, Lucas. That's the very definition of being calculating *and* a prick."

"Aren't you a little firecracker today?" He laid both his elbows on the bar behind him and leaned back. "Why are we even allowing her to continue? She broke the rules."

"She shifted to help Matt," Frank said, his bushy white eyebrows shadowing his eyes.

Lucas snorted. "He would've been fine."

"Still," Eric said, "empathy is commendable."

Lucas's nostrils flared. His hatred for me was as acrimonious as the sweaty half-moons staining his gray muscle tee.

"Ness, why don't you take a seat so we can discuss the second trial?" Frank tipped his head toward the barstool between Liam and Lucas.

Like hell I would sit there.

"I'm good standing." I leaned against the built-in bookcase that was stacked with hundreds of books. Horrible Heath had apparently been an avid reader. Too bad it hadn't made him a kinder person.

Frank rose from the couch and grabbed a wooden box from the coffee table, then walked over to Liam and Lucas. "An Alpha should be cunning." He waved the box in the air. "You might be wondering why we decided to hold the meeting here. There is a reason for our choice of location. When Heath was sworn in, he was ordained to protect a very valuable pack artifact, which rested within these six little walls." He slowly pivoted the box. "I use the past tense because it was stolen."

"Maybe Heath got rid of what was inside," I suggested.

Frank raised a single bushy eyebrow. "Why would he have broken the lock?"

"Because he misplaced the key?"

Eric grunted. "We've known about the theft for some time but haven't acted upon recovering it until now. First we needed to locate the artifact, and we have. Julian Matz has it."

Goose bumps the size of mosquito bites coated my arms. "So someone from the Pines stole it?"

"We don't know who took it; we just know they have it." Frank turned to Lucas. "So you see, Ness's sociability with the Pines might serve her in this second trial."

Lucas huffed.

"What exactly is it that we're looking for?" Liam asked.

Although Frank looked at Liam, I didn't. If I could, I would never, ever set my gaze on his face...*ever again.*

"A piece of petrified wood."

"Seriously? We're hunting down a piece of wood?" Lucas crossed his beefy forearms.

The barstool creaked as Liam shifted on it. "What's so special about it?"

"Its properties only concern the Alpha, and us." Frank pointed to himself and the four other older wolves.

That raised my curiosity a couple dozen notches. "And if we find it, can we know what it is?"

"If you become Alpha, Ness"—he side-eyed the graying wolves—"you'll be privy to the information."

From the way he'd glanced at the others, I could swear that he'd sooner believe in leprechauns prancing around Boulder with pots of gold than in me, Ness Clark, a girl, becoming his Alpha.

Little did he know I had Julian's support.

Julian's support...

Whoa.

Julian had said he'd help me become Alpha. Like the rocks that had trampled my body during the first trial, understanding knocked hard into me. Frank was right. Julian *must've* stolen it. He *must've* known they'd come searching for it.

A new scenario played out in my head: *Heath finds out Julian stole from him, gets angry, threatens Julian, who comes over or sends over a thug—like Justin—and has Heath quieted forever.*

The possibility that *I* hadn't killed Heath thickened my blood, making it slide sluggishly through my organs.

"Do you think"—I moistened my lips with the tip of my tongue—"Julian had something to do with Heath's death?"

"No." It was Liam who answered. There was no hesitation in his voice.

I set my eyes on the black leather boot he'd crooked on his opposite knee. "How can you be sure?"

He hesitated a second before saying, "Because he knows the consequences of killing *or* backing the killing of another Alpha."

"Which are?" The laces on both his boots were untied. I supposed it was on purpose. One boot would've been a coincidence, but not two.

"He and his entire pack can be razed."

"Razed? You mean killed?"

"Yes."

Well, there went my shred of hope. The vein in my neck palpitated with disappointment. I stuffed my hands into the pockets of my white denim shorts so that no one would spot how terribly my fingers trembled.

"What if they destroyed the piece of wood?" Lucas asked, which I hated to admit, was a relevant question.

Frank rubbed the day-old white growth on his chin. "Let's hope they didn't."

"How long do we have to find it?" Liam asked next.

"Well"—Frank glanced behind him at Eric—"Robbie's wedding is next weekend, and they've invited our pack to attend."

"Hell, no. You can't be serious." Lucas flipped the baseball cap on his head from side to back. "It's a trap."

"We've considered this, Lucas, and although we don't believe it's a trap, we've decided that only me, Eric, and the three of you will be attending. It'll give you the opportunity to locate the artifact without breaking and entering." Frank opened the box and held it out toward me.

I frowned as I peered at the bare interior. Did he want me to confirm it was empty?

"Smell it, Ness."

Oh. I dipped my nose and sniffed, and my eyes watered from the rancid odor. It was the way I imagined rotting bones smelled—dry chalk and tangy decay.

Frank moved to Lucas next, who took a deep whiff. "That's foul."

He held the box out to Liam. I didn't look at him but imagined he wrinkled his nose, too.

James, the thick-waisted elder, rose from the couch and hooked his thumbs underneath the suspenders holding up his khakis. While the elders still turned into wolves on full moons, the rest of the time, they were humans with normal, slower metabolisms.

"The wedding's taking place on Julian's estate," he said. "We believe our artifact's stored on the premises, thus our reasoning for sending you all to the wedding. You boys will need tuxes and you, Ness, will need a gown. You all got some?"

"Yeah. Sure." Lucas snorted. "Got a whole closet full of tuxes."

"Rent one, Lucas," Eric said. "Liam?"

"I have one, but I don't know if it still fits. I'll try it on tonight."

"Ness?"

"No ball gowns in my closet. Is there a place I can rent one?"

"I wouldn't know," Eric said.

"Why don't you ask one of your customers to buy you one?" Lucas shot out.

I snatched my hand out of my pocket and flipped him off, which just made him smile.

"I can ask the wife if she's got one," Eric offered. "She's about your size."

I blanched at his suggestion. If his wife was as old as he was, then I couldn't imagine her owning anything I'd want to wear. But beggars couldn't be choosers.

"Maybe Taryn has one she could lend Ness. They're about the same height." Liam's suggestion made me as rigid as the bookcase.

I'd rather wear a vintage dress than anything owned by Terrible Taryn.

Lucas didn't answer. I bet he was glaring at Liam.

I pinched my lips and muttered, "I'll find something."

A thought crawled into my mind. Perhaps I could ask Julian, as part of the package of helping me out.

"Okay, then." Eric clapped his hands once to signal that the meeting was adjourned.

"I have one last question," Liam started.

I scrutinized my grass-streaked sneakers.

He continued, "There's only one thing to find and three of us."

"Good question, son," Frank said. "The person who finds it gets to choose his or *her* adversary for the last trial."

I snapped my neck up, and my gaze collided with Liam's. His dark eyes glinted with brutal hope...hope to disqualify me. I bet Lucas and Liam would even work together to retrieve it. Little did Liam know that Julian would give it to *me*.

I could finally eliminate Liam.

My heart pounded, and the adrenaline bled into my eyes. I felt them shifting. I blinked the transformation away.

When I cracked my lids, everyone had risen.

I peeled myself away from the bookcase and voiced the concern that had been gnawing at me for the last twenty-four hours. "Why wasn't my father's death avenged?"

Everyone froze. Great waves of shame rolled over the elders' weathered faces, excavating their wrinkles. Or maybe I wanted to believe it was shame. Maybe it was simply discomfort. There was an elephant in the room— *me*—and I was forcing them to acknowledge it.

"We haven't avenged Heath's death either," one of the elders said, and a chill spider-crawled up my spine.

My eyesight dotted as blood pounded against my temples. Would the fact that it had been an accident sway them to spare me?

"I'm not talking about Heath right now." Keeping my voice steady, even though my lungs felt vacuum-packed, I said, "I'm talking about my father. Why is Aidan Michaels still alive?"

No one spoke for a painfully long minute. Eric palmed his bald head, and Frank sighed.

"Why—" I was about to reiterate my question when James interrupted me.

"'Cause he's got a detailed file on us, complete with pictures of us shifting."

"So? Werewolves aren't a secret," I said.

"Just because a handful of people know about us in these parts doesn't mean we want the entire world to find out werewolves are real. Do you realize how many crazies that sort of news would attract?"

I chewed on my bottom lip. "But if Aidan is dead, the file disappears. So it would be a win-win."

"If he dies, the file *gets* released."

"How?"

"He's made copies, Ness. He's given it to key people," Frank explained. "Too many to track down. I'm sorry, but we just can't risk it."

I pursed my lips. "Was he punished at all, or did he get off scot-free?"

Frank scrubbed a hand against the back of his neck. "Heath reprimanded him. Told him that if he ever killed again, he'd stop doing business with Aidan."

Heat scorched my eyes. "You're kidding me. All Heath did was *threaten* to end his business dealings?" My voice echoed shrilly against the exposed wooden beams running across the ceiling. "Did he hate my father? Is that it? Did he hate him because he had a girl instead of a boy?"

"Ness..." Frank started, but I held up my palm.

"I thought Alphas were supposed to put the pack before everything else. I guess I was wrong." My chest pounded with fierce breaths and fiercer heartbeats. I stalked out of the living room, out of the house like a wild creature, my gaze going in and out of focus.

I needed to calm down, and I needed to do it fast or my body would shift and rip up my favorite shorts and T-shirt, *and* force me to enter the inn in my birthday suit—again.

I yanked my phone out of my back pocket and typed Aidan's name in the search engine. A second later, pages of data on him spewed over my screen. Only one thing interested me though. The minute I found it, I memorized the information, then I downloaded a recording app.

I would exact my own justice.

THIRTY-ONE

When night fell, I borrowed a mountain bike from the inn's private fleet and pedaled the three miles of rough trails that led to Aidan Michaels's estate. Maybe he wouldn't be home, but I was a patient person with a desperate need for answers and nothing better to do on a Wednesday night.

I could wait.

Fortunately for me, his palatial glass and stone house was lit up, cutting tall squares of light on the landscaped bushes and peach flagstones tiling the path to the front door. I pedaled harder, checking for security cameras. I was pretty sure I caught sight of several glowing red dots, but that could've been my overactive imagination.

I leaned my bike against the manicured bushes by the front door, then slid my phone out of my bag and turned on the microphone. After carefully placing it back inside my bag, I walked to the front door and punched the doorbell. Like a gong, the sound reverberated against the lofty panes of glass…against the walls of my chest.

As I waited, I licked my lips which felt chapped. Footsteps sounded inside the house, claws skittered on stone, and then a lock clicked and the door opened.

"Ness!"

Aidan grabbed the collar of his dog and held him back. The dog growled, not at his owner, but at me.

I'd forgotten he had a dog. I swiped my tongue against my lips again, praying he wouldn't let the hound charge me. I'd have to kick it, and I didn't like the idea of striking a dog.

"Is this about the discount?" he asked.

I jerked my gaze back up to Aidan. "The money?" I didn't want *that* on tape. "No. It's about my father."

"Your father?" Behind his wire glasses, Aidan's gaze roved over the darkness surrounding me as though searching the night for my father.

"The man you shot six years ago?" I sounded aggressive. I needed to cool down or he'd slam the door in my face. Or worse, he'd release his dog.

It growled again, slobber dripping down its jowls. My wolf bristled within.

"You must be mistaken. I've never shot a man." Aidan's navy eyes met mine with a disconcerting steadiness.

"He wasn't a man when you shot him. But you know that. You know everything about *us*. Isn't that why you asked me to dinner? Did you get lots of interesting material for your blackmail file?"

His lips thinned. "Careful, Ness. One phone call to the police, and I'll show them your escort profile. I don't think they'd take too well to a minor—"

"Because you think they'd take well to an old man paying said minor."

His mouth quirked. "I'm not that old. Besides, I never paid *you*."

The money in my account had been wired from the agency, but cops could trace his payment to the agency, unless it was made in cash. "Look, I didn't come here to blackmail you into apologizing for what you did to me or to my father. I don't even care if you took me out to dinner to gather information on my pack. The reason I came here was to get closure. To understand *why* you shot him."

His gaze flicked again to the darkness, and it dawned on me to check the hand that wasn't holding the dog—check for rifles or knives or whatever weapon a crazy, werewolf-hating recluse could wield. The fingers of his right hand were empty, simply toying with his earlobe.

"I shot a wolf that was on my property. I didn't shoot your father."

He was careful with his words, as though he was aware I was recording him. But he couldn't know. My phone was wedged deep inside my bag.

"Then why didn't you shoot the other wolf he was with?" I asked.

Aidan studied my face. "The little one wasn't *threatening*."

"The big one wasn't threatening you either."

"It was on my property," he repeated, as though that was a sound reason for murder.

"So was the little one."

His eyes bore into mine. "In hindsight, I should've shot the little one."

"But you didn't shoot…*me*."

His Adam's apple bobbed and rippled the lax, stubbly skin of his neck. "Want the truth, Ness Clark?"

I crossed my arms in front of my tank top, which stuck to my back. "That's what I came here for." Sweat beaded between my breasts but quickly absorbed into the fabric of my hot pink bra.

"Packs have Alphas. Alphas are larger than other wolves."

I frowned, but then his words sunk into me like the perspiration into my clothes. "My father wasn't the Alpha."

"It was dark. And there was a small wolf next to a larger one. How was I to know it was a pup?"

"So you meant to kill Heath? My father's death was a…a *mistake*?"

Aidan nodded.

Damn. Speak the freaking words! I tried to rephrase my question so it required a verbal response when his hand skidded off his earlobe. In the next instant, he'd released his hound and grabbed a rifle which he pointed at my chest. I shut my eyes, expecting the hound to pummel into me, but it flew toward the tall pines hedging the property.

I started inching backward when he hissed, "You move, I shoot."

His hound snarled, and then it didn't. Bones snapped. And then silence.

I strained to look behind me, but my vision was hazy with fear.

"They just killed my dog," Aidan whispered, a manic inflection to his tone.

Who'd just killed—

He shoved the barrel of his rifle into my chest, jerking my attention back to him. "They leave me no choice but to kill theirs."

Theirs? Was he referring to me? Adrenaline spiked through me, clearing the haze. I gripped the barrel and shoved it upward. A shot detonated. I jammed the butt of the rifle hard into his shoulder blade. His grip faltered, but he didn't drop the weapon.

Growls resonated behind me, and Aidan's eyes turned wild with bloodlust. He cocked the rifle. I tried to ram it into his shoulder again, but sweat had slickened my palms, and my hands slipped. Aidan ripped the rifle from my fingers and pointed it at the wolves behind me.

The wolves who'd just come to help. Who didn't deserve to get shot.

"Go!" I yelled as I stepped in front of the still-warm muzzle.

My heart spun like a flicked top. I shrieked the word again, but neither wolf moved. I could smell them mere feet away from me, like I could smell the sharp stench of gunpowder.

Aidan's knuckle flexed.

My body reacted. My fingernails lengthened into claws. I punched the rifle away again. The shot flew wide. As he actioned the bolt, I swiped my claws over his sideburns, ripping hair and skin. Blood dribbled down his throat.

"You little cunt," he growled.

I bounced away from him as he stared at his bloodied fingers, momentarily forgetting about the weapon in his hands. Why had I stepped back? I shouldn't have stepped back… I needed to take the rifle from him.

I lunged for him again, and he swung the rifle into my cheek. My neck cracked, but I didn't fall. The hot metal barrel scorched my skin, and the blow had my ears ringing.

"Crazy bitch!" He shouldered his rifle again.

"Better not shoot me in human form," I said. "You wouldn't be able to pass it off as a…*hunting accident*."

He angled the gun's muzzle on my thigh. My ears rang louder. If he spoke, if the wolves behind me howled, the sounds were lost to me.

Aidan smiled, and his knuckle whitened on the trigger.

The stink of gunfire tore through the air at the same time my body rocketed sideways. My head glanced against the flagstones so hard pale stars exploded in the corner of my vision. I blinked sluggishly. The world came back into focus, but all I could see was darkness.

Dense, soft blackness.

I reached out, and my fingertips met fur.

Even though moving made my skull scream in pain, I shifted to see past the fur.

A black wolf lay on top of me.

He'd knocked me out of the bullet's path, but now he was crushing my lungs. I shifted again, this time extricating my body from underneath the beast.

A volley of snarls and screams echoed next to me. Gritting my teeth, I twisted toward the cacophony. A gray wolf was on top of Aidan, fangs bared at the psycho's ashen, pulpy face. Aidan's lips moved. The bastard was still alive. How I wished he were dead.

He spit at the wolf. It struck the man's face with its giant paw. Aidan's cheek slammed hard against the sticky, wet stones. His purple-veined lids slid shut, lashes fluttering against sallow skin.

I pressed my shaky palm against the ground and heaved myself into a sitting position.

The gray wolf magicked away his fur and claws and fangs. *Lucas.* He whipped his head toward me. The area around his mouth was tinged crimson, and his black hair was as wild as his blue gaze.

"Liam!" he yelled as he jumped off Aidan and soared toward me.

Liam?

Liam had saved me?

"Liam!"

He lay still, as still as Aidan and the hound.

A new wave of terror beat at the back of my throat.

Lucas rolled Liam's large lupine form over and pressed a hand against his flank. When Lucas drew his fingers away, his palm was dyed a deep red. "Call Matt!"

Sick chills pulsated through me.

"Ness! Fucking call him!" Lucas hollered.

Hands shaking, I dug through my bag for my phone. I managed to grasp it, but it slipped out of my slick fingers and tumbled on the stones.

Lucas, who'd pressed his hand back against the wound in Liam's side, growled at me. "Are you waiting for him to die?"

"N-No." I seized my phone again. Entered the wrong code. Twice. The third time I managed to unlock it. I began scrolling through my contacts when I remembered I didn't have Matt's phone number. "I d-don't have it."

Lucas barked the number at me.

Fingertips tap-tapping against the screen, it took me several attempts to get the number entered right.

Matt's voice came on before I could even speak. "Who's this?"

I was trying to gather my voice, but it kept jamming behind my jumpy breaths. "M-M-Matt…"

"Ness?"

I nodded stupidly.

Matt couldn't hear me nod.

Lucas growled and tore the phone from my inept fingers. While he spoke, I touched Liam's neck. I felt a soft flutter nip my fingertips.

I smoothed the fur on his cheek. "He-He's alive."

"Barely," Lucas muttered. "The fucker probably used a silver bullet." He twisted to look at Aidan, who hadn't moved.

His chest still rose and fell, but he was out cold.

"If Liam dies, I'm going to shred Aidan Michaels's body with my claws, then tear his carotid out with my fangs, and then I'll watch him bleed the fuck out."

It was petty, but the pack's double-standards stung.

"Fuck. I can't staunch the fucking blood."

"Here." I pulled my tank top off, then balled it up and handed it to Lucas.

He wadded it against the hole.

"Is there an exit wound?"

Lucas blinked at me, and then, clutching my T-shirt, he lifted his friend's leg and felt blindly for a puckered hole. "I can't goddamn see anything!"

I scooted over and prodded the velvety flesh, seeking depressions. Found none. The bullet was still inside Liam.

And if it was made of silver...

I shuddered then returned to Liam's head and pressed my palm delicately against his nose. It was wet and cold, pulsing weak breaths against my clammy skin.

It should've been my leg that leaked blood.

It should've been me.

Why did you do that?

As I stroked his fur, a car engine roared and rubber squealed.

A silver sedan glinted in the darkness.

Matt was here.

THIRTY-TWO

M att must've ground his foot into the brake, because the tires shrieked as the Dodge vaulted to a stop. He opened his door, and then, face as pale as the clouds twisting over the moon, he pumped open his trunk, took out a heavy blanket, and jogged toward us. Without uttering a single word, he spread the heavy fabric on the blood-soaked flagstones, then shoved me aside, crooked one arm underneath Liam's neck, and snared his forepaws.

"Ness, hold it down!" Lucas jerked his head toward my tank top still wedged against the gushing wound.

I scrambled to my feet and gripped the sodden fabric.

Lucas hooked his arms around Liam's rump, and on Matt's signal, they hoisted their friend onto the blanket. Then they crimped its edges with white-knuckled fingers and heaved. I straightened in time with them, keeping a steady pressure on Liam's flank.

I only let go when Matt shouted at me to open the passenger door. He placed his end of the body inside, then loped around the car and crawled onto the backseat. Breathing jaggedly, he tugged the blanket until Liam was entirely sprawled on the backseat, then flung the door shut.

I got in next to Liam. Laid his head on my cold, goose-fleshed thighs. And then I resumed pressing my tank against his injury. Car doors slammed, and then tires screeched and headlights burned a white path down the road.

As we zipped through the darkness, I heard snippets of Lucas's and Matt's conversation—*he was trying to shoot her…out cold, but not dead…silver bullet, I think…Greg is on his way.*

"That's not the way to the hospital," I said when Matt hung a left instead of a right.

He twisted around long enough to glare at me.

"We're not going to the hospital. We're not going to a vet either." There was no humor in his voice. Just anger.

He was angry with me. I wondered if it had solely to do with tonight, or if other factors—like the engagement party I'd attended on the arm of the enemy pack Alpha—contributed to his antagonism.

I stared down at Liam, my fingers moving gently through the long, silky black strands on his neck. His fur began shortening, retreating inside his pores. Next, his snout receded, and his ears migrated back to the sides of his face.

"Guys, he's shifting." The dark shape draped over my legs became a human face with sallow skin and a pale, gaping mouth.

"Fuck," Lucas said.

I guessed it wasn't a good thing. But why, I had no—

My hand stilled on Liam's brow.

My father had shifted back when the silver had leaked into his heart, draining his werewolf magic and then his life.

My vision tilted and blurred, and the fingers gripping my balled, sodden top curled so hard around the fabric that rivulets of blood ran over Liam's burnished thigh.

Liam was dying.

THIRTY-THREE

I t had started to rain during the drive over to Liam's house. Soft drops pelted the windshield and then the navy cover wrapped around Liam.

My bare stomach was covered in goose bumps that had little to do with the weather and everything to do with the direness of Liam's predicament, and the memories of another time when another silver bullet had pierced the flesh of another wolf. I crossed my arms in front of me, to cover myself and to ward off the chill in my bones.

Seconds after we arrived, a middle-aged man wearing rubber Crocs and navy scrubs knocked on the door. "Where's Liam?"

I assumed this was Greg, the doctor Matt had mentioned in the car. The man was neither part of our pack, nor did he smell like a wolf. From the way he dressed, I took it he was a real doctor. He blustered in, squeezing a black nylon duffel in one hand. I trailed him inside Liam's dusky bedroom, keeping my eyes averted from the cadaverous-looking body nestled underneath a brown fleece cover.

Even though my gaze was fixed to the painting of an oversized peacock feather that hung over the stone fireplace, cocooned in a Plexiglas box, my attention was on the hushed conversation whirring around Liam.

"You're going to have to help me, Matt," Greg was saying. "Hold him down."

My teeth ground hard as I heard metal clink—probably surgical tools.

"Ready?" Greg asked.

Matt must've nodded because the next thing I knew, a hoarse cry shredded the room. Liam was definitely not dead. As suddenly as it arose, the cry abated, and the room oozed with silence.

Abysmal silence.

"I see it," Greg said. "Hold him down again."

I squeezed my eyes tight.

This time, the cry was muted, as though Liam's ability to form sounds had gotten bogged down in a web of sticky breaths.

Metal pinged against metal. Footsteps. The gush of water. Was it over? Was Greg washing his hands? Had he retrieved the bullet?

I peeked toward Liam, who was out cold. His face was pale and shiny with sweat, like melted candle wax. A matching sheen of perspiration gleamed on Matt's large, furrowed forehead. He was talking softly, steadily, using gentle words and shared memories to bring his friend back to life.

Lucas stood vigil on Liam's other side, wearing a pair of low-slung jeans surely borrowed from Liam. When his murky gaze met mine, I jolted my eyes toward my bare, bloodied midriff.

I was an intruder… I had no right to be here.

So I left.

The living room was bright. Too bright. I rubbed my eyes, wishing I could rub the horror of the night out. Waiting for news, I perched on the edge of the couch. I tried to pray like Evelyn did when I accompanied her to mass, but then remembered how many prayers I'd sent upward for my mother and how deafening the answering silence had been.

The tangle of male voices in the bedroom had me perking up. The conversation was still hushed, but I caught a lilt to the tone. Greg must've gotten the bullet out... Or maybe it wasn't made of silver.

That would be good.

A moment later, Matt emerged from the bedroom, shoulders hunched but forehead smoother.

"Is he— Did—" Nerves tore the volume from my voice.

"Greg got the bullet out. It was whole."

I raked my clammy palms over my thighs and exhaled a deep sigh.

Matt tossed a piece of fabric at me—a plaid shirt. Since he was still wearing his, I assumed it was one of Liam's. I slipped it on, and the scent of Liam enveloped me.

"Thank you." I didn't dare meet Matt's gaze. Just the heavy, reproachful feel of it was painful. "Was it made of silver?"

"Yes."

I shuddered, then rubbed the right side of my skull that tingled from a lump the size of an egg.

The couch cushion dimpled as Matt took a seat next to me. "You okay?"

"I'm fine. Just shook up."

Matt's lips were pinched. "We told you to stay away from Aidan Michaels, but you didn't listen." He shook his head. "I don't get you, Ness. I thought I did. I thought I had you all figured out. I thought you were some shy, sweet girl trying to act all tough to fit into the pack, but I don't think you're shy. And I don't think you're trying to fit into the pack."

I swallowed, twining my fingers together in my lap. Like Matt, I was no longer sure I knew who I was and what I was doing.

"Why did you go see the Pines, Ness? And please don't tell me it was for money, because we'll all pitch in and give you the amount you need. You'd have to ask, but we'd do it." He touched my knee lightly, and I flinched. "Asking for help isn't a weakness. It's not a flaw either."

My eyes went hot. With shame. But also with gratitude.

How I wished I could unburden myself, but if I told Matt my reasons for visiting the Pines, I'd be inking my death sentence.

"It was a job," I lied, and then I repeated the words I'd heard Mom yell at Evelyn, "I don't want charity." That was true at least. Like my mother, I had my pride. She'd worn it throughout her life like armor, and it had earned her the respect of many.

Matt loosed a rough sigh. "And what were you doing at Aidan Michaels's house?"

This time, I told him the truth. How I'd hoped to understand why he'd killed my father. How I'd planned on entrapping him with a recorded confession.

Matt snorted.

"What?"

"Aidan Michaels is the biggest benefactor of the Boulder PD. He's got every officer crawling around this town in his pocket. If I can give you some advice—which I hope you'll actually listen to this time—don't...*ever*...go to the police. Some people in the department are aware of our existence, and they share Aidan's view—that we're abominations. If they weren't scared shitless of what we would do to their families if they waged an attack, they'd have tried to eliminate us a long time ago."

Lucas came out of the bedroom, and we both looked up at him expectantly. "The good doctor needs alcohol." He swiped a bottle of tequila from the rollaway bar tucked in the corner of the living room. I must've frowned, because Lucas added, "To disinfect the wound. We're not celebrating...yet." He flicked his gaze to Matt, then vanished back inside the dark bedroom.

"How did they know I was there?" My voice was as quiet as the cold air murmuring through the vent in the ceiling.

"Aidan is enemy number one of the pack. We've breached his security system, so we have eyes on him at all times. My brother, Cole, is a tech prodigy. He's constantly monitoring the dude. When he noticed you there, he called me. Liam and Lucas were with me. Liam...he flipped." Matt scratched a spot behind his ear. "He said you got real upset earlier over Heath's decision not to seek retribution. Anyway, he was sure Aidan was going to kill you, or do...worse things to you."

Guilt ravaged me. But then the conversation I'd had with Aidan played in my mind.

"Aidan shot my father because he thought it was Heath. Could Aidan...could *he* have killed Liam's father?" I sounded so pathetically hopeful.

Matt stared long and hard at me.

"Like I said, Cole monitors him," Matt said slowly. "Aidan was inside his house all night."

"Maybe he got someone else to do it for him?"

"Maybe."

That little word buoyed me more than Julian's support.

Lucas padded back out into the living room. He wasn't smiling, but his mouth was softer. "The wound's closing up. He's healing."

Air whooshed out of Matt's lungs. "Thank God."

"I'd thank Greg, not God." Lucas's voice pinged around the glass walls enclosing the living room. "I need to go debrief the pack."

His relief was making him jumpy and borderline giddy. I half expected him to hug Matt and pound him on the back, but Lucas did neither. He just asked his friend for a ride.

As though remembering I was there, Matt offered to drop me back at the inn. I rose just as Greg came out of the bedroom, wiping his hands on a steel-gray towel that reminded me of the one Liam had tied around his waist the night he—

"He's asking for you, Ness," Greg said.

THIRTY-FOUR

I sucked in air so harshly I coughed. "He wants to see *me*?"

Greg nodded, while Lucas and Matt exchanged a silent, weighted glance.

"You staying, right, Greg?" Lucas asked.

"Sure."

Lucas pinned me with his blue stare. "Just until one of us comes back."

Did Lucas fear I would finish the job the bullet had botched, or was he scared Liam might need a doctor on standby? I hoped it was the latter but believed it was the former. Sadly, Lucas and Matt had every right to be distrustful of me.

"I'll stay out here." Greg sat on the sofa, then picked up a large book from the wrought-iron coffee table. *The History of Wolves*.

I wondered if it mentioned werewolves.

"We should be back in a half hour max," Matt said.

"That's fine," Greg said. "I'm not on call tonight."

So he *was* a real doctor.

He put his feet up on the table and feigned great interest in the reading material on his lap.

"You gonna be okay in there, Clark?" Lucas asked.

I doubted he cared if I would be okay. What he cared about was if Liam would be okay with me in the same room. Still, I said, "Yes," before I advanced toward the bedroom. Even though the door was ajar, I knuckled it. "Can I come in?"

A hoarse, "Yes," answered me.

Without looking back at the others, I entered the bedroom, leaving the door open to show I had no ill intent. Liam was propped up on three pillows. Although still pale, some color had returned to his cheeks and some life to his eyes. In the darkness, they gleamed disquietingly bright, their beam ensnaring me. The hard set of his jaw told me he was angry.

Really angry.

The front door banged shut, and I jumped.

"Close the door." His voice was deep and raspy, as though the bullet had scraped his throat.

My heart banged like Aidan's shotgun.

"Please." His Adam's apple bobbed in his corded neck.

I bit my lower lip, eyeing the doorknob. Finally, I wrapped my fingers around the cool metal and pushed it. The click of the latch bolt against the strike plate echoed harshly in the quiet room.

I'd decided never to lay eyes on him after what he'd done to me, and here I was locking myself inside a bedroom with him. The night was stretching the limits of my sanity. I crossed my arms and raised my gaze to his.

"I know you can't stand to look at me after what I did to you." He watched what his words did to me.

My nostrils pulsed. The coppery scent of blood mixed with the smell of his skin was making my head spin. Or maybe it was the intensity with which he was studying me.

"I wish I could erase my actions, Ness. I wish I could go back in time and let you go without acting like a...a"—even though his voice wavered, his gaze didn't—"a savage. I am so deeply ashamed of what I did to you." His voice was soft like the patter of the raindrops tapping against the window.

"Is that why you took a bullet for me tonight? So I would forgive and forget?"

"No." His lids slid shut for a long second. When they lifted, his eyes were even brighter than before. Wolf eyes. "I'd understand if you never forgave me."

My chest tightened like a fist.

"Please say something," he croaked.

Pressing my arms against my abdomen, I said, "I'm glad you're okay."

"Are you?"

"Yes."

He hitched up an eyebrow, as though not truly believing me. But it was true, and he must've seen this on my face because his eyebrow slowly fell back, aligning with the other.

"Why did you do it?" I asked.

"Because I was hurt and"—he looked at the painting of the feather over his fireplace—"jealous."

My arms loosened. "Jealous? Of Aidan?"

His gaze jolted back to me. "What?" A flush creeped over his jaw.

I swallowed. "I asked why you took a bullet for me."

"Oh." Clearly, his answer hadn't been intended for this question. He looked away again and a deep groove appeared between his eyebrows. "I reacted. That's all." His lips barely shifted, yet his words stirred the air that had gone very still.

I barely heard his answer over the loud echo of his previous answer. *Jealous*. "What did you think I was asking you about?"

The tendons in his neck shifted as he sat a little taller, as his shoulders pressed a little harder into the pillows. "Why I lost my mind when you came to my house." He closed his eyes, then leaned his head back against the wooden headboard. "This conversation is more painful than being shot."

A breath snagged in my chest. "You *like* me?"

His eyes remained closed. He was so still I checked his chest was rising with breaths.

Liam had feelings for me?

"Are you trying to torture me some more?" His voice broke the spell of his confession.

"No. I— *Why*?"

His eyes flew open and set on me. "Why do I like you?"

"No one else does."

"First off, that's not true. Second off, I have no clue. I just do. But apparently the feeling isn't mutual." His tone was rough. "So if you can forget I said anything, that would be great." He turned his face so that he was facing his bathroom door.

"I was scared tonight. Scared that you'd die." My blood simmered in my veins, heated my skin.

I toed the tufted rug that stretched over almost every inch of the wooden floor and examined the long fibers, trying to decide if they were purple or maroon. In the obscurity, it was hard to tell.

"I don't hate you, Liam."

Purple. They were purple. A deep, almost electric purple.

Bare feet flattened the looped filaments and stopped inches from mine. My heartbeats quickened like skittish trout.

The heat from his bare skin permeated the slim divide between us. Warmth meant he was better, unless he was coming down with a fever. Was his wound infected? I didn't dare move. Didn't dare look up. But Liam crooked a finger underneath my chin and tipped my face up.

"I almost died tonight, Ness, and that reminded me that I'm not immortal. That none of us are. We might be stronger than humans, but we don't get to live forever."

My throat tightened.

"Do you know what I thought about when the bullet hit me?" His pupils throbbed, burned a path straight into me.

"What?" I breathed.

"That I'd hate to die with you thinking I was a bastard."

I removed my head from its perch. "Liam—"

"Let me finish." His tone was gentle but tremulous, as though severing the connection between his finger and my chin had shaken his confidence.

I'd been about to say that I didn't think he was a bastard. At least, not anymore. Not since he'd taken a bullet for me.

"And the second thing that entered my mind"—he combed an unruly lock of hair behind my ear, and I shivered—"was that I didn't want to die before getting to kiss you."

I blinked. "You want to kiss me?" If I'd heard him wrong, and he'd said *kill me,* then…well, that would be so many shades of embarrassing.

"Yes, Ness Clark. I'd like to kiss you."

It struck me then that Liam didn't think I murdered his father. I closed my eyes. "Don't, Liam. Don't like me. I'm no good. For you…I'm no good."

My eyelashes dampened. *No, no, no*…I couldn't cry. Not in front of Liam. Oh, God, I was such a mess.

"Why shouldn't I like you?"

"Because…you shouldn't." The tears snaked out.

Perfidious tears.

I felt his thumbs swipe over my cheeks, felt his fingers close around the sides of my face, tilt it back toward his.

"You're going to have to give me a better reason."

I looked at him then, and my heart beat so wildly it almost tripped right out of my chest. A better reason was the truth.

"Tamara." I blurted out the redhead's name, not knowing what else to say.

"Tamara?"

"She likes you, Liam. I couldn't do that to her." My excuse was pathetic, eye-roll-worthy pathetic.

"Let me make something very clear, I don't give a crap about Tamara."

"But—"

"Go out on a date with me."

"Liam—"

"One date. And I promise to wear clothes." One side of Liam's mouth quirked up.

Of course, *that* made me acutely aware that he was naked. "Lucas said there was no dating within the pack."

"Lucas is a dumbass, and it's a bogus rule. I know for a fact that two of the wolves in our pack are together."

For the briefest of moments, I wondered who, but then I focused back on the matter at hand. "We're opponents. Opponents can't date."

A nerve jumped in his jaw. "Says who?"

"It wouldn't be ethical."

"Really?" His face loomed over mine.

I licked my lips that felt as dry as my throat. "Yes. Really."

"Drop out then."

That snapped something in me. I ducked away from him. "Is that what this is about?"

"What?" His forehead grooved.

"You're trying to make me drop out?"

His eyes darkened, and he gave his head a little shake. "Why don't *you* drop out?"

His jaw clenched. "I've been working my entire life toward this, Ness. You only want this to piss me off."

"That's not true," I blurted out. But it was true.

So. Damn. True.

He crossed his arms in front of his blood-flecked torso. "You didn't go against me because you hated the idea of having a Kolane in charge?"

Instead of answering him, I used the momentum of our quarrel to drive in my previous point. "See? We can't date, Liam."

He snorted but didn't disagree with me. Then again, his bedroom door flew open.

As he took us in, Matt's eyebrows shot up. "Everything all right in here?"

Liam glared at me. For someone whose dying wish had been to kiss me, he seemed over it.

"Yeah," I mumbled, planting my gaze on the large oaf of a man standing in the doorway instead of on the infuriating one standing inches from me.

Matt flicked his attention to Liam, who remained as still as glass.

"Can you take me home?" I asked Matt.

"Of course."

I started walking away when Liam's voice made me halt. "Why do you want to lead this pack, Ness?"

My cheeks burned from being put on the spot. "I don't have to explain my reasons to you."

"I just hope your reasons are noble, because these are good men. Men who deserve someone honest, with the pack's interest at heart."

I stared at Matt's dirty boots.

I swallowed over and over, but my saliva kept getting jammed up. Finally, I managed to wheeze out, "And they'll have someone deserving of them."

For the first time in a long time, I was speaking the truth.

Because it wouldn't be me.

I would make sure to lose the next test. I wasn't sure how yet, but I was sure it would come to me. If I lost, Julian couldn't hold that against me. Could he?

He probably could. He'd probably rescind his offer to speak to the PI. Or if he'd already spoken to him, he'd call him back. But it wouldn't matter because Liam would already have heard it from me.

After the next test, I'd confess.

I'd confess it all and free myself of the debilitating guilt. And if that meant groveling for my life, then I would drop to my knees and grovel. My only hope was that Liam would show me the mercy his father had been incapable of showing my mother.

THIRTY-FIVE

I spent every minute of the next three days with Evelyn. If these were to be my last hours on this earth, there was no one I wanted to spend them with more than Evelyn. Several times, she asked me what was wrong. *Nothing.* That was my answer. *Nothing* plus a cheerful smile.

But she knew me better than that. She also knew there was no point in pushing me. That when I walled myself off, there was no breaching my brick-and-mortar shell.

Next week, my fate would be sealed.

I thought about the wedding with a heavy heart. Remembered I still needed a dress. I tried to call Everest for help, but Lucy told me he'd gotten dire news about Becca and that he'd hit the road to clear his mind.

I didn't want to hold his sorrow against him, but I was sad he'd left me behind. I didn't wallow too long in my loneliness, though. After days of avoiding August's calls and messages, I'd answered him that morning. Like a dying person, I was putting my life in order, and part of that order was thanking August for caring, even though I didn't really understand why he cared about me in the first place. I was no longer the innocent little girl whose hair he'd ruffled and whom he'd taught to whittle wood into animal statues.

As I wiped down wine glasses in the pantry, my heart squeezed so tight a sharp pain spread through my chest. I was wallowing again. God, I didn't want to wallow. I drove my focus outward, on the chirpy conversation of the two servers who worked nights and weekends at the inn. They were discussing going clubbing at The Den.

One of them, the one with a pixie cut and a gazillion silver hoops in her right ear—Emmy—must've noticed I was listening, because she asked, "Want to come with us, Ness?"

I almost dropped the glass I was drying. Emmy and the other server—Skylar—were at least a decade older than I was and had never spoken to me before. I'd assumed it was because I was so much younger than them *and* related to their boss.

"I'm only seventeen."

"You don't look seventeen," Emmy said. "Besides you're too pretty to be turned away from the door. Plus, DJ Wolverine's spinning. She's awesome."

DJ Wolverine… It took my mind a second to connect the dots. DJ Wolverine was Julian's niece, Sarah. She could help me get in touch with Julian.

"Okay. I'm in."

I'D NEVER GONE CLUBBING, so I didn't know how people dressed. Although sporting the black dress I'd worn when I'd visited Heath made my skin itch, it was the only nice thing I owned. Well, that and the red dress, but there was a small tear in the side seam—probably from when I'd ripped it off my shifting body.

The black sequins sewn over the material caught every flick of light, casting tinsels over the dashboard of Emmy's little car that rumbled with club beats.

"You okay, hun?" Skylar asked. She'd swept her bleached hair into a high bun that sat atop her head like frosting on a cupcake. "You seem real down."

I bit the inside of my cheek. "I'm okay."

Emmy turned down the music. "Is it your momma?"

"My mom?"

Just two mornings ago, in that slim moment between sleep and wakefulness, I'd reached for my phone to call her for advice. Only when I couldn't find her contact did I remember she was gone. I'd lain in my bed a long while, watching the dove-gray light of dawn turn pale gold.

Emmy glanced toward Skylar. "We heard you lost her a couple months before coming out here."

Skylar spun around in her seat, her manga-sized blue eyes roving over my face. "I lost mine last year, and although I ain't gonna say our pains are the same"—she didn't sound like she was from around here—"if you ever need to talk, well, you can talk to me, hun. We can bitch and lament together. I'm real good at bitchin' about life."

"It's one of her many talents."

Emmy grinned, while Skylar chortled.

Intent on shifting the spotlight off the woman I missed so much, I asked, "How long have you two known each other?"

"We met two years ago." Skylar placed her hand over Emmy's and brushed her knuckles. "We started working at the inn at the same time."

Emmy loosed a light sigh. "It was love at first sight."

My lids fluttered. "Oh...you two...you're together?"

"For a year and a half already! Time flies," Emmy said. "What about you, Ness? Are you seeing anybody?"

I stared out my window at the moon that was growing fatter and fuller every day. "No."

"No one's caught your eye?"

"Not really."

"Maybe you'll meet someone tonight," Skylar said. "The Den's full of hotness."

"Maybe."

Soon, we were parking across from a brick building illuminated by a huge blue flickering neon sign. A beefy bouncer stood by the closed metal doors, turning away three gangly boys, before letting in a gaggle of chattering girls who wore too much makeup and too little clothes. I'd never felt overdressed before, but in this moment, as I trailed Emmy and Skylar, I felt extraordinarily self-conscious. It didn't help that people from the long line awaiting to get into the club were staring.

I started walking toward the end of the line when Skylar looped her arm through mine and tugged me to the front. Grumbling erupted behind us, but neither Emmy nor Skylar seemed to care.

"Hey, Bobby!" Skylar chirped.

The bouncer turned toward us. "Skysky." He tipped his head down toward me, hiking up an eyebrow. "Who's your little friend?"

Little friend. Skylar had a couple inches on me, but I was far from little. Unless he meant age-wise. That was probably what he'd meant. My palms slickened. *Don't ask to see my ID. Don't ask to see my ID.*

"Ness's my little sister. She's visiting from LA." The lie rolled off Skylar's tongue so naturally that Bobby pulled the heavy metal door open.

Music whooshed out and battered against the dark street.

"Be good," he said.

"Aren't we always?"

"Em is." He smirked at Skylar. "You, not so much." He winked at us as we passed by him and then closed the door.

Swirling neon lights illuminated the cavernous building, which must've housed an old power plant once upon a time. Exposed metal tubing and air vents crisscrossed the high ceiling like a rat maze, reflecting the swinging strobes. In the middle of the dancefloor stood a wide square bar manned by several bartenders. Partygoers spilled around the bar, moving their bodies to the deafening beat. On a metal mezzanine, people sat at tables, pouring long drinks from liquor and juice bottles. Some were leaning against the railing, gazing down at the crowd below.

"Where's the DJ booth?" I yelled into Emmy's ear, my mouth coming in contact with some of her silver hoops.

My lips instantly blistered, and I jerked away. I licked the tiny sores, then squashed my mouth shut when I caught her staring at it.

Nostrils working, she pointed to the top of the stairs that led to the mezzanine floor. There, in an open booth, pink headphones nestled in a mane of wild curls, stood Sarah aka DJ Wolverine.

Emmy tapped my shoulder. "Is it me, or is your mouth smoking?"

I licked my lips. "Must be you."

She frowned.

"I'm going to go say hi to someone," I said.

"Okay. We'll be right here."

I nodded, then strode across the room, slaloming between the bodies.

Another burly bouncer stood at the bottom of the stairs. He stuck out his hand when I approached.

"The DJ's my friend," I said.

He gave me a grumpy, meaningful look. He wasn't buying it.

"Ask her," I pleaded.

"I can't interrupt her set."

"Please. Her name is Sarah. Her uncle is Julian Matz. Her brother—"

The bouncer grumbled. "Fine. But I'm keeping an eye on you."

I slid by him before he could change his mind. When I reached Sarah, she was fiddling with some dials on her turntables.

"Hey!" I yelled.

Since my voice didn't carry through her headphones, I gesticulated my hands. That caught her attention. She looked up from her laptop. A frown gusted over her face, but then she recognized me, and a sizeable smile curved her lips. She held up a finger, tapped on her laptop—probably cuing up the next song—and then she lowered her headphones.

"Welcome to my den. Did you just get here?"

I leaned over the tall booth. "I need Julian's phone number."

"Why?"

"I need to ask him something."

"Ask me instead."

I supposed I *could* ask her. "I've been invited to your brother's wedding, and I need a dress."

She frowned, her thin eyebrows slanting over her wide brown eyes. "Not sure what you heard, but my uncle doesn't wear dresses."

I balked at her answer. "I was just hoping he could help me get one."

"Why would he help you get one?"

"Because he offered to help me the other day." Before she could jump to any conclusions about her uncle's reasons for aiding me, I added, "He pities me for being the only girl in my pack."

Not my best lie ever, but it seemed to appease Sarah because her forehead uncrumpled. She raised a finger again, then set the headphones back on her ears and cued up the next song. The beats overlapped seamlessly, before the new song glided over the fading one.

She pushed the headphones down again, then sized me up. "You're what, a four?"

I nodded.

"You can borrow one of mine. Come over to my place tomorrow."

"Really?"

"Yes, really." She rolled her eyes. "Now, go dance. I need to concentrate on my set."

I started to turn away when I remembered I had no clue where *her place* was. "I don't know where you live."

"Give me your phone."

I entered my password and passed it over.

She typed in her contact information, then handed the phone back to me. "Don't come before twelve! I'm dead to the world in the morning."

"'Kay. Thanks."

She fluttered her hand in a *don't-mention-it* gesture, then stuck her headphones back on and bobbed her head.

I clambered down the stairs, past the bouncer, who'd lost interest in me after ascertaining I wasn't some crazed fan. I zeroed in on Skylar and Emmy's location at the bar and threaded myself through the mass of bodies.

The newest song Sarah was playing had people jumping and pumping their fists in the air. Twice, my feet got trampled. The first time, the person didn't apologize—they probably hadn't realized. The second time, though, the *trampler* caught my arm and leaned over to apologize. The boy's breath reeked of beer and bad dental hygiene.

"It's okay," I said, shrugging him off.

His gaze skimmed over my face, then dipped to the V-shaped neckline of my dress. *Subtle.* "Can I buy you a drink?"

I was about to turn him down when someone beat me to it.

Liam loomed over the boy. "No. You can't."

The boy turned toward him before backing away faster than a spooked rabbit.

"Maybe I wanted a free drink," I said.

Liam's eyes flashed dangerously. "Then *I'll* buy you a drink."

Not the answer I was expecting. "Forget it. I don't want anything to drink."

"Did you come with Everest?"

I shook my head. "He's out of town."

Liam's jaw tightened. "Of course he is."

What was that supposed to mean?

"Did you come alone?"

"No! I came with two coworkers from the inn."

Someone shoved into me, and I momentarily lost my balance. Liam shot out a hand and caught my elbow, steadying me. Once he'd established I could stand on my own two feet, he let go.

I rubbed the patch of skin he'd touched. "I should go find them."

"Females or males?"

My forehead furrowed at his strange question.

"Your coworkers, are they women or men?"

"Women. Why?"

"Just asking."

Uh-huh. Weirdo. "I should go find them."

Heart pounding to the hectic rhythm of the bass spilling from the surround-sound speakers, I made my way toward Skylar and Emmy. They'd met up with another couple—Francine and Lark. Francine was petite and feminine. Lark was something else. In spite of the buzz cut and the baggy AC/DC T-shirt, Lark didn't strike me as a man. But maybe he was.

They were all very nice and included me in every conversation, which was more than the pack did. At some point, I found myself looking upward at the mezzanine, right into Liam's shadowy gaze. His forearms were propped on the metal guardrail. Matt stood next to him, and behind them sat the rest of their posse and their harem of girls.

When a thin, pale arm snaked around Liam's midsection, crumpling his black V-neck, I looked away. Three days ago, he'd proclaimed he'd wanted to kiss me, that he didn't care about Tamara, and yet here she was, wrapped around him like string around a birthday present.

His fickleness stung way more than it should.

THIRTY-SIX

I'd been standing for what felt like hours in the bathroom line, and it had barely shortened. What did women do in there?

I started tapping my foot to distract myself from the spasms in my bladder. When that didn't help, I took out my phone. I wasn't socially connected—no Facebook, no Instagram, no Twitter, no Snapchat—so I checked the news, especially what was happening overseas. Even though August had said little could kill a werewolf, I worried about his safety. What if a blood-thirsty rebel set fire to his camp?

I shuddered just thinking about it.

By the fifth article I read, I was two people closer to my destination. I contemplated the men's room entrance that swung like a revolving door. Boys were in and out so fast I suspected they didn't wash their hands. At this moment, I wished women would sacrifice hygiene for speed. Just as I had that thought, the boy's bathroom door flapped again, and lo and behold, Liam Kolane stepped out.

I swung my gaze to the short ponytail of the girl in front of me, feigning great interest in her purple hair tie.

When her head swiveled and her mouth fell a little open, I momentarily shut my eyes. I could smell Liam next to me, feel the heat from his hulking body.

"What do girls do in there?" he asked.

I loosed a sigh, then opened my eyes. Why was he always there? Did he have some internal radar that displayed my location at all times?

Barely moving my lips, I mumbled, "Beats me."

"Come."

That made me look up. "Where?"

He nodded toward the guy's bathroom.

"I can't go in there."

"We have toilets too."

They also had urinals and probably a long line of boys doing their business. "With doors?"

One side of Liam's mouth curled up. "Yes."

He leaned down until his mouth was leveled with my ear. I shivered when his hot breath pulsed against my lobe.

"If you become Alpha, you'll need to get over your prudishness."

I raised my gaze toward him. *But I won't be Alpha, Liam. I won't even be part of a pack come next week. Maybe I won't be part of this world either.* I didn't say any of these things. Instead, because I was going to seriously pee myself if I didn't get to a toilet soon, I accepted his proposal and trailed him to the guy's bathroom. Two boys tried to go inside, but Liam told them to wait. He opened the door. Three guys were standing at the urinals. *Great.* Not awkward at all.

"Get out," he said.

My jaw prickled with embarrassment when I realized he was kicking people out. The three guys turned—just their heads thankfully—and gaped at Liam. When they noticed his serious expression, they zipped up quick, and bypassing the sinks, they filed out.

"You didn't have to kick everyone out," I said, going toward a stall.

He leaned against the door to keep it closed and gave me a smug smile. "You'd rather have had an audience?"

No I wouldn't. I locked myself up in a stall, and squatting over the piss-covered toilet seat, I emptied my throbbing bladder. I tried not to think about Liam standing just outside.

As I flushed, there was banging. Liam must've cracked open the door because music blared against the black tiles.

"The bathroom's out of order," he bellowed, just as I came out of the stall. He leaned against the metal door then planted one boot on it.

I washed my hands with the pink soap that smelled like antiseptic and artificial cherry.

"I saw you talking with Sarah Matz."

Of course he'd had an angle for helping me out and clearing the bathroom. He wanted information. Instead of beating around the bush and asking if it was illegal to chat with a Pine wolf, I said, "And you want to know what I discussed, I suppose?"

He didn't respond, just studied me as I approached him, wiping my hands on my dress. The sequins weren't very absorbent.

"I asked her if I could borrow a dress for her brother's wedding," I said.

His eyebrows shifted over his eyes that looked amber in the bathroom's red florescent lighting. "Why did you ask her for a dress?"

"Who else was I supposed to ask? My aunt is twenty sizes bigger than me, and Evelyn doesn't own any fancy apparel. I looked online, but unlike tuxes, there's no shop that rents dresses in Boulder."

The door pulsed behind him. He opened it and barked, "It's out of order," then leaned against it again.

"I'm done, Liam. You can let them—"

"*I'm* not done."

I balled my fingers into fists. "That's all I talked about."

"Taryn must have a dress."

"I don't want Taryn's dress."

"I'll take you shopping tomorrow."

I jerked back. "No way."

His gaze ground into mine, and my pulse skittered. I tried to breathe to calm myself. After the fourth not-even-remotely-close-to-soothing breath, I mumbled, "Stay locked in here with me any longer, and it'll start rumors."

"I don't give a shit about rumors."

"But Tamara will give a shit."

"Please stop using Tamara as an excuse to push me away."

"I'm not using her as an excuse. She was groping you earlier! I saw her."

His pupils expanded and bled darkness into his irises. "You were watching me?"

Heat pulsed against my jaw. "I was looking around and happened to see her *and* you."

"You're the first girl who's turned me down."

So this was what his strange behavior was about? No longer feeling threatened, I unclenched my fingers. "I'd say get used to it, but I doubt you'll ever need to get used to it."

He didn't smile, didn't even react to my indirect compliment.

"Seriously, can you let me out now? This place reeks." When he didn't, I reached around him for the doorknob.

He swiped my arm and spun me around so fast he had me pinned to the door with his forearms bracketing my head.

I'd been wrong to relax. Liam was unpredictable.

"Ness"—the way he spoke my name, all rough and low, had my stomach swishing—"I'm not like my father."

I'd expected him to say many things but not that. "Then don't hold me against my will."

His breaths shuddered against my forehead. Slowly, almost painfully, he pushed himself off the door…off me.

And he let me go.

THIRTY-SEVEN

At four the following afternoon, I entered a modern-looking building not too far away from the The Den. I checked my phone for Sarah's floor number and pressed on the button that had a big six on it.

As the elevator rose, so did my nerves. What if her generosity was a ploy? What if she'd called up a bunch of other Pine shifters and they were going to ambush me?

I massaged my temples as the elevator doors swept open on the sixth floor. Where was all this anxiety coming from?

I hadn't slept much last night, getting to bed way too late and getting woken up by Lucy way too early. It was as though she wanted to make me pay for going out. Or maybe she was making me pay for the missing bike—the one I'd left at Aidan's house the night he shot Liam. I told her someone had stolen it while I'd gone into the DMV to get the sign-up forms. It beat explaining what had really happened to it.

I'd contemplated retrieving it, but I didn't want to risk Aidan putting a bullet in my skull...if he was even home. Considering his injuries, he could be bandaged up like a mummy in a hospital bed.

When I arrived in front of Sarah's door, I pressed on the buzzer. A long minute later, there was grumbling followed by footsteps. Sarah opened the door, a pink silk sleep mask that read *Go Away* wedged up on her forehead. Smudged crescents of makeup framed her squinty eyes.

"Shit. Is it noon already?"

I smiled. "It's 4:00 p.m."

"Shit," she said again.

The outfit she'd worn last night was draped over the back of a lavender velvet couch. Her buffed, white stone floors were strewn with various other articles of clothing. She nodded for me to come in.

"For a girl who wanted a hundred bucks for headphones, you live in a mighty fancy place." I studied the crystal chandelier that dangled over a leather coffee table. Each crystal was shaped like a raindrop and hung at different heights. "Are your parents in?"

"No. Why would they be?"

"Don't you live with them?"

"God, no. The second I turned eighteen I was out the door."

"So this is all yours?"

"Yes, ma'am."

"Do you have a roommate?"

She scrunched up her nose. "I don't do roommates."

"I wish I could live alone too."

"You live at the inn, right?"

"Yeah," I said with a sigh.

"Sucks."

"Tell me about it."

Over her black sleep shorts and black tank, she wore a turquoise silk bathrobe with a heron print.

"Want a glass of water? Or coffee? Or—"

I smiled at her attempt at playing hostess. "Just a dress."

"I need coffee first." She padded away toward the open kitchen. The stainless-steel appliances shone as bright as the gray ceramic tiles around them. The place was seriously sick, straight out of a lifestyle magazine. As she filled a percolator with ground coffee, I put my bag down on one of the many stools propped under the marble kitchen island. She flicked the switch, then gestured me toward a doorway that was twice the size of a normal doorway.

Like the rest of her apartment, her bedroom was monstrously oversized and covered in clothes.

"You can't afford a housekeeper?" I asked before realizing how critical that sounded.

Then again, she was a slob, and she didn't strike me as ignorant of the fact.

"I don't like people touching my stuff."

"Yet you're okay with letting me borrow a dress?"

She cocked an eyebrow as though just grasping how egregious that was. Then again, everything about this girl was a contradiction. She drove a Mini yet lived in a marble palace; she DJed in a club yet obviously didn't need the money.

"Dry clean it before giving it back." She flashed me a smile that pried her sleep-filled eyes wider. She slid a mirrored door open with great flourish. "I'm wearing the yellow one. Take your pick from the others."

I stared at the row of hangers dripping with silks and satins and tulle and sequins. "Are you a gown hoarder, or do you really attend that many fancy parties?"

"That many fancy parties. But I do like clothes. A lot."

My gaze swept over the rest of her closet, over the teetering piles of sweaters and T-shirts, over the lineup of jeans in every wash imaginable, over the column of shoes that ranged the gamut of sneakers to crystallized heels to every style of boots on the market.

"You're drooling."

I snapped my mouth shut. I *was* drooling—metaphorically speaking. I didn't have saliva dribbling down my chin or anything.

"Another reason I would never get a roommate… She'd steal all my clothes."

"Only if she was your size."

"She'd probably get to my size to fit into my clothes." She dropped down on her bed, then stretched her arms over her head.

I fingered the material of a black dress.

"You shouldn't wear black to a wedding."

"Okay."

"Or white. Try the red one. Red usually looks good on us blondes." She stuck her sleep mask back on.

I plucked the red one out and marveled at it.

The coffee machine gurgled, and then it beeped, and Sarah rolled back up.

"Stop eye-fucking it, and try it on." She tossed her silken sleep mask on top of her mussed-up sheets, then got to her feet and walked back out to the kitchen.

While she was pouring coffee, I pulled off my T-shirt and slid the fluid, backless halter number over my head. Once the fabric settled, I unbuttoned my cut-offs and kicked them off. I stepped in front of the mirror. The dress was stunning. Too stunning. What if I ripped it or stained it or—

"Told you it would look awesome." Sarah was leaning against the gigantic doorframe, clutching a mug of coffee between her fingers. A gold-foiled word was stamped on it—*Princess*. How appropriate.

"It's really nice, but maybe…*too* nice?" My voice sounded slightly high-pitched.

"Would you rather wear something ugly? 'Cause if that's the case, I don't have anything for you."

"No. It's just"—I smoothed the fabric of the flowy skirt—"it's expensive, isn't it?"

"Probably. Mom gave it to me." She pushed off the doorjamb. "Look, I'm not going to force you to wear something you're not comfortable with, but know that I most probably won't wear it again. I try not to wear the same thing twice. So if you're worried about ruining it, don't. There are plenty more where that one came from."

"That's really generous."

She shrugged, and her silk robe fell off her shoulder. She hiked the slippery material back up, then returned to the bed, where she sat cross-legged. "I had a question for you."

I stopped admiring the dress.

"Why are you the only girl in your pack?"

"I always assumed I was a fluke of nature." I bit the inside of my cheek. "Do *you* know why I'm the only girl in my pack?" It struck me I used the possessive pronoun, so I switched it out for, "I mean, in the Boulder Pack?"

"Nope. No clue." She sipped her steaming coffee. "Must be weird... Weirdly cool."

"It's definitely weird but not cool at all. I wish there were others."

"You get all these hot guys to yourself. Why would you ever want to share?"

"They're not *all* hot. Besides, none of them like me." *Anymore...*

"Babe, pull off your blinkers. You know the way you were checking out the dress. Well, Liam was staring at you the exact same way all fucking night. Seriously, I almost screwed up my beat-juggling because of you two."

"He stares at me because he doesn't trust me. None of the Boulder wolves do. After he saw me talking with you, he was all up in my face about what we'd discussed."

She rolled her eyes. "The Boulders think everyone's out to get them."

"And they're wrong?"

"Well, yeah. Not *everyone's* out to get them. The dudes are Neanderthals. Hot Neanderthals, but Neanderthals nonetheless. What would my *very evolved* pack need with any of them?" She downed the rest of her coffee, then set her mug down next to a half-empty bottle of water. "They don't have anything we don't already have."

"They're all males."

She frowned. "So?"

"They're all stronger than I am."

"Just because your muscles aren't as big doesn't mean you're weak, Ness." She tapped her index finger against her temple. "This'll sound corny as shit, but the greatest strength comes from here."

I pursed my lips, not because I thought she was wrong, but because I thought she was idealistic. It was easy to be idealistic when you possessed everything—from riches to security to status to family. I had none of those things.

She tipped her head to the side. "Here I thought you were this self-confident, arrogant girl, but you're not, are you?"

"I make a good first impression, don't I?" I raised a smile I wasn't really feeling. "You're also surprisingly different than I assumed. You're actually nice."

"Ha. I think you're the first person to say that." She twisted her long curls in a makeshift bun that held by itself. "Can you please tell my mother that on Saturday? I'd *love* a front-row seat to that reaction…"

My smile turned genuine.

Sarah's stomach growled long and hard. "I need food. Want to grab some lunch?"

I glanced at the glowing red digits on her bedside clock. "It's 4:30."

"Perfect time for lunch." She walked over to another doorway and slid it open. Behind it sprawled a white marble bathroom. "So? You in?"

"Sure."

While she showered, I delicately pulled the dress off and folded it neatly, then put on my denim cut-offs and navy T-shirt that felt incredibly ratty in comparison. I asked her twice more if she was sure about the dress. Both times won me headshakes and *yes*es.

We had food at Tracy's, where I expected to run into some member of the Boulder Pack, but instead we ran into a couple Pines. Thankfully none of them were Justin Summix.

When I mentioned his name, Sarah wrinkled her nose and leaned over, burger suspended in midair, meat juice dripping onto her creamy coleslaw. "He's the worst."

I liked her more after that. And I already liked her quite a bit, so that was saying a lot. How I wished she were a Boulder wolf. But then I wondered why I wished she were part of a pack *I* wasn't even part of. And what did it matter anyway? In the end, she was a wolf like me. Just because we didn't answer to the same Alpha—I answered to none for that matter—didn't mean we couldn't be friends.

THIRTY-EIGHT

Although we'd made plans to hang out mid-week, Sarah had to cancel for some wedding stuff. The bored sound of her voice told me she wasn't looking forward to whatever her family had planned for her.

I stayed in most of the week, shifting into my wolf form only once to go for a run. I didn't stray too far up the mountain, but I did pound the earth from sundown to twilight, exerting my pent-up nerves.

All week I'd tried to call Everest for news, but he didn't answer his phone. I was beginning to think he didn't want to talk to me. Maybe he thought that associating with me was shameful considering what I'd done to his Alpha. Whatever his reasons, I added his silence to the long list of things that perturbed me.

I spoke to August a few times—always steering the conversation toward him. We talked battle strategies and hot deserts, grenades and religious indoctrination. Lighthearted subjects.

At the end of our last call, I asked him when he was coming home, and he asked me if I missed him, and it triggered a painfully awkward stretch of silence, which he put an end to by saying he needed to get geared up because his squad was waiting for him in a Humvee.

Truth was, I did miss him, but I tacked that up to being a lonely pariah. It was probably better that he was away. If he'd stayed, he might have hung out with me out of pity, and I would've hated that.

When Saturday rolled around, my stomach roiled with nerves. I'd been too nervous to eat, too nervous to do much of anything besides the chores Lucy had assigned to me. I'd asked Evelyn if she wanted to go for a walk, but she told me her head was hurting.

Before leaving for the wedding, decked in my red gown, I stopped by her bedroom where she was watching Law and Order reruns. She blinked up at me from a flowered armchair that seemed as old as the inn, then her eyes glittered and she repeated, "*Que linda*" so many times, the tips of my ears glowed as bright as my dress.

"How are you feeling?"

"How are *you* feeling?" She narrowed her black eyes at me.

"Fine."

Her puckered brow told me she didn't believe me.

"I'm going to be late if I don't hurry." I bent over and kissed her forehead.

She caught my hand and squeezed it. "You'll tell me all about the wedding tomorrow?"

"Yes." I lingered by her bedroom door, staring at her calm, screen-lit profile.

What would happen to her if Liam didn't forgive me? Would Jeb and Lucy keep her on, or would they chase her away?

When she caught me staring, I razed the anxiety from my face and pasted on a smile. I shut the door before she could ask me what was wrong, then walked briskly away in case she decided to go after me.

Jeb, who'd been sitting in the office filling out a spreadsheet, followed me outside to await Frank. Even though the sun was beginning to arc down, it was a couple million degrees out, yet the heat did little to ward off the chill skittering over my bones.

"You don't have to stay out here with me, Jeb."

My uncle squinted at the setting sun. "Today's part of the Alpha contest, isn't it?"

"Yes."

He pursed his thinning lips. "Why are you still competing? Are you trying to prove something to someone?"

As I stared out at the sinking ball of fire that gilded the crowns of the tall pines, I nibbled on the inside of my cheek. "Not anymore."

"You really want this?"

I didn't answer him. Instead, I asked, "Is Everest mad at me?"

A frown touched Jeb's wrinkled brow. "Why would he be mad at you?"

Everest must not have shared what had happened to Heath if my uncle was asking me this.

When I failed to answer, Jeb said, "Lucy told me he got bad news. Apparently, Becca's parents have decided to take her off life support." He sighed. "So sad… She was so young and seemed like such a nice girl."

"Seemed? You didn't know her?"

"Not well. Everest didn't bring her around much. My son is a very private person." I felt him study me in silence for a long second. "Speaking of knowing people, Ness, how well do you know Evelyn?"

His frown made a tremor zing up my exposed spine. "Very well. Why?"

He hooked his thumbs through his belt loops, shifting from one loafered foot to the other.

"*Why?*" I repeated.

He stopped shifting. "The other day, a guest wanted to meet our new cook, and when I introduced them, the woman called her by another name—*Gloria*. Evelyn said she didn't know any Glorias, but her eye twitched. I'm no behavioral expert, but I think—"

"Evelyn's not a liar. She's never even been to Boulder." I was annoyed my uncle was trying to destroy my faith in the only person I trusted.

He nodded. "I was just putting it out there. In case—"

"You shouldn't put things out there if they're hurtful."

His mouth gaped a little. I could tell he wanted to say more on the subject, but my expression must've dissuaded him. Thankfully, a car rumbled up the driveway. Frank was coming. When I spotted giant wheels, the relief I'd felt evaporated.

It wasn't Frank who was picking me up.

The car slowed to a stop next to me. Lucas was riding shotgun, decked out in a black tux that strained in the shoulders. He had his arm slung out the open window.

"Hey, Mr. Clark."

"Hi, boys." My uncle inclined his head before pulling open the back door and holding out a hand to help me up. "You're all looking mighty dapper tonight."

"Well, you know the Pines and their hoity-toity events."

Jeb offered a small smile that didn't reach his eyes. "You boys keep my niece safe, now. I don't like the look of them young'uns."

"Oh, Ness doesn't need us for that," Lucas drawled. "Especially now that she's besties with Julian's niece."

Jeb blinked at me. "You're friends with Sarah Matz?"

"Is that not allowed?" I wasn't in a good mood. Not at all. But it had little to do with Lucas's comment and everything to do with Jeb's.

"Is Ness ever in a good mood?" Lucas asked my uncle.

I growled as I strapped myself in.

My uncle didn't answer Lucas, too busy scrutinizing my face.

Evelyn wouldn't lie to me.

She wasn't a woman called Gloria.

"Are you sensing you're going to fail miserably? Is that it?" Lucas chirped.

Liam glanced into his rearview mirror, and our eyes met for the briefest of moments. I looked away before he did.

"You're so astute at reading people, Lucas." I didn't want to fight with him tonight.

He simpered at me before rubbing his hands together. "Should we get this party on the road? I'm dying for some canapés or whatever dainty shit the Pines feed on."

The entire way to Julian's estate, Liam didn't speak once, but there was never a dull moment, because Lucas was a freaking word-mill. The boy *loved* the sound of his voice.

When we passed through the gates that were manned by two burly wolves in skin, I nibbled on my lip before remembering I'd slicked on bright-red lipstick to match my dress. I checked my reflection in my phone's camera, fixed my lipstick, then smoothed the glossy curls I'd made with my mom's old flat iron after watching ten tutorials on YouTube and failing nine times out of the ten at recreating them.

Julian's home loomed at the top of a knoll like a pale cloud. During the ride over, Lucas had informed me the Pine Alpha's inspiration had been a French castle.

"The dude thinks he's a fucking king," Lucas had said.

As I took in the smooth stone façade and the grid of diamond-cut window panes that seemed to stretch an entire acre long, I had to agree with Lucas—Julian definitely fancied himself a sovereign.

A valet dressed in black pants and a high-collared red jacket drew open my door and held out a gloved hand. Before I could latch onto it, Liam rounded the car, stepped in front of the parking attendant, and extended his own hand.

I hesitated to touch him, and he sensed it because his gaze grew stormy. He didn't lower his hand, though. He held it out stubbornly. I gathered the folds of red chiffon in one hand and then yielded to Liam's will, grasping his fingers. Angering him would work against me when I pleaded for my life.

As soon as my feet touched the ground, I removed my fingers from his. His shoulders tightened, creasing the fine fabric of his tuxedo. Lucas walked ahead of us through the mammoth front doors, his head swiveling from right to left. Either he was ascertaining threats or he was admiring Julian's black-marbled lair. Gold finishes accented the dark furnishings, and crystal vases overflowing with scarlet roses adorned every table in sight.

"Did Julian ever marry?" I asked.

"Why? Are you interested?" Lucas shot back.

I rolled my eyes but caught Liam observing me. Even though I hadn't planned on answering Lucas's inane question, Liam's weighty stare made me say, "Of course not. He could be my father."

"I didn't think age mattered to you," Lucas said.

I snapped my attention to the shaggy-haired male who drove me insane. "Can you cut me some slack tonight, Lucas? I'm really not in the mood."

A server approached us with a platter of champagne flutes. I grabbed one and downed it in a very un-ladylike manner. I didn't care, though. Tonight was going to be rough, and I needed as much liquid courage as I could get. I set the stemmed glass back down on the man's platter before emerging from the black entrails of the house onto the packed terrace.

A hush fell over the crowd as all heads swiveled toward us. Although many stared my way, most looked at Liam. Between his chiseled jaw, his artfully gelled hair, and his black tux, he looked like he'd just stepped out of a GQ spread. Perhaps that wasn't the reason they looked at him, but I bet it was the reason why some of them *kept* staring.

The unremitting gurgle of water from a large round fountain projected noise against the mosaic-tiled floor, chipping away at the oppressive silence. I inhaled slowly, trying to iron out my nerves, but all that did was fill my lungs with the sickly-sweet smell of the roses spilling over the flat wooden trellis that roofed part of the terrace. Orange dregs of sunlight slid around the velvety petals and sharp thorns, dappling the crowd in shards of light. Candles flickered on tall skinny tables wrapped in white cloth, and glowing spheres of frosted glass hung from the trellis like miniature moons.

Lucas stood close to me; Liam even closer. Both narrowed their eyes at the quiet, observant crowd. Julian appeared then, in an emerald tux. He pressed past his people to reach us, a tumbler in one hand, a woman in the other. First I thought the woman was his date, but the resemblance between them was so uncanny that I guessed she was Sarah's mother.

"Welcome, welcome." His voice trumpeted out of him, cheerful and loud. "My sister Nora and I are so glad you could make it." He let go of his sister's hand to take mine and lifted it to his lips. "Ness, there are no words to describe how you look tonight."

"I can think of a few," Lucas muttered. "Red, for example. Half-naked."

"What a poet you are, Mr. Mason," Julian said, tossing a chilly glance Lucas's way. "The women must just love you."

"They do actually."

Liam shifted to stand in front of me, which forced Julian to let go.

A broad smile curled over Julian's face.

"Well, aren't we a little possessive?" he said under his breath.

Liam didn't answer.

Thankfully, Lucas spoke. "Frank and Eric aren't here yet, are they?"

"You are the first to arrive." Julian's eyes sparked as newcomers made their way onto the twinkling patio. "Mingle and be merry." He took his sister's arm, and together they walked to greet their new guests.

Soft string music started up again. Although the Pines remained alert, tossing sporadic glances our way, conversations resumed.

"Is he expecting us to actually chat with his people?" Lucas muttered to Liam.

"Damn, girl, I was right." A burst of yellow popped into my line of sight. Sarah walked over to us, blonde corkscrews tumbling over the buttercup dress that stuck to her curves like a bandage.

She pressed a kiss to my cheek, which had Lucas and Liam gaping. They'd heard we were friends, but apparently they didn't believe it.

"You Neanderthals clean up nicely, too," she said.

Lucas, who'd grabbed a glass of champagne from a passing tray, choked on his drink. "Neanderthal?"

I grinned.

"Yes. Neanderthal. Especially you, Mason," Sarah said. "From what I hear, you're a particularly devolved male specimen."

Lucas's eyes turned a neon shade of blue. "Figures you and Ness get along. Both shrews."

"Lucas…" Liam said.

Lucas turned on his friend. "What? I'm not the one tossing around hurtful observations."

"Was shrew supposed to be a compliment?" Sarah asked.

Lucas smirked. "Compared to what I was really thinking, yes."

Her eyes glittered with mirth.

"Are you deejaying tonight?" Liam asked, and I wondered how painful it was for him to act convivial.

"After dinner, I'm on."

"Damn. I forgot my earplugs." Lucas downed his champagne.

"Oh, I saw you dancing to my beats on Thursday night."

"Must've mistaken me for someone else. I don't dance."

"Not well, but you do."

Lucas rolled his fingers into a fist and cracked his knuckles. "Why were you even looking at me, blondie?"

"It's part of the job. I keep an eye on my crowd. I need to make sure you're all hearing what you want to hear."

"Then you're reading me all wrong."

Sarah crossed her arms in front of her. "Really? What is it you want to hear?"

He scraped his hand through his black hair. "Anything but that crap you play."

"You're an ass, Mason," she said. "A real ass." They glared at each other for so long I started to pull her aside, but she stood her ground.

"Sarah, darling! Come greet our guests." Nora's voice rang over the courtyard.

Still glaring, my friend whipped around and strode over toward her mother and uncle.

"Is it completely impossible for you to be nice, Lucas?" I asked.

His gaze, which had trailed after Sarah, snapped back toward me. "Are her lips and tits even real?"

"Oh my God, shut up," I said.

"What? Am I not allowed to ask? They don't look real."

"Lucas—" Liam started.

"Don't tell me you weren't wondering the same thing…" Lucas turned to look at Sarah again.

"I wasn't wondering the same thing," Liam said in a low voice.

Lucas shifted his attention back to his friend. "Right." His eyes flashed to me then to a waiter carrying a platter of mini club sandwiches. He grabbed three and chucked them into his mouth. "See you kids later."

I didn't ask where he was going, because I already knew. He was going to start the hunt for the piece of decaying wood.

After Lucas left, I asked Liam, "Shouldn't you go?"

"It would look suspicious if I left too, don't you think?" Liam peered at something beyond me.

I turned and found the focus of his attention—Justin and his two cronies from the music festival.

"Do you have any idea why the thing we're seeking is so important?" I asked softly.

Liam's gaze tracked back to my face, then lower, to my collarbone dusted with glittery powder. "No."

My heart scudded. "Not even a guess?"

He shook his head as he lifted his gaze back to mine. The intensity of his attention pressed my lungs hard against my ribcage. No one had ever looked at me so intently. Then again, no one had ever tried to see into my mind as desperately as Liam Kolane. I lowered my lids, hoping the delicate skin would hide my machinations just a little while longer.

THIRTY-NINE

Lucas returned a few minutes before the ceremony began—empty-handed and pissed. He shuffled past Frank and Eric and the latter's wife to reach the seat Liam had saved.

Lucas exchanged quiet words with his friend, probably telling him where he'd looked. No doubt remained in my mind that they were performing this test as a tag team.

Liam was about to sidestep past me, when he stopped and leaned in, his breath warming my earlobe. "I'm not being very polite. Why don't you go?"

Musk lifted off his smooth skin and slid into me, momentarily hazing my mind. God, he smelled so good. Why couldn't I just be repulsed by him? I tried to put some space between our bodies, but the backs of my knees hit the seat of the chair.

"I want to see what the bride is wearing." I sounded as hoarse as a heavy smoker.

Liam straightened, eyebrows casting shadows over his amber eyes. "Don't you want to beat me?"

"Just because I'm letting you go first doesn't mean I won't win."

The tendons in his neck shifted as he studied my face. Could he tell it was a lie?

He started to dip his head back toward my ear when the first notes of the wedding march began. All those who'd been sitting rose to their feet in a rustle of chiffon.

"You better go," I whispered.

Liam stepped past me and into the outer aisle, distancing himself quickly from the ceremony.

HE RETURNED AFTER THE ceremony, wearing a disgruntled expression. I took it he'd failed to locate the artifact.

"Wasn't the ceremony just marvelous?" Julian was standing in the petal-strewn aisle by our row.

"It was lovely," Eric's wife said, tucking a short white curl behind her ear.

Unlike Eric, Frank had come alone to the ceremony. Maybe he wasn't married. I realized I didn't know much about the elders. All I knew was that both men had had sons, but only Eric's was still alive, and both had fourteen-year-old grandsons who were part of the pack.

"Are there any weddings on the Boulder Pack horizon?" Julian asked.

Frank glanced at Lucas, then at Liam. "None of our boys are committing yet, but we'll be sure to keep you updated, Julian."

Our boys. Salt in my wound.

Julian smiled a frigid smile then turned his attention to me. "Ness, may I have the pleasure of your company before dinner begins?"

Prickling from Frank's exclusion, I moved past *his boys* and hooked my arm through Julian's extended one. I knew what it looked like but was too slighted to care. We drifted away from the festivities, toward the glossy green hedges forming a manicured maze.

"Ah…the Boulders and their boys." Julian let out a soft snort. "It's a real shame wolves can't pledge their allegiances to another pack. I'd welcome you with open arms."

"That's kind of you, Mr. Matz."

"Julian, please. Mr. Matz makes me sound like an old college professor with a penchant for tweed." He wrinkled his nose. "How's the contest going?"

"It's going." I lowered my gaze to the red chiffon swirling around my ankles.

"Then why are you putting off competing?"

I faltered and would've faceplanted if he hadn't been holding me up. It didn't help that my skinny heels kept burying themselves in the soft earth.

"I'm not putting it off—"

"Ness, spare me the lie. I'm not an idiot. While Lucas and Liam roamed my house, you stayed planted on my lawn like a gloomy poppy."

He led me around a sharp, leafy corner, then around another. I was disoriented. Not only by the thriving labyrinth, but also by his admission. He knew why we were here. How? I opened my mouth but not to speak. Just to gape.

"Did you assume my invitation to attend my nephew's wedding was sent out of geniality?"

I tried to shut my jaw, but it hung open, its hinges shattered by shock.

"I possess something dear to your pack, and McNamara knows it. It was a matter of time before he sent his *boys* to retrieve it."

I finally got my mouth to work. "But how... How did you know it would be part of the contest?"

"I made sure it became a part of it by tendering an invitation onto my estate."

A loud squawk sounded. I raised my eyes to the sky to spot the bird capable of releasing such an ear-splitting sound but saw nothing flying overhead.

"If I'd been Frank, and your pack held something of mine, instead of breaking and entering, I'd jump on the opportunity to stroll through the front door."

"So your pack really did steal it?" I whispered into the dusky air.

"No."

"But then...how—"

"Someone gave it to me in exchange for a favor. I knew it was of great importance because Heath had paid me a visit a couple days before he died to demand I return it to him. At that point, I had no idea what in God's good name he'd been raving about. But of course, his request rendered me extraordinarily curious. And when what he'd been pursuing dropped into my lap some time later...well, you can imagine my absolute delight."

Julian stopped walking, pulling me to a stop too. He frowned and released my arm. I assumed someone was coming but heard no footsteps, smelled no other body. Then again, it was difficult to smell much of anything over the sour scent wafting in the air. He reached around me to pluck a leaf that stuck out from the smooth green wall of vegetation.

The reason we'd stopped.

My skin turned bitterly cold as I realized that if I stepped out of the line he'd drawn for me, he'd probably snap my neck like he'd snapped that poking imperfection.

Julian returned his attention to me. I took a step back, my bare shoulder blade brushing against the bristly hedge. What had gotten into me to follow him deep into a maze he knew like the palm of his hand?

The sky had dimmed to a periwinkle blue that matched Julian's eyes as he drank in my dread like a man savoring a delectable vintage.

He held out his arm. "Shall we?"

I swallowed, forcing my limbs to move, even though the mere thought of touching Julian had goose bumps pebbling my arm.

As we started walking again, he said, "Shortly before we met, I contacted McNamara to let him know I held what Heath had been so desperately seeking and promised to hand it over if he explained its importance."

My throat moved with another swallow. "He mustn't have told you if you still have it."

He tsked. "Ye have little faith in me, Miss Clark."

My eyes widened, soaking up the silvery outline of his gelled hair. "He told you?"

"Yes."

"But you didn't return it."

Another loud squawk. I tipped my head upward again.

"I had every intention of giving it back—until I heard what they used it for. Then I had every intention of destroying it, but I held off, waiting for a new Alpha to rise to power in your pack. It is more challenging to barter with ashes."

"What do they use it for?"

Julian stopped walking again, but this time, it was simply to face me. "Have you really no idea?"

I shook my head.

"They grate the wood into the drink pledges have to ingest the day they join your pack."

I frowned.

"Have you never wondered why only males are born to the Boulder Pack? Did you truly think it was an evolutionary trait like your elders claim?"

The world held still for a moment, and then it tipped. Julian slid his palms underneath my elbows to hold me upright.

"I hope this will renew your desire to compete."

A gust of wind cartwheeled through the maze, blowing against the glossy leaves that waved at me like tiny hands. Anger bloomed in my chest, chasing away the chilling numbness I'd felt all week long.

"Once you become Alpha, you can destroy it and change the course of your pack's future."

Color must've seeped into my cheeks, because Julian raised a wide smile that barely crimped his too-smooth, too-shiny brow.

He leaned in close. "Shall I tell you where I'm keeping it hidden?"

"Why are you helping me?"

"I've already told you. I want a friend in your pack, and I think you'd make a good friend."

"You already have Everest."

"I would not call your cousin a friend. Merely an effective purveyor. But if you'd rather not be my friend, then—"

"Where is the damn stick?"

A slow smile drew his pouty lips upward, revealing the perfectly polished enamel of his teeth. "That's my girl."

"I'm no one's girl."

He scraped a dry finger against my cheek. His hand smelled so strongly of acetone and lotion it momentarily dispelled the repulsive scent blistering the air.

I bristled away from his touch.

"Take every right turn from now on. At the center of this maze, you'll find the cage in which I keep my glorious pets. What you're looking for is inside."

A cage? Was that the source of the squawking and revolting reek?

Julian handed me a little key. "You will be needing this."

I closed my fingers around the gold key and started walking away when Julian called out to me.

"After you were born, your father came to me."

I didn't turn around, but I waited, spine tight.

"He asked if I could enlighten him as to why he'd been given a daughter."

"He must not have drunk the celebratory concoction," I said drily.

"Perhaps. Anyway, at the time, I didn't have an answer for him. I told him he should ask his Alpha. He told me that he had. Would you like to know what Heath told him?"

"He instructed him to kill me and try again. Oh… and he also suggested a paternity test." My tone dripped with acid.

The ensuing silence told me Julian hadn't expected me to answer.

But then his voice rose again. "I know you feel guilt, Ness. I sense it weighing heavily on your shoulders. Cast it away. Heath Kolane was not a good man. Besides, think of your father. Think of what a victory it would've been for him to see you, his strong, beautiful daughter, rise to the highest rank of a pack who cast her away because of her gender."

My heart hardened to steel. My resolve too. I didn't delude myself into thinking Julian was my friend. He was an oily, manipulative man, but he'd just given me two tools—courage and knowledge—to right one of the many wrongs inside my pack, and for that I was grateful.

I started up again and took the first right.

The first of many rights.

FORTY

E ven if Julian hadn't shared the directions to his birdcage, I would've found it from the smell. His vibrant-colored and cacophonous parrots reeked. As I approached their cage, eyes prickling from the aggressive stench, I lifted a hand to block my nose.

No wonder he'd hidden the fossilized wood inside. The birds' awful stink would cover up the artifact's. I wasn't sure what the old thing I needed to find would look like and regretted not having asked what color it was or where it rested in the cage. When Julian had mentioned a cage, I'd imagined a smallish thing, not one I could step into without hunching over.

The birds turned their beady black eyes toward me, growing still and quiet at my advance. I uncovered my nose and sniffed the air for what I needed to find. My eyes watered, but I kept sniffing, strolling slowly around the cage. I caught a whiff of cold rot and stopped. Both parrots had swiveled their neckless heads to watch me, their sharp beaks buried deep in their puffy red chests.

I crouched to see if the smell emanated from the wood-chipped floor. My nose burned. The rancid odor was definitely worse below. In the pale light of the moon, I tracked my gaze over the woodchips until I found a disturbance in their evenness. Something glinted among the dull carpeting like polished bone.

Pressing one palm over my nose, I made my way back around the cage to the door and slid the key into the lock. When the latch clanked open, I pushed the door open and slipped inside, shutting it back quickly so Julian's prized pets didn't flock out. Keeping one eye out on the quiet birds, I moved toward the irregular patch of flooring and dug out what I'd seen.

Thick. Yellowed. Shiny. Putrid.

The key to gender selection.

How had anyone been able to swallow a drink sprinkled with this was beyond me. I would've thrown up at the mere smell.

Perhaps that's what had happened to my father. Perhaps he'd thrown up the vile thing.

I wrapped my fingers lightly around the disgusting object and exited the birdcage. The parrots hadn't fluttered a single feather. I turned the key, then buried it in the palm that wasn't holding the Boulder relic.

As I turned, I bumped into a body.

A tall, broad body with glowing yellow eyes.

FORTY-ONE

Liam stood in front of me, jaw so hard it could cut glass.

My pulse raged from his presence, from his nearness.

"You found it." The low timbre of his voice rolled toward me. He was angry. Terribly angry.

I pressed the key harder into my palm. "I did." I should probably have dropped the key into the grass and prayed he wouldn't see its shine, but I didn't drop it. I didn't dare move. "You've arrived too late."

"You wouldn't have had any help, would you now?"

"Would it matter? The rule of the game was to find the artifact. They didn't specify our method for finding it."

A rough smile perched on his lips. "You're good, Ness. Sneaky, even."

I tried to step around him, but he blocked my advance. "Get out of my way, Liam."

"You cheated."

I glared up at him defiantly. "I used my connection to find it. How is that cheating?"

"Your connection...or your mouth?"

I uncurled my fingers from the piece of wood. It tumbled onto the grass at the same time as my hand flew into Liam's jaw.

How could I ever have considered letting him win? "I've never ever touched a man that way!"

"Then why is Julian helping you?" he asked, rubbing his jaw.

"Maybe because he thinks I'd make a better Alpha than any of you." I crouched to pick up the fossil. Woodchips had caught in the hem of my dress, but I didn't bother brushing them off. My hands trembled too fiercely to do much more than focus on clutching the key and the wood.

I shook my head as I rose and passed by him, knocking my shoulder into his chest on purpose.

"You're going the wrong way."

"It's away from you, so it must be right." My vision had tunneled from anger and adrenaline. I'd find my way outside of this maze eventually. I was in no rush. I walked briskly, my heels poking into the ground and popping out. I took every left turn I could find. Instead of finding myself on the great lawn, I found myself back in front of the birdcage.

I growled out of frustration.

At least Liam was gone.

I tried again, this time focusing. I remembered I'd emerged from the maze on the side facing the cage door, so I walked back that way, and then I took a left, and another left, and another. On the ground beneath my feet I spotted the spindly branch Julian had ripped. Bolstered by the knowledge I was heading in the correct direction, I concentrated on recalling how I'd gotten to that point. It took me three attempts to figure it out.

When I burst out of the maze, I released a deep breath but then sucked in air anew when I caught sight of my welcoming committee.

Liam, Lucas, and Frank stood there. All of them had their arms crossed.

"What? No applause?" Apparently anger made me snarky.

"You had help," Lucas said.

I shot my gaze to Liam who met it straight on. He didn't even flinch. "Perhaps I did, but as far as I can remember, that wasn't forbidden."

Lucas whipped his head to shift his hair off his forehead. "That's cheating."

"I didn't come up with this test, Lucas. The elders did."

"Frank, come on…" Lucas said, untying his arms and waving his hands around. "You can't let her win."

I fixed my gaze on Frank and dared him to disqualify me.

Slowly, his chest rose with a sigh. Even more slowly his lips parted, and he said, "Let me see it."

"Can't you smell it?" I was pretty certain the odor would never wash away from my skin, even if I dipped my hand in bleach.

"I need to ascertain it's whole."

I raised my chin up a little higher and walked closer. I held out my palm and opened my fingers. When he tried to pluck it out, I snapped my fingers closed around the noxious wood and hid it behind my back. "I'm not giving it back."

Frank cocked a bushy eyebrow. "If you don't give it back, you'll be disqualified."

"I know what it does," I said, shaking with anger.

He dipped his chin into his neck. "I assumed as much."

"How could you use this? How could you perpetuate such savagery?" I murmured disgustedly.

Liam and Lucas turned their attention to Frank.

"Could we discuss this in private, Ness?"

"Why? Are you afraid of how *your boys* will react, Mr. McNamara?"

One of his eyes twitched. "No. Actually, go ahead and tell them. This shouldn't be a secret anymore."

He was bluffing. He had to be bluffing. The Alphas and elders had kept this a secret for a century.

"It's too late anyway," he said. "For their generation at least, it's too late."

"What does it do?" Liam asked.

Frank raised his gaze to me. "Shall I tell them, or should I leave you that honor?" When I didn't move my lips, Frank said, "A trifling amount of the wood is mixed into your pledge drinks. It destroys female sperm."

Both Liam's and Lucas's eyes widened. Both their mouths gaped. They'd really had no idea.

"Genius," Lucas said.

I balked at his answer. But of course he'd find it genius. I looked at Liam, waited to see his reaction, but besides a slackening of his stance, he didn't utter a single word.

"Not the reactions you were expecting, are they?" Frank said.

To think my father had had to answer to him as a boy.

"Do you also find it genius?" I asked Liam, loathing how desperate I was for him to say no.

He blinked but didn't speak.

"I don't think the pack could've dealt with more girls," Lucas said, which made Frank's lips quirk up.

I wanted to whack the smile off his face and almost swung the yellowed fossil into his cheek, but I held myself back.

"At least," Frank said, serious again, "we don't kill off female embryos like they do in the other packs. Because that's what happens in the other packs. Women interrupt pregnancies when they find out their offspring is female."

"Not the Pines."

"*Even* the Pines. Why do you think there aren't as many females to males in their pack? They just cover it up better than the other packs."

"That's a lie."

"No, Ness. It isn't a lie."

I wanted to growl, and I did.

Frank held out his hand. "Last chance to stay in this contest."

Shaking my head, I slapped the rancid stick against his palm. He could have his evil gender selection tool back. If I became Alpha, I'd destroy it. And if I didn't rise to the top, I wouldn't have to worry about the damn thing, because I would no longer be part of the Boulder Pack.

"Did Callum not drink it, Frank?" Liam asked. "Is that why he had Ness?"

I held my breath.

"He drank it," Frank said, "but it made him sick. We believe that's why it didn't work on him."

I released the captive air, hating how much relief Frank's explanation brought me.

"Aw, man…" Lucas grumbled. "I had a bet going that Ness wasn't a Boulder."

"You bet that my mom cheated on my dad?"

"Lucas," Frank chided him. "Not only is that inappropriate but—"

"Oh come on, Mr. McNamara. Wasn't that one of the reasons Heath didn't accept Ness's pledge? Because he wanted to spare her the heartache of uncovering her heritage through a communication glitch?"

"What are you talking about?" I all but snarled.

"If you're not a Boulder," Lucas said, "you won't hear the Alpha."

Silence caked the warm breeze. I tucked a long tendril of hair behind my ear before remembering the hand I used had been the one to clutch the pack artifact. The lingering stench made my eyes water.

"Do you also doubt my lineage, Mr. McNamara?" I asked.

Frank hooked a finger into his black bowtie and tugged as though it were on too tight. "Your mother was a good woman."

A non-answer.

"I suppose we'll find out for sure if you win, Ness," Lucas continued. "If none of us can hear you—"

"Enough! Enough." Frank's face was so red it made his eyebrows appear whiter. "Who will you choose as your opponent for the last test, Ness?"

I hated the uncertainty that had again crawled underneath my skin. I exhaled an annoyed breath, then looked at Lucas and Liam—a rock and a hard place.

I finally made my choice.

"Liam," I said. "I pick Liam."

And then I walked away, finding my way home the same way I'd found my way out of the maze.

Alone.

FORTY-TWO

I'd tried to drown my overactive mind in a book, but to no avail. After three pages, the contents of which had pinged against my skull without leaving a trace, I tossed the book aside and turned off the light on my nightstand. I shut my eyes and prayed sleep would devour me.

But it didn't. My nerves were too raw to sleep.

"Oh, Mom," I murmured. "Whose child am I?" A tear slid down my nose and into my pillow.

I rolled onto my back, and then I stared at the immaculate white paint on the ceiling, crumpling my comforter between my fingers. I felt a nonsensical bout of nostalgia for the water stains that had adorned our ceiling back in Los Angeles.

A knock on my window had my pulse spiking. I sat up quickly, and the world spun. Had I imagined it? Another knock, this time more insistent. I got out of bed slowly, swiping my room key off my desk and fitting it between clenched fingers.

Who would knock on my window? Everest maybe—

I drew the drapes open.

Liam stood on my balcony, barely distinguishable from the night in his dark clothes. Only his face stood out, pale as the moon behind him.

Nerves shrilled in my ears, and I shut my curtains.

"Ness, let me in." He banged on the glass again, and I felt his fist inside my chest. "I'll wake up the whole damn inn if you don't let me—"

I shoved the curtains aside and opened the door, and then I backed away from him, fingers wrapped tightly around the key.

He thrust the door closed so hard it sucked in a piece of beige curtain.

He scowled as his gaze caught the glint of metal in my fist. "I'm not here to hurt you."

I didn't loosen my grip on my makeshift weapon. "Why are you here then?"

"I'm here for answers." He inhaled a rough breath. "Why are you Julian's puppet?"

"I'm not his puppet."

"Oh, come on!" Liam smacked an open palm on my desk. I jumped. "You vanish into a fucking maze with him, and then you come back out all victorious and smug."

"Is it so hard to believe he might enjoy my company?"

Liam let out a cruel laugh. "It is, actually." His voice was hostile. "Julian is a manipulative bastard, and don't tell me you don't realize that, because you might be a lot of things, Ness, but you're not dumb. Now, please tell me what the fuck is going on, because I am this close"—he held out his index finger and thumb, which were a hairbreadth's away from touching—"to my breaking point."

I pressed my lips shut, not to keep my confession from sliding out, but to keep Liam from seeing how they trembled. I squared my shoulders for the same reason.

"Did you think Lucas wouldn't kill me? Is that it?" he asked.

My heart punched my ribcage. "What?"

"Don't tell me you weren't aware that the last test is a kill game."

Those two words should never have been part of the same sentence. "A-A kill game?"

A shadow lapsed over Liam's brow. "Winner takes all. Including loser's life."

The key tumbled out of my slack fingers and clinked against the wooden floor.

His eyebrows writhed in surprise. "What? You didn't know?"

"They're going to—" I swallowed, but it did little to displace the lump expanding like a vacuum bag inside my throat. "Make us—" I'd convinced myself I'd meet Liam's punishment with my chin raised high—whatever that punishment may be. But that was because I hadn't really believed he would kill me.

I wasn't ready to die.

I didn't want to die.

"Is this some sick joke?"

"No. It's not. I wouldn't joke about something like that." Liam raked his hand through his hair, ramming back a lock that had fallen over his forehead.

A thought whispered across my mind. He'd planned on selecting Lucas as his contestant. Had it been to spare me? "You would've been ready to kill Lucas?"

"I wouldn't have had to kill Lucas, because the elders would've let one of us concede. They wouldn't have wanted to eliminate a pack member."

His words trickled through me like grains of sand in an hourglass, and like those grains of sand, they were marking the time I had left.

I realized then that this was the perfect way to get rid of me for good. "But because it's me—a non-pack member—they'll take conceding off the table?" I swayed a little but caught myself on the back of my desk chair. My knuckles whitened. "Is that why you're here? To finish this stupid contest?"

His gaze turned a forbidding shade of black. "Do you really think I could kill you?"

Silence rang in my ears. "You want to become Alpha more than you want anything else, Liam, so yes, I think you *could* kill me."

He dropped down on the foot of my bed and let out a gravelly sigh. "It's true. I used to want it more than anything else. For my father, for the elders, there was no doubt I would be the next leader. It was what I was reared for."

I tucked a piece of hair behind my ear. My fingers shook. "And you'll make a great Alpha, Liam," I admitted softly. "I didn't use to think so. I assumed you were like Heath, and sometimes, you do remind me of him, but you also remind me of your mother, and she was a good woman who always cared for others more than she cared for herself. At least, that's what my mother told me. I don't remember her very well."

He snorted. "You don't have to be nice to me. I'm not going to kill you."

I released the chair and went to sit next to him on the bed. "I mean everything I just said." I twined my fingers together in my lap and marveled at how quickly my fingernails had grown back, how strong they'd become, almost as hard as my wolf claws. "I entered this contest to spite you but stayed in it because I'm proud and hated to be considered lower than low because I'm a girl. I wanted to prove to you, to the pack, and to myself that I was worth something, but I wasn't planning on even trying to win the last contest. That's why I picked you and not Lucas. Because…because I wanted *you* to win."

"Ness—"

"Let me finish." I squeezed my fingers together. "I don't want this, Liam. I don't want a pack that doesn't want me. And certainly not at the cost of a life."

I'd killed once.

Never again.

Never again.

"I'll leave Boulder and never come back. They can't make you kill me if I'm gone, right?" I turned my head to look at Liam, who was staring back, eyes wide.

"No."

"It won't work?"

He shifted, and one of his knees knocked into mine, creating a spot of heat on my cool skin. "You shouldn't have to leave your home because of me."

"*My home*?" I let out a soft snort. "I don't have a home here, Liam." I lifted my eyes to the untainted ceiling. "I live in a hotel. With an aunt who, for some reason, really despises me and an uncle who doesn't think very highly of me. My only friend was my cousin, but he up and left me. And my newest friend is a girl I keep being warned not to be friends with because she's the enemy. The only other person who was nice to me is off fighting in the Middle East. I might have a roof over my head, and a woman who cares about me like I was her own granddaughter, but I don't have a home."

One of Liam's hands came up to my face, his fingers cradling my chin, angling it toward him.

"You can't leave," he said, his voice a husky whisper.

"Why not?"

His warm breath rushed over my face. "Because then I'd spend my days tracking you down instead of focusing on the pack. What sort of Alpha would that make me?"

I lowered my lashes. "You think they'd make you track me down?"

"No one would make me do it."

The room was so quiet I heard him swallow.

"Do you...*feel* anything for me...besides contempt?" His lips worked on a smile but tumbled nervously back into a straight line.

"Would it change anything if I did?"

Emotion flared over his face, fast and bright like lightning. "It would change *everything*." He spoke the last word so slowly goose bumps erupted over my bare legs and arms, over the slice of bare stomach peeking between my sleep shorts and tank top. "Do you?"

The goose bumps breached my skin and skittered over my ribs. "What do you think?"

"I don't want to think; I want to know. Do you?" Even though his grip on my chin was gentle, his fingers were not. They dipped into my skin as though trying to leave marks.

"Yes," I whispered.

Before my next heartbeat, he'd splayed both his hands on my hips, lifted me, and propped me onto his lap. I bent my knees around his thighs. And then one of his hands was in my hair, his other on the base of my spine. And his lips...his lips were on mine, hard and soft, punishing and kind.

A series of explosions went off in me.

I was kissing Liam Kolane.

Liam Kolane was kissing me.

When his tongue swept over the seam of my mouth, my entire body rocked with a shiver. My hands, which had been resting lightly on his biceps, reached up to grip his shoulders. I burrowed my fingertips into his T-shirt, afraid that if I loosened my grip, I would tumble off him.

I parted my lips and took his tongue in. He growled into my mouth, his hands pressing harder into my skin. In his bruising grip, he scooped me up and stood. I locked my legs around him, locked my mouth on his. He walked to one side of the bed, knelt on the mattress, then lowered my body beneath his. Slowly I untangled my legs from around his waist and stretched them out underneath him. He braced himself on his forearms and pressed his lips against mine, tangling his tongue with mine.

Kissing Liam Kolane felt like running through a starlit field in my wolf form—the purest form of power and sensation there existed in this vast, dark world.

I ran my fingers over the runnel of his spine, then dipped my hands beneath the fabric of his black T-shirt to touch the warm, tanned skin I'd barely ever dared glimpse. His muscles roiled underneath my exploring hands; tendons pinched, flesh tensed.

He broke the kiss.

"Not fair," he whispered hoarsely.

I arched an eyebrow.

He rolled me over so that I was on top, so that his big hands could slip underneath my tank top.

"I've been dying to touch you, Ness. Every fucking inch of you. My turn."

His hands stroked my spine, the sides of my body, the indents of my waist before traveling upward, his thumbs trailing over my stomach, my ribcage, the underside of my breasts, stilling on my nipples. His touch sent so many tremors through my bent arms that I almost collapsed over him. He drew a line of kisses from the edge of my jaw all the way down to the hollow of my collarbone.

I moaned. Embarrassingly loud. And not just once.

He fit his mouth back over mine and swallowed the rest of my sounds, then slid his thumbs back down.

"You are so fucking perfect," he murmured against my lips.

Those words were my undoing. And not in any romantic way.

I began to cry, hundreds of tears.

If he knew what I'd done to his father, he wouldn't think me very perfect.

He wouldn't want to kiss me.

He wouldn't want to touch me.

"Hey." He slid me onto my side, then brushed his knuckles over my face to dry my wet cheeks. "Hey. What's going on?"

A savage sob raked up my chest, erupting from my mouth. I threw the back of my hand against my trembling lips and bit the thin skin to silence myself.

He combed a lock of hair behind my ear. "Tell me what's going on."

The words shivered on the tip of my tongue but never made it out. I couldn't tell him.

I tried to turn my face away from his, but he forced me to look at him.

"Do you also think my mother cheated on my father?" I croaked. It wasn't what had set me off, but it was troubling me almost equally.

The tension burst from his taut features in time with his breaths. "You have his dimples. And his smile."

Were dimples and smiles proof of genetic affiliation?

He caressed the side of my neck. "Is that all that's bothering you?"

I swallowed before I lied, "Yes."

"Good." He smiled, the slow scrape of his nails agonizingly pleasurable.

I shivered, and not because of how good his touch felt, but because I knew, with unfaltering doubt, that the next time his fingers would come in contact with my neck, it wouldn't be to caress it, but to snap it.

FORTY-THREE

L iam left a little after midnight. I'd pretended to have fallen asleep so he wouldn't soil his lips further on mine. The guilt of having let him kiss me was tenfold-worse than the guilt of having drugged Heath.

In the gray hours of the morning, glum thoughts turned my mind the same dull shade as the sky. I got up and walked onto my balcony. A warm wind combed through the tall evergreens, making them shiver, making me shiver. My skin itched to shift, and I let it. I pulled off my tank top and sleep shorts and transformed into my other self, and then I jumped over the balcony and raced away from the inn, not caring if any guest had awakened. They all looked forward to wolf sightings anyway.

The lavender sky was no longer littered with stars, and the air was calm, abuzz with the beating wings of oblivious things. By a stream, I ran into a herd of mule deer. Even though I meant them no harm, their perky ears twitched at my approach. When their large, shiny eyes zeroed in on me, they pranced away in a blur of gray-brown fur.

I watched them leave, like everything else in my life.

Only Evelyn remained.

Evelyn...

I needed to get back to her. I needed to speak to her. But what would I tell her? I hadn't decided what to do. To leave or to stay?

I stared at the horizon.

I *could* run.

Right now, I could run. As a wolf, I'd cover a lot of ground.

But Liam could run too. I had no doubt he'd track my scent with ease. Even if I had hours on him, his legs were so much longer than mine that he'd catch up. And then what?

A fly buzzed by my ear, droning loudly. I flicked my ears.

If I could get away, I'd have to relearn to live only as a human, my body frozen in a single shape. I'd done it once. I could do it again, but did I want to? The need to shift had become visceral, part of me, like the blueness of my irises and the blondeness of my hair.

I watched the horizon as it yellowed and greened, and then I turned and started to run back, savoring each tread of dewy earth, each crunch of crumbling rock, each crush of springy grass. I breathed in heavy lungfuls of the sweet dawn, cherishing them as though each breath were to be my last.

I thought of Liam. Of his mouth and hands. And my muscles swelled with adrenaline. I was thankful for last night. Thankful to have felt desired. I almost wished I hadn't pretended to sleep, that I'd stripped Liam of his clothes and let him peel mine off my body so I would finally know what so many accused me of taking against payment.

But it would've been greedy and unfair.

I was grateful for what we'd shared, even though I was haunted by the hatred he'd feel once he knew who the girl he'd called *perfect* truly was.

Ahead of me stretched the hedge of pines that separated me from the inn like a picket fence. I slowed.

If these were to be my last moments in wolf form, I'd savor each second.

I MADE IT BACK TO the inn without being discovered, leaping onto the little balcony Liam had scaled just a few hours ago. I trotted back into my bedroom, my claws clicking on the hardwood floors, and then I changed back.

Swift as it had appeared, my fur retracted, leaving behind flushed skin. Sweat salted my lips. I licked it away as I pushed off the ground and rose to my feet. I headed toward the shower but stopped when I spotted a folded sheet of paper by my bedroom door. Muscles tensing, I approached and snatched the letter up, unfolding it in the same breath.

IF YOU WANT TO SEE EVELYN AGAIN,

GO THROUGH WITH THE LAST TRIAL.

SPEAK ABOUT THIS NOTE AND SHE DIES.

My fingers turned as cold and hard as ice chips and crimped the paper. I read the words; reread them. The letters blurred and fragmented, then knit back together and smoothed.

Who would do this to me?

Someone who was aware of how much I cared for Evelyn. I'd never made it a secret, but still...how many people possessed this knowledge? She so rarely left the inn that it would have to be someone close to me.

Who could possibly want to blackmail me into killing Liam?

Or was their intention to get *me* killed by Liam?

Could it be Julian? He'd guessed Liam cared about me— made several allusions to it last night—and wouldn't want to murder me, which would force *me* to kill Liam and become the Alpha Julian so desperately desired as an ally.

But Julian didn't know about Evelyn. Or did he? I'd told Sarah about her when we'd had lunch. Had Sarah been spying for her uncle? Was her friendship an act?

My stomach turned as cold as my fingers.

But Julian had seen how determined I was last night. He couldn't possibly know I'd chicken out of the last test. Unless he'd heard what it entailed...

Something hardened inside my mind. Whoever sent me this note knew what the last test would be. They knew blood would be spilled. Mine or Liam's. Whose death were they rooting for?

Lucas hated me and had never hidden how much he wanted Liam to become Alpha. It wouldn't have been difficult for him to find out about my relationship with Evelyn. I could go to him and confess my plan, but if he hadn't sent me the note...

I brought the paper closer to my nose—crushed flowers. The scent could've drifted from the dirt embedded underneath my fingernails. I sniffed the paper again. There was another scent. Something almost sour but also a little sweet. I inhaled so many times that my head started to spin, and all the smells melded together. I crumpled the paper and tossed it against the door.

A violent chill curled around my skin but was soon replaced with heat. My body smoldered with anger. One person would die today...and it wouldn't be me or Evelyn or Liam.

It would be whoever fucking wrote this.

FORTY-FOUR

I tossed on the first things I found in my closet and then flew through my bedroom door.

Evelyn's door was unlocked, her bed unmade. Whoever had taken her had snatched her from sleep, because she always made her bed. I touched the creased pillow—cold. And then I crouched next to the bed. The fabric smelled faintly of menthol but also of something else—cold smoke.

Evelyn didn't smoke.

Which meant her captor did.

My phone vibrated in the back pocket of my shorts. I straightened up, staring at the unknown number flashing on my screen. Could it be the kidnapper?

Slowly, I slid my finger across the screen to answer the call. "Hello."

"Ness? It's Frank."

His voice shrink-wrapped my hope.

"McNamara," he added.

As though I could've forgotten… "What is it, Mr. McNamara?"

"We'd like you to meet us at your father's old factory. The one the Watts took over."

Blood beat against my skin, making every inch of it tingle. Just what I needed. A trip down memory lane. "Why?"

"We need to discuss a...*development* with the pack."

I looked toward the sash windows that gave onto the employee parking lot. When we'd arrived, I'd tried exchanging my room with Evelyn's so she could have a better view, but she insisted that being on the ground floor was better for her. I didn't see how it had benefited her in any way considering she so rarely went out.

The edge of Evelyn's curtain fluttered. I lunged forward and drew it open so briskly a handful of tiny hooks ripped off the metal rod.

Heart twitching, I stepped into the parking lot.

"Ness? Are you still there?" Frank's voice sounded tinny.

"Yeah. I'm here." I shaded my sore eyes from the sun spiking through the fir trees lining the lot and scanned the premises.

"Liam came to speak with us."

My stomach knotted like a climbing rope. Had Liam asked them to cancel the last trial? Had he told them I was ready to concede? What would happen to Evelyn if they voided the contest?

"We need you to come see us. The pack is waiting for you. Your uncle said he could take you."

"Now?"

"Now."

His firm response made my fingers curl hard around the phone. "I'll be there as soon as I can."

The warm air smelled of car exhaust, rancid garbage, and evaporated dew. Dark stains dappled the asphalt. My heart gave a shudder. Forcing my stiff legs to bend, I crouched and sniffed.

Oil.

Not blood.

My phone vibrated with a message from an unknown number. Frank must've forgotten to tell me something.

The message said: **Tick tock.**

Not Frank.

A car honked so shrilly I bounced onto the balls of my feet. A black minivan with the Boulder Inn logo backed into the employee lot. Another honk. The strident sound shrilled in my skull.

"I tried to call your room," Jeb said, leaning out the driver's side window to peer at me. "What are you doing out here?"

"I stopped by to see Evelyn."

I watched his face as I said this. He glanced toward the open window, but didn't ask me how she was doing. Did he know she wasn't there?

"Did Frank get ahold of you? The pack's expecting us at the Watts's warehouse."

"I had him on the phone."

"Are you ready to go?"

No. I wasn't ready, but did I have a choice? I threw open the passenger door and got in.

Tick. Tock. The words echoed through me at the same time as a deafening deliberation. My aunt was a heavy smoker.

"Where's Lucy?"

"She's with Everest."

"Where?" My voice was so brusque my uncle frowned.

"I don't know, Ness."

Could Lucy have taken Evelyn? Forcing me to compete in a death match would be a convenient way of getting rid of me. I stuck my elbow on the door handle and cradled my pounding forehead.

"I wish you'd listened to me." My uncle's voice broke, and a thick sob lurched out of him. "I wish you'd never entered this contest."

I pried my head off my fingertips.

My uncle was crying.

Over *me*.

He was crying over me.

Surprise momentarily displaced my raging edginess.

"I failed your mother," he croaked, wiping his eyes.

I didn't think anyone besides Evelyn would ever mourn my death, but apparently I was wrong. Apparently Uncle Jeb would.

"I'm not dead yet." My words were thin, flat. I couldn't deal with his grief or his remorse. Not now. Maybe not ever. To each their own. "Can we please just go? I want to get this over with…"

That set him off all over again. Hearing a grown man cry used to irk me, but as I sat there, watching the tears drip around his mouth, I was numb.

When he still hadn't started driving, I repeated, "Can we please go?"

He inhaled deeply, stared at my stony expression, and finally…finally started driving.

The world smeared into one long strip of color outside the window. I hadn't taken this road in years. It had changed. There was still the Mom and Pop ice-cream shop with the flickering neon cone and the gas station—empty at this early hour, but new buildings had sprouted on the sunburned grass. All of them carried the word Watt.

August and his father had expanded the business. I was glad it had been so profitable even though seeing their name on those plaques instead of my father's pinched my heart.

The flat-roofed gray warehouse—the original workshop—materialized in the distance. It looked the same as it had the dusty afternoon Mom and I had driven over to hand Nelson the keys and the deed.

Jeb parked in front of the loading bay, which was gaping wide. I climbed out of the van and then closed the door.

A figure stepped out of the shadowy workshop, cutting across the lot.

Liam. Mute sunlight played over his handsome face, danced across his lips.

My heart became very quiet. When he reached out for me, I took a step back. If he touched me, I'd break. Shading my eyes, I stared around the lot, then back at him, at the slant of his eyebrows.

He stared around the lot too. "Are you expecting someone?"

"No," I said fast.

Jeb came around the car. "Morning, Liam."

One glance at my uncle's tear-streaked face, and Liam's eyes widened, as though he understood my moodiness.

"The fight's off," he said. "But only if we both concede."

Uncle Jeb squinted his red-rimmed eyes. "Then who becomes Alpha?"

"Lucas," Liam said.

As though he'd heard his name, Lucas stepped out of the warehouse, his black hair devouring the rays of pale sun.

A chill swept up my spine. If he became Alpha, then Lucas wasn't the one blackmailing me.

Unless he didn't want the title.

No. He wanted it. Even though he wouldn't have willingly taken it from his friend, there was no way he would turn this down.

Maybe it really was Lucy, but wouldn't my uncle be aware of his wife's machinations?

Unless Julian was behind the whole thing.

"You need to tell the elders you're conceding." Liam placed his hand low on my back to guide me into the warehouse. His pressure was light, and yet I felt like his fingers were imprinting into my flesh.

Every set of eyes fixed on me. On Liam. On the place where his palm connected with my body.

The warehouse was so quiet. Or maybe I couldn't hear anything over the deafening sound of my thundering pulse. My phone vibrated in my pocket. I jumped. My gaze sped over every man and boy. I checked their hands for phones. None of them held one.

With rigid fingers, I extricated it from my pocket. The silicone cover caught on the crumpled note, which slipped out and tumbled onto the sprinkling of sawdust like a cluster of down. I watched in horror as my uncle crouched to retrieve it. Time slowed as he rose, the paper tucked in his palm.

The world tipped, and Liam's fingers curled around my waist.

"This fell out." Jeb handed it to me without so much as glancing at it.

My knuckles seemed to have fused with my phalanges, yet somehow, I managed to hold the paper and stuff it back into my pocket.

A groove materialized between Liam's eyebrows. It deepened when I stepped away from him to read my newest text message.

I tried to reason that it could be from anyone.

Maybe it was from August.

The number was unlisted. **I see you.**

Nothing else. Nothing more.

My throat locked up.

Someone touched my shoulder, and I jumped.

"Everything all right?" Jeb asked.

I powered off my phone. If they were watching me, that meant they were here. That meant they no longer had to communicate with me through enigmatic text messages. I wanted to yell at whoever was sick enough to toy with me to man up and step forward, but I didn't yell. I barely breathed.

"Has Liam filled you in on what we're offering?" Frank's white hair frizzed around his leathery face like a halo.

I gave a sharp nod.

Eric frowned at me, light pinging off his bald head. "It's a great sacrifice he's making to save your life."

"Do you forfeit, Ness?" Frank asked.

The cement floor shifted, yet everyone remained upright. The strips of lights on the ceiling droned like wasps. Mouths moved, but voices didn't reach my throbbing eardrums. I wanted to scream *yes, I forfeit*, but the words on my phone seared my corneas.

I. See. You.

Julian wasn't here.

Unless he was seeing me through a surveillance camera.

I swallowed, choking on my saliva. I coughed.

Liam stepped in front of me, face tipped down toward mine. "Ness?"

"No." The world lurched out of me like a bullet. "I don't forfeit."

Liam's gaze cut through me like a knife. "What are you doing?"

"But I want to fight in wolf form because I don't stand a chance in human form." I prayed Evelyn's captor wouldn't figure out the true reason I wanted to fight in wolf form.

"You're a cheat, Ness," Lucas hissed. He stood next to Matt. Matt who'd once looked at me with kindness. There was no more kindness in his green eyes. "If you win this, I will never answer to you."

Matt lowered his gaze and then he turned and stalked away, his big body graying in the shadows of the warehouse.

Frank glanced around him. After the other elders nodded, he said, "We agree to your terms."

"I don't agree to them," Liam blurted out.

"You'd rather fight in skin than fur?" I asked him.

His temper flared. "I'm not fighting you."

"Please."

"Please?" He scraped his hands over his face. "What's wrong with you?"

"Nothing's wrong with me. But something's obviously wrong with you if you don't fight for what you want."

"I *am* fighting for what I want."

That splintered my heart. My lids fluttered closed a moment. *Be strong. Be strong.* When I opened them, my resolve was back. "Should we shift, Mr. McNamara?"

"You may proceed. But remember, conceding will no longer be allowed after this."

I nodded, then kicked off my shoes and yanked off my tank top.

Liam stepped in front of me, blocking the sight of my body with his. He radiated anger. His taut muscles pulsed with it. "Ness, this is crazy."

I unbuttoned my shorts and let them fall to the floor. I didn't bother taking off my bra or underwear. I'd never get them back anyway.

The dead had no use for undergarments. Or any garments for that matter.

Before my teeth turned into fangs, I whispered, "Don't make me wait too long."

And then I dropped on all fours.

Come on, I begged, but all he would hear was a whimper.

As wolves, we understood human speech.

As humans, we didn't understand wolf speech.

I pawed at the sawdust, impatient for him to be able to hear my last confession.

My last apology.

FORTY-FIVE

L iam shouted something at Frank that I didn't try to understand. I was too busy looking around me to see if someone else would shift.

No one shed clothes. No one transformed. Most were too busy gaping between me and Liam.

Sawdust puffed beneath me as a black T-shirt hit the floor. I craned my neck up as Liam kicked off his jeans, swearing beneath his breath.

In seconds, he became a black beast with gleaming eyes.

Don't react at what I'm about to tell you, I said.

His nostrils flared.

I'm being blackmailed. Someone took Evelyn, and they said they would kill her if I didn't go through with the last trial.

He turned so still I bared my fangs and lashed at him, nipping his neck.

Fight me or they'll know I'm talking. I dug the tips of my fangs into his skin. *Damn it, Liam, figh—*

He released a blood-curdling snarl and then tossed me off him with a hard shrug. I yelped as I landed on my haunches, a pale cloud rising around me like smoke.

He advanced toward me.

They sent me a message saying, I see you. *So they're here. Or they're watching me somehow.*

When he started to turn his head—a dead giveaway I was talking—I launched myself on his back like an arrow. He wrung his massive body, and I tumbled off, falling hard on my spine. He stepped over me, pinning me to the ground.

What now? he growled. *'Cause I sure as hell won't kill you.*

Yes, you will.

A deep, guttural sound rose out of him and made my fur stand on end. *The fuck I am!*

You will once you know…once I tell you what I did.

He became as still as an ebony carving. *What did you do?*

I shut my lids so I wouldn't see his reaction. *I…I killed your father.* Nothing happened for so long that I peeked through my lashes at him. *I am the reason he's dead.*

His pupils turned pin-sized. *What are you talking about?*

The crowd tightened around us, but still no one transformed.

I started working at the escort agency to land a meeting with Heath. I knew he wouldn't let me into his house and listen to me otherwise. I wanted to see him to speak my piece. I slipped him three pills—I swallowed, but my throat felt wadded up with cotton—*that made it impossible for him to shift. And then I told him that I knew what he'd done to Becca Howard…to my mother.*

Shock rushed over Liam's features, but soon that shock turned into something else. Something that whittled his expression. *What did he do to your mother?*

He didn't ask about Becca, which meant he already knew.

When she begged him to let me into the pack and train me, he…he raped her. I dragged in a rough breath. *I hated your father, Liam, but I never meant to kill him. It truly was an accident. If I could rewind…if I could just—*

Ness, my father didn't die because of any drug.

I know how he died, Liam. I know he drowned. My eyes were so hot that the cold air made them sting. *But he drowned because of their effect.*

You think he fell into his pool and somehow spasmed to death? His gravelly voice turned almost shrill. *Oh, Ness...* He nudged my cheek with his wet nose.

But Everest said—

What did he say? His tone was as dark as his glistening fur.

I didn't answer him. I couldn't. My throat had squeezed as tight as a fist.

My father did die in his pool, but he was strangled to death with a silver cord.

The air eddied between us, cold and hot, loud and silent.

Strangled? I whispered.

Your pills might've slowed him down, but they didn't kill him. Liam's large black face dipped heavily. In a slow, even voice, he added, *I wondered why my father hadn't shifted.* And then, *Everest knew about the pills, didn't he?*

He suggested them. I only wanted to give your father one, but Everest recommended three. He told me Alphas weren't built like normal wolves.

Suddenly, everything made sense. How quickly Everest had been to blame me. How swiftly he'd pushed me toward the enemy pack to make me look like a traitor. How he'd up and left Boulder. Why he'd blackmailed me to compete in the last trial.

My death would mean his secret was safe.

Liam's death would mean my cousin would be free of retaliation.

What he hadn't counted on was for me to figure it out and share my findings with Heath's son.

My head swam, but my heart, it shot up from the depths it had been wallowing in. *I have to go. I have to go.* I tried to wriggle out from underneath him, but he pinned one of my shoulders with his giant forepaws. *Liam, I have to go! Let me go! Everest took Evelyn. I have to save her.*

I spun my face to see my uncle. He was watching on as intently and curiously as the others. Was he in on his son's scheme? Was he the one who *saw* me?

I writhed, but Liam wouldn't get off me. I snarled at him. *I need to find her.*

I'll go with you.

You come with me and they'll know I talked.

What am I supposed to do? Let you leave to face Everest on your own?

Yes.

No. His yellow eyes sparked like fire.

He'll kill Evelyn if you come with me.

He might kill her and *you if I let you go on your own.*

We're wasting time. I writhed like a snake. *You want to help me?* I growled. *Then shift back and tell them I'm running away since I can't forfeit. That'll give me time to find her, and it will lead Everest astray.*

Ness—

I spun so briskly to the side that he faltered. He tried to trap me again but ended up swiping his paw across my face, his claws catching in my cheek. The wound wasn't deep, but it stung.

Liam folded his ears back. *Shit.*

I could see my reflection in his gaze; I could see the red seeping over the white. Using his surprise, I flipped onto my stomach, my cheek weeping blood on the cement floor, and leaped out from underneath him.

I burst into the sunlight, speeding away from the boy who made my heart beat fiercely, from the warehouse that held cherished moments of my childhood, from the pack I'd wanted to become a part of even though I'd claimed otherwise.

FORTY-SIX

L iam didn't come after me, which led me to think he'd changed back to his human form and indulged my plea. I prayed his explanation would get back to Everest, and that he wouldn't hold my supposed desertion against Evelyn.

I flew toward the inn like a lightning bolt, pounding the earth so violently I thought my heart would crack. The urgency and the adrenaline dimmed the horror of what I'd just learned...of what my cousin had done.

When I reached the inn's property line, I slowed to make sure there weren't too many humans but then realized I was wasting precious minutes. To hell with sightings. I was not an impressive creature, not like Liam and the rest of the boys. They couldn't pass for real wolves; I could. I muscled my way through the prickly fir trees and bounded into the parking lot. Evelyn's sash window still gaped wide.

As I trotted toward it, I lowered my nose to the hot asphalt and inhaled. There it was again. The ashen scent of a crushed cigarette laced with Evelyn's minty ointment. Everest didn't smoke... Or did he? Did I even know my cousin?

The odor of arthritis cream ran the length of the parking lot, tempered with that of gasoline fumes. He'd taken Evelyn in a car. How was I supposed to trail a car?

I ran, but not fast, clinging to the edge of the road. I discovered a cigarette butt, coated in dry saliva, then picked up more hints of Evelyn's salve. I prayed it wasn't my addled mind conjuring up smells that weren't there.

The sun baked my hide, but thankfully, the whiteness of my fur repelled some of the heat. I walked and walked, losing the invisible trail more than once, but retrieving it each time. Like a fractured chain, it hung in the stifling air. The only explanation I could come up with was that her captor had left the car window open.

A fork split the road in half. I smelled the air but froze as I took in my surroundings.

No…

NO!

I'd followed an old scent. Despair limning my vision, I stared at the steep hill with the pockmarked road that led to my childhood home. My heart thudded. I backed away but stepped in a spot of mud that sucked at my hind paw. I yanked my leg free, noticing tread marks beneath my paw print.

Fresh tread marks.

A car *had* come by here.

Maybe I hadn't followed an old trail.

I sped up the hill, pulse lurching savagely. Tucked behind the house was a black minivan with the Boulder Inn logo. Part of me had held out hope that I'd been wrong. That it wasn't my own family that had done this to me. The van trampled that hope.

Wolves didn't have goose bumps, yet my fur tingled with thousands.

I swayed but steeled my nerves as I inched closer to the house, ears perked up for sound. Through the grimy window of my old living room, I caught a sight that sucked all the oxygen from the air.

Evelyn was strapped to a chair, her snarled black hair spilling over her hunched shoulders. My eyesight narrowed as I took in her legs hooked to the chair rungs with duct tape, her arms taut and stretched backward, her hands bound with a zip tie. I tried to see her chest, see if it still rose and fell, but she was angled away from me.

The desire to sink my fangs into flesh and spill blood seized me so hard my muscles jerked.

One of Evelyn's fingers twitched.

She wasn't dead!

A voice, scratchy yet feminine, rose from within. "She didn't go through with the trial."

My vision blurred and sharpened.

Lucy!

I circled around my house toward the broken window pane of my bedroom. The second the crackled glass would fall against the hardwood floor, Lucy would know I was here.

My stomach seized as the scent of cigarettes and menthol blasted into my pulsing nostrils.

Now!

Glass bit into my flesh and rained over the floor.

Something thumped lightly in the living room. And then everything turned quiet-quiet. I lunged toward my open door and shoved it wide, claws skittering over wood. My aunt's mouth rounded with a gasp as I leaped onto her, slamming her against the floor. Her skull cracked like an eggshell, or maybe it was one of the bones in her body because her eyes were still wide, still seeing. I bared my teeth and growled.

The sharp tang of urine and fear filled the room.

"Ness!" she shouted, but it sounded like static to my buzzing ears.

I barked, and she blinked wildly.

Suddenly, something collided into my side and tore me off my aunt's heaving, urine-soaked body.

FORTY-SEVEN

I was half expecting to see my cousin, but it wasn't Everest who'd flung me off Lucy; it was Liam. He'd caged her underneath his massive furred body.

What are you doing? I hissed.

Lucy was muttering, "It's not what you think."

He growled at her so roughly she shut up and turned as white as the towels I'd laundered for her day after day.

Liam spun his face toward me. *We need to find Everest, and Jeb doesn't know where he is, but I bet she does.*

I stared at him wide-eyed. My uncle wasn't in on it? How could he not have known? How—

The others are on their way.

I turned toward the wrap-around windows, and sure enough, vehicles were rolling up the drive. Suddenly, the room was filled with human bodies.

Frank rushed toward Evelyn, who was shaking with sobs. The second he freed her, she slung her arms around his neck. He whispered into her ear words I couldn't pick up. And then he kissed her cheek.

And she let him.

But then Liam stepped in front of me and blocked out the rest of the room. He licked my cheek, and the warm wetness stung, and then he tried to lick my shoulder, and I realized he was trying to get the blood off me.

I shoved him aside. I'd tend to my injuries later. First, I needed to ascertain Evelyn wasn't hurt.

Cole and Lucas were hauling Lucy up. I felt them look my way, but I didn't look at them, utterly focused on Evelyn. She released Frank and limped toward me. Slowly, she kneeled, pain excavating each one of her wrinkles, and then she extended her arms, and I walked into her embrace.

I trembled when her fingers combed through my fur.

"*Querida*," she murmured croakily. "She told me you needed me, that you were here." She took my face in her hands, then pressed her forehead to mine. "*Lo siento*. I am so sorry for going with her." Evelyn swept her shaky, dry palms over my muzzle.

A bone-deep shudder raked across my body, and tears skimmed off my eyes, tangled with my bloodied fur. Fear, relief, anger, and tension swept through me in waves.

Evelyn was safe.

She was safe.

I tried to tell her I loved her but remembered I was still a wolf. She wouldn't understand me. And then I realized this was the first time she saw me in my beast form, and I froze.

She threaded her shaky fingers through my fur again, stroking my neck over and over.

She wasn't running off, screaming.

I relaxed into her embrace, but then a hand touched my haunches. I snatched my head out of Evelyn's hands and snarled at the person who'd dared pet me. Frank pulled his arm back to his side, as though fearing I would bite.

I licked Evelyn's hand. She stared at the skin my tongue had touched, then stared at me, and I felt like I'd done something wrong. But then her pallid face split with a startled smile, and she wrapped her arms around my neck and crushed me against her.

Her scent rushed through me, reaching the places her arms couldn't, and like the petals on a limp rose, my wolf form tumbled off my spent body.

Several things happened at once. Evelyn gasped. The air turned colder. A shirt whispered over my naked backside. A loud voice rose over all the others, demanding that everyone get out. Frank's. Large hands lifted Evelyn and helped her back to the couch, and then those same large, papery hands wrapped around my taut and trembling arms.

"Someone, get her clothes!" Frank's frantic voice reverberated off the cracked plaster walls. "I'm so sorry. We didn't know."

I bobbed my head, half nod, half tremble.

Frank rose and someone else crouched in front of my huddled, naked form. *Liam.*

"Here," he said.

I kept my eyes on the dusty, water-stained wooden slats my father would oil every two years. Whoever had bought our house hadn't cared for it at all.

Liam fit a roomy T-shirt over my head, then lifted my hands one after the other and guided them through the sleeves. He tugged the hem low over my thighs. And then he crooked my chin on a finger to make me look at him.

"She's safe, Ness. You saved her." He smoothed my hair back, and then he collected my trembling body against his solid one, and held me.

The room swayed and then it blurred and darkened before finally vanishing completely.

FORTY-EIGHT

I sprang awake so fast my head spun and my vision fragmented. "Evelyn!"

"I am right here, *querida*." She eased me back down, then leaned over me, her fingertips curving over the sides of my face, tracking over each one of my features.

I blinked at her. "You're okay?"

"I am okay."

"Did Lucy...did she hurt you?" I whispered.

"No."

I closed my eyes and saw my aunt's protruding eyes, saw Evelyn hunched in a chair. I forced my lids up. My mouth tasted sour, and my body reeked of wet-dog. I stretched my arms and legs then sat up, slower this time, my cheek pulsing. I lifted my fingers and felt a patch of puckered skin.

Evelyn wrapped her hands around my bicep. Although I didn't require her support, I let her guide me to the bathroom...I let her tend to me. She closed the lid of the toilet and sat me down. As she warmed the water, I peeled my T-shirt and shorts away. I didn't remember putting them on.

When steam curled up from the shower nozzle, I stepped into the bathtub, sat, and raised my face, letting the hot water beat down on me. Evelyn squirted soap into her hands and cleaned my body. And then she rubbed shampoo between her palms and washed my hair. She lathered in conditioner next, her careful fingers working out the knots.

She rinsed and rinsed and then turned off the water. As she picked up a towel, I clamped my fingers around the rim of the bathtub and heaved myself up and out. She patted down my body and then my hair, and I felt like I was a toddler all over again. She forced me to sit back down on the closed lid and went to get me clean clothes: leggings and a tank top. I pulled both on. She dried my hair some more and then combed it out.

As I stood, the world spun a little, and my stomach rumbled as though it hadn't been fed in days instead of hours.

"You need to eat something." She steered me to the armchair that was creased and warmed from her body. "Sit here and don't move."

"I won't." I leaned my head back and shut my eyes, relishing the tranquility.

Sometime later, she was back with thick slices of chewy bread topped with thin slivers of turkey. I ate slowly, the food dropping into my stomach like clumps of blizzard snow. Evelyn pulled the sheets off my bed and tucked in new ones. For a long time, the rustle of fabric and the floorboards creaking under Evelyn's lopsided footsteps were the only sounds inside the room. I thought about the day. About Lucy and Everest and Jeb. And that made me think of what my uncle had insinuated.

She was fluffing my pillows when I finally spoke. "Evelyn?"

"Yes?"

I peeled a piece of crust off the bread and shredded it into dark dust between my fingers. "Can I ask you something?"

Like an articulated toy, she straightened out. "Anything."

"Is your real name…is it Evelyn?"

Even though her pupils were almost indistinguishable from her irises, I saw them pulse, or maybe I sensed them pulse. For seconds that stretched into full minutes, she stared at me. Then her gaze moved off mine, settling on a spot beyond my shoulder. Her long lashes swooped down and skimmed her pallid cheeks.

I hadn't wanted to believe Jeb; I still didn't want to believe him. But her evasion… "Who's Gloria?"

The silence turned barbed. Slowly, she raised her lashes. Tears burned in her eyes as brightly as the stars blazing in the night sky behind her. The plate slid off my knees. It didn't crack, but crumbs peppered the rug, and the remaining slices of turkey dropped like crumpled tissues.

She sat on the foot of the bed and linked her hands in her lap, her black hair falling around her lowered face.

"You're Gloria, aren't you?" I murmured at the same time as she said, "I am sorry."

Heartache bloomed inside my chest. I hadn't wanted my uncle to be right.

I blinked away the sudden blurriness. "Was it a coincidence we met?"

She shook her head.

I gripped the armrests.

Her lips trembled behind the fence of bottle-black strands draped around her face. "It does not change the way I feel about you, Ness."

I studied the perfect arc of light cast by my nightstand lamp on my white wall. "Just tell me everything."

Evelyn—no, not Evelyn—*Gloria* sat up straighter. "My name *used to be* Gloria. I changed it to Evelyn so my husband wouldn't find me."

I frowned. *Husband?*

"I was born in Mexico, but I moved to the U.S. as a child. To pay for college, I took up housekeeping jobs. That is how I met...*him*. I married him for papers, and he married me because his grandmother refused to give him access to his trust fund as long as he was a bachelor."

My gaze leaped off the wall and back onto her.

"The romantic in me believed that maybe we would fall in love. He was handsome and well-educated, but he had a lot of secrets. Dark secrets. He would spend most of his days locked in his office, and when he left the house, he would lock the door. I became so terrified of him that I confronted him." Her mouth set in a grim line. "He told me that if I ever questioned him again...if I ever went into his office, he would have me deported, so I stopped prying and kept my distance. Well, as much distance as you can put between two people sharing a house.

"One day he forgot to lock his office door. I feared it was a trap and almost did not go inside, but I was desperate to know what sort of man I was living with. What if he was a serial killer? Or a terrorist?

"It *was* a trap. He caught me before I could find anything, and then he blackmailed me. He said that if I wanted to stay in America, I had to do something for him." She turned to look out the window. "He made me seduce a man. That man was Frank McNamara."

Shock pinned me in my seat. "Frank?" The memory of their encounter before the music festival flashed inside my mind. And then the kiss he'd placed on her cheek earlier...

"You're from here?" I croaked.

Without turning away from the window, she nodded. "I was so scared, Ness, that I did as my husband told me. Frank was a married man. Seducing him went against all of my beliefs." She held a knuckle underneath her nose and drew in juddering breaths. "Frank fell for my act. But soon it was no longer an act." She closed her eyes, and a tear slid down her pale cheek. "We fell in love, and I told Frank the truth. And it was terrible."

She bit her lip that had started to tremble.

"After I told Frank the location of all the listening devices I had planted, he made me leave. I went back to the house I hated, to the man I detested. I only had months left to get my papers, but I could not stay so I packed my bags. My husband came home then. He already knew I had removed the surveillance equipment. I told him I was done. He said he would call the police, and I told him I no longer cared. I made the mistake of turning my back on him."

She stretched her bad leg in front of her.

"He shot me. The bullet was meant for my heart, but a wolf attacked him, and he missed. And then Frank was beside me. I do not remember much, but I do remember something...something that did not make sense until a couple days ago. I remember seeing the wolf turn into a man. For years—decades—I thought it was a delusion brought on by loss of blood."

Her voice broke on a sob and then on another. For a long moment, she wept.

"I had deceived Frank, spied on him, and yet he saved me."

Every fiber of my being urged me to go over to her, but my muscles had gelled with shock.

"He took me to a man who fixed my leg as best he could, and then he drove me out of Colorado and into Arizona. He had a great aunt who lived in Tucson. He asked her to take me in, and she agreed. She was such a kind lady."

Evelyn—*Gloria*—rubbed her hands together slowly, the same way she did when her palms were dusted in flour.

"Before he left, he got me new papers. I became Evelyn Monroe. I lived with his great aunt for many years, and during all those years, Frank visited only once. For her funeral." She closed her eyes and inhaled a deep sigh. "Frank allowed me to live there, in his house, many more years. I cleaned stores and offices but never made enough money to pay him back for all he had done for me.

"He came back into my life six years ago. I thought he was bringing me news of my husband. That he had finally died." She looked up at me. "But it was not that. He came for a favor, which I agreed to. I would do anything for this man."

My ribs trembled from the rapid drumming of my heart. I knew what was coming.

"He asked me to move to Los Angeles to watch over you and your mother. He knew that if he sent anyone else to care for you, your mother would have made you move. He did not want to lose sight of you. He did not tell me why you were important. Not that he needed to explain himself to me. Especially not after telling me..."

Silence as thick as my duvet settled between us.

"What did he tell you?" I whispered.

She raised her eyes to mine. Like moonlit ponds, their black depths shivered. "That it was my husband's fault you had to leave Boulder."

My mind whirred with rapid calculations. None of them made sense, and yet I asked, "You were Heath's wife?" Had he had a second wife?

"No, *querida*. I was married to another monster."

There was a more monstrous man than Heath Kolane?

She pursed her lips in shame. "I was married to the man who shot your father."

I swallowed, and my throat smarted as though I had consumed shards of glass, then I sputtered as though the glass had embedded itself into my lungs.

"*El diablo*."

I couldn't draw a full breath. "Y-You were married t-to Aidan Michaels?"

"Keep away from him, you hear me?"

I gave a sharp nod. The dinner I'd sat through made me want to throw up. "Is that why you don't leave the inn?"

She squeezed her lips. "*Sí*."

"You shouldn't have come back here, Evel— I mean, Gloria."

"Do not call me Gloria. I am not her anymore." She stood, walked toward me, then took a seat again, this time in front of me. She held her hands out, palms up. When I didn't touch them, she said, "I might have found you for the wrong reasons, but please do not doubt how much I love you. You are like a granddaughter to me, Ness."

My throat clenched.

"Please, *querida*, do not hate me for my lies. I cannot lose you. *Te quiero tanto…*"

My heart bounded in time with my hands that landed on Evelyn's. She closed her fingers around mine as though afraid I might change my mind, but I wouldn't. I could never change my mind. It didn't matter how she got into my life. What mattered was what she'd done since she'd been in it, and all she'd done was love me. As deeply and fiercely as my parents had.

I had so many more questions, but one took precedent over the others. "You really didn't know what I was?"

A slow smile curved her lips. "No. I did not know that men or women could change into wolves."

"Frank never told you?"

"No. After the night he saved me, I never dared ask him. I think part of me did not want to know the truth." Her mouth stayed curved a while longer. But slowly, her lips settled back into a soft line. "He came by to check on you a few hours ago." Her thumbs traced the tops of my hands. "He asked me to convince you to join the...*pack*."

I inhaled so sharply the air seared my nostrils. Was this a possibility now?

"I told him I would do no such thing. That it had to be your decision. But..." She tapped her thumbs on the back of my rigid hands.

"But...?"

"But I think you should consider it. I worry for you, *querida*. I worry that without the pack's protection, someone could hurt you."

"My father had the pack's protection, and he's dead."

Her thumbs stilled as horror leached the color from her already insipid skin.

"The pack can't protect me from everything, Evelyn. Look at what my own family did. To you." *To me*. Did she know that Everest had made me take the fall for his crime?

"I suppose you are right." She fell silent for a long moment, her eyes directed on the crescents she was sketching over my skin. "Frank says my ex-husband did not murder Heath, but I think he says this to reassure me. It is probably just my imagination." She exhaled a deep sigh. "What a relief that you know everything. What a relief."

I trembled to tell her the truth about Heath—if only to reassure her that it wasn't the monster she'd married who'd killed him.

I was about to launch into that convoluted story when she said, "Liam is outside. He has been waiting to speak with you all day."

I jerked my gaze toward my balcony.

The corners of her lips tipped up further, and then she laughed. "You think I would let a man linger outside your bedroom?" She shook her head. "He has been waiting for you on the inn's porch all day. Frank came, but so did Liam...so did Liam."

FORTY-NINE

I didn't run off right away after Evelyn left. I spent long minutes processing everything she'd told me, coming to terms with the facts that our encounter hadn't been motivated by a random act of kindness; that she'd once been married to the man who'd killed my father; that Frank had cared enough to send someone to watch over me. I'd been convinced everyone in the Boulder Pack detested me.

My heart sped up when I closed my fingers over the doorknob and turned it. The walk down the carpeted corridor seemed interminable, and my lightheadedness made the floor feel as though it were swinging like in a fun house. Several times I had to lean against the wainscoting to steady myself.

The cavernous living room was dimly lit and occupied with a couple of guests sipping wine. I was surprised the inn hadn't been shut down after what had happened. Was Jeb even here?

I scanned the terrace for Liam, found him leaning over the balustrade. I stared at him for a long moment, watched how the white moon delineated his long body. The summer night was warm and frosted with a perfect round moon.

The elders must be running with the pack. It was strange to think there would come a time when I could no longer change at will.

Liam hadn't sensed me yet, or maybe he had but didn't dare acknowledge me, afraid to spook me. I walked over to him slowly, then placed my forearms over the balustrade even slower.

He kept his gaze fixed to the sprawling, jeweled immensity stretching before us. "I'm sorry, Ness."

"What are you sorry for?"

"For not catching Everest before he fled. For what my father did to your mother. For having rejected your plea to enter our pack after your father died. For hurting you." He touched my cheek, the marks he'd clawed there, then his gaze dipped lower, and I knew he was apologizing for another night.

"I incapacitated your father, Liam. And then I went after something you wanted just to annoy you. If anyone needs to apologize, it's me." I surveyed the gentle sway of the tall pines that were almost as green as during daylight in this bright darkness. "To think I befriended Julian because Everest told me the Pine Alpha could protect me from your retaliation once you found out what I'd done." My eyes were so hot that the cold air made them sting.

He shifted so that his entire body faced mine. "Is that why? I thought you were having an affair with him."

"God, no." I shuddered.

He mistook my shivers for a chill and coasted his hands up my bare arms. That just made me shiver harder.

He frowned. "Are you cold?"

"No."

A smile started on his face. He glided one of his palms over my shoulder, toward my neck, settling his thumb in the hollow of my collarbone. His four other fingers rested lightly on the knobs of my spine. My frenzied pulse pounded against the pad of his thumb.

"You know, the night it happened—probably moments after you left—my father called me. He was agitated and drunk. And angry. Really angry. He ordered me to set fire to the inn. He said your family would be the pack's downfall. I told him he was drunk and crazy, and that no one was setting fire to anything. And then he called me a coward. A coward like my mother. And then he said—" His fingers clenched almost painfully around my neck.

I wrapped my hand around his and dragged it away.

His lids slipped shut.

"What did he say?" I murmured.

He squashed his lips hard. So hard I thought they would never open again. But they did. "He said that he'd hoped getting rid of her would make me more of a man."

My hand froze against his. "Getting rid of—"

"Dad would beat Mom. Often. The night she died..." His voice juddered. I squeezed his hand to steady him. "They fought because of something I did." His voice broke on a strangled sob. He pressed his lips tight again, but again, they reopened along with eyes blackened by tears. "I always suspected that he'd beaten my mother to death, but I'd never known it for certain. Not until he confessed to it. I lost my shit then. I told him I would kill him. And then I hung up."

My heart shattered like Liam's stance. He sagged against me, sobs rolling out of him. I wasn't sure if they were for his father or for his mother. I led him to an Adirondack before the weight of his sorrow could knock us both over. He pulled me down with him and hugged me like a frightened child hugged their mother, clutching the fabric of my tank, crying against my collarbone.

Liam's sobs finally subsided, but he didn't raise his face from where it pressed against me. "Lucas and August had been sitting next to me, so when my father was found floating in his pool mere hours later, they were convinced I'd killed him. They went so far as to discuss this with Frank. I went ape-shit crazy on them and carried out my own investigation. I hired a PI and had him look into you. I'd smelled you on my father's couch. I didn't think you'd killed him—at least not alone."

I ran my fingers through his hair, hoping my touch could soothe him a little.

"It took Everest leaving town for it to suddenly click into place. I'd learned about Becca by then and made the connection. And then, when Frank told me Everest had stolen the Boulder relic—"

"Everest stole it?"

He nodded.

"Why?"

"I'm not sure. For leverage?" He sighed, and his warm breath pulsed against my skin. "Tomorrow, I'll start looking for him, but tonight… Tonight, I want to spend the night not thinking about my father. Not thinking about Everest. Not thinking about the heart attack you gave me when you asked me to end your life…"

He released the fabric of my tank top and gazed up at me, his hands finding purchase on the small of my back. His breaths slowed, evening out. The heat of them raised goose bumps *everywhere*.

I was suddenly conscious that it wasn't a child who was holding me, and my fingers faltered. His lips connected with the sharp bone in my shoulder and stayed there—not quite a kiss. I never thought a shoulder could be so sensitive, but every nerve ending in my body converged in that one spot.

He raised a hand to the base of my skull and tugged my face infinitesimally closer.

"Frank wants me to join the pack," I blurted out.

"He's not the only one."

With the tip of his index finger, he traced a line down the center of my face, down the middle of my throat, stopping only once his finger reached the patch of skin underneath which my heart beat a fevered rhythm. He spread his fingers and pressed his palm there.

"You really think Frank would have had us fight to the death?" I asked, my voice a little hoarse.

"Probably not, but there was no way I was going to risk your life to find out."

His eyes glimmered in the violet darkness, reflecting the sheet of stars suspended over our heads.

He leaned toward me and fit his lips to mine. The fragrance of his skin tangled with that of the forest and of the moon and of the warm earth. His hold became crushing as his mouth parted mine, as his tongue twirled around mine.

Liam kissed the same way he did everything else in his life, with a deep, savage, territorial hunger.

In the distance, a wolf howled, and I swear my body responded, my skin bristled. Liam's too. Soft, hot skin transformed beneath my fingers into softer fur.

He broke off the kiss to curse.

"Full moon," he explained.

I frowned.

"It makes our bodies crave turning more than anything else."

I was pretty sure I craved *him* more than anything.

"Fuck it. I'd rather stay in skin tonight."

Another howl tore through the dark fabric of the night, alluring and deep, an invitation. My fingers tapered into curved claws. Liam's eyes glowed an inhuman hue, and the slightest hint of fang appeared over his lip.

"Do you have any plans tomorrow?" I asked him.

He frowned, and his teeth shortened. "No."

"Want to spend the day with me? In human form? We could get to know each other…and not just in the proverbial sense."

Heat stained my jaw.

He pushed a strand of hair off my face. "I didn't think Ness Clark ever blushed." He placed a kiss on the base of my neck.

I shuddered. "Run. I need to run."

"Hmm…is that what you need?"

I swatted his shoulder, and he winked. Tightening his grip around my waist, he stood, then set me down.

Another howl punctured the night.

Liam weaved his fingers through mine, and then together, we raced down the staircase that was carved in the side of the wide deck and crossed the moonlit field.

Someone yelled for us to watch out for the wolves. I glanced back at the inn, my hair whipping my face. Guests stood against the railing, gazes plunged on the forest beyond. Their mouths moved, but we could no longer hear them. I guessed they were discussing the reckless girl and boy running toward certain death.

I understood then why the pack hadn't avenged my father. What would these people do to us if they found out magic ran in our blood? Would they be holding rifles loaded with silver bullets or recording devices?

Neither scenario was pleasing.

And yet letting a man like Aidan Michaels live was the least pleasing of all.

FIFTY

I n the cover of the forest, Liam stripped. My gaze caught on the perfect shape of his anatomy. It wasn't the first time he'd been naked in front of me, but it was the first time I let my gaze slip lower than the sharp dents at his waist.

"Your turn."

I jerked my gaze up to his face. He was smiling, his incandescent eyes more yellow than brown, burning a path straight for me.

"R-Right." I needed to get naked to change or I would have no more clothes left in my wardrobe. Checking that no other sets of eyes glowed my way, I awkwardly removed my tank top, getting my hair stuck in the process.

Not that he'd been far away, but Liam stepped in closer and reached over my bare shoulders to help me untangle the mess of cotton and blonde strands. His chest brushed against my bare breasts. I could tell it was calculated because after he tossed my tank top on the ground, he moved again...

And again...

"Need help with your leggings?" His voice was as soft and husky as a caress.

"No," I breathed, hooking my fingers into the elastic waistband. "Turn around."

His pupils pulsed. "Really?"

"Really."

"I've seen you naked, Ness."

I was about to ask when but remembered. The first trial. He'd been the one to carry me back to the inn. If he'd seen me, it probably meant the rest of the pack had had an eyeful too. *Damn*.

"I was unconscious, so it doesn't count."

He shot me a crooked smile, and ever so slowly, he turned, smearing a hot trail across my navel that glistened in the moonlight falling around the pine branches.

When seconds passed, and I hadn't looked away from the mark he'd left on me, he asked, "Are you sure you don't need my help?"

I hurried to remove my leggings, kicking them aside. However turned on I was, my first time wouldn't be in the middle of the woods against a tree. I shut my eyes and flipped that small switch that transformed me from human to animal. When I blinked, I was on all fours beside a looming dark beast. He nuzzled my neck, and it sent a delicious shiver down my spine. Although chaste, the gesture felt almost as intimate as a kiss.

Liam tipped his face toward the sky and let out a long howl. A moment later, a deep keening answered us. The pack was on the Flatirons.

We took off toward them, Liam gentling his speed to match my own. Every so often, I would stop watching the dark forest floor and glance over at him. The irony of how much I enjoyed running beside him and being with him didn't escape me. I'd spent my formative years despising both Kolane men, believing they were equal in deserving my contempt.

Son and father were nothing alike.

As Liam ran, he looked at me, his eyes glowing so bright they resembled fragments of stars. *Did anything ever happen between August and you?*

His question made me trip and stumble on a sliver of rock that nicked my hock. Liam stopped so suddenly his claws dug into the earth and raised dark dust. Startled, it took me a second to regain my footing.

He bent his long neck toward the warm trickle seeping from the slice on my hind leg and licked the blood away. Again, my whole body quivered.

No. Nothing ever happened, I finally said. *But it's not the first time you ask. Why don't you believe me? Did August say something?*

He shook his head. *I smelled you on him the night he left.*

Weird. But then I remembered my last meeting with August in the laundry room. *I did hug him.*

The fur on Liam's forehead rippled with a frown. *He smelled like you'd mated.*

I blinked at him. *You mean, like we'd had sex?*

He looked off into the distance, as though embarrassed to be asking this question.

Liam, I've never had sex with August, or with anyone else for that matter.

He swung his head back toward me. Gone was his embarrassment. In its place was pure astonishment.

Oh, God, he really thought I'd whored myself off.

Never? He took a step closer, and his nose bumped into mine.

I only became an escort to meet your father.

And Aidan.

Ugh. My shoulders tightened at the sound of his name. *Dinner with him was an accident. Well, not an accident. I told the escort agency I was no longer interested, but apparently Aidan insisted on meeting me. I said no, but he offered three thousand dollars. I regret every second of that dinner.*

You were so mad when I dragged you out.

Because you think I would've admitted to you how relieved I was? I was still convinced you were the devil's spawn.

His eyes turned somber. *I was...I am.*

I'm sorry. That came out wrong. I—

It's the truth, Ness. My father was a horrible man. He didn't speak for a long while after that. Just drew in breaths, one after another.

I licked his muzzle, and that jolted him out of his dark deliberations. *You're* nothing *like him.*

Well isn't this sweet?

Liam whirled around, stepping in front of me to block me from the sight of the whiny-voiced wolf. It didn't take me long to figure out who it was. A skein of wolves spilled out on either side of the creature who'd spoken.

Julian, Liam said tightly.

I thought one of you would be dead by now. Personally, I was hoping it would be you, Kolane. No offense.

Plenty taken, Liam gritted out.

Julian walked around Liam to see me. Not that I was cowering behind Liam. I was just too busy gauging the intentions of the Pines to move a muscle.

Ness, darling, I believe we need to have a little chat.

I searched for Sarah in the lupine faces and thought I saw her, but it could've been one of the other females of Julian's pack.

I lost. Sorry, I said, distracted by the flash of teeth from a dark-brown creature. I'd lay my paw in a snare it was Justin Summix.

Sorry? Well, then so am I. Shall I tell Liam what you did, or would you like to?

Go right ahead.

The brown wolf snarled at me—probably from the lack of respect I was showing his Alpha; I snarled right back.

Julian remained quiet for so long that I finally looked up at him. He was much more impressive in fur than he was in skin, and yet he inspired no fear in me.

Turns out I didn't kill Heath, I said.

After a long moment, he said, *It was Everest, wasn't it?*

It's none of your business, Julian, Liam growled.

An Alpha killer is every Alpha's business.

My father wasn't targeted because he was an Alpha. He was killed because he was a cruel man.

That took Julian a long, long second to process. He was still and silent for such a slow stretch of time that I started to think he would never recover from his shock. *Perhaps I have misjudged you, Liam.*

He had.

Like I had.

Who will become the next Boulder Alpha then? Julian asked.

Lucas Mason, I said.

My answer elicited intakes of breaths and ragged chuffs. I deduced that Lucas wasn't much admired by the Pines. I shared in their antipathy, but he was Liam's friend. Maybe he wasn't as bad as I deemed him to be; or maybe he was, and Liam was blinded by their shared history.

A feminine voice rose above the others. *Ness?*

Sarah? I asked.

Sorry. I was chasing after a rabbit. She advanced toward us, her wavy gold fur gleaming with sweat and moonlight. *What did I miss?* Blood was smeared over her smile. She licked her muzzle.

Lucas Mason will be sworn in as the next Boulder Alpha, Julian said.

No effing way, she said in a low, rumbling voice.

She stopped beside me, sniffed the air, then sniffed my fur. She frowned, and then her eyes snapped very wide.

Lots of surprises in the Boulder Pack tonight, huh? A wolfish pout-smile flourished over the Pine Alpha's face. *Word of advice, in fur, it is equally pleasurable.*

My body temperature soared so fast the air around me surely trembled. Sarah made a noise that sounded like a chuckle. I shot her a death-glare. She was still laughing softly when Julian called her away.

Julian, why did Everest give you the Boulder relic? I asked.

He stopped and turned his neck to face me. *He said it was to help you.*

Help me? More like help himself. My cousin didn't care about me. He'd been willing to sacrifice me.

May you have a truly enjoyable night, Julian said, and then he was off.

The sound of paws thundered through the forest as the Pines raced after their Alpha. Liam stared after them in silence for so long that I nipped his neck. He twitched back to life. And then his head curved toward mine.

How will you punish Everest? A gust of wind tickled my fur.

That will be for Lucas to decide.

My stomach writhed with nerves. *He'll kill him…*

Liam watched a bird take flight in the tree above us, disrupting the rustling stillness. *Doesn't he deserve to die?*

I hated my cousin. There was no doubt about that. But did I wish him dead?

He nuzzled a spot next my ear. *Don't worry yourself with that now.*

All thoughts of my cousin puffed out of existence as Liam slid his wet nose down the length of my neck and back, taking the scent of me deep into his lungs.

A delicious shiver ran through me as his hot breaths pulsed against my taut flesh. *You marked me on purpose, didn't you?*

He circled around me, lowering his face to mine. *Are you angry that I want everyone to know you belong to the Boulders?*

How hard my parents had fought for me to belong. How hard I had fought for this myself.

To me? he added raspingly.

No. I pressed my cheek into his jaw, feeling the sprint of heartbeats beneath his black fur.

His pulse matched my own.

That wasn't true.

My pulse wasn't sprinting.

My pulse was dancing.

EPILOGUE

the following day

E ven though I was still undecided whether to pledge myself to Lucas Mason, I decided to attend the ceremony held at the Boulder headquarters.

I was going for Liam. Sure, he promised he was fine about having lost out on the chance to rule the pack, but I believed he was saying this to assuage my guilt.

"Did you think it over?" He reached out across the center console of his car to take my hand in his. His palm was calloused from his midnight run, his nails jagged, and yet it was the gentlest hand I had ever held. "Ness?"

I jerked my gaze away from our twined hands. "What?"

"Please pledge yourself."

I bit on my bottom lip. I would be lying if I said last night, running with a group of men who were like me in every way, except anatomically, hadn't been magical. Because it had been. But how much of that magic was due to Liam?

If he'd been the one to become Alpha…

"Does the offer come with an expiration date?" I asked.

"Of course not, but I want you with me, Ness." He slowed to a stop at a traffic light. The last one before the winding path that led to the headquarters. "Wasn't last night incredible?"

"It was."

"Then why are you hesitating?"

Keeping my gaze fixed on the windshield, I said softly, "It was incredible because of you."

He tugged on my hand, dragging me nearer. "Look at me."

I looked. At his swept-back hair, his dark eyes, his full upper lip, his slightly thinner lower one.

"I once told you about my oldest memory, but I never told you about the memory that's marked me the most. The one that's been playing on a loop in my mind for the past six years. You, tiny, skinny, fragile you, coming into the headquarters and asking us to train you, to accept you."

The memory crimped the edges of my heart. "You all said no. Well, all of you except August, Nelson, and Everest." I tried to snatch my hand from Liam's, but he tightened his grip. "I let you go once—*we* let you go—and it was a mistake. I would love to blame it all on my father, but that would be unfair. Truth is, we were cowards. Almost all of us. We were a brotherhood. We thought having a girl in our midst would change us, would change everything. And it does change everything, Ness, but the Boulders are ready for change.

"A new Alpha will rise tonight. A new era will begin. Be part of it. You are as strong, as cunning, as resilient as the rest of us. And a hell of a lot better to look at."

"Stop it."

"Stop what? Telling you the truth?"

"You already won me over, Liam."

A smile tipped his lips. "And you won over the pack."

I rolled my eyes.

"I'm serious. Matt still talks about how you saved his paw. And then Frank told us about your life in LA, how you cared for your mother until the end, and for Evelyn. And then I caught some of the elders discussing how smart and strong you'd turned out, just like your father, but with your mother's fiery temper."

"Seriously, stop it." I knuckled a tear from the corner of my eye but smiled at the mention of my mother's temper. My mother had always blazed brighter and hotter than most women.

"Ness, you've earned their respect. You've earned everyone's respect."

"Except Lucas's."

Not that Lucas's respect mattered. Lucas didn't matter to me.

"Babe, last night, you let me stay out with them. When I insisted on going back with you, you insisted I stay with them. Lucas's greatest fear is that a girl comes between us."

"That's not seriously his greatest fear...?"

"It sort of is. Lucas lost his parents young."

Lucas had been involved in a car crash a couple years after I was born. A shard of glass had sliced through his eyebrow, leaving behind the nasty scar he still bore. He'd survived because he'd forgotten to wear his seatbelt. His father and mother hadn't been as lucky, and when the car tumbled down into Coot Lake, they hadn't managed to unstrap themselves.

"And then, when his granddad died," Liam continued, "we were all he had left. He doesn't hate you."

I blinked wet eyelashes at Liam. The air shimmered around his face. I blinked again, and the shimmer was gone, but his face remained.

Solid.

Real.

I reached out and touched his jaw. "I'll think about it."

He stopped the car on the side of the road. "You're not still worried about not being a Boulder, are you?"

I bit my lip.

Giving his head a little shake, he leaned over his gearshift and closed the distance between our mouths, forcing my lips to open. The kiss dimmed my gnawing anxiety.

When we pulled apart, the sky was a rosy lavender, and the pines a gilded green.

We drove the rest of the way in silence. I wasn't sure what he was thinking about, too concentrated on all I was thinking about. How I longed to tell my mother about Liam, about the trials, about Frank's invitation to join the pack. I closed my eyes and saw her eyes glitter with a smile. The memory flickered behind my lids like birthday candles. I thought about my father next. About how he'd taught me about constellations and crafted stories of strong, alien, warrior princesses sprinting through clusters of stars. His princesses were always blonde, always had dimples, and always had wide blue eyes, like me. Each night, thanks to his boundless imagination, I would live a new life, on a new planet, face new challenges, new enemies. I wouldn't always be victorious, though. *A loss will teach you more than a win,* Dad would tell me on the nights my alter-ego alien-self returned home to her parents, defeated.

I no longer had parents to run home to when I lost.

But I did have Evelyn.

And now I also had Liam.

He stroked the top of my hand. "We're here."

We rolled through the open rusty fence and parked next to a long row of cars. I smoothed my hair into a knot at the nape of my neck, then tucked my mother's ring into my sky-blue camisole so the gold band rested against my heart.

Liam walked around the front bumper of his car and then collected my hand in his. We strode slowly toward the stone building that glowed with yellow light. Bodies milled inside. Excitement rippled through the glass windows that had been propped open to let the warm July evening in.

When we entered the spacious room, gazes fell on our twined fingers. Liam let go of my hand, snaked his hand around my waist, and tucked me closer.

Matt stepped in front of us, holding out a wicker basket full of razor blades. "Less pain than claws." Liam took one, but I didn't—even though Matt waited a long time for me to change my mind.

"The Alpha will slash the skin over his heart, and the rest of us will slash our wrists then touch them to his chest," Frank was telling the younger ones. I felt him glance my way, and then I felt him glance beyond me, and something shifted in his expression.

A new scent layered itself over the ones rising from the broad bodies around us. One I hadn't smelled in weeks—sawdust and Old Spice. It suddenly nulled all the other smells. My heartbeat fluttered as I glanced over my shoulder, daring to hope August was back.

There he stood, in a dusky corner, body steeped in shadows. When our gazes met, a smile broke over my face. He didn't smile; he froze.

I swiveled back. "You didn't tell me August was coming home."

Liam's jaw set a little tightly. Wasn't he happy to see his friend? His brother?

"Give me a second." I pried Liam's rigid fingers from my waist, then walked toward August who seemed to burrow deeper into the wall behind him. "You came back!"

He palmed his buzzed hair, muscles twisting beneath his dark-copper forearms. "Yeah, but just for the ceremony. I deploy in a few hours." His green irises eddied. "So you and Liam, huh?"

I looked behind me. Saw Liam staring at us, shoulders squared, expression stern. Was he still mad at August for having assumed he'd been involved in Heath's death? Or was Liam jealous?

I took a small step back but felt a hard tug forward that destabilized me. I checked August's hands, assuming he'd held me back, but his hands were shoved deep inside the pockets of his army fatigues.

Frank clapped, and I jumped. "We are all here, so let's begin."

A circle formed around Lucas.

August walked off first, and I felt him distancing himself from me like a mooring line stretching tight. *What the hell?* I returned toward Liam slowly, palm pressed against my navel.

Liam watched August, who'd situated himself across from us, arms crossed firmly, gaze sunk on Lucas.

"Are you okay?" Liam asked me.

I nodded, then added a smile when I noticed my nod hadn't seemed to reassure him.

Lucas slashed one of his wrists. Crimson ribbons of blood leaked down the inside of his forearm.

"Your chest, son," Frank said. "You have to slice here." He tapped two fingers against his heart.

But Lucas disregarded his instruction. He walked over to Liam. "Take off your shirt, Kolane."

A deep groove appeared between Liam's eyebrows. "What are you doing?"

"I'm not taking this from you."

"Lucas, I don't—"

"Shut the fuck up and strip, man." Under his breath, Lucas added, "Never thought I'd say that to you, huh?"

When Liam didn't pull his shirt off, Lucas said, "Hope you weren't too attached to this thing." He yanked on Liam's shirt and sliced through it with the razor blade and then shoved the limp material aside and carved a narrow slit over Liam's heart.

I gasped.

Lucas pressed his wrist to Liam's wound and then kneeled before his friend. "I pledge myself to thee, Liam Kolane, for as long as I shall walk the world in fur. Long may you live and rule."

For a moment no one moved, and then everyone moved at once. Even though men shoved me to get close to Liam, to swap blood with their new leader, he held on tight to my hand, anchoring me at his side.

When it was Augusts's turn, a hush fell over the room. He slashed his wrist, then pressed it to Liam's rising chest. Rivulets of red ran down the carved planes of his stomach, absorbed into the waistband of his jeans, tinting the blue a dark crimson. August didn't speak any words. I supposed words weren't necessary for the magic to bind them together.

He tipped his head toward Liam and then left without so much as a passing glance at me. And again, I felt something tighten behind my belly-button, stretch thinly, coming close to snapping when his pick-up's taillights vanished past the rusted fence.

"May you lead us well, son," Frank said, gripping Liam's shoulder and giving it a short squeeze.

The ceremony took almost an hour for everyone to pledge themselves. When it was Jeb's turn, my uncle walked over, eyes and cheeks more sunken than I'd ever seen them.

He shot me a pained look, then, trembling, he sliced his wrist and touched his blood to Liam's.

"Thank you, Jeb," Liam said.

Jeb's lips quavered, and then his shoulders hunched and he retreated to the back of the room. Frank went to him. I watched them talk, watched my uncle cry as he nursed a reddened tissue around his wrist.

And then I stared back at Liam and pried the razor blade from his grip. He looked at me, at my fingers guiding the blade over my wrist. When blood beaded there, wonder shimmered in his umber eyes.

I pressed my wound to his slashed skin. His chest pumped harder as I spoke my own version of the pledge. "In fur and in skin, I belong to you, Liam Kolane."

He didn't smile, but he caught my wrist in his hand and held it there, against his heart. Something palpitated inside my chest, but it wasn't my heart. It felt as though a link were clicking into place, fastening me to my Alpha.

He raised my wrist to his lips and kissed it. When he brought it back down, his curved lips red with my blood, I heard words in my head, *As I to you*.

I blinked back tears. "I heard you," I whispered hoarsely. "I heard you."

His smile grew and grew, as did the noise level around us. The air vibrated with the thrill and significance of the moment we had all just shared.

My uncle's soft wail snapped me out of my enchantment. I retracted my arm that was still stretched toward Liam and went to Jeb.

"Did you know what Lucy and Everest had planned?" I asked him.

"No." The word came out garbled. "I swear I didn't, Ness."

Suddenly he hugged me, and I let him. I even patted his bowed back.

"I'm so sorry. So sorry," he kept repeating.

And I believed he was.

"I'm so ashamed of what was done to you."

Frank placed a hand on Jeb's shoulder and squeezed. "You're getting blood all over her pretty top." The elder's smile deepened his crow's feet.

Jeb jerked away from me.

"Don't worry. Evelyn taught me a foolproof way to wash blood out of clothing," I said.

"Meat tenderizer mixed with water," Frank said.

His answer had me gaping, until I remembered Evelyn's earlier confession.

"Thank you for putting her in my life," I told him.

Jeb frowned so hard his brow scrunched up. "Evelyn?"

"Mr. McNamara sent her to watch over me and Mom."

"What?" Jeb gaped at Frank.

"Ness, please call me Frank. As to Evelyn, she and I share a tumultuous history," Frank explained, which just had Jeb gape wider. At least he was no longer sobbing. "I owed it to Callum to take care of his little girl. He was a good man."

At the mention of his brother, a strangled sound jerked out of Jeb's mouth. He dug his fists into his reddened eyes.

"I'm glad you joined the pack, Ness." Frank touched my cheek, then leaned over and placed a kiss on my forehead. "Welcome to the family."

Little butterflies whirled around my stomach, and I smiled gratefully up at him. "Can I ask you something, Frank? Would you have made us kill each other?"

He smiled a little as he said, "That, you'll never know."

But I did know. His expression told me all I needed to know. Frank wouldn't have made us spill blood. That was something Heath would've done.

I stayed next to my uncle after Frank left. "Where's Lucy?"

Jeb drove the heels of his hands into his reddened eyes. "Eric…Eric locked her up in his basement"—his words were labored—"until she talks. Until she reveals where Everest is hiding."

She'd sooner die than hand over her only son. "What happens if she doesn't talk?"

"They'll make the pack track him down."

I'd meant to her, but I didn't clarify my question. This was hard enough on Jeb.

"Let's hope he went far, far away then," I whispered just loud enough for Jeb to hear.

His puffy eyes widened, as though he couldn't believe I wasn't first in line to rip out his son's jugular.

I wanted answers, and corpses don't talk.

I gave Jeb a tight smile, then started to turn away when he called out my name.

"I have something that belongs to you." He dug through his jeans and produced a key that he tucked into my palm. "It took me a couple years to get the money, but I bought back your house."

That was how Lucy had gotten in…

I pushed that morose insight away as he continued, "It's in your name."

"I can't—"

"You can."

"But it'll take me years to pay you back."

"It's a gift."

"Jeb…"

He closed his fingers around mine, forcing the key into my palm. "I couldn't prevent Aidan from killing my brother. I couldn't prevent Heath from hurting your mother. And more recently I couldn't prevent my wife and son from using you to terrible ends. Let me make amends."

"But none of those things were your fault."

"Please, Ness. Please take it. It's in a dire state, but Nelson said he could help you. Or maybe August—"

"Thank you." Heat blurred the sight of his pale features. "What'll happen to the inn?"

He sniffed. "It'll keep running. I'll hire a new manager." He stared down at his brown loafers. "Maybe after the summer, maybe I'll close it down for a little while. I don't know yet."

I supposed working would keep him from dwelling on the fate of his family. "I'll help out."

"You don't have to—"

"I want to."

Can I get you back now?

The voice in my mind jolted me. Liam hadn't moved from where I'd left him, and although he was surrounded by his pack, his full attention was on me.

"Thank you again for"—I nodded to my fist—"this. It means more to me than I could ever tell you."

Jeb squeezed a smile onto his collapsed face.

I weaved myself between the large bodies until I reached Liam.

"Hey, sister from another mister." Matt enfolded me in a bone-crushing hug, lifting me off my feet.

"We're good again?" I asked once he'd set me down.

"As long as you're good to my man, you and I are good, Little Wolf." The warning was sugarcoated but clear.

Lucas held my gaze for a second. We didn't exchange words. Unlike what Liam had told me in the car, I could sense I was far from Lucas's favorite person. Maybe we'd grow on each other. Maybe not. We didn't need to be best friends, but we would need to be friendly, for Liam's sake.

Fingers gripped my chin and lifted my face gently.

A vein throbbed in Liam's temple. *Come home with me tonight?*

Like the feather duster I'd been carrying when we'd met after so many years of being apart, Liam's voice swept everything in the room away: the feral, rowdy men encircling us, my uncle's intractable heartache, August's strange chilliness. Even the musky male scents seemed to dim in the beam of Liam's dark gaze.

"Yes."

He smiled and then he kissed me, and whistles and cheers erupted around us. When he lifted his mouth off mine, I was completely breathless. And I could've sworn the tie that bound us together tightened a little harder.

ACKNOWLEDGMENTS

I've had a fascination with werewolves since I was a little girl, so it was about time I indulged myself and wrote a story featuring my beloved humanoid wolves. The plot took shape in my mind after an extremely brief night of sleep, and then thickened during an exhausting drive back down from the mountains. Who knew staring at bumpers could fuel creativity? It did help that I had a fabulous passenger by my side.

Vee, thanks for being such a great sounding board and leading me to the idea of a magical pledge drink without which an all-male pack would have made little sense. Also, thanks for being a kick-ass sister. How I wish we could live in the same country!

Katie, Theresea, Astrid, my three favorite readers and authors, how lucky I am to have you girls in my life. Thank you for reading each one of my manuscripts and challenging me—even if this leads to a lot of rewrites! My plots and characters grow and mature thanks to your input.

To my editor, Krystal, this was our first collaboration but definitely not our last. You saw the potential in my story, and coaxed it to the surface. Not only did you improve my prose—often by simplifying it—but you also perfected the story's flow and rhythm.

To my awesome proofreader, Josiah, thanks for catching the pesky errors that blend into the forest of my words.

To my designer, Monika, I love how you encompassed the darkness and magic of A Pack of Blood and Lies into a single image. It's everything I wanted and more.

To my publisher, may you soar.

To my children and husband, I love you guys to the furthest reaches of the universe and back. You inspire me each day.

To my parents, I would be nothing without you…literally. Thanks for making me. And for loving me, even when I'm not all that loveable.

Last but not least, to you, dearest reader, thank you for coming along on this lupine adventure. I hope you've enjoyed Ness's tale and will read on. I have so much more in store for her in the next installment.

Be sure to visit http://oliviawildenstein.com and sign up for my newsletter to stay up to date on all the happenings.

OTHER BOOKS

YA URBAN FANTASY

The Lost Clan series
ROSE PETAL GRAVES
ROWAN WOOD LEGENDS
RISING SILVER MIST
RAGING RIVAL HEARTS
RECKLESS CRUEL HEIRS (coming 2019)

A Pack of Blood and Lies series
A PACK OF BLOOD AND LIES (Spring 2019)
A PACK OF VOWS AND TEARS (Summer 2019)
A PACK OF LOVE AND HATE (Summer 2019)

YA MYSTERY

Masterful series
THE MASTERKEY
THE MASTERPIECERS
THE MASTERMINDS
THE MASTERPLAN (coming 2020)

YA STANDALONES

GHOSTBOY, CHAMELEON & THE DUKE OF GRAFFITI
HARSHVILLE (Spring 2020, SwoonReads)